FATE'S FINAL SEASON

MAIDENS OF THE MYSTICAL STONES: BOOK 5

LEIGH ANN EDWARDS

TULE
PUBLISHING

Fate's Final Season
Copyright© 2023 Leigh Ann Edwards
Tule Publishing First Printing, September 2023

The Tule Publishing, Inc.

First Publication by Tule Publishing 2023

Cover design by Covers by Christian

ISBN: 978-1-961544-11-6

DEDICATION

For my late father-in-law, Brian Knowles.

When I began the Maidens of the Mystical Stones series there were to be four books—one for each season. I have four grandchildren, therefore it made perfect sense to dedicate one book to each. Except—then I needed a fifth book to complete the many storylines and give the four heroines their happily ever afters.

While I was writing this series my father-in-law passed away. I thought it only fitting that I dedicate this book to him. Brian was very interested in my writing and never failed to ask about it when we did video chats on Sundays. He used to check the ratings and reviews on Amazons and Goodreads, too.

He even urged me to write him into one of my stories as "*the cad.*" That used to make me laugh for I thought of him as a reserved, charming English gentleman. I will definitely create a character based on him one day and try to make him a little caddish.

Brian loved to read and enjoyed travelling and nature. I miss those weekly chats and hope he's resting easy in a beautiful garden with lots of trees.

PART ONE

CHAPTER ONE

Medieval Times
Near The Wessex/ Cymru Border

RHIANWYN HAD BEEN barely conscious since the horses galloped off. She was thankful when they finally stopped, for her unsettled stomach lurched. Dizzy and disoriented, with trembling hands, she unfastened the belt holding her, slid off the tall stallion, dropped to her knees, and spewed.

The crescent moon shone above, but heavy ground mist hung in the air. She focused on the rich brocade of the garment she'd barely avoided soiling. Lilliana's gown. Memory of the infernal soul-switching pact returned, clearing her head slightly but adding to her pain. She was Rhianwyn in spirit but the body she inhabited was that of the princess. She heard rushing water nearby. Probably a river. The River Severn separated Wessex and Cymru, or Welshland, as most Saxons referred to it. Could they have already journeyed that far?

She glanced at Dubh, Broccan's immense black steed, experiencing pangs of guilt. He'd be worried about his beloved horse. She'd appropriated the stallion from the castle's stable yesterday but didn't intend to keep him— certainly not to take him on a long journey. She didn't want to distress her true love. Or did she? Anger and pain warred within her even though she couldn't recall why.

Stumbling, she went to Dubh, placed her cheek against his taut neck, and unfastened the reins holding him and a white mare together.

"Go back to Broccan, beautiful boy."

The horse bobbed his head at Rhianwyn, then affectionately nudged the mare with his soft nose and snorted.

"I know you're torn. But soon she'll not want you near her, for I suspect you've sired her foal."

The stallion stared at Rhianwyn like it was her he shouldn't leave.

She swatted his rump. "Go home, Dubh!" she commanded. He whinnied, turned to her once more, then took off running. He was loyal to Broccan. She prayed he'd make it home safely.

She held her aching head; thinking took such effort. Should she return to Hengebury? As Princess Lilliana, she'd have to face King Thaddeus, her friend's oppressive father. Rhianwyn shuddered. She'd go to Cymru, her late mother's homeland, instead.

With her walking stick steadying her, and only mild protests from the temperamental mare, she grasped the reins and pulled herself upon the large white beauty. *Gwynna*. She remembered with relief that the horse belonged to Prince Tyven, Lilliana's Welsh husband. Wasn't she displeased with him, too?

Gwynna leaped about, threatening to rear. Squeezing her knees against the horse, Rhianwyn spoke soothingly. The mare finally settled. Fearful she'd lose consciousness again, she tied the reins to her belt and tucked the walking stick inside the tether. Gwynna obviously knew where she was going and set off again.

At the river's edge the fog was even thicker. Surely there'd be someone to ferry them across. When the horse abruptly plunged into the swift-running river, Rhianwyn gasped as icy water soaked her to her hips.

The frigid water and worry for her life should've fully roused her, yet she remained distressingly groggy. What had caused this impairment? She vaguely recalled Agnes, Princess Lilliana's former maidservant, passing Rhianwyn a potion claiming it calmed the uneasy stomach Lilliana suffered during journeys. Maybe she'd reacted unfavorably. Had it been poisoned? She shouldn't have ingested the concoction knowing Agnes harbored animosity toward the princess.

Even if it was a poison—and one she could identify—if she had a remedy to counteract it, she could barely control her shivering body now. Maybe she should return to Broccan. If she *was* dying, she'd long to see him again. But she wasn't in her true form and had already caused him so much pain and confusion.

"Should've waited for a ferry," a sleepy, high-pitched voice said.

Something tugged her cloak. Rhianwyn glanced down. A tiny creature with large protruding eyes, wide-spaced front teeth, a small body, and translucent wings peeked out from her pocket.

"Good gracious; you look even worse!" he exclaimed.

"Agnes's remedy might've been poisoned," she managed, thick-tongued and befuddled.

"I suppose that won't much matter if we drown in this blasted river. Still, I would've thought you'd be more cautious," he tut-tutted.

Rhianwyn widened her eyes, then squinted. Everything looked blurry. Gwynna snorted, breathing heavily as she swam. She must be remarkably strong to stay afloat in the fast-moving water.

"What are you doing?" Rhianwyn asked the tiny person climbing up her cloak.

"Your pocket is filling with water. My, it's warm under your lovely smelling hair."

Couldn't he fly away?

Two glowing orbs appeared in the darkness. Perhaps they were angels here to accompany her to the beyond. She blinked. Only lanterns hanging seemingly in midair; then a large raft came into view.

"Why didn't you use my ferry?" a man called. "Not many horses could ford the River Severn with its danger-some undercurrents. If not crossing here at the narrowest spot or if the tidal water was swelling now, you'd be carried out to sea."

Obviously, things could be worse.

"Steer the horse closer," he shouted again. "I'll tether the beast, so it won't tire."

How the hell was she supposed to do that?

The wee person nudged Rhianwyn. Memories came in disjointed snippets. *Teg...* She finally remembered his name, and that he was an ellyll, a magical Welsh creature.

"What ails you, woman?" the ferryman asked. "If

you've a sickness maybe you shouldn't come closer."

"I might've been poisoned," she managed.

"God's nails!" the man replied.

The current pulled them toward the ferry, but Gwynna frantically fought. In her agitation, she went under, taking woman and ellyll with her. Rhianwyn held her breath till she felt her lungs might burst. They truly might drown here! Her heart sunk. She'd never see Broccan again.

They were suddenly pulled up when the ferryman caught the mare's bridle with an oar. Rhianwyn and Teg sputtered, gasping for air.

Alert with terror and cold, she searched for the positivity her mother had instilled in her. At least, with her garments drenched through, she wasn't recognizable as Princess Lilliana.

"I'll leave you there on your horse lest you're contagious, but I've tied a rope to your mount's bridle. I won't charge you coin. Here, take this." The man threw a blanket over her shoulders. From beneath her dripping wet hair, Teg secured it with her brooch.

"If you're needing a healer, there's few in these parts." The ferryman's voice echoed. "You're not frothing at the mouth or spewing blood. If it's poison it must be slow-acting."

Rhianwyn trembled uncontrollably; her head lolled as fatigue washed over her once more.

"Don't fall asleep again, Princess," Teg whispered. "Or you mightn't awaken."

She wasn't the princess...was she? Her mind was as foggy as the air around them. She was Rhianwyn the healer.

No…that wasn't correct either. She'd once been a healer. She'd also been married to her beloved, Broccan— until…until…until the infernal magical pact that despoiled everything.

And hadn't Teg told her she was likely cursed? With her body failing, feeling heartsick and soul-weary, she wondered if it would be a kindness to just slip away.

No! If there was a sliver of hope she'd return to her life with Broccan, she had to fight.

Fight a poison…maybe a curse?

Surely impossible. It was unlikely Broccan would want a future together if he learned she'd agreed to the pact that had caused such despair. It *was* better she didn't remember. Guilt wouldn't plague her then.

The ferry docked and the horse was untied. Gwynna bounded up the rocky shore and shook herself while Rhianwyn clung tightly to her mane. Quaking from her sopping garments and whatever noxious potion coursed through her, Rhianwyn was grateful for the threadbare blanket. Even if it smelled of unwashed man and strong woodsmoke.

No longer winded, the mare galloped off again. Rhianwyn laid her head against Gwynna's neck and wove her fingers into her mane as she was roughly jostled about.

"Try to stay alive, Princess. How might I assist?"

She opened one eye. Teg was still tucked in the crook of her neck.

"You could p-p-pray," she stuttered, teeth chattering.

"Pray?" He didn't sound hopeful.

Finally, she simply gave way to slumber.

"EEK!" TEG'S SHRILL shriek woke her. "We're headed for the precarious mountain passes and it's bloody well started snowing. The steep path will be treacherously icy. We're sure to fall to our deaths." He placed his hands over his prominent eyes. "You could untie the belt so only the horse would fall, but then we'd just freeze to death."

Teg evidently wasn't given to finding positivity. Snowing? Wasn't it summer? Rhianwyn couldn't even muster fear. It would be tragic if Gwynna died just trying to get home. Teg could fly; surely, he'd save himself.

She now heard unusual flapping and forced her eyes open. A lone man stood before them on the narrow, winding ascent. Dawn was breaking. Although stunningly beautiful, the sparkling mountainous terrain looked rugged and dangerous. As did the man. Tall and muscular with blond hair and gold eyes. Should she recognize him?

"Did you actually steal my brother's horse?" The man grinned. "I'm surprised Gwynna'd permit you near her, much less let you mount and ride her from Wessex to Cymru. Not that *I'd* be opposed to that!" he snickered.

Even in her failing state, she saw him smirk. She didn't have the strength to rebuke his impropriety. He spoke in her Saxon tongue but with a Cymruian accent.

"You don't look in fine feather, sister-in-law."

Sister-in-law? She couldn't discern that connection, but she wasn't certain she knew who she was any longer, much less who he was.

"She's poisoned, likely cursed, and affected by uncommon magic."

"Who said that?" The man looked around him.

Teg moved from beneath the blanket.

"By *Dduw*!" The man stepped back. "A bloody ellyll. Did you poison or curse her?"

Teg clucked his tongue. "If I did, do you suppose I'd admit it?"

"You might gladly take credit. Ellylls are damn mischievous!"

"I'll take no credit for this," Teg snorted. "I'm bonded to the princess by Morwenna's magic, so I'd not want her dead."

"That'd be strong motive if you'd be free of her."

"I've grown rather fond of the princess," Teg said.

"Tyven sent me to search for his horse. He'll be surprised I've found his missing wife, too."

Voices still echoed unnaturally before everything went black.

FEELING HERSELF BEING lifted and carried, Rhianwyn moaned.

"Are you alive, Princess?" Teg whispered, tickling her ear. She swatted with a mostly useless arm.

She heard voices. Cymruian. Her mother's language. As a child, she'd taught her some. How could she remember that but not know how she'd gotten here?

"She moved!" a woman said. "I thought maybe she was dead."

"She's still breathing," the man carrying her replied. "Likely not for long if we don't employ a healer."

She liked the warmth of his bulky body—his powerful arms around her.

"Maybe we should let her die." The woman sounded serious. "She is Saxon."

"That's cold, Buddeg! Our brother wouldn't want his wife dead—certainly not without leaving him an heir." That was a different man's voice.

Rhianwyn briefly opened her eyes, but her eyelids were...so...damn...heavy.

"Best take her to the infirmary chambers then, Gronow," Buddeg suggested. "Whether poisoned or cursed, there's only two who might save her."

"Bronwyn wouldn't think a Saxon woman worthy of his time unless Father requested it. I doubt any of us want to involve either of them," the other man said.

"That leaves Morwenna," Buddeg replied.

Probably trying to revive her, Gronow shook Rhianwyn as he walked. "It's unlikely the princess will survive to be taken to Morwenna and the sorceress certainly won't come here."

"We haven't time to wait till Tyven returns to decide," the other man said.

A door opened and closed. She smelled smoke, food, and ale. Felt welcome warmth but then a change of temperature. A cool stairwell. She was taken up several winding stairs. Yet Gronow wasn't breathing heavier and didn't appear to tire. Another door opened; a musty smell met her nose. The chamber was damp and cold.

"I'll remove her wet garments," the woman said.

"You'll not manage without help," the man carrying her replied.

"That would be a hardship, Gronow, for you to disrobe a woman. Did you give her a potion so you could do just that?"

A rumble across Gronow's chest preceded a snort.

"I'm offended! There's no denying she's beautiful, and it isn't that I haven't lusted for her since they married, but she *is* my brother's wife. Tyven and I enjoy battling for sport, but I wouldn't cross him. Besides, I prefer my women fully alert, participating in the bedding."

Rhianwyn smelled burning wood. Someone must've started a fire. As her garments were removed, she heard a whistle, and felt her bare skin upon cool bed linens. Something was tugged over her head and covers placed upon her. If she died now, at least she'd be warm and dry.

"Who'll fetch Morwenna?" Buddeg asked.

"You go, Madok. I'll wait here," Gronow suggested.

"Perhaps together we'd be able to convince her," Madok said, gruffly. "At least it's not Tyven asking for favors."

Madok sounded intense. Gronow, the man who'd carried her, was given to humor.

"I won't remain here and perhaps be blamed should she perish before you return," Buddeg snapped.

"I doubt you'd be suspected, *dear* stepmother." Madok sounded sardonic.

"Does Tyven know she's here?" Buddeg asked.

"He was searching for her in Wessex but instructed me to follow his horse," Gronow replied. "I used magic to catch the swift mare. I've sent word by enchanted carrier pigeon that I found Lilliana and Gwynna…"

His voice trailed off. Rhianwyn heard footsteps and a door close, then silence but for the fire crackling and spitting as a log settled. Something flitted near her face. A midge maybe, but then Teg lifted her eyelid and stared straight into her eye.

"Stop that!" she ordered.

"Stay awake, damn you. Are you still there, Princess?" He nudged her cheek with fluttering wings.

"I'm not a princess," she replied. "I'm Rhianwyn Mulryan in Lilliana's body."

Her head hurt fiercely, remembering, and she winced.

"You do still have some wits about you. However, mentioning that could be fatal. You're not to speak of the soulswitch pact, correct?"

She groaned. That confounded pact she didn't want to recall.

"True. Especially when my mind's addled and I'm so weak I can barely move." With effort she raised her hand, but it dropped back down with a thud.

"If Morwenna agrees to assist, hopefully she'll save you. She's the powerful sorceress who bonded me to you."

"Morwenna? She also created a remedy to alleviate pain and gave it to Agnes for Lilliana, back when Selena inhabited this body."

The pact was confusing when fully lucid—now, it was impossible.

"Perhaps the combination of potion and remedy was unsafe," Teg suggested.

Rhianwyn recalled Agnes's deep despair when last she'd seen her. She was resentful of Lilliana, therefore Rhianwyn suspected it *was* intentional. Why had she ingested the potion then? She remembered being angry herself and filled with drink, but still.

"Teg, you said I might be cursed," Rhianwyn managed. "Is the dark cloud around me still visible?"

"Regrettably, it is." Teg patted her forehead tenderly despite his stubby fingers.

Perhaps Agnes had poisoned *and* cursed her. Lilliana once said Agnes descended from a family of sorceresses.

Rhianwyn heard peculiar flapping. A large bat or a bird? It sounded much larger even than the birds of prey royals might keep. It perplexed Rhianwyn's already befuddled mind. Hurried footsteps approached.

"That might be King Eurion," Teg warned and dove beneath the bedcovers. With one eye partially open, Rhianwyn was startled when Prince Tyven entered. By firelight she noted his rigid stance and strained features.

"Dammit, woman, you stole my horse and left without farewell!" He sounded furious.

Hadn't she liked him before? He'd chivalrously defended her against King Thaddeus. Seeing Tyven twigged another memory. He and Broccan had done something that enraged her. But if it was that distressing, why couldn't she recall what it was?

Upon noticing her dire state, Tyven's expression turned to concern. He rushed to her side, taking her hand.

"What's happened to you, Lilliana?" He sounded distraught.

"A curse and a potion, she suspects," someone said though Rhianwyn hadn't been aware anyone other than Teg was here.

"A curse? A potion?" Tyven asked, confused.

"You weren't aware of it?" the other person said.

"Woru, I only knew my horse and my wife went missing from her father's Wessexian kingdom where I participated in a tournament. Gwynna was spotted galloping off with another horse and a peasant woman. Lilliana must've dressed in peasant garb. She *was* displeased when last I saw her. Yet I wouldn't have believed she'd foolishly leave unaccompanied. When Gronow sent word they'd been found, I came straightaway."

"It was foolhardy to use one of your limited transformations to fly here, Tyven."

Fly? Rhianwyn was more confused.

"You shouldn't be offering advice, Woru. Your reckless disobedience cost you your life."

Tyven was speaking to someone who'd died? Rhianwyn had occasionally seen and spoken with her dear Anslem's spirit.

"I needed to know Lilliana and Gwynna were well," Tyven said. "My horse evidently fared far better than my lady."

"Our brothers—the two most liable to beguile women, have gone in search of Morwenna," Woru said.

Tyven's hand tightened on hers. Even in her failing state, Rhianwyn felt him tense.

"That's pointless," Tyven scoffed. "She's mostly immune to men's charms and loathes the Dafyddsons. She'd *never* do me a beneficent deed."

"Then it's likely you'll be widowed…again!"

Had Rhianwyn been aware Tyven was married before?

"Lilliana." Tyven leaned closer speaking in her Saxon tongue with an agreeable accent. She had an affinity for men with accents. "Who did this to you?"

Before she could attempt reply, voices approached, and the door was flung open.

CHAPTER TWO

"I CAN'T BELIEVE you had the gall to look for me, much less insist I come *here*!"

A woman with long unbound red hair and a tattered green cloak entered the chamber with Gronow and Madok. There was something familiar about her. Even through blurred eyesight, Rhianwyn saw her glare at Tyven.

"I thought *you* were in Wessex. If I'd known you'd returned, I wouldn't have come." She turned and went straight back out.

"I didn't request your presence, Morwenna," Tyven called. "My wife hasn't wronged you. Please determine if you can better her condition."

Morwenna sighed, but stepped in. She glanced about the massive chamber. A pained expression crossed her face as though remembering something sorrowful. She inhaled, composed herself, loosened her cloak, then motioned for Tyven to move.

Rhianwyn sensed a strong connection to her. Familial perhaps? Rhianwyn's mother had haled from Cymru. Morwenna's eyes seemed oddly familiar.

Rhianwyn believed the sorceress felt the connection, too, for she stared intently, maybe trying to discern how they were linked.

"By the pernicious cloud surrounding her, she's clearly been cursed."

She leaned over and smelled Rhianwyn's lips.

"Poisoned, too with dwale…deadly nightshade. It's usually fatal. Why have you lived through this, girl?" Morwenna mused softly.

Rhianwyn well knew that toxic plant. It had a light scent. Why hadn't she suspected? Perhaps the other potion masked it or affected her sense of smell.

"Your princess isn't the same as before she left for the Saxon land!" Morwenna said. "The peculiar magic previously affecting her has shifted."

Tyven shook his head. "I wasn't aware she'd been touched by magic." He sounded dumbstruck.

"Apparently, you've barely been together in the moons since you've been wed. How would you know?" the sorceress asked.

"Do you suppose she wouldn't be changed if she's been cursed and poisoned?" Gronow used notable sarcasm.

"I don't mean that," Morwenna snapped. She grazed Rhianwyn's cheek, then pulled her hand away. "How can this be?"

"What is it?" Tyven asked.

Morwenna didn't reply but placed her hands on Rhianwyn's head.

Tyven stood tapping his foot. "Are you able to create an antidote for the poison and reverse whatever dark magic's cursed her?"

"You don't ask for much!" Morwenna's said, acridly, still holding her hands to Rhianwyn's head.

She felt something altered within her—the weariness lifted at least marginally. Had Morwenna used healing magic?

"Who poisoned you?" Morwenna asked.

"I believe it was Lilliana's...er...my former lady's maid, Agnes."

Morwenna cocked her head. "I sensed the servant's contempt but it's doubtful she'd poison you—certainly not curse you. She was happy to return to Wessex to her true love or some such drivel."

"Agnes confided in you?" Rhianwyn's voice was hoarse.

The sorceress narrowed her eyes. "Do I seem like someone others would confide in? I sensed it with my intuition."

She opened a pouch she pulled from her cloak.

"What's caused the unusual transformation within you, girl?"

"Also magic," Rhianwyn replied. "But the source must remain hidden else peril will follow."

If Rhianwyn didn't mention more, perhaps the crone's magic wouldn't harm them. She now recalled the mystical old woman's warnings last autumn at the sunstones. It was to be kept only within the circle of friends who'd agreed to the pact.

"Powerful dark magic," Morwenna affirmed. "You obviously have a hardy constitution, a strong will, or a good reason to live, girl, to have survived this poison. I'll give you an antidotal remedy to manage any residual effects. However, the curse, and the other magic affecting you...those are entirely different kettles of fish."

"What's to be done?" Tyven looked truly distressed.

His green eyes clouded, and he brushed his long hair from his face.

An attractive man, like his brothers, Tyven emitted raw sensuality that she supposed appealed to women…well women who weren't presently suffering a curse, a poison, and a wretched pact.

"She must be taken to an isolated location." Morwenna sounded firm. "Remembering her past appears to worsen her condition. I'll see to her healing, but *you*…the lot of you—" she gestured to the men "—must remain distanced."

"I doubt that'll be possible…the three *draig* moons are nearly upon us," Gronow, the most talkative of the brothers, said. "She'll also be coming into season. Father will insist on the mating."

What a crude way of phrasing it. They weren't animals.

"Damn your father to hell!" Morwenna stomped her foot. "This woman's body is severely weakened and her mind's fragile. If you want her to survive and not be left a mindless imbecile, you *will* entrust me with her well-being. If not, she'll soon be dead, which might be a less cruel fate than being linked with you."

Tyven's face paled. He looked stricken. "I don't want her to die."

"It'll happen eventually anyway," Madok replied.

"Don't slather the truth with honey, Brother!" Gronow said.

"You're an unfeeling clodpoll!" Morwenna glowered.

Madok shrugged. "Just stating the truth."

"Please try to save her." Tyven sounded desperate.

"So she'll live to face a more dismal fate?" Morwenna's intense strangely recognizable eyes became tormented again. Pulling a vial from her pouch, she placed it to Rhianwyn's lips.

She turned her head away, refusing.

"Drink it, girl, for I'm your only hope of living and regaining any semblance of wellness or sanity."

Rhianwyn opened her lips and drank the liquid expecting bitterness. Yet it was sweet. Now more alert, she lifted her head, noting the high ceiling and gray stone walls in the castle's bedchamber. She felt the heaviness. Many had died here and someone close to Morwenna.

She espied Tyven, and Gronow, the brother she'd seen in Wessex and again on the mountain path. The other brother, Madok, she hadn't met before today.

Remarkably different in appearance, each was almost mesmerizing with striking good looks. All tall and brawny, but each had different hair and eye color. Tyven had brown hair, Gronow blond, and Madok black. Tyven's eyes were green, Gronow's gold, and Madok's brown. None blue like her beloved Broccan's. She clutched her suddenly throbbing head and cried out.

Morwenna touched her hand. "Don't try to remember, girl. Memories obviously cause that pain."

Rhianwyn nodded.

Tossing her wavy red hair, Morwenna stood, looking at Tyven. "If you permit me to take her, you must stay away. It's imperative she doesn't encounter anyone from her past while I endeavor to discover if the curse can be lessened or ended and learn what other magic has affected her. However…" she waggled her finger in warning "…if her healing's interrupted midway, it could cause irreparable damage. If her memories should suddenly all return, it'll likely be with vengeance." Morwenna widened her eyes for effect. "She might be driven to utter madness or violence."

That didn't sound good.

"I'll not go with you." Rhianwyn tried to sit but the room spun. "I just want to go home to my husband!" She began to weep.

"This is your home, Lilliana, and I'm your husband." Tyven's voice was soft, his touch gentle when taking her hand.

Seeing that, Morwenna turned sharply. "You actually care for her?"

Was Morwenna jealous? It seemed unlikely. She must be older than Tyven and appeared to dislike him. Had he spurned her?

An urgent knock thudded against the door, then it opened without instruction. Presumably a servant, by her plain garments, stood trembling.

"Milords, your father's here," she said before scurrying off.

TYVEN LOOKED AT his brothers gauging their reactions.

Good at hiding behind humor, Gronow seemed unaffected. Still, Tyven could tell he wasn't pleased they'd be made to confront their overbearing, often violent father.

Madok was more transparent. His face showed anger,

distaste, perhaps fear and Madok, the warrior, feared little. Even Woru's spirit appeared distressed. King Eurion was gruff, cruel, demanding, intimidating; not a man anyone would want for a father.

Eurion and Tyven maintained the least volatile relationship. Because now the eldest, he was in line to be king. Tyven also went along with his father's penchant for warring. However, like numerous times in his life, he wished he had a different sire.

Heavy footsteps approached. Tyven watched Lilliana. She'd met Eurion once—at their wedding. He'd briefly appraised her beauty and fine womanly form surely hoping she'd produce a strong grandson. He'd arranged the political union with her father, a Saxon king.

Morwenna despised his father—more than she despised Tyven. Even though Tyven was to blame for her losing her only child, his first wife...his beloved Seren. He shook his head at the painful memories.

"This should be delightful!" Gronow, the jokester, said.

The doorway was soon shrouded by the tall, broad-shouldered man. King Eurion Dafyddson. Even at past five decades, he was handsome, but austere. He wore armor in battle or at rest. Always cautious, suspicious, and ready to meet enemies.

Eurion growled a greeting—affording his sons a quick glance. Morwenna stood—not in respect by her steely glare.

"Why is *she* here?" Eurion thundered.

"Do you honestly think I'd want to be anywhere near you or your ill-favored spawn?" Morwenna held her head high. "I was summoned to see to your daughter-in-law's maladies. I'm hoping to better the plight of another woman tragically linked to your lot."

"I should've taken your head decades ago," the king hissed.

"Someone should take your cock!" she said defiantly.

Few would stand up to Eurion much less purposely infuriate him. But Morwenna unnerved his father like no other. She'd once slighted him, after her sister had done the same.

Tyven had only heard stories of the mysterious sister…whom his father apparently was smitten with. Tyven doubted that. Eurion saw women only as a means to ease male desires and provide them with heirs. No matter the tragic cost to the women. His father's marriage to Buddeg was a ruse to make them appear a typical royal family. They shared no affection nor a bed.

"Be off with you, witch. Get out of my sight!" Eurion blared, stepping toward Morwenna.

She held her palm up. "If you want your son's wife to survive, I must take her with me."

"You cannot," he countered. "The three draig moons are soon upon us. She'll be in season and must be impregnated then!"

He looked at Tyven demandingly. That *would* be expected.

"If the poison isn't managed, she'll not live till then," Morwenna said. "Should she carry a child while afflicted by a curse and perhaps a dark magical spell, too, it's unlikely you'd want to see what that offspring might be." Morwenna's mouth curved into a devious smile. "It might be less favored than the halflings."

"You'd wish that upon the house of Dafyddson?" Eurion's voice was menacing.

She sneered. "You think I'd shed a tear if all of you died a gruesome death?"

Eurion stepped closer, hand on his immense broadsword. Morwenna didn't flinch. Her eyes glowed eerily, and she produced a small wooden wand from her pocket.

"I dare you! Will your draig powers compete with the magic of the bloodline that cursed yours all those centuries ago?"

Eurion's eyes changed, too. A low rumble reverberated from his chest.

"Go ahead," she taunted. "Become so angry you can't control the transformation. Show your daughter-in-law your other form."

"Morwenna," Tyven interrupted. "I'll agree to any healing you deem necessary. You have my permission to take my wife."

"What by the blazes of *Uffern*, Tyven?" Eurion roared and the entire chamber shook.

"If Morwenna doesn't heal her there'll be no heir conceived." Tyven tried to appeal to what mattered to his father.

"There damn well must be; time grows short."

"Then Morwenna must take Lilliana."

His father growled. Those with draig powers would see smoke rising from Eurion's nostrils—sense his body heat rising. If not soon calmed, he *would* transmute.

"You do want me to ensure our legacy continues?" Tyven dared to touch his father's arm and another growl erupted.

"You must!" Eurion snapped, wisps of smoke curling from his nose and mouth now.

Tyven smelled the pungent sulfuric scent that preceded changing to dragon form.

"Father, trust me, the next *draig brenin.*"

Dragon king. Something Tyven never wanted. Something that should've been Woru's fate.

Eyes now more reptilian than human, Eurion snarled, turned, and left them. Tyven dared to breathe again, and several relieved sighs were heard.

Being unwell, Lilliana must've been unaware. But Morwenna wore a satisfied smile. Her magical ability to disappear would protect her, but even his sons mightn't survive Eurion's temper in an enclosed space while he was breathing fire. Not without transforming themselves.

Tyven touched his wife's hand. It was worrisomely cold. "This is to protect you, Lilliana. When you're well enough, you'll return, and we'll speak at length."

She didn't reply. Maybe the potion had numbed her, or she didn't know how precarious the situation was.

"Take her, Morwenna," Tyven insisted. "Before Father sends for the sorcerer, Bronwyn."

She nodded. "Don't come near her...any of you!" Morwenna warned again. "I'll keep her at the *clom* cottage by the black waters. Provide sustenance but don't approach. She's to see no one bar me."

"I give you my word." Tyven held out his hand.

Morwenna seemed loath to touch him, but finally shook his hand.

"As the draig moons approach the draw to her will become visceral. But you *must* resist until she's healed."

Madok crossed his arms, clearly annoyed. "We're not rutting about like stags!" He snorted indignantly.

"Stags in rut might be more civilized," Morwenna accused with a glare. "You obviously underestimate the animalistic need that will surge through you."

"How would a damn woman know anything of that?" Madok asked.

Morwenna glowered again. "Too often women suffer the lust of men, even those not cursed with dragon blood."

Tyven nodded. The need had become far greater. It was said it would increase the longer time went on without a healthy heir beyond their generation.

Morwenna pursed her lips impatiently.

"Well…take her then, before we're unable to control ourselves and violate her even when she's near death." Gronow's tone was mocking.

"You dare jest!" Morwenna glared.

"You dare linger when apparently you're the only hope of saving my brother's wife from death or defilement," he replied.

"I should place a curse upon you, Gronow. Perhaps make your ever-wagging tongue shrivel and fall off."

"Imagine how many women would be disheartened should that occur." He arched his brow and puckered his lips. Morwenna's eyes flashed, but Tyven saw even she wasn't completely unaffected by his brother's notable charm.

Taking Lilliana's hand, the sorceress chanted words Tyven recognized as a language of the elders. Both women disappeared.

CHAPTER THREE

AWAKING WITH A start, she glanced around a small cottage. Hadn't she been in a castle? Why was she having trouble remembering...everything? The more she tried to recall, the less she seemed able. Her name was...what? They called her Princess Lilliana. She looked at her plain nightdress, tangled unbound hair, and the simple cottage. Clearly, she wasn't a princess. Her name was...

She pressed her hands against the throbbing in her head.

"Drink this potion, then rest again." The sorceress's voice was stern. "Don't attempt to remember. That impedes your healing."

She'd best abide the woman.

DAYS COULD HAVE been weeks or months in her bedridden state. The healer tended to her, offering broth, and providing potions, elixirs, herbs, and remedies, some familiar, others entirely foreign. Then she was alone. She moved from the straw-filled mattress to the table and back again, blissfully unaware of who she was. She ate the bread, meat, and cheese that appeared each day, drank the diluted ale, and took the potions.

The small looking glass reflected pitch-black hair and large dark brown eyes. But she had pale blue eyes and light brown hair. Didn't she?

Beyond the open meadow, outside her lonely cottage, stretched a dark lake and a foreboding forest. Craggy-cliffed mountains rose in the distance.

The summer days were warm and as her strength grew, she walked in the sunshine, reveling in nature's beauty. She wore no kirtle, only her plain shift. Her waist-length hair was always unbound, and she went barefoot. She couldn't recollect how long she'd been in this cottage or where her food came from but wasn't concerned. There were berries and herbs nearby and fish in the lake. The healer had left sufficient potion for whatever ailment afflicted her. It must be working, for the stranger in the looking glass had clear eyes and rosy cheeks. Her memories would surely return eventually.

THE HEALER—OR WAS she a sorceress?—came to her one evening.

"Why are you here?" she asked. "You never visit when darkness is falling."

"You'll need protection tonight and two nights following, Lilliana," the healer said brusquely, before stepping inside the cottage. "I'll place a protection spell ensuring no one can get to you."

"Who'd want to get to me?" she asked, perplexed. The

healer still called her Lilliana, which wasn't accurate, but she didn't know why. The woman claimed it was best she didn't remember, that she'd been cursed, affected by unknown magic as sinister as it was powerful.

"Drink this elixir. It'll make you less fearful."

"I'm not afraid."

"Perhaps you should be." The healer scowled.

She drank it. Later, she heard a peculiar flapping of wings, yet nothing harmed them. The sorceress spoke very little but insisted they remain inside. On the morning following the third night, the woman left without explanation of why she'd been in danger or from what.

ALL WAS DELIGHTFULLY pleasant. She adored listening to the birds' songs and watching the wildlife—deer, foxes, rabbits, and squirrels. She feared for nothing in this lovely, unfettered life, though sometimes she thought she should remember someone. Food continued to appear mysteriously by the cottage door, and sometimes the tiny hairs on the back of her neck prickled, as if someone was watching her, yet she saw no one.

One morning, as she knelt in the grass selecting herbs for tea, she caught sight of a shadow. A man, she thought, near the woodlands.

She leaped to her feet and shaded her eyes from the sun.

"Show yourself!" she demanded, but only the birds replied.

Sometimes beyond the dark water, she heard large birds, but the healer had said she was safe here and she trusted her.

Mostly.

ONE NIGHT, WIND rattled the cottage walls; heavy rain battered the door. Thunder rumbled overhead. Even through the drawn shutters she saw lightning flash. She wasn't usually afraid of storms. Was she?

Thunder boomed again. She shrunk into bed and pulled the covers over her head, trembling. Maybe she didn't like being alone after all. Maybe she'd prefer having someone hold her.

A man's face flashed in her mind. Wavy shoulder-length dark brown hair…very blue eyes and a smile that melted her heart. Her heart raced, but also…something stirred within her—a longing, innate and primal. She knew nothing about this handsome stranger, only that once she'd been his and he'd been hers, and she wanted him again, desperately.

COME MORNING, SHE assessed the storm's damage. Tree branches were strewn about outside the thatched-roof cottage. The kettle had been tipped over. But the wind had calmed; the air smelled fresh after the rainfall. She bent to right the kettle and placed it over the fire, then jumped hearing heavy footsteps.

"I didn't intend to frighten you."

A tall man with copper-colored hair and light amber eyes stood there. He held his hand up, signaling he didn't intend harm. He had a string of three fish.

"I thought you might like a change from the rabbits and ducks my brothers and I hunt for you."

"Who are you?"

"Cynfawr Dafyddson. We've been leaving food. Morwenna instructed us not to let you see us, but seeing me shouldn't matter. We've never met and it's not as though I'd try anything inappropriate. I thought you might like company."

She nodded, realizing he was talking about the healer. "I have begun to feel lonely."

"I could tell."

"How would you know?"

He cleared his throat.

"Well tell me!" she ordered.

"As an empath, I've felt your loneliness and, as a man, I sensed your…womanly yearning."

She certainly remembered that powerful yearning. It kept her awake long after the storm ended.

"That's absurd. How would you…?" She tucked her hair behind her ear. "Never mind. I appreciate the fish but won't speak of such personal matters."

"My brothers will also be aware of your needs. It'll be more difficult for them to stay away."

"What in bloody hell are you on about?" She was becoming most annoyed. Her hands went to her hips—

perhaps a habit from her previous life.

"Our kind sense things. We smell fear, hunger, and desire. Especially in a woman and especially when a woman's in season."

"Your kind?" she asked.

He sighed, a lengthy sigh that came from deep within.

"The *draig* people. Our senses are exceptionally keen."

Dragon. He spoke the Saxon language, but the word was Welsh. Dragon people. She was intrigued.

"Why wouldn't you be tempted when your brothers would?"

"Tyven, Gronow, and Madok certainly would. Tomos seldom slakes his desires. I'm not tempted because if I were to bed any woman, I'd die. No matter how strong natural base needs are, they aren't worth dying for."

She was bewildered again.

"How would you know that's true? You obviously haven't tested the theory."

He snorted. "Nor am I about to. It's the curse on the Dafyddson line. We're all affected by a different branch. Best we don't talk about it."

She nodded. "I made a magical pact once that wasn't to be discussed either."

Those words came without conscious thought. Had she made such a pact? She'd begun to suspect Morwenna's potion was what ensured her memories were veiled. Was it suddenly not working? People could become immune to remedies. She recalled that knowledge from her time as a healer. Had she been a healer? Was she simply going mad?

Again, the face of the handsome man who'd filled her

thoughts, and caused deep desire the previous night, came to her. Now, she envisioned his tall, muscular body which further fueled her desires. But thoughts of him brought anger, also. The last time she'd seen him, she'd been furious. He'd done something to gravely displease her.

"Are you unwell?" Cynfawr asked. "You've become pale. Should I fetch Morwenna?" His face clouded. "But then she'd know I spoke with you, and she'd be right annoyed."

"You needn't fetch her. I'm well enough. I'll cook the fish and we could share a meal."

His eyes lit up. "I'd like that. I'll clean them now."

He went to the stream, and she followed, then watched him slice the fish and pull out the innards.

"You're not afraid of Morwenna?" she asked.

He shrugged. "Anyone in their right mind should be afraid of her. Her family has always claimed powerful sorcery. Father wanted to wed her or her sister in hope they'd end the curse or maybe produce a more powerful magical lineage."

"Will you at least tell me my name?" she whispered.

"You're Princess Lilliana. My eldest brother, Tyven's wife."

She shook her head. "I'm not a princess and not married to him. I'm wed to...an Irishman, I think." She held her hands to her forehead. "His name is...and my name is..." She growled, frustrated, for it seemed on the tip of her tongue.

"You're truly bedeviled," Cynfawr said. "I assure you; you are Princess Lilliana of Wessex, and you *are* married to my brother, Prince Tyven."

"What are you doing here?" a stern voice called.

She turned to see Morwenna although she hadn't heard her approach.

Cynfawr held up a fish, daring to smile at the unsmiling woman.

"I've asked Cynfawr to dine with me," she informed Morwenna. "Would you join us?"

"I told you, you're not to have contact with others," Morwenna snapped.

"I've become lonely," she argued.

"She's nearly in season and fraught with desire." The man raised his eyebrow. "Not a good combination, but better me or Tomos discover that than our other brothers."

Morwenna scowled. "That's true."

"If you're intent on keeping them away, you'll need to think of something soon. If Father senses it, he *will* demand Tyven do his husbandly duty. Or he'll mate with her himself."

"Are you offering to help protect her?" Morwenna asked.

"I wouldn't be able to keep them away. Not when the first draig moon has passed and the second's soon here. Your magic mightn't even prevent that."

Morwenna's brow creased. It was the first time she'd seen the sorceress appear daunted.

"Tell me what you speak of. I'd especially like to know my true name. I'm not the damn *princess* as he claims." She motioned to Cynfawr.

Morwenna stared as though deciding.

"By outward appearance you *are* Lilliana, a Saxon princess. However, I agree, your soul is not of that woman. I cannot determine what magic has caused this soul transference, but it's of a dark origin—as potent as any I've seen. Pagan. Perhaps Druid. Maybe Celt but not Cymruian."

"What of me being in season?"

"You're fertile. The Dafyddsons, brothers and father, will be compelled to have you. If you've not mated soon, they'll become frantic."

She looked from Morwenna to Cynfawr, disbelievingly. Hadn't someone told her she wouldn't conceive?

Cynfawr nodded, placing the cleaned fish on a rock. "If it hasn't occurred by the third draig moon I suspect even I'll be filled with frenzied lust. Tomos, too. The need to procreate will likely overpower all thought...or morals."

Morwenna chewed on her lip, wearing a strained expression. "She'll have to be taken away."

"The craving we'll experience if the wedded mate of the next draig king is in season and her heightening desires aren't met during the draig moons might be uncontrollable. Even if you hide her or send her back to her Saxon kingdom, Father would insist we follow. Perhaps he'd order all of us to mate with her."

"You sound like animals!" she accused. "You said you'd die if you were with a woman."

"That wouldn't distress Father." Cynfawr scoffed.

Morwenna inhaled deeply. "You'll have to be intimately joined with a man before then...and not a Dafyddson. Someone who'll sate your base hunger, but not endanger you."

"Explain straightaway!" she ordered. "I'll not be bloody *mating* with anyone!"

"You shouldn't have come, Cynfawr! You've distressed her." Morwenna's tone was caustic.

Cynfawr shook his head. "It's not only me who's unsettled her."

"I must learn more." She clasped Morwenna's arm.

"She has a right to know," Cynfawr said. "I'm surprised you haven't warned her of her eventual fate."

Morwenna's eyes became glassy, and her body tensed. "Even coupling with a Dafyddson can be dangerous. If you should be impregnated with whatever offspring that might be, it'll cost you your life as it did my daughter."

Glancing at the walking stick propped against the cottage, she now remembered that cudgel and felt driven to retrieve it. As she held it in her hands, it began to glow, and scattered memories returned.

Morwenna gasped. "You have abilities in your own right, woman…strong magic not there before you went to Wessex. But something in the Saxon land caused a soul shift. Were you a victim of a soul thief?"

"It's because of a pact," she whispered. "Between me and three friends. If I speak of it, we might die." She looked at Morwenna and Cynfawr.

"It's unlikely," Morwenna argued. "I've recently been sworn protection by the elders, and I'll protect you. And if he dies." She shrugged. "There'd be one less Dafyddson."

"I've never wronged you, Morwenna," Cynfawr scowled. "I could seek revenge on you for your line cursing us."

"I suppose so." Morwenna's voice softened marginally.

"Although your fury's clearly greater," Cynfawr mused. "It's said you ripped out your own womb so you wouldn't be forced to carry a Dafyddson offspring."

She stared hard at Morwenna.

"I wish my daughter had done the same," Morwenna whispered, sadness back in her eyes.

Impulsively, she went to the sorceress who backed away. Still, she placed her arms around her and held tightly.

"You must be foolish or fearless, girl, to dare embrace me."

"Mam said a firm embrace during times of joy or sorrow leaves both people better for it."

Morwenna pulled away, green eyes wild now. "My mam used to say that, too, nearly word for word. She died years ago. Whose soul inhabits this princess's body? Who was your mother?"

She held the wand, feeling power flowing through her. "Mam's name was Mererid," she whispered when that knowledge abruptly came to her. "And I'm Rhianwyn...Albray. No, Rhianwyn Mulryan." She smiled.

It was a great relief to finally know.

CHAPTER FOUR

ORWENNA'S FACE TURNED pasty. She lowered herself to the ground, trembling. Rhianwyn sat beside her and took her hand. The sorceress didn't protest.

"Why does the mention of those names distress you?" Rhianwyn asked.

"You must leave!" Morwenna said to Cynfawr.

He hesitated, but nodded to the sorceress, then to her.

"Thank you for the fish," Rhianwyn called before they watched him walk away. "Now you must tell me," she urged Morwenna.

The sorceress took a deep breath. "I sensed a connection between us that night at the castle. Finally, I know. Dear Mererid was my sister. Her daughter, Rhianwyn, I saw only once when she was a child."

Rhianwyn cocked her head—another memory overtaking her. "You and Mam met at a castle ruin under cover of darkness. I slipped away from my father and followed her."

Eyes wide, Morwenna nodded. "You truly must be my niece, Rhianwyn. You did follow that night, which made your father fretful—the young Saxon mage, William Albray, who'd fallen in love with my sister while traveling Cymru. His veiling magic permitted her to escape marrying Eurion."

"Mam was to wed that atrocious man?" Rhianwyn now remembered seeing Eurion in Tyven's castle.

Morwenna nodded. "Our parents only agreed to the union hoping that, as his wife, she'd catch him unaware, and her powerful magic would kill Eurion. She would've been his third wife. Woru and Tyven had already been born. Their mothers died giving birth. After Mererid disappeared, Eurion, his father, and his brother searched far and wide. When she couldn't be located, I was to have the despicable fate of being his next wife."

Morwenna sighed. "Using my veiling spells, I hid away for years. Eurion wed thrice more; three more women died bearing three more sons: Gronow, Madok, and Cynfawr. When Eurion eventually found me, I already carried a child by the man I loved." Her voice broke. "He died of a fever even I couldn't cure. But being with child bought me time. Eurion's oddly compassionate regarding pregnant women.

"After my daughter was born, Eurion and I were to be wed in hopes I'd give him another son...a magical son, perhaps, who might end the curse. But I couldn't risk dying giving birth, thus leaving Seren at his mercy. I feared he'd eventually pair her with one of his sons or marry her himself."

"That's when you ripped out your womb?" Rhianwyn couldn't imagine anyone being that desperate or how it would even be done.

"With magic." Morwenna nodded. "Done in the presence of Eurion and his kin, it alerted them to how greatly I objected being paired with him. If only Seren had done the same."

"Your daughter was Tyven's first wife?" Rhianwyn asked. It was all becoming clearer.

Morwenna nodded, closing her eyes.

"With a spell, I led Eurion to believe my girlchild was born still so he'd not one day try to match her with one of her sons. Without a womb, I was of no use to him. Seren and I escaped to the Cambrian Mountains, where using veiling spells we hid for many years. Yet, it seemed fated that Seren and Tyven would meet and fall in love.

"Though I did everything I could, magical and otherwise, to keep them apart, they ran off and were wed. Enraged, Eurion surely would've killed them but when he learned Seren was my daughter, he celebrated. I didn't see her again until ripe with child, she requested Tyven come for me and take me to her at his castle. She was already laboring."

Morwenna looked weary and older now. Rhianwyn doubted she usually shared personal information. Perhaps because she believed her soul was that of her niece, she felt compelled to explain.

"Tell me more about the Dafyddson curse," Rhianwyn pleaded. "Tyven explained some to my friend, Selena, who was in Lilliana's form then. He said he couldn't have sexual relations at that time, for it would be dangerous."

Morwenna cleared her throat of her sorrow. "Mating with a Dafyddson will always prove dangerous, but certain times are worse."

"Who cursed the brothers?" Rhianwyn asked.

"I don't know what's truth, myth, or embellished tales. I've heard a woman of my ancestry was wronged by a man of the ancient Dafyddson line. Presumably raped, she cursed him with the *draig* legacy. The dragon within the man."

"I don't understand." Rhianwyn shook her head.

"They transform into dragons," Morwenna said, impatiently. "The shifts can occur during moon phases, or with their moods, but sometimes by choice."

Rhianwyn must've looked dumbfounded. It was quite enough to believe that she and her friends had switched human bodies, their souls inhabiting each body for a season because of a pact. But cursed to change into a beast?

"If your ancestor was harmed by a man, why would she create dangerous creatures who'd only wreak more havoc?" Rhianwyn asked.

"How would I know?" Morwenna barked. "If she was brutalized it was probably done impulsively."

"Is there a way to end this curse?" Rhianwyn asked.

Morwenna nodded. "It's said someone of my lineage must undo it. I don't know how, when the curse was uttered long ago. Few are left of my...of *our* line."

Curious to learn more, Rhianwyn sat closer. "There's others besides you and me then?"

Morwenna looked around perhaps thinking Cynfawr might remain near and be listening. She didn't reply to her query.

"How would we discover how to finally terminate the curse?" Rhianwyn asked.

Morwenna shrugged. "My grandmam spoke of a book containing that information. Apparently written in the language of the elders, torn into three sections, each placed in different locations. It's said one is hidden in those caves." She pointed to the craggy cliffs. "Perhaps that, too, is only myth."

"How would anyone discover the truth with only that to go on?" Rhianwyn held out her hands, perplexed. "Why wouldn't everyone want the curse ended?"

Morwenna's eyes clouded, and she shrugged. "It's said the Dafyddsons must show remorse first, but I suspect ending it would be a daunting quest. I would've attempted to learn more when Seren was with child, had I known earlier. But alone, it's likely beyond my ability."

"How did your daughter die?" Rhianwyn asked despite knowing this would be difficult for Morwenna.

"Like every woman who bears a Dafyddson offspring whether the mating's done by choice or by force. She died giving birth. Fortunately, their *child* died with her." Morwenna's voice sounded bitter now.

Rhianwyn wondered why that would be fortunate?

"It tried to claw its way from her womb; she died of blood loss," Morwenna explained without her asking.

"Claw?" Rhianwyn gasped, horrified.

"Mad for each other, she and Tyven failed to heed the warnings to wait. She didn't conceive during the draig moons; therefore their offspring was in dragon form."

"I'm terribly sorry." Rhianwyn touched her aunt's hand.

She didn't reply.

"How did the eldest brother die?"

"In love with another, Woru defied his father by refusing to marry the woman Eurion chose for him. His father ordered he and his woman beheaded, their heads placed on pikes."

Rhianwyn gasped. God's teeth! What monster would kill his own son? What madness had Lilliana married into?

"Does the curse affect all brothers the same?" Rhianwyn asked.

"Tyven can apparently sire children who'll be born human and remain human unless they choose to transform...but *only* if he mates during the three draig moons."

"But the woman would still die giving birth?" Rhianwyn guessed.

Morwenna nodded solemnly. "Unless she has powerful magic, but that's never been proven, for as I said Seren wasn't impregnated during the draig moons."

Rhianwyn shook her head at the curse's tragic complexity.

"Heartbroken after Seren's death, Tyven didn't wish to remarry, but valuing his head, he married the bride Eurion chose. A Saxon from a far-off kingdom whose kin wouldn't suspect anything untoward if she died giving birth. It's common for women, even those who don't birth a draig blood."

"That's true. Mam died in childbed when I was four and ten." Rhianwyn fought tears, remembering that tragic day.

Morwenna nodded. "William thoughtfully sent word of Mererid's death...my beloved twin sister."

"You were twins?" Rhianwyn said. "Mam was evasive about her past. Now I understand why. But when she left Cymru, did she know it would be your fate to wed a

Dafyddson?"

"I delved into dark magic more than Mererid and insisted I'd create a spell to render me barren. Although I knew I'd miss her terribly, I urged her to go as fast and far as possible, for Eurion was besotted with her. She was sorrowful to leave. She dearly loved her family and Cymru.

"Young and starry-eyed, William gladly took Mererid away. I hoped his different magic might protect her. I suppose it must have. Eurion never found her."

"Why would she risk coming back here when I was a child?" Rhianwyn asked.

"Our parents died," Morwenna explained. "Mererid came to pay respects and lay claim to her castle and land."

"Mam had a castle and land?" Rhianwyn was stunned.

Morwenna nodded. "They now belong to you. I thought William would inform you when you reached adulthood. Perhaps he didn't want you near the Dafyddsons."

"Don't you live there?"

"I have my own castle, but I reside in the ensorcelled glen," Morwenna replied. "I never much liked castles."

"How are the other brothers cursed?" Rhianwyn wanted to learn. "Even in my befuddled state when I arrived, Gronow appeared to favor women."

Morwenna nodded. "It's said Gronow will father no children unless he should fall in love. Therefore, he can mate endlessly and apparently does. Yet if he beds and impregnates a woman he loves, they'll probably produce full dragons."

"Love is hardly something we can control," Rhianwyn

said.

Morwenna shrugged. "Madok can mate, too, but it's likely he'll produce only full-draig offspring. Therefore, he apparently chooses older women no longer able to bear children, those known to be barren, or harlots who'd dispose of a child should they conceive.

"And Tomos, the bastard son, whose mother was rumored to be a halfling, appears hideously grotesque. If he mates, it's likely to be by force or during dark of night."

"What of his offspring?" Intrigued, Rhianwyn couldn't stop asking questions.

"I doubt anyone knows for certain. It's all allegedly recorded on scrolls in a secret chamber in Eurion's castle."

"And Cynfawr can't mate because he'd die?" Rhianwyn asked. "Therefore, he can't even be with women of advanced age or barren?"

Rhianwyn now recalled Heledd, Lilliana's maidservant mentioning something else.

"Is it true Vala is Tyven's mistress?"

Morwenna bobbed her head. "Eurion sees that she tends to Tyven's sexual needs. She remains attractive, though beyond childbearing age. It's unlikely he'd want to mate only three moons a year. No man would be content with that."

"Yet Cynfawr's not permitted to mate...ever?"

"Not with humans." Morwenna scowled.

"What?" Rhianwyn wasn't sure she wanted to know.

"During certain moon phases Cynfawr becomes full dragon. There are female dragons in the draig caves beyond the black waters." Morwenna motioned to the nearby lake.

"I'd like to witness a transformation," Rhianwyn said.

"You would not!" Morwenna warned, emphatically. "You daren't force that simply to satisfy your curiosity."

"Force it?" Rhianwyn shook her head, not understanding.

"Strong emotion sometimes causes transformation; however, they're permitted few changes per moon or per annum before they remain in dragon form. But enough about the damn Dafyddsons." Morwenna scowled.

"But what's a halfling?" Rhianwyn asked.

"Half human, half dragon, but some in varying degrees. I've only ever seen one. They're pitiful creatures, some known to be dangerous. I don't wish to talk of dragons any longer."

Rhianwyn shrugged.

"Is the princess's soul in your own body now, Rhianwyn?" Morwenna asked.

How odd to be referred to by name.

"Yes," she replied.

"You said you couldn't speak of this without something untoward occurring?"

"It was part of the pact," Rhianwyn said.

"Maybe there's no threat to me knowing," Morwenna suggested. "Perhaps only those in your kingdom would fare unfavorably."

Rhianwyn nodded. "Maybe."

"Do you know who's responsible for this dark magic?" Morwenna asked.

Rhianwyn recalled the mysterious aged woman.

"An old crone. I don't know anything about her," Rhianwyn whispered glancing around, fearful she might appear. Lost in her thoughts Rhianwyn grasped the walking stick tightly.

"You said your name's Albray, then claimed it's Mulryan." Morwenna's voice startled her. "You're married?"

Rhianwyn's heart beat faster.

Morwenna put up her hand. "No. Don't attempt to remember. It might be unfavorable recalling something that evokes deep emotion."

The face of the handsome dark-haired man she'd thought of and lusted for last night came to mind again. She was confused—heartsick missing him, yet angry with him, too.

Morwenna passed Rhianwyn a vial. "This will veil the memories that cause sorrow."

With these distressing emotions she wasn't ready to fully remember. She drank the potion, hoping Morwenna had her best interests at heart.

RHIANWYN STIRRED THE soup in the pot over the fire outside the cottage. She was Rhianwyn Mulryan. Every day she'd repeat that, so she'd not forget everything again. Her soul was in Princess Lilliana's body. She'd begun scratching those truths on the stone floor beneath the bed.

Deep in thought, she jumped when Morwenna approached.

"You're edgy. Aren't you taking the remedy?"

"I am," Rhianwyn replied. "Why are you here?"

"I've determined more about the curse."

"Rest by the fire and tell me." Rhianwyn pointed to the ground.

The two women sat together.

"From what I've gleaned of the curse that the servant placed upon you, believing you were Lilliana, it was in retribution for something hurtful the princess did. I believe she wants Lilliana miserable and discontented, unable to recall anything or anyone who brought her joy. She'd tried to kill her with the deadly nightshade. The curse was probably an alternate strategy should the poison not work."

Living, but always unhappy, would probably be worse than death.

"Why didn't the poison kill me?" Rhianwyn asked.

"Your soul has unusual magic."

Rhianwyn gestured to her torso. "Still, shouldn't this body have died?"

"Perhaps the crone's magic protects you," Morwenna suggested. "But for now, I've reasoned you shouldn't appear entirely healed. If Eurion knows, you'll be returned to Tyven to be bred, for the whole moon draws near."

Rhianwyn shivered at the thought of a beast clawing its way from her womb. Her cousin's tragic fate. The woman Tyven had loved. She sensed him near sometimes. Yet, abiding Morwenna's warnings, he kept his distance. She hadn't seen anyone, even Cynfawr, since the day she met him.

"You also have two spirits who hover near," Morwenna said. "Since I don't know their intent, I've veiled them from you. I believe one is Saxon, the other Norse."

Rhianwyn shrugged unable to remember.

"Now, I'll leave you." Her voice pulled Rhianwyn from her thoughts. "Take the potion daily."

Morwenna walked away, then simply disappeared.

SHE WOKE WITH a sigh—loneliness weighing upon her. She rose, washed, dressed, brushed her hair, ate, cleaned the already tidy cottage. How damn tedious. Even the previous joy of the birds' song, animals, and nature was fading. She missed people, especially the man she'd once loved.

She'd been gradually taking less of Morwenna's potion, needing to remember. When she held the wand it helped; however, certain memories still caused the sharp pain in her head. She definitely didn't want to feel as disoriented as the night she'd arrived.

How odd she'd not seen Teg since then. Wasn't he bonded to her?

"Teg?" she called after stepping outside. "Are you near?"

"Don't tell me you've missed me, Princess?" The ellyll materialized almost instantly.

"I suppose I have."

The small creature grinned. "My, you're looking better."

He glanced at her short sheer shift, the low neckline revealing her ample cleavage. She hadn't expected to see anyone, certainly didn't know saying Teg's name would summon him.

"Your color's returned, and you look voluptuous in that garment."

His buggy eyes bulged further, and he waggled his eyebrows.

"You're a hopeless miscreant."

"I'm only appreciating your beauty."

"Where have you been?" she asked.

"Here and there…not far, for yes, I'm still bonded to you."

"Why would Morwenna keep us bonded?"

The ellyll shrugged. Spotting some fungi, he spread his wings, fluttered down and plucked some. Shoveling it into his mouth he munched noisily. "Why not ask her?"

"She's not always forthcoming."

"Did you expect a sorceress to be entirely trustworthy?"

"I suppose not," Rhianwyn replied.

"Why did you summon me, Princess?"

"I'm feeling lonely."

"Probably not for long." He glanced up at the sky.

"What do you see?" She only saw fluffy white clouds in the summer sky.

"The moon's nearly full—the second to last draig moon till next year. Soon you'll become unsettled. When they sense your desire and you sense their male need to mate while you're in season, you *will* want a man."

"I very much dislike that term! I'm not an animal."

He shrugged. "You'll be fertile. All species have primal tendencies regarding mating…to coupling if you prefer. Even humans. Especially men. However, you're a healthy young woman with desires not presently being met and memories of when you shared passionate love with a man."

"Morwenna says she'll protect me. The first dragon moon passed. None of the Dafyddsons came near."

"You were ill and having Morwenna with you was a deterrent. Now, you look healthy and enticing. If they draw near or use magic to envision you, they *will* want you."

"You're bloody blunt," she accused.

He grinned. "I suspect Morwenna's been lacing your potion with monk's pepper or water lily to lessen your thirst to couple, but it won't be enough. That's probably why she doesn't want you to remember your Irishman."

Rhianwyn turned sharply. Her head always throbbed trying to recall him.

"At any rate, I'm glad you lived. I worried you wouldn't."

"I appreciated you being with me then, Teg. You could've flown away when we were in that river."

"Don't make me out a hero. My wings were wet."

"You could've left me before that."

"It *was* my fault you were in that predicament. I did tell that determined mare to go home."

"True. It really was all your fault." She smiled.

He laughed his odd high-pitched laugh. "I didn't curse or poison you. Morwenna told me to keep away, said if you remembered me, you might recall other things that would thwart your healing."

"Do *you* trust her?" Rhianwyn whispered.

"She's evidently your kin. I doubt she'd harm you."

"I hope not. She appears to have loved Mam even

though her absence made Morwenna's life difficult."

"Morwenna was sorrowful after Mererid left. They were close."

"Teg, did you know my mother?"

Misty-eyed, the ellyll wiped away a tear.

"She and I were friends before she left. I was sorry to hear lovely Mererid passed."

Again, Rhianwyn's heart ached remembering her mother's death.

"Always darker than Mererid," Teg said, "Morwenna has become disenchanted with what life's dealt her. She lost her sweet daughter. Seren was more like Mererid. I see why Tyven fell for her. She loved him, too."

How devastating for Tyven to lose the woman he loved and their child.

Emotional now, Rhianwyn sniffled. "I think I'll go walking."

"I'll remain eating these delightful fungi. There's none so fine as here in Cymru." He belched loudly.

She smiled and shook her head. "Thanks for your company, Teg."

He bowed. "Anytime, lovely lady."

TYVEN ENTERED THE small unadorned *clas*. He preferred it to the grander abbey. He started on seeing Morwenna kneeling near the altar. She must've heard him. She turned. On first glance, he saw her resentment. She stood and nodded, knowing why he was here today—the date he'd lost his beloved Seren.

Four years had passed; they both mourned her still. Morwenna moved to a bench pew. He dared to sit at the other end.

"Has there been improvement in Lilliana's condition?" He had to make conversation. "She's been in your care for a moon and a fortnight. Father's asking when she'll be recovered and…"

"Recovered enough to share your bed," Morwenna interrupted. "Enough to conceive your child? To die giving birth?"

That was more like the woman he'd come to know. Her words cut him to the quick. Seren *had* been her only child. Of course she blamed him.

"I loved Seren beyond measure, Morwenna. I would've died for her."

Morwenna's grim expression softened. "And she you. Else she wouldn't have been foolish enough to lie with you. I warned her it wasn't safe."

Tyven felt the familiar agonizing heartache.

"She admitted she initiated the coupling." Morwenna let out a breath. "I suppose no healthy man would deny her."

His late wife had been enticing, determined, and passionate. Tyven looked away and cleared his throat. Thoughts of Seren still aggrieved him. He should've turned her away when lust consumed her, but they'd waited so long and wanted each other desperately.

He'd known if not conceived during the draig moons, the chance of a woman, even one with magic, surviving the birth when impregnated by someone of *draig* lineage was unlikely. But his lovely optimistic wife adamantly opposed his father's suggestion of Tyven slaking his needs with a woman beyond child-bearing age. Vala hung about him until, jealous and infuriated, Seren sent her away with a spell.

He loved Seren so. Wildly eager to make love with her…it had occurred. Then she'd hidden her pregnancy for a time, knowing he might suggest she end it.

Despite her optimism and Morwenna's magical healing during the labor, neither Seren nor their child had lived. Tyven's heart was forever shattered. Seeing the unimaginable amount of blood after she'd died had gutted him. He mourned her still.

He hadn't expected to feel anything for the Saxon princess. He hadn't…other than a brief lustful drunken night a few moons earlier. He'd kissed and caressed her, then come to his senses and gone to Vala. It temporarily eased his frustration yet always left him feeling he'd betrayed Seren's memory.

When in Wessex, Lilliana seemed changed. Brighter, more alluring, and her feistiness reminded him of Seren. Unexpectedly attracted to Lilliana, he mostly avoided her.

Worried when she'd gone missing, he'd used magic to transform to dragon form enabling him to fly…which he rarely did.

When he believed she might be dying, he realized he'd come to care for her. Now, he was in a damn dilemma. Even if he abided his father and a child was conceived during the draig moons, the child would probably be born healthy, but a mortal woman had never survived the birthing.

Eurion said if Tyven married a Saxon woman—a woman of their enemies, he wouldn't suffer when she was lost providing him an heir. That she was merely a vessel for the draig child to grow. How heartless! Had his father felt nothing for his mother or his brothers' mothers?

"Are you suddenly deaf, Tyven?"

"What?" he asked, shaken from his dark memories.

"You looked far away." Morwenna tugged her shawl tighter.

He only nodded.

"You do intend to bed Lilliana, regardless of the consequences?"

"If I value my own skin," he answered truthfully. "It's not as though Father wouldn't kill his own son."

Morwenna stiffened. "You feel your life's worth more than hers? Because you're a man? A prince? Or do you abide your father's skewed opinion that the *draig-pobl* are superior?"

Tyven's own temper piqued. "I do not!"

"You *could* have another man sire her child. Your princess would be more likely to survive. Eurion's never disposed of any newborn."

Tyven let out a long breath. He'd suggested that moons ago when he'd seen Lilliana looking fondly at their groom. He'd sensed their attraction. When he broached the subject, she'd become embarrassed. He hadn't brought it up again.

Now Lilliana seemed changed...more passionate, and

he'd sensed her growing desires. Perhaps she'd accept such a proposal, especially if he explained it could save her life.

If she conceived with another man's child, it would spare her...at least temporarily. Maybe King Eurion would be killed by one of his many enemies...mortal or magical. Tyven and his brothers would be free of his tyranny. The curse would remain, but much *would* change for them.

Eurion was clever and suspicious, yet perhaps too arrogant to believe his own sons would wish him dead, much less carry out the murderous plot. It wasn't that they hadn't considered it especially after Woru was killed by their father's order. But Eurion had guards and spies always watching. Some possessed magic, too. The vicious halflings also did his bidding.

"If you haven't the courtesy to reply, I'll be leaving." Morwenna's stern voice jarred him.

"I once suggested Lilliana be with a man she seemed to fancy. She wouldn't be party to adultery. I've yet to fully explain what might occur if she bears my child."

"She'll surely flee once she knows."

Tyven shrugged. "Where would she go? Father would have her hunted. Her own father barely tolerates her."

Morwenna eyed him closer.

"There's something else you should know," she said. "Besides being cursed, your wife's affected by dark and powerful magic I've never seen before. Should she conceive your child while so affected, I'd not want to consider what might be created."

"Why do you alert me? You despise me and surely have no fondness for a Saxon woman."

There must be something Morwenna wasn't telling him. Why was she interested in Lilliana?

Her next words startled him.

"My daughter loved you and believed you're an honorable man. I've come to believe so, too."

Did she mean that or was she deceiving him?

"I hope to make Seren proud of me still," he said.

Morwenna nodded. "Find another man to bed your princess. Someone she's attracted to. Save her, Tyven. Surely, you're the only one who can."

He sighed, lost in memories of the past and concerns for Lilliana and their future, as they parted.

CHAPTER FIVE

Wessex

B ROCCAN STOOD IN Brockwell Manor's great hall dwelling on the message just delivered.

"Why would the king send for you?" Matty's thin face was wrought with concern after hearing Broccan give the king's messenger assurance he'd be at the castle tomorrow as requested.

Broccan shrugged. "Damned if I know. But don't worry of it."

"Tell me what you're thinkin', Broccan. I see your botheration."

"Maybe he wants to congratulate me again on bein' top competitor in the recent tournament." He grinned, trying to lighten her concerns.

Matty pursed her lips, obviously having none of it.

Broccan sighed. "If you must know, I'm hopin' it's nothin' to do with the new bishop. It's said he's damn unpleasant. And he's uncle to the late Sheriff Percival and his bastard of a son, Godric. If amorality runs in bloodlines, the bishop's probably a right lout and one with power aplenty."

"I'd tell ye not to speak ill of the dead, but Percival and Godric hadn't a hint of decency 'tween the two of them."

"You'll get no argument from me. I'm relieved no one has to deal with them any longer."

Six weeks had passed since their death. The day his friend Ulf had been killed, too. Everything had been mostly peaceful since. Thank God, for there'd been enough despair and calamity in recent months to last a lifetime.

He'd been much relieved when Dubh, his beloved stallion, returned home unharmed. He was surprised to learn Lilliana had taken him when she'd left Wessex with Prince Tyven's mare.

"You look deep in thought, husband," Rhianwyn said on entering the hall.

He smiled, greeting her with a kiss and an embrace. Thankfully he and his wife had begun to put some of the unpleasantness that had occurred in their marriage behind them. It wasn't precisely how it had been before he'd gone to Mercia all those moons ago, but it was improving. She seemed back to herself...or nearly. People did change and they'd gone through a lot together. He'd changed, too.

"What has you so preoccupied?" she asked.

"Broccan's been requested to take audience with King Thaddeus," Matty answered still wearing a careworn look.

"It wasn't a request so much as a demand," Broccan said.

Rhianwyn looked into his eyes searchingly. She, too, now bore a worried expression. "What do you suppose he wants?"

Broccan shrugged and touched her lovely light brown hair. "I'll find out tomorrow. Don't think on it further, either of you." He looked from Rhianwyn to Matty.

His wife's chin lifted as though she might push, but she only sighed and sat upon a chair. She glanced at Matty with a hint of disapproval. Recently Rhianwyn seemed resentful of the woman who'd raised him. They'd once gotten on well. Now, it was as though Rhianwyn didn't want Matty taking his time away from her. She had become possessive.

"I'll go and let you break fast before you must go to the knights' trainin' field." Matty tipped her head to Rhianwyn like she might expect the reverence. That was peculiar. Rhianwyn didn't usually request such formality.

As soon as Matty left, Broccan gazed at his wife.

"Have you and Matty fallen out?"

She shook her head. "What makes you think so?"

"You seem a bit short with her lately," he replied.

"I'm certainly not." She sounded short even with him. "I simply wish we might have one conversation without her hovering about."

Broccan felt defensive of the older woman. "I never feel Matty's hoverin'."

"You'd think she was your mother and not merely a servant the way she's always in our business. I find her meddlesome."

Broccan stared at Rhianwyn.

"Matty raised me from infancy and has been with me much of my life. I do love her as a mother. I certainly don't think of her as a servant. She's invaluable to the manor."

Rhianwyn's head rose, nostrils flared. "I resent that you confide in her more than me. Would that not distress most wives?"

Wanting no quarrel, Broccan tried to appease her.

"Matty was here when the messenger arrived. Naturally she'd want to know what plagued my mind upon reading the king's note."

Rhianwyn looked down, straightening her skirts, then nodded, reluctantly he surmised.

"What have you planned for this day?" Broccan changed the subject, heartily setting into his biscuits and gravy, pork, and eggs.

"I thought I'd have Chester take me to the village market."

Broccan nodded. "Will you be meetin' Selena and Elspeth as you once did?"

She tensed. "We haven't seen each other recently."

"I thought you wanted everythin' to return to how it once was," he said. "You've been friends for years."

She sighed, heavier now. "I find it off-putting being with them after all that occurred. You wouldn't really expect me to maintain our friendships after you've had *relations* with them?" She narrowed her eyes disapprovingly.

Broccan was startled she'd speak of the subject that was ever avoided. He bloody well didn't want to have that discussion either.

Rhianwyn exhaled again. "Selena appears happy to be *working* at her aunt's brothel, which is completely ludicrous. Evidently, other than performing her castle duties, Elspeth mostly keeps to herself."

"I don't pretend to know why Selena's chosen to be employed there when Fleta doesn't expect it. But I believe Elspeth's deeply mournin' the loss of Ulf and Agnes,"

Broccan said.

Agnes had been found dead in a village cottage. Poisoned with deadly nightshade by her own hand as deemed by the king's physician, for there was evidence the potion was created there. Broccan mightn't have trusted the incompetent man, but the healer, Radella, had confirmed it.

"Elspeth did love Ulf and Agnes," Rhianwyn said.

She didn't sound empathetic. Rhianwyn's kindness and empathy were part of why he'd fallen in love with her. Sure, she'd always harbor jealousy because of the absurd soul transference that had occurred. She refused to further explain, claiming it might cause whatever dark magic that brought about the occurrence to resurface.

She only said it was forced upon her. Broccan longed to find who was responsible for the magic and make them face their comeuppance. How could he discover that truth if Rhianwyn wouldn't or couldn't speak of it?

Maybe it was best he didn't know. Things were nearly back to what they'd once been. He'd not want to threaten their renewed closeness. He shouldn't have brought up Selena or Elspeth, yet he didn't want Rhianwyn to lose those longtime friendships. She'd surely become discontented without her healing, too.

Dorsett had taken on healing duties when Rhianwyn couldn't during the tournament after she'd suffered a dog bite. He remained head physician and Rhianwyn was once again disallowed.

"You'll peruse the market alone?" Broccan returned to their previous conversation.

"Unless you'll accompany me?" She smiled, yet he caught something off in her tone.

Was she melancholy? Lonely? Other than when he was training, he was with her. Was she still insecure about their relationship because he'd strayed? He'd never have done so without the damnable soul switch.

Rhianwyn *had* become more demanding of his time. He presumed she was making up for all they'd lost when they were parted—that she, too, wanted it like it once was between them.

"Maybe Severin will allow me time off today, keepin' in mind I'd have to make it up tomorrow after I meet with the king."

She sighed, frowning. "No, I won't likely be long anyway. Chester will take me in the wagon and might accompany me through the market. Pray Mirtha and her vexing little brother don't beg to come along."

Broccan stared again. "Now you sound like Cassian regarding that lad. You adore children. I thought you found Fairfax amusin'?"

"He cusses like a sailor, and I certainly don't wish to be seen with Mirtha wearing those unbecoming breeches. She'd look much more feminine in gowns."

Broccan's eyebrow rose. Rhianwyn never used to judge or find fault in others. Maybe she was discontented.

"I don't know that Chester and Mirtha have been spendin' much time together lately."

"You take note of her whereabouts? Are you attracted to her like all men seem to be?"

He tilted his head and eyed her closer. Was she jealous

of Mirtha? The Mercian woman was undeniably beautiful. Most men followed her around nearly drooling. She'd once seemed smitten with him, but he'd never looked her way. Well...he'd done no more than look, other than that kiss in Mercia but that was only to lure Doirean into a trap. He'd best console Rhianwyn. He wanted no more woes.

"I could take you in the wagon," Broccan said.

She sighed, theatrically. "If you accompany me, you'd have to leave almost straightaway. You're always cautious not to annoy Severin. I couldn't view the market stalls at my leisure."

Broccan cleared his throat. She seemed disagreeable today. He pushed his plate aside and stood although he hadn't finished the food. Rhianwyn had barely touched hers.

"I'll go then and let you speak to Chester."

She batted her eyelashes and grazed his forearm.

"Don't leave without a farewell kiss, husband," she said.

As if he ever did. He bent to kiss her. She returned the affection, but no longer closed her eyes when they kissed. She'd once professed he took her breath away and she'd become hopelessly lost in his kisses, like it was a dream.

"Be cautious while training today," she called.

"I will...as always," he replied.

Something niggled him. Maybe they hadn't mended their marriage as he'd believed. He hoped he was wrong.

AFTER CONVINCING SEVERIN to allow him time with his

wife, Broccan glanced across the market and spotted her straightaway. She wore a fancy garment for attending market. She had been attired in more lavish gowns recently and was having more made. The tailor would be well pleased getting the business. Her hair was fashioned fancily, too.

Presently Rhianwyn wasn't surveying the market wares but standing on the cobblestone street gazing at knights' field. When he approached, she seemed startled. Her cheeks turned pink.

"What lustful thoughts have caused that blush, Rhianwyn?" he jested.

She cleared her throat and lifted her chin. "I was merely trying to catch a glimpse of my handsome husband training."

She seemed oddly nervous.

"I wasn't trainin' there. Cassian was with me on the field beyond the keep. As per Severin's advisement, we're tryin' to keep Cassian and Zachary parted."

The two knights remained at odds for Chester, Zachary's twin, and Cassian had both fancied Mirtha. Zachary was still displeased with his half-brother Cassian, too, because he'd once bedded Selena, the harlot Zachary loved. Everard, Cassian's full brother, was caught in the middle. It made it awkward for Broccan, too, being friends with all of them.

Severin frequently warned the brothers to keep their differences from the training field and the knights' keep, but ignoring the animosity when spending so much time together was difficult.

"I suspect Severin will be forced to make cuts if this rivalry continues," Broccan said.

"Who'd be cut?" Rhianwyn sounded tense.

"Not Cassian." Broccan shook his head. "He's been in the order for years. As the late Sir Rodrick's son, Cassian has the king's favor. And as joint knight commander, he'd be least likely to be let go."

Rhianwyn's eyes became stormy. "Although not legitimate, Zachary's also Roderick's son. They'd truly let Zachary go simply because he defended Chester? Is Cassian not also to blame? Chester didn't force Mirtha's affections."

The romance between Chester and Mirtha had cooled because of the tension between Cassian and Chester.

"True. But Zachary hasn't been long with this order. He might be sent to another or follow a banneret if he wishes to continue with this pursuit. Although a natural with the sword and proud to be a knight, he's been unsettled lately. If he and Cassian can't work it out, that's likely to be the way of it."

That seemed to distress Rhianwyn. Avoiding his eyes, she looked as though she might weep. Why was she suddenly bothered about Zachary? Months ago, when she'd been withdrawn and uninterested in their marriage bed, Broccan had caught her looking at Zachary with interest. But that was when she was Selena and afflicted by magic that was no longer happening.

Rhianwyn was surely only concerned as a friend. She'd discovered the Thorton twins working at a raucous neighboring village tavern and sleeping in a stable. Longing to improve their situation, she'd employed them. Chester was a fine horseman and an asset to Brockwell Manor. Zachary was an honorable man, too. Rhianwyn likely just didn't want the twins separated. Nor did Broccan.

"Should we walk through the market together then?" Broccan was now unsure.

"Perhaps I'll return to the manor," she replied sullenly.

He followed her gaze, spotting Selena and Elspeth. He couldn't be outright rude and nodded to the two women. Rhianwyn looked like she didn't approve of that innocent gesture.

Maybe things weren't as rosy as he'd hoped. And tomorrow he'd meet with the king. Why in bloody hell would he demand a private audience?

HOPING TO CALM his rising temper before he spoke, Broccan took several deep breaths. He glanced around the massive castle chamber where the king offered rulings and made judgments.

"And if I refuse, Your Grace?" Broccan fought to keep his tone respectful.

King Thaddeus scowled. "My son-in-law has asked that you provide protection for my daughter. Surely you wouldn't turn down such a vital request. Lilliana is Wessexian and my knights are sworn to protect anyone of my kingdom."

Broccan curled and uncurled his fists. "She doesn't reside in your kingdom now. Besides, Tyven has a dozen of his own knights as skilled as me."

"Surely you're not still fretting about her taking your damn horse?" Thaddeus asked. "Your steed was returned unharmed."

"This has nothin' to do with my horse. May I speak plain?"

The king snorted. "You've never been one to hold your tongue, Broccan."

"I don't want to leave just now. My wife and I are… We need time to…"

"King Thaddeus is ordering you to go to Welshland!" Hankin, the irksome advisor, interrupted as he passed him the decree.

Broccan fumed on reading the written orders.

"Refusing to protect my daughter could be seen as treasonous." The king's tone was solemn.

Broccan tucked the damn orders in his tunic pocket and pulled his hand through his hair, frustrated and wanting to cuss. But at whom? The king, Hankin, Prince Tyven? Maybe Severin, for he *was* the one who'd forced him to return to the knighthood. He longed to hit something or thrash his sword about, to alleviate his fury.

"When am I to be there?" Broccan realized he had no choice.

"To protect my daughter, obviously you must leave straightaway!" The king gave an arrogant grunt. "The journey *will* take nearly two days."

"Am I to go alone? Have other knights been requested?"

"Only you," Hankin said. "Perhaps because you were victor in the recent tournament."

Bloody hell. Was that it? Was it truly even Tyven making this request? Lilliana had, on more than one occasion, been forward saying she'd favor time alone with Broccan...even though she'd been good friends with Rhianwyn then. He'd heard whispers of the princess's habit of taking knights to her bed.

"May I leave tomorrow mornin' after a hot meal and a decent night's sleep?" Broccan asked. "I must break this news to my wife since I've no notion how long I'll be gone."

"You're not honestly thinking your wife's bruised feelings are to be considered when my daughter's very life might be at risk." The king's voice was brusque, his face reddening. That wasn't a good sign. "If what the rumor mill's been spreading is true, not long ago, you developed a fondness for other women and weren't even faithful to your wife despite being so damn eager to wed her. Is Lady Brockwell fearful you'll stray again?"

Enraged, Broccan was sure his own face was red. He bit his tongue until he tasted blood.

"It's unlikely *anyone* in Welshland could compare to my wife's beauty," he finally said.

The king cast Broccan a disapproving glare at the slight toward his daughter.

"I'd suggest you procure your horse and gear and be on the road before midday." The smugness in Hankin's tone made Broccan want to run him through with his sword. The man thought he had the power of a king.

"So be it, Your Grace." Broccan bowed.

The king nodded with a pompous smirk.

Upon leaving Broccan met a man about to enter the king's hall. By the rich fabric of the vibrant green bejeweled robe and the stiff pointed miter headdress, he was the bishop. At first glance Broccan disliked the man. He had an air of superiority that might surpass that of the king and Hankin. With the same cold eyes and broad jaw, he also reminded him of Godric—that misbegotten shite.

Broccan nodded to the clergyman. As a knight it was expected, yet the man lifted his hawk-like nose and looked away. Apparently, a king's knight, even one of the knight commanders, didn't dignify acknowledgment by the visiting bishop.

Conceited bastard!

Entering the castle's expansive corridor leading to the arched main doors, Broccan nearly ran into Oliver Barlow, who didn't look joyful either.

"Lord Barlow. Are you to meet with the king?"

Oliver nodded, unenthused. "I've been named one of the king's advisors. I should be honored, but in truth, I don't relish the position. Unfortunately, I have no choice. I'll have to put up with the other unyielding advisors, the stubborn king, and the bishop whom I'm told is a difficult man."

"I've heard the same. And from what I've just seen, I believe it. I know precisely how you feel." Broccan felt his own forehead furrow.

"Have you been named advisor, too?" Oliver asked.

"No. I've been ordered to Welshland to help protect the princess."

Oliver narrowed one eye. "Why would she need protection from a knight of Thaddeus's order? Doesn't Prince Tyven have dozens of his own knights?"

"Why indeed?" Broccan replied, unable to come up with a reasonable explanation.

Oliver continued speaking. "I've never longed to be advisor and especially now. I've enough to contend with trying to discover if my sister had something to do with the recent messy business at the brothel."

"You mean the murders?" Broccan thought stabbings and murder were more than messy. Although always unlikeable and manipulative, Broccan wasn't sure Corliss Barlow was capable of murder. However, she'd likely once conspired to have Rhianwyn enslaved so that Broccan might wed Corliss instead. Apparently, her own brother suspected she *was* somehow connected to the murders. She'd also apparently threatened Halsey Winthrop. Halsey and her girlchild were presently staying with Sir Severin and Mabel. There they'd be protected from Corliss and her threats.

Oliver and Broccan planned to meet with Friar Drummond to help Severin find out who'd adopted Mabel's daughter several years ago. That would have to wait.

Oliver sighed. "Well, safe journey, Sir Broccan."

"Good luck with your new position, Lord Barlow," Broccan replied.

"I might like to trade places," Oliver said. "Though I suspect Princess Lilliana can be as difficult as her father."

That was true. Broccan didn't fancy being in her company. He tipped his head to Oliver as he left.

Because Oliver had once bid for Rhianwyn's hand, Broccan had never been on overly friendly terms with him. Strangely, he now thought of Oliver as an ally if only because they were equally wretched. Misery did love company.

"YOU CANNOT GO to Welshland!" Rhianwyn lifted her chin defiantly. "I simply won't have it!"

Broccan looked at his wife with some impatience. They'd discussed it in the hall over a hurried meal, and now again in their bedchamber in a more heated exchange.

"Rhianwyn, we've been through this. I've no choice."

"Why would the king make this request?" She threw her hands before her in frustration that matched his own.

Broccan shrugged, hastily tossing a few garments in a sack and rolling up a blanket. Now, late summer, he wouldn't need a heavy cloak or fur bedroll. He was expected to ride straight through to Welshland, which was impractical. He'd be wearied should he encounter anything untoward on the journey or upon arrival. What would the princess need protection from? And why him?

Broccan tossed the decree with his orders on the bed.

"Read this over for yourself, Rhianwyn."

She glanced at the parchment but didn't take time to read it.

"Why must it be you?" she asked.

"Prince Tyven requested my presence and honestly, Rhianwyn, I don't know more than that."

"That's absurd. Tyven has a full order of knights...surely a sheriff and his men-at-arms, and an army of barbaric Welshmen."

Barbaric Welshmen? Her mother hailed from Welshland. Rhianwyn had always spoken fondly of it.

Broccan shrugged again.

"You should refuse to go," she said, bossily.

"Sure that'd earn me a place in the dungeon if not the block."

She began to pace when her face suddenly brightened. "Then I'll accompany you."

He eyed her closer, shaking his head. "Rhianwyn, you don't even ride any longer; there's no time to take a wagon. Besides, if Lilliana is in peril, I don't want you anywhere near."

"You suspect she's not actually in peril?" Her eyebrow arched.

He filled his cheeks with air, then blew out his breath. Obviously, he couldn't say anything to appease her.

"I've been given a detail in Welshland. As a sworn knight I must accept, and I can't take you, for it might be bloody dangerous."

He'd expected she'd be unhappy they'd be parted but didn't think he'd be made to explain again and again. She well knew a knight must obey orders.

Rhianwyn's full lips pouted untypically. "Then promise you'll stay away from Lilliana."

There was that jealous tone again.

"I suspect if I'm to protect the princess, we may need to be in close proximity."

"Then swear to me you'll not bed her!"

Broccan pivoted to face his wife. "God's bones, I wouldn't!"

"Lilliana's been interested in you from when first you met that night at my cottage. She's made no attempt to hide that."

That was true.

"The princess and I are both wed now. At her husband's request, I'll protect her and nothin' more."

"She's very beautiful. You find her attractive."

"If I bedded every attractive woman..." He tried to make light of this impossible situation. "I'd be utterly exhausted and unable to fulfill my duty of protectin' her."

Rhianwyn's pale blue eyes flashed furiously. He went to her and took her in his arms. But as he bent to kiss her, she pulled away.

"Do you know of the princess's reputation with knights...that she orders them to her bed? She's even insisted women join them and perversely watches others sharing intimacies."

Broccan stared. "Did Lilliana admit this...or are these only rumors spread by gossipmongers?"

Why was he defending the princess? He'd heard similar notions, though none so deviant as what Rhianwyn mentioned.

"I know some is true." She stubbornly crossed her arms.

"Sure we've all done somethin' in the past we aren't proud of," Broccan began. God knew he had. "As I've said, Lilliana's married and surely true to her husband. Why torment yourself frettin' of this, Rhianwyn? I swear I wouldn't betray my marriage vows."

"You mean *not again?*" This time she threw him a caustic glare.

"Not unless a magical spell should make me unable to determine the true identity of my wife and unable to resist her no matter what form she's in." He dared to broach the distasteful subject they mostly avoided. "But since you've assured me all that's over with, there'd be no reason for you to suspect any indiscretions in that regard. Isn't that so?"

She lowered her head, finally nodding.

"Are you so riled about me leavin' that you won't let me love you before I go?" He waggled his eyebrow.

A slow smile crossed her face as their eyes met. "You'd defy the king by not leaving straightaway?"

He grinned. "He can't know how long it takes me to ready myself for the journey and Dubh's a swift steed."

He lifted her into his arms and carried her to their bed.

CHAPTER SIX

ALREADY BONE-WEARY, BROCCAN led Dubh onto the ferry. He'd spent longer than intended with Rhianwyn in her reluctance for him to leave, and twice expended considerable energy in exuberant coupling. He sighed. After this river crossing there'd still be hours of riding. The road consisted of hills leading to treacherous terrain. Maybe snow in the mountain passes.

He shook his head, petting Dubh's neck. He wouldn't run him ragged and risk injury getting there. Sure whatever Lilliana needed protection from, Tyven and his knights could hold off until Broccan arrived. It seemed unreasonable he was needed at all. There must be more to it.

He'd worked for Tyven a few times before…rid him of enemies in hiding, or when Tyven wanted no one to know the Dafyddsons were involved. It was back when Broccan did that for a living…sought out dangerous sorts whose deaths meant innocent lives would be saved.

The ferryman made conversation. "That's a large horse."

"Over eighteen hands." Broccan nodded.

"Saw a white mare nearly that big a few weeks back. The owner, a peculiar woman, said she'd maybe been poisoned. Not sure if she lived. The bedeviled horse took off when the ferry docked."

"What'd the woman look like?" Broccan asked, thinking it too much of a coincidence that Lilliana left for Welshland with Tyven's white horse...the largest mare Broccan had seen. They would've probably crossed here.

"Pretty sort. Long, black hair. She barely spoke but sounded Saxon not Welsh. The horse was swimming across. Might've both drowned if I hadn't towed them."

Broccan was lost in thought. There'd been much speculation about why Lilliana would leave for Welshland and steal Tyven's horse. It seemed out of character. Maybe Lilliana and the horse had a spell placed upon them. Perhaps she needed protection from something of an unnatural origin. That might explain why Tyven had requested him.

There were rumors Tyven's kin were associated with dragons. Some even claimed they were shifters. Tyven's father was believed to be. Most people wouldn't give that much credence, but previously in Welshland, Broccan had been called to destroy some of the halfling creatures who'd become more feral and begun killing humans.

Raised in Ireland, Broccan's father was high king in Tara. They were descendants of the *Tuatha Dé Danann*, the Fae. Though he'd turned from his own magical abilities, Broccan had witnessed too many things only explained by magic.

Hell, he'd once been involved with Doirean, a vicious shapeshifting creature. Leofwine, bounty hunter and soul seer, had recently sent word he'd tracked Doirean to her homeland, the Isle of Skye. If she left again, Leofwine warned he'd pursue her. Broccan prayed she'd stay put. He had enough to contend with.

He also couldn't discredit magic when his own wife had been involved in a soul transference. At least that's what she claimed. It would finally explain why he'd been attracted to Selena and Elspeth. God's teeth, he was glad to be done with that.

"Where you headed?" the ferryman asked.

"The Dafyddson kingdom," Broccan replied.

The man grunted. "What takes you there?" He glanced at Broccan's chain mail and knightly arming sword.

"I've been summoned."

Not that it was any of his business.

"I'd keep my wits about you. They're a portentous lot."

The man spoke in broken Saxon with some Welsh. Ireland and Welshland both had Celtic roots. Broccan likely understood more than most not native to Welshland.

"I'll take that under consideration," Broccan said, passing the man the required coin after they docked.

With the sun already setting, he'd take lodging at an inn. A warm meal, some ale, and a decent bed would make the remainder of the journey less harrowing on the morrow.

"We'll find you a nice stable, Dubh."

The horse neighed agreement. If whatever Broccan would be protecting Princess Lilliana from was of an otherworldly origin, he'd better be well rested.

RHIANWYN HAD BECOME far more discontented. Her mind was clearer without the potion. Still, her memory hadn't fully returned. Maybe Morwenna had magically prevented her learning everything from her past. Was she protecting her because she was her niece?

As twilight neared, Rhianwyn looked toward the cliffs, spotting bright yellow flowers. Hawkweed. She recalled being presented with that flower by a tall red-haired man. He'd smiled as though he loved her. Oddly when recalling the memory, she was taller with blonde hair. Wait…that was her friend Elspeth. She hadn't thought of her friends in a long while.

Suddenly she remembered standing within a stone circle with Elspeth, Selena, and Lilliana. She recalled saying words she didn't want to speak to an old woman she didn't trust. Why would she do that?

She closed her eyes. Although it didn't hurt so fiercely when remembering, her head spun.

"Don't look so glum, Princess."

Teg's voice didn't cheer her.

"I'm weary of this uncertainty."

"I told you, you're restless in needing a man."

She gave him a dismissive wave of her hand. "Is that *all* males think about?"

"So you're not kept awake remembering the Irishman and what you once shared in a bed?"

"I am not," she lied. "Besides he did something to infuriate me, and I don't want to see him again."

Teg shrugged. "Has Morwenna rid you of the curse the princess's servant placed upon you?"

"She said the curse is ended."

"By her magic?"

"No. She claims the curser must've died, for she cannot sense her on this earthly plane."

"Would that terminate a curse?" he asked. "Why wasn't the curse on the Dafyddsons ended long ago then?"

They were interrupted by strumming, a profoundly sad melody—like every night. When she'd asked Morwenna about it, she'd said Tomos Dafyddson was playing. It was probably a lute.

"That music would make the cheeriest soul despond-ent," Teg said. "I suppose if I was seen as hideously ugly and could never do any sarding, I might create sorrowful tunes, too."

"Sarding? That's a Saxon word," Rhianwyn said.

Teg grinned. "I thought it might amuse you."

"My friend Elspeth uses the term at will."

"Do you miss your friends…the others you made the pact with?"

"I haven't remembered them enough to miss them. When I do recall, I feel angry with them, too."

"What did they do?" Teg looked eager to hear.

"I don't remember. But when I left Wessex, I was mightily vexed at them and the Irishman. If I should see any of them, I might…"

Teg flitted about, his eyes extra wide. "Well…what might you do, Princess?"

"Probably nothing!" she sighed. "I made a promise to my mother to cause no harm. Although I believe I broke that promise."

They were quiet for some time. The evening breeze pleasantly rustled her hair, but the dismal music tugged at her heart as she stared into the fire. The sunset colored the sky with glorious pink and purple hues.

"Do you fancy some undiluted ale?" Teg asked. "The Dafyddsons keep a store nearby."

"Show me." Rhianwyn stood. "Maybe strong ale will drown the solemness of that damn music."

Teg flew to the winding stream, then pointed. "Just there behind that rock."

Rhianwyn waded in. She sometimes bathed here, but with summer evenings now cooler, the water was cold. She gasped, reaching behind the rock to find a jug.

"Why would they leave their ale here?"

Teg shrugged. "How would I know why cursed princes do much of what they do?"

After they'd returned to the fireside and drank more than their fill, Rhianwyn felt more lighthearted. She took the jug of ale, picked up the walking stick, and started toward the mournful sound.

"Where're you going?" Teg sounded drunk.

"I must meet this maker of maudlin music."

"He could be far away. Music's often carried on the wind. Besides, why would you want to see someone who's grotesque?" Teg darted about zigzagging, clearly affected by the drink.

"I've grown accustomed to *your* grotesqueness." She, too, slurred and broke into laughter seeing his wounded expression.

"That's cruel, Princess."

She giggled. "In truth, I find you quite comely. You've grown on me, Teg. If I truly found you unsightly, would I speak of it?"

He only drunkenly flitted, following her up the path that grew steadily steeper as the night became darker. She struck the walking stick, smiling when rewarded by the bright glow. Teg grinned. When they'd gone for some time following the music, it stopped abruptly.

"He knows we're coming and doesn't want to be found," Teg whispered.

"Tomos," Rhianwyn called. "Might you play something cheerier?"

"Why are you here?" The voice sounded angry.

When a hooded man leaped before them, Teg shrieked and Rhianwyn nearly teetered over the ledge.

"Well don't frighten us half to death!" Rhianwyn rebuked.

"Why are you here?" the man repeated.

"Are you Tomos?" she asked.

"Why do you need to know?"

"If I must be subjected to your melancholy music, you could at least answer my query." Unsteady on her feet, she finally sat on the path.

"How do you even know it was me playing the music?"

"The lute on your shoulder might be a giveaway." Rhianwyn rolled her eyes.

He grumbled and leaned forward, his hood falling down.

"Why do you conceal your face? It isn't as though you'd want me to be attracted to you when that attraction would be fatal if we...were more than friends. No, wait...that's Cynfawr. You wouldn't die if we mated; that would be me." She hiccupped.

"I didn't know my brother's bride would be so blunt or given to overdrinking."

"Have you ever met me?" Rhianwyn asked.

"Well no...but you're a Saxon princess. I thought you'd be refined and mannerly."

Teg snorted and slapped his tiny knee. "She's not."

"Come share our fire and drink our ale. Well...I suppose it's your ale," Rhianwyn slurred. "Maybe you'll be cheerier, and we could request happier songs."

By the pale waxing moon, he shook his hooded head.

"Why would I be bothered whether you're pleased with my songs?"

"Because, if I'm made to listen to your bloody mournful melodies much longer, I might toss your damn lute into the sarding sea." She gestured toward the cliffs.

He growled, crossing his arms. "What makes you think you could get my lute even if you weren't drunk?"

"Going to transform into a mighty dragon and fly away?" she asked.

He snarled again. "Why would you be so unkind as to take my only way of expressing my misery?"

"Just come with me." She shakily stood, reaching for his hand. "After you drink some ale, you'll feel less woeful, I promise."

He yanked his hand away and she nearly fell. "You can make no such promise, Princess."

"I think you're happy wallowing in misery."

"I don't give a damn what you think!" he snapped.

She shrugged. "So be it. We'll leave, Teg. Tomos thinks himself the only one displeased with his lot in life. Poor, wretched Tomos." She placed the back of her hand to her forehead.

She turned to go but Tomos followed. She winked at Teg.

"You've no right to condemn me, Princess."

"I suppose being wed to a man who'll soon impregnate me so I'll die gruesomely giving birth—probably to a beast—would be a fate envied by many then?"

"I suppose not," Tomos conceded.

Before long they were back sitting by the fire drinking. Tomos was ever cautious to keep the hood over his face.

"When you look at your reflection, do you see yourself as revolting?" Teg asked.

"Why do you keep bringing up my appearance?" Tomos asked.

"It's the first time I've spoken of it." Teg grinned.

Tomos grunted. "Perhaps I should tell you what I think of ellylls."

"I think," Rhianwyn said, feeling delightfully drunk and warm from the fire, "you should play a merry tune and Teg and I will dance."

Tomos laughed. "I might like to see that. A Saxon princess dancing with an ellyll."

"Or Teg could play, and I'll dance with you."

"I do not *dance*, and I doubt he plays." He gestured to Teg. "I wouldn't permit him to touch my lute."

"Then I'll have the lute play while we all dance." Rhianwyn giggled drunkenly.

"How would that be done?" Teg sounded curious.

"Wand." She looked at the walking stick. "Make the lute play, so we might make merry till light of day."

When her walking stick glowed and his lute began to play with no one touching it, Tomos jumped up, his hood falling back. Rhianwyn stared. Snarling, he reached for the cloak's hood.

"No, you needn't cover your face," she assured him. "You're as handsome as your brothers. Your golden hair and blue eyes are most pleasing."

He looked doubtful. "No one is ever to see me as anything but ghastly."

She shrugged. "You're attractive to me. Now, play a cheery tune."

"You're lying!" he charged. "Only so I'll play happier tunes?"

"Your lute's already playing happily…therefore I needn't speak falsehoods. Just come dance, fair Tomos."

"Is she lying?" Tomos looked at Teg.

"She's not turning away unable to bear the sight of you. So, dance with her…but keep your distance so neither of you become desirous."

"I only want to dance." Rhianwyn grasped Tomos's hand and pulled him to his feet.

They danced for some time with Teg fluttering about in his drunkenness, too.

"I'm wearied now so play something slow and dear to my heart," Rhianwyn said to the wand.

A song began, and her chest tightened. Tears threatened to fall. A song written by the man who loved her, whom she loved as well, but she couldn't fully remember. Raising her hand, the music screeched unpleasantly before stopping. The wand sailed across the fire, hit the cottage wall, and then fell to the ground with a thud.

"Why did you do that?" Tomos asked, eyes wide.

"How did you do that?" Teg stared. "It's one thing to use a wand but quite another to use your hand to direct magic against the wand. That takes potent magic."

"I only know I've had too much to drink. Thank you both for spending time with me. Might I request you douse the fire before you leave, Tomos?"

He nodded and Teg followed her inside, as did the wand.

"Whatever's wrong?" Teg sounded understanding even in his drunkenness. "Why did that song rattle you?"

"My true love composed it for me. Thinking of him hurts too much." She touched her chest. "Good night, Teg. Stay if you wish, but I must sleep off the drink." She fell upon the bed without removing her garments.

BROCCAN WAS ODDLY disoriented. He always had an impeccable sense of direction and he'd been to Tyven's castle before. He took the road he knew led there, but peculiarly kept ending up on this unfamiliar path. Was it magic? A spell perhaps cast by whomever he was to protect Lilliana from? Someone not wanting him to get to her? This could be dark magic indeed.

He found himself in a valley. From here, he could see the six Dafyddson castles. He'd had several dealings with Tyven, met the other brothers once, and seen Gronow in Wessex, too. He wasn't sure he'd care to meet King Eurion. He'd yet to hear anything complimentary of him even beyond rumors he was a heartless dragon-born shifter.

Broccan looked up easily distinguishing Tyven's castle with the unusually high parapets. He started up the incline again only to find himself back on the path.

"What in bloody hell? What magic's afoot this day?"

Dubh snorted and started off in another direction.

"Go wherever you like, boy. Your guess is maybe better than mine."

RHIANWYN SENT TEG away. He'd asked questions about the song that saddened her. She'd rudely told him she couldn't listen to his annoying chatter when her head throbbed from drinking undiluted ale in excess.

She stood out in the sunlit meadow inhaling the scent of the late summer wildflowers. She was dressed in her frayed shift—sleeves torn off and hem ripped to mid-thigh, so it didn't snag when walking through long grass. She liked the sun's warmth on her skin. While walking barefoot she'd become skilled in avoiding nettles and thistles.

Tomos wouldn't likely return. That was just as well, for being near a man made her remember persistent womanly urges. Clearly the prospect of something clawing its way from her womb should deter her from spending time with any Dafyddson.

Holding her hands to her throbbing head, she dropped her wand when she spotted feverfew. She reached down to pick some. It'd be better crushed, made into paste and boiled with willow bark, but in a pinch, this might abate her aching head. She chewed, ignoring the bitterness. Perhaps she should search for monk's pepper or water lily to take away these unignorable surging desires.

BROCCAN SPOTTED A woman across the meadow. Attired in a short, ragged shift, she was wandering aimlessly, occasionally holding her head. Bloody hell, now she appeared to be picking and chewing grass. Was she starving? No, she seemed curvy enough. Perhaps born addleminded—or had something untoward happened to her?

Whatever the reason, she wasn't his concern. He couldn't even find his bloody way to a castle he'd been to before. Yet as a knight who prided himself in protecting women or anyone in need, he kept glancing at her.

Damned if Dubh didn't head straight for her. Her back was to them. Her long pitch-black hair flew about when she twirled with her eyes closed. There was something familiar in that movement.

After dismounting, he tied Dubh to the nearby tree. He hadn't seen how close the woman was to the cliffs. Did she not notice? Would it matter to her?

Walking closer, he was wholly astounded. She was Princess Lilliana, though she looked no more like a princess than he did. Her garment was indeed a tattered rag, soiled with earth and grass. Her tresses were unbound, even tangled. Had she been accosted? Had the danger he'd been called to protect her from already occurred?

Where were Tyven and his knights? Perhaps she'd witnessed them killed and her mind was left damaged. Maybe she'd been violated. Yet her face, legs, and arms bore no bruising; there was no blood on her shift. She didn't appear tormented. In truth, she appeared mindlessly unencumbered.

"Lilliana," he called quietly, not wanting to startle her.

Her dark eyes flew open. Upon seeing him, they became wild. Maybe she had been raped. He'd seen similar terror of men in women who'd been assaulted.

"Go away!" she spat.

"Lilliana, don't you recognize me? What's happened to you?"

He stepped nearer.

"Don't come closer!" she warned bending to pick up a stick.

Was that the walking stick that once belonged to Rhianwyn? He hadn't seen it for some time.

He held his hands before him. "I won't approach. Tell me what's happened. Where's your husband?"

"My husband?" She sounded entirely befuddled.

"Prince Tyven?"

She backed up.

"Mind the cliff's edge, Lilliana. Don't fall over."

He looked beyond. The drop would be perilous.

"Go away! You can't be here. She said you couldn't.

I'm not even to think of you."

"Who is *she*? Think of me?" He was now more per-plexed. "Do you know who I am, Lilliana?"

She shook her head hard, eyes like a trapped feral ani-mal. She backed up farther. He considered grabbing for her. Better she was frightened than for her to go over the edge. But she wasn't letting him near her. He'd put himself between her and the dangerous crags.

When he moved, she ran at him, shoving him hard. That took him off guard. His knees buckled and he fought to right himself. Then she charged again like an enraged bull. Although he was more prepared, and considerably larger than her, the ground beneath him wasn't sound...apparently no more sound than her mind.

As he began to fall, she clung to him, pounding at his chest as they both plunged downward. His heart sped and his mouth went dry. He was about to die.

CHAPTER SEVEN

S URPRISINGLY, THEY LANDED on a ledge part way down. Broccan heaved a sigh, then groaned. His shoulder must've taken the brunt of the fall. He supposed it was better than his head. Still, it was agonizing and in her unstable state, he couldn't be sure Lilliana wouldn't pull them both over. He moaned, keeping her at a distance with his good arm, holding her hand so she wouldn't go over.

In excruciating pain, he grunted and writhed, but there wasn't space to afford him that.

"Broccan?" She sounded like she recognized him now.

He didn't reply.

"Broccan," she whispered. "Oh, Broccan, I'm sorry. What have I done?"

She looked up at the cliff above and then to the drop below.

"Don't move," he managed.

Christ's cross, his shoulder throbbed. She reached for him.

"Don't bloody well touch me, woman."

"Why are you here?" she asked, now apparently lucid.

"Because you pushed me over the sardin' cliff!"

"Why aren't you in Wessex with your wife?"

"At your husband's request, King Thaddeus ordered me

to come protect you."

Her eyes became pensive.

"How did you get in this state, Lilliana?" He glanced at her shift's low neckline. The garment barely covered her breasts. Her shift was so short it afforded him a clear view of long, shapely thighs. It was difficult not to stare. However, natural male interest was secondary to his present agony.

She didn't reply but reached for his injured shoulder. He shook his head, which sent pain down his arm.

He growled. "God's nails, stay still; *do not* touch me!"

"Your shoulder might be broken, but it's more likely dislocated," she said. "It'll need to be adjusted."

How would a princess know anything of that?

"Maybe so, but not here. In truth, I don't want you near me. I admit I've no notion how we'll get out of this predicament. No one will see us down here. Dubh's tied to a tree and..."

"Dubh?" She smiled brightly. "I've missed him."

"Since last you saw him, when you stole him."

"He and Gwynna were drawn to one another. Admittedly, I wasn't thinking straight. I'd been poisoned and cursed."

She spoke like those were everyday occurrences.

"You sound cursed even now...the curse of an imbecile."

She pulled a face. He wasn't bothered if he insulted her but really shouldn't anger her if she was given to madness. If she'd been poisoned, perhaps it had affected her mind.

Maybe she wasn't the one who needed protection after all. He began envisioning all sorts of fresh hell. Maybe she'd killed Tyven and his men. Surely not. She was *one* woman. They'd have weapons and protect themselves no matter how capricious she might be. Again, she had no blood on her.

Broccan's mind raced. In pain, he broke out in a cold sweat. She reached for his face, but he gasped and pulled away.

"I wouldn't hurt you, Sir Broccan."

He laughed humorlessly. "I beg to differ. You've caused me ample pain."

He stretched his legs, sending another shot of agony through him.

"Don't fret." She touched his hand gently. "I'll call for Teg. He'll get Dubh, tie a rope to his saddle, and throw it to us."

"Oh is that all?" he said sarcastically. "Who the hell's Teg when he's at home and how, pray tell, am I to get up that cliff when I've only one good arm, even if I had a sardin' rope?"

"You're being very difficult!" She placed her fists on her curvy hips and scowled.

"I suppose I should be celebratin' then? Dancin' maybe?"

"How I've missed your Irish accent." She smiled again, which further irritated him.

That was important now. He groaned, attempting to wipe sweat from his brow before it dripped in his eyes. She tore a strip of her already inappropriately short shift and placed it to his forehead.

"Teg's an ellyll, therefore you mightn't see him. He's a

lewd magical creature with an affliction to drink. But still, I'm fond of him and he's bonded to me…so he'll help if he's able."

By God, she *was* utterly mad. He stared as she spoke on.

"Since you're originally from Tara and some believe you might have magic, maybe you will see him."

"Maybe you should be pushed off the cliff and put out of your misery!" he snapped.

"Dear Broccan, I'll not hold your cantankerousness against you. Men in pain are often ill-tempered." She cupped her hands. "Teg, if you're near, you must find the tall black horse, untie him, and lead him here."

Broccan watched her. She seemed to believe this magical creature would simply appear.

"If you're thinkin' you're distractin' me from my pain by speakin' such absurdities, it's not workin'."

"Me speaking absurdities? Only weeks ago you claimed Elspeth and Rhianwyn needed protection from a diabolical shapeshifting woman whom you once cared for! Then you and my friends created the ridiculous notion of a soul shift so you could…sard them. You and Teg might get along famously, for you're a bit lewd, too!"

Broccan tensed. "Shut the hell up. You don't know what you're talkin' about. Although I've never injured a woman, I might be tempted. Who'd even know if I pushed you over this ledge?"

She snorted. "I doubt you're able in your present condition. I might have Teg only help me and not you or…maybe I'll use my wand and leave you stranded here since you're so churlish!"

Her wand? Having no desire to banter, he didn't reply. He'd been in many difficult spots, but this just might be the least enviable and all because of her. She stared as though deep in thought. What madness would she spout now?

"I could attempt to right your shoulder. I've successfully done such healing before...not on a narrow cliff ledge, mind you. That would be chancy."

"You're not comin' near me, Lilliana!" he blared, sending pain through his body again. "Sardin' hell!"

Thinking he might pass out, he moaned, leaning his head against the rock.

"Teg, I swear if you don't come here this instant, I'll request Morwenna use dark magic on you," she hollered.

When Broccan saw a small peculiar-looking creature peek over the ledge above, he thought the pain must've driven him mad.

"I was getting the horse, Princess. Don't be so damned impatient. You'd think I was your infernal servant."

God's teeth, was he hearing things, too?

"Teg, meet Sir Broccan. He's a knight originally from Ireland, but presently living in Wessex and married to my friend, Rhianwyn." She winked at the small creature.

"Is he now?" The peculiar creature's bulging eyes bulged further.

Temporarily distracted by the wee being, Lilliana abruptly grasped Broccan's arm, placed her foot in his armpit and yanked hard. He bellowed so loud his voice echoed. She jumped away, grasped the walking stick seeming to hover mid-air. His mind truly was affected by pain. Yet come to it, the pain had mostly subsided.

"You could thank me, Sir Broccan." Fluttering her eyelashes, she was surely purposely trying to annoy him.

"Thank you for sendin' me over a cliff?"

"Do you suppose we should leave him here, Teg? Since he's whingeing and ill-tempered?"

"Wouldn't your friend Rhianwyn be displeased?" Teg grinned.

She shrugged. "As the ungentlemanly Sir Broccan once told me, who'd ever know if he fell to his death?"

"Oh you've the devil in you today, Princess." Teg guffawed.

"You're not amusin'—either of you." Broccan cautiously stood.

"My, he is a tall one, isn't he? Almost a giant." Teg chuckled.

"Throw down the rope. I'll get myself up, then we'll decide what's to be done about him." She winked again.

"I *should* throw you over the ledge," Broccan suggested. "Since Tyven isn't here to rescue you... You didn't murder him and his brothers, did you?"

"Not yet." She smirked disturbingly.

No longer racked with pain, he couldn't help noticing her womanly attributes. The swell of her high, firm breasts in the thin shift, the dark nipples beneath and her long uncovered legs. He cleared his throat. He *was* a man with a beautiful half-naked woman so near he could feel her body heat.

She reached for the rope and her shift rose higher. He

looked away.

"Christ's cross, woman, your damn arse is bared."

She spared him a glare. "Avert your eyes then. However, I require your help. It seems I haven't the strength to pull myself up that far."

"You'll maybe need to place your hand on her pleasingly formed arse, Sir Broccan," Teg called down.

"I will not," Broccan replied.

Instead, he cupped his hands and motioned for her to step onto them.

"You intend to stand below and watch," Teg snickered.

"I'll not look!" he snarled.

She stepped into his hand. Grasping the rope, she made it up. If she hadn't just pushed him over the cliff, he might've stolen a glance.

"Now, tie the rope around your waist," she called down. "Otherwise your shoulder could become displaced again."

That idea probably had merit.

"The rope's tied to Dubh's saddle. I'll lead him away slowly."

"He'll not let you."

Although he must've allowed the strange wee creature to lead him.

"He did permit me to take him to the Cymruian border. Granted he was enamored with Gwynna. They'd just mated. I must tell Tyven she's most likely with foal."

"By God, you natter on, woman. Just bloody well see this done if Dubh's willin' to heed you."

She glanced down and rolled her eyes. "You're the most

impatient, ungrateful…"

"Woman, pull me up this instant!" Broccan roared.

"You didn't tell me you were ready," she muttered.

Broccan felt himself being lifted.

"THAT'S HIM THEN, your husband?" Teg asked, widening his prominent eyes.

"Shhh," Rhianwyn whispered. "Yes. But Broccan must continue to believe I'm the princess. I hope he'll soon return to Wessex."

"Why is he in Cymru?" Teg asked.

"Apparently Tyven wants him to protect me. From what I can't say. Why wouldn't he have his own knights protect me?"

"I'd like to discover that, too," Broccan said as his head came into view over the edge of the cliff, followed by the rest of him.

Rhianwyn shouldn't look at his ruggedly handsome face or impressive muscular body. The desire she'd recently been feeling was intensifying tenfold. It was just as well he was furious with her.

When she'd spotted him today, her emotions, along with her memories, and fury from when she'd last seen him, came rushing back and she couldn't control herself. Though she hadn't intended to knock him over a cliff, she was more than happy to send him on his arse. Now she wanted to throw herself at him for something entirely different. Her body thrummed with need.

Broccan untied the rope from his waist, throwing her another angry glare.

"Why are you in this state?" He gestured to her hair and shift.

She glanced down at the garment, uncertain what to tell him.

"Why is a princess clad in rags and nowhere near her husband's castle?" Broccan reached for Dubh's reins.

Their conversation was disrupted when several knights on horseback rode toward them.

"We're to take you to Prince Tyven's castle, my princess," the lead knight said.

Rhianwyn recognized Sir Cadfael. He'd been at the tournament in Wessex.

"I can't go with you," she replied.

"It's by your husband's order." Sir Cadfael glanced at her then looked away.

"Morwenna said I must abide only her," Rhianwyn argued but was startled when the sorceress herself suddenly stepped from behind a tree.

"You may return with them." Morwenna nodded before she turned away and seemed to disappear.

"Sir Broccan's to accompany us, too," Cadfael said.

Rhianwyn watched Broccan's face. He obviously didn't like being ordered about. But he mounted his horse, looking marvelously grand.

"I must speak with Prince Tyven and learn my true purpose for bein' here," Broccan said.

Reaching behind his saddle, Cadfael retrieved a blanket.

"Put this around you, my princess."

She did as instructed, then took the walking stick.

"Who am I to ride with?" Rhianwyn asked.

"With me." Gronow appeared behind them riding a brown horse as large as Dubh. He lifted her in front of him, then wrapped his arm around her waist. They galloped along the road leading to the castles above.

CHAPTER EIGHT

Rhianwyn BATHED IN a chamber, apparently Lilliana's. She was helped into her garments by a maidservant she didn't know. She then remembered Heledd. Why wasn't she here? Perhaps she'd remained in Wessex with Cassian. Rhianwyn recalled they'd seemed attracted to one another.

The woman helped plait and tie her hair. Rhianwyn glanced in the mirror. She looked more like a princess in her fine red gown. The servant indicated by gesture she was to follow her.

She was led down a dark corridor to a great hall, as grand as the hall in King Thaddeus's castle. Only half the candles on the many round iron chandeliers, hanging from chains, were presently lit. She espied two men at a table near the front of the hall. The servant pointed toward them, curtsied, then left.

Rhianwyn felt oddly shy seeing Prince Tyven and Broccan. By Broccan's grim expression he remained displeased with her. Still, he stood respectfully. Tyven also stood, then nodded.

"Please sit, Lilliana." He pulled out the chair beside him and across from Broccan. They were all seated.

"I trust you're much improved from when last I saw

you. You do look nearly radiant this night."

"I'm certainly in better health than when I arrived, Your Grace."

"Sir Broccan informed me of the disturbing incident this day. It's fortunate you're both still alive."

She glanced at Broccan, wondering how much he'd told Tyven.

"It was rather frightening," she admitted.

Tyven gazed from one to the other wearing a peculiar expression, then looked away.

"Why have you summoned me, Prince Tyven?" Broccan sat straighter, still favoring his shoulder. "Your wife appears not to be in danger as I was led to believe."

"Let's sup before we speak of business."

Tyven was being evasive.

They ate. First cawl, the delicious lamb soup with seasonable vegetables, then both fine venison and pheasant served with thick bread and gravy. The men spoke companionably of horses and weaponry while she remained silent only speaking when asked a question.

Broccan fidgeted, probably impatient to learn why he was here. She was curious, too. She tried to keep her eyes on the food, her thoughts from her powerful attraction to Broccan and memories of the passion they'd once shared. That he remained furious with her aided in that regard. Any looks he spared her were those of contempt.

She was considering excusing herself when a servant brought another tray. She removed the cloth covering it. *Bara brith*. Rhianwyn's mouth watered seeing the cakes that Mererid, her Welsh mother, used to make. She'd not tasted them since her mother's death. Remembering her, she couldn't hide emotional tears. She dabbed them, pretending to wipe a stray lock of hair.

She hadn't thought Tyven would notice but his intense green eyes softened, and he touched her hand.

"Does something trouble you, Lilliana?"

"I'm weary and should like to return to my chambers, Your Grace."

"Of course. If that's your wish, go now."

They stood, he pulled out her chair, then took her hand and kissed it. She saw the interest in his eyes...and the lust. He was attracted to her. Admittedly, she found him appealing. Thoughts of sharing intimacies with Tyven had crossed her mind, but not when being with him could end her life...and certainly not with Broccan here, the true source of her present arousal.

She took a *bara brith* and curtsied. Tyven drew nearer, his lips grazed her cheek.

"Sleep well, lovely Lilliana. On the morrow I must speak with you on a matter of grave importance."

That sounded ominous.

Broccan rose then, too, nodding his head. "Princess," he said stiffly.

"Sir Broccan," she replied equally cool before she left them.

"Tyven, I'd appreciate you tellin' me why I'm here!" Broccan demanded, gulping his ale.

The prince sighed and wouldn't meet his eyes.

"You've done deeds for me in the past," Tyven said taking a long drink from his own tankard.

"I have." Broccan nodded.

"All of a secretive nature. I chose you knowing I could count on your sworn confidentiality. In truth, had I not trusted you entirely, it's likely you would've been killed soon after you completed those tasks."

Broccan narrowed his eyes but met the other man's stare. He supposed that was true. He had killed King Eurion's brother, a heinous man. He'd also disposed of some of the violent halfling creatures that escaped the caves.

"What distasteful deed do you require now, Tyven? I doubt it has anythin' to do with protectin' your wife."

"It does, Broccan. In truth it will probably save her life...or extend it at the very least."

"You want me to take her to Wessex?" Broccan guessed.

"Would that it were that easy, my friend, I'd see it done myself. My father wouldn't permit it. As wedded mate to a Dafyddson, her fate is to remain here till her death...or mine."

"Don't beat about the bush, then? Tell me what you need done."

Tyven took a long breath and looked away. "You must share my wife's bed...impregnate her and..."

Broccan thought the man was only jesting. Yet by his solemn expression he was serious. Broccan jumped up, stunned. "You're as bloody mad as she is!"

"Sit down," Tyven said. "I assure you, I've thought this

through. You have coloring like mine. Tall and powerfully built, you'd surely produce fine, strong children. You draw women like a moth to a flame and you appeal to Lilliana. Her heart beats faster when you're near. Her skin becomes heated."

"I *will not* bed your wife," Broccan avowed, remaining standing.

He'd go to the stables, find Dubh...leave straightaway.

"But you must. Surely, you've heard rumors of what befalls women who carry a Dafyddson's child?"

"I pay little heed to gossip," Broccan replied.

"So you've never considered that my line is connected to dragons, even after disposing of those volatile creatures in the caves?"

Broccan didn't respond. His mind was whirring.

"My mother died giving birth," Tyven said, "as did the mothers of all my brothers...as did my first wife."

Broccan pulled his hands through his hair.

"Many women die in childbed," Broccan argued.

"Not like this!" Tyven sounded stricken.

"Even if that's true, find another man. Sir Cadfael seems enamored with Lilliana. Many men are. She's a beautiful woman."

"You do find her attractive, then?"

"I'll not bed her," Broccan repeated. "Have you mentioned this absurd notion to her?"

Tyven grasped his tankard tighter. "Months ago I suggested she share intimacies with another. She didn't seem in favor. I wouldn't push her into it, but the second draig moon begins tomorrow night—this time coinciding with her being in season and fertile. She's already experiencing intense natural base urges. The coupling and conception must happen then."

Broccan's neck was tight. He moved it from one side to the other. "Then have Cadfael or another man…do what's necessary. If your wife isn't in agreement, will you have the man force himself upon her?"

"I hope it won't come to that," Tyven whispered. "But even violation would be better than her dying as violently as my Seren did."

Broccan clenched his fists. He needed to talk his way out of this.

"I'm married and committed to my wife. We've experienced difficulties before. I'll not further disenchant her by sharin' another woman's bed."

"Are you about to tell her?" Tyven shrugged. "Being far distanced from Wessex, she's not apt to learn of it."

Beginning to believe he might be in peril, Broccan glanced at the guards at the door. Too far away to hear the conversation, but undoubtedly there not only to protect Tyven but also to prevent Broccan from leaving.

"If I attempt to walk out—" he gestured toward the doors "—will I meet discord?"

"You are the man my wife favors. Perhaps the only one she'd agree to lie with."

"You didn't answer me." Broccan placed his hand on his sword's hilt when four brawny men entered the room. The other Dafyddson brothers.

"It could be worse, Sir Broccan." Gronow grinned, seated himself and reached for the ale. "She could be old, unsightly or grotesque like my brother." He nodded to Tomos, the brother whose face was hidden behind a hood.

"The princess is beautiful," Madok added. "Desirable, young."

"You'll kill me if I don't go along with this ludicrous demand?" Broccan asked.

"If you comply, no one will speak of it again," Cynfawr suggested.

"We've all become fond of our sister-in-law," Tomos added. "We don't want her dead in mere months."

Broccan blew out a breath. "I'd suggest you have a battle on your hands convincin' Lilliana. She's strong-willed and I'll not rape a woman...even if I should meet your swords if I refuse."

"You'd die to protect her?" Madok sniffed.

"You are noble." Gronow grinned. "No wonder women fawn over you."

"I'll convince her," Tyven said. "Leave that to me, Broccan. Until then you may stay and drink with us or go to your chambers. However, should you try to leave, my knights have been instructed to strike you down."

Broccan snarled. "I believed you to be my friend and an honorable man. Much different than your father and uncle. Apparently, I was wrong."

Tyven sighed. "I've come to care for the Saxon princess. You are my friend, but to save her life, I would end yours."

"Killin' me would end your demented strategy," Broccan growled.

"I'll find another man by the next full moon...if my father doesn't force himself upon her by the last night of this draig moon. He'll be aware if she's been bedded…and know if her womanly desires are met satisfactorily. Which I presume you'd see done. I've seen women's entrancement of you and heard of your reputable prowess in pleasing them."

How the hell would he have heard that?

Broccan didn't want to consider any of this. He supposed Eurion, whom he'd heard might be a dragon at least some of the time, would have keen senses of an animal—perhaps smell a man's seed left when a woman was bedded. But how he'd know if she was satisfied, Broccan couldn't fathom.

"A satisfied woman no longer gives off the same essence as a wanton woman," Gronow, the most candid of the brothers, answered Broccan's unspoken question.

"The innate primal desire all men experience, but draig-born feel to an unimaginable degree is lessened," Madok added. "Like when a bitch is no longer in heat, males don't hang about any longer."

Broccan was disgusted and infuriated. Yet he couldn't best five men, the guards, and the others who'd be waiting if he attempted escape. He'd need to find a way to avoid this infernal situation.

BROCCAN WAITED OUTSIDE the door while Tyven spoke with Lilliana. Madok and Gronow stood with Broccan. He wasn't tethered but his sword and knife had been taken. There were guards at both ends of the corridor.

"I will not agree to this," she roared through the closed door. "I'm a princess, not a common whore who can be ordered to lie with a man who's not my husband."

Broccan presumed Tyven would be listing the reasons this must be done, just as he had explained to him. When the door opened, Lilliana stood rosy-cheeked, dark eyes flashing with temper. Broccan stepped back. His arm was improved, but still not optimal.

"You're in favor of this…this…lunacy?" she snapped, sparing him a glower.

"I am not!" Broccan replied. "Even if I was inclined to betray my vow of faithfulness to my wife, I'd not choose a princess given to madness who only yesterday damaged my sword arm and nearly caused my death."

"Do you suppose I'd choose you, Sir Broccan?" She lifted her chin. "You really are bloody full of yourself."

She blew out her breath, making her fringe flutter. By God that did something undesired to his loins. He was immediately hard.

"Will you kill me if I refuse?" She glowered at Tyven, holding her slightly pointed chin higher.

Tyven didn't reply but dubiously looked toward the large arched window at the full moon rising. Madok stepped forward.

"You won't be killed, sister-in-law. But in the morning, we'll have him—" Madok gestured to Broccan "—beaten and thrown in the dungeon; then he'll enjoy a day in the torture chamber before being killed."

"You wouldn't dare kill a Wessexian warrior!" she warned, hands on her hips. "One of my father's most prized knights!" She glared at Madok, then Tyven. "That could cause a war."

"Who in your kingdom would ever know what fate befell him?" Madok argued.

"Sir Broccan could've been killed by bandits in Wessex wanting his fine sword before he ever crossed the border...or perhaps drowned in the Severn," Gronow added.

Madok stepped nearer. "We couldn't be linked to his death if his body's fed to hogs or he's left rotting in the dungeon till he's dust."

Looking like she might pitch a fit, Lilliana threw her husband a daggered gaze. "I don't know your brothers well enough to determine their honorable traits, but I didn't take you for an amoral man, Tyven."

"Simply spend three nights with him, Lilliana." Tyven reached for her arm, but she pulled away. "You fancy him and needn't deny it. I can sense it."

"Even if I do—" she lifted her chin again, defiantly "—he's furious with me."

Tyven looked at Broccan. "There's passion within his fury...even if Sir Broccan denies the attraction. I suspect he's aroused even now."

She shook her head, pushed past the men, walked back into her chambers and slammed the door.

"That went well." Broccan crossed his arms and leaned against the wall.

"You will go in there and charm her, Broccan," Tyven said. "Convince her or take her as you see fit. Whatever should transpire in that chamber has to be better than what befell my lovely Seren when the beast-child within her ripped its way from her womb."

Sickened by that consideration, Broccan closed his eyes and shook his head. "Even if I should follow through, there's no sayin' she'd conceive."

"I suspect you have strong seed, Sir Broccan."

"My wife has yet to carry my child," Broccan argued.

Doirean had been infertile, and he knew of no other children he'd fathered. Selena or Elspeth hadn't become with child after he'd coupled with them either. Should he mention that?

Tyven pointed to the door. "Go to her now!"

The prince clearly wouldn't be swayed.

"As long as she's bedded, it will ease her growing desires and our father's insistence," Gronow said.

Tyven stared at Broccan. "I do hope you leave her with child. If not, it will still buy time till the next draig moon...or until my father is no more."

"You should've hired me to kill him. That might be less harrowin' than beddin' her."

Madok touched his sword. "If we thought it could be done so easily, our father would already be dead."

CHAPTER NINE

B ROCCAN AND LILLIANA shared a silent, uncomfortable meal in her expansive bedchamber. She wouldn't meet his eyes and barely nibbled her food. The knock on the door startled them both.

She jumped, but didn't call for the knocker to enter, so Broccan pushed his plate away and went to the door. Pray God Tyven had come to his senses and changed his mind.

But it was Gronow, wearing a damn smirk that Broccan longed to wipe from his face.

"Servants have a bath drawn for you, Sir Broccan." He glanced inside the door. "They'll come to prepare one for you, too, Princess."

Lilliana's face colored. If looks could kill, Gronow would be dead.

"The serving girls could get you in the necessary aroused state, if you wish," Gronow continued, "since my sister-in-law doesn't seem overly warm to the notion."

"Sard off, you miscreant!" she spat.

Gronow laughed uproariously. "I think you dislike that notion."

"Go to hell!" She waved her fist, then picked up her plate and threw it at Gronow.

He jumped away and the plate shattered against the

stone wall, scattering food across the floor.

"Clearly, Lilliana, you don't see we do this to protect you. It's not as though Sir Broccan isn't a handsome, tempting man. I suspect he knows what to do to ensure a woman likes the joining."

"If you don't leave this instant, I'll take a shard of crockery and slit your throat!"

Gronow held up his hands, still grinning. "I might like to see you try. However, I'd probably find it highly arousing and it's not my arousal we're after."

Lilliana glowered and Gronow finally left them.

Broccan would go bathe. Whether only to be taken to the dungeon was yet to be determined. She looked angry, still, but her lip quivered. He was tempted to take her in his arms. He supposed that would occur later.

SOAKING IN THE hot bath didn't soothe Rhianwyn's anxiousness. She dried off and donned the lacy shift left for her. She ached to be with Broccan even if this was being forced upon them both. Lilliana *had* always seemed eager for that. But what would that do to their already crumbling marriage?

Rhianwyn hoped that Broccan believed she'd returned to her own body, that he had made amends with his "wife" and been happier these past weeks. But if she lay with him now when he believed she was Lilliana, it would surely undo all that.

She sat on the bed, thinking. Should she go along with

it? But he was angry and didn't want to look at her, much less…have her. How degrading to be forced to lie with her when he was opposed? And unsettling for her who wanted him but had to pretend she didn't.

There was a soft knock.

"Enter," she called.

He stood there looking devilishly handsome, yet sheepish. He no longer wore his chain mail, but a white tunic and tight black breeches that revealed his muscular thighs. His wavy freshly washed hair wasn't plaited and looked undeniably sensual. He carried a bottle…wine perhaps.

"Tyven said there were goblets here." He placed the bottle on the table, then slumped into a chair.

"We will sleep together and only sleep," she said, decisively. "For three nights and then you'll return to Wessex unharmed."

He shook his head. "Apparently they'll be able to sense if we've been together intimately."

"Perhaps that's only a falsehood they use to force us."

"Perhaps." He didn't sound convinced.

"Drink if you wish." She gestured to the bottle.

"I'd need more than that to…"

"To bed me?" she quipped. "You're insinuating you'd have to be drunk to take me to bed?"

"I'm not exactly feelin' anythin' other than annoyance just now. With you for what occurred yesterday, and with your husband and his damn family for what they expect of us."

"Drink then," she said. "I suspect they'll bring more if required. Tonight we'll only sleep and determine whether they'll know in the morning."

"Suit yourself, Princess."

It wouldn't be her who was beaten if they sensed the truth.

THEY SLEPT ON opposite sides of the bed, not daring to touch one another. Rhianwyn presumed it was a sleepless night for both.

She pounded on the door the following morning. It was opened and two knights stood guard.

"I'll break fast in the great hall," she demanded with a haughtiness she'd seen in Lilliana and felt now herself.

"Sorry, milady. You're to remain here. Food will be brought to you."

"I wish to speak with my husband straightaway!"

"He and his brothers have gone hunting, milady."

That might work in their favor. Perhaps she and Broccan could find a way for him to escape.

"I'd like to go to the gardens or perhaps go riding, then."

The knights shook their heads. "As we said, you must remain here."

"Will you kill me if I try to leave?"

"No, but we've been ordered to take your companion to the dungeon after a sound beating."

That couldn't be true. How would Broccan follow through with bedding her if he'd been beaten?

"Go on then. Take him."

Broccan came to the door and scowled at her.

"I assure you, we'll stay here as Prince Tyven request-ed." He closed the door and she glared.

"You'd risk me beaten, perhaps tortured?" He placed his angry face close to hers.

She shrugged. "By how you look at me, I thought that might be preferential to taking me to bed."

"I suppose you find it insultin' that it's your husband orderin' me to your bed and not you makin' such de-mands."

She glowered.

"It's a bit ironic, for my wife told me to stay clear of your bed. She mentioned other knights called to your chambers for more than standing guard. Now…it seems I'll have no choice but to join that lot."

Rhianwyn felt a tinge of worry. Was Lilliana warning him off in hopes of keeping Broccan for herself? "If I'd had any say in it, I might've requested Sir Cassian. Maybe even Sir Zachary."

He turned his head quickly at that.

"Sir Cassian and I have a lengthy history," Rhianwyn continued, recalling what she knew of Lilliana's past. "Even though he's been in love with *your* wife for a long while. And Sir Zachary…well I've not had the pleasure of him in my bed, for he was enamored with Selena, but he is young, fine, and fit. Why would Tyven pick you?"

"Don't let on you haven't been attracted to me since first we met, Princess," Broccan said. "That first night you kissed me."

Male pride was damn predictable.

"I'm attracted to many men, Sir Broccan, but perhaps those besotted by other women are the ones who most appeal. I welcome a challenge. Like men, in that regard, I suppose."

"You think angerin' me when I'm already riled will make me want to sard you?"

She smiled. "I suspect I should attempt to learn what arouses you. Else you might be taken to be tortured." She attempted a wry smile.

If this had to happen, they might as well get on with it. It seemed she was to be with him during each season of the pact, in all three of her friends' bodies. Though this time it was being forced upon them. Still, she couldn't deny the always powerful attraction.

"Do you want to wait till after we break fast or should we simply…?" She looked at the bed.

He shook his head, sat on a chair, and crossed his arms.

She turned down the bed, removed her outer garments, and began unlacing her shift when someone knocked. She jumped.

"Your food is here," a guard called from outside the door. She heard it being unlocked and pulled a bedcover over her.

One guard carried a tray; the other stood with his sword unsheathed. Both kept their eyes from her. As soon as they were alone again and the door locked, Broccan reached for a piece of ham and groaned.

The healer in her couldn't bear to see him in pain, but she lifted her chin in regal diffidence. "I could place your arm in a sling. It's a simple enough task—one I've seen

Rhianwyn do. That would take away some of the discomfort and make you less likely to reinjure it."

"I didn't injure it in the first place," he snarled.

She rolled her eyes. "I've apologized for hurting you. Brooding doesn't suit you, Sir Broccan."

That was a damn lie. He dripped with sensuality even in his moodiness.

Sensing his lack of interest, she donned her garments, and they ate another silent meal. Rhianwyn loathed how awkward this was. She thought of when they were first in love, their lengthy conversations, constant affection, and heated lovemaking. The pact had changed everything.

She went to the window, pulled open the shutters, and leaned over. Looking down nearly made her dizzy. She hadn't realized how high they were in the castle. There was a wide moat below.

"It's too far to jump if that's what you're thinkin', for I've been considerin' it myself."

She made a face. "How deep do you think that moat is?"

She used to dive from the hill above the lake.

"Not deep enough," he replied.

"I might chance it."

"I once saw a man dive into water not deep enough; he struck his head and from that day forward was unable to walk or move anythin' beneath his waist."

"I suppose that might deter you more than me," she said, sarcastically.

She slumped upon the window seat, trying to determine their options, then sighed yet again. "Perhaps if it was done after dark, no kisses or caresses, no affection, just do...what must be done."

"You have it all determined then, Princess?"

She threw him a glare. "I don't see you trying to find another solution to this confounded situation."

He put his head in his hands and winced again. She pulled a linen off the bed.

"I suppose they took your knife?" she asked.

He gave her a look that suggested she was an imbecile. "They didn't even give us a knife with our food, Princess."

The bedsheet was too large to create a sling, a pillow-case too small. She set the platter on the bed and folded the tablecloth into a triangle.

"Will you permit me to get close enough to tie this around you?"

He shrugged, indifferently.

"Remove your tunic first."

He grumbled, then winced as he complied. By God, he was an impressive man. She glanced at his muscular chest and arms, his rippled stomach. She placed the makeshift sling around his neck, then gently put his arm through it and tied it. Inhaling his musky scent made her nearly swoon. Her body responded with instant arousal. She wanted to kiss his lips and run her tongue down the slightly salty skin of his chest, push him back upon the bed and mount him straightaway.

"It will restrict movement and allow your shoulder to heal," she said, instead.

He tested the tightness. "You have surprising skills, Lilliana. You learned all this from watching my wife?"

"The window in my castle chambers faced the knights' training field. I saw Rhianwyn attend many injuries incurred by the men."

He nodded but looked around like a caged animal.

"Do you play chess?" she asked.

"Do you see a chessboard anywhere?" he snapped.

He was in uncommonly ill temper.

She looked at the two plates. Clearing the food remnants, she wiped the plates clean, then one at a time, shattered them against the stone wall. They crashed loudly.

"Bloody hell, Lilliana! What are you up to?" Broccan jumped up, wincing as he jostled his arm.

"I'm not about to slit your throat. Nor my wrists. Not that you'd likely worry if I was about to harm myself. I'm making chess pieces."

She knew she'd piqued his interest. First, she took a jagged shard and scratched the necessary squares on the wooden table. Then she spent considerable time breaking bits into chess pieces.

"Obviously, we must use our imaginations, but this should work. At least it'll pass some time."

He nodded and pulled his chair closer to the table, smiling for the first time since she'd attacked him.

BROCCAN HAD TO admit he was surprised. Lilliana had always seemed pompous or manipulative with her friends, and haughty or forward with him. Although he'd known from the start she wasn't a typical princess, today he'd discovered she was an interesting woman.

They'd played two lengthy and admittedly enjoyable games of chess and they were evenly matched. He won the first, she the second. She'd laughed at his continued pessimistic comments.

Then she'd drawn lines on the wall and suggested games of noughts and crosses. Her cheeks colored when she reached to eagerly place a winning symbol and his hand touched hers. He couldn't deny he felt the spark, too. He supposed that was favorable if they were truly to carry through with the absurd notion of coupling.

"You should lie on the bed and rest your shoulder."

She sounded like a damn healer or a wife mollycoddling him.

"What'll you do while I rest?"

"I might draw upon the walls. They're rather unadorned for a princess's chambers."

He looked at the gray walls, heavy dark bedcovers and curtains around the canopied bed and the window. It was a dreary chamber even with sun streaming through the open windows.

He nodded, stretched out upon the bed and must've drifted off.

When he awoke, he was startled to see the sun had set. She'd lit the candles and now sat at the table. She'd been watching him, for she turned away when their eyes met. Then he looked at what she'd scratched upon the wall. He gazed at her disbelievingly and whistled.

"I had no notion you could draw so well."

She only shrugged as he went to examine the large etching. If it had been painted on cloth it would make an impressive tapestry. He smiled at the image of a woman, a princess by her opulent garments. Flanked on one side by an immense dragon breathing fire. On the other was a knight in full armor, sword raised. But instead of the knight battling the dragon, the princess stood in the middle holding swords toward both.

"You see Tyven and me as your enemies?" he asked.

She pushed a strand of hair behind her ear and blushed again.

"I see you as two powerful men who presently dictate what happens next in my life."

"And if you had swords, would you slay us?" He couldn't fight a smile. "I saw you throw that knife the night of the feast in Wessex when you were displeased with your father. Do you know the way of a sword, too?"

"I can't use a sword. Ulf taught me how to throw a knife."

Another knock on the door disrupted their conversation. "Your evening meal is here, Princess," the guard called.

Broccan went to the door as it opened.

"We'll require more plates," Broccan said.

The guard glanced inside, spotting the broken crockery.

"Do you aim to use those shards as weapons?" He looked at Broccan, assessing his strength.

"I doubt they'd do well against your swords even if I didn't suffer from an injured arm."

Still, the guard seemed relieved. He carried in a tray and looked at the bed. Was the man to report to Tyven whether it appeared they'd had relations?

"You'll not be disturbed again. We'll leave food outside your door come morning and knock to alert you."

Lilliana stared at the guard who seemed put off by her gaze.

"Do you believe you'll be permitted to live much longer?" she asked.

One knight's face turned white; the other stared at her, uncertainly.

"Knowing I've spent days and nights alone in a bedchamber with a man who's not my husband, do you suspect the Dafyddson brothers will permit you to live?"

"We're loyal to our prince," the knight outside the door said.

"But you aren't top knights in his order," she persisted with an air of superiority. "Else you'd have been at the tournament in Wessex. If my husband wanted me ably protected, why wouldn't he request his most favored knights?"

Neither man replied.

"I'll tell you why." She tapped her chin, sounding confident. "Because Tyven wouldn't want to behead them. They're too valuable in competitions and warring. But you two...you're expendable."

The knights shared an uncomfortable look and soon closed the door.

Broccan smirked. "You enjoy unsettling men?"

"Don't you agree with my assumption?"

He nodded. "Those men aren't likely to know longevity."

She crinkled her nose prettily. "I'd like to eat and not think about their fate or ours."

Broccan sat down, catching the scent of her hair. She was an enticing woman. Although he didn't agree with what was expected of them, he doubted there was any way out of it. But would his fate be the same as that of those two guards, regardless of what occurred in this chamber?

CHAPTER TEN

RHIANWYN WAS NERVOUS. Spending time with Broc-can had only fueled her womanly desires—her powerful, primal need for him. She'd attempted to find activities to fill their time that didn't involve… She glanced at the bed despite herself. Her heart beat faster and her breath quickened.

"No one came to issue you a beating today?" She had to make conversation.

"The day's not over," he replied.

As though on cue, someone pounded on the door. That was not the guards who'd gingerly knocked.

The door was unlocked and thrown open. Madok stepped in wearing a dour expression. He lifted his head, nostrils flared. He was determining by scent if she and Broccan had coupled.

"How was your hunting, brother-in-law?"

He scowled. "You don't take this seriously!" Madok accused.

"Why are you here?" Rhianwyn asked.

"Because Tyven's too soft-hearted and Gronow jests about everything. I'm the most likely to see things done."

"Permit Broccan to return home. Then you could *see it done?*"

"You want to mate with me?" Madok cocked his head.

She wet her lips. "I don't *want* to mate with anyone, but it seems I've no say. Why must we involve Broccan?"

"He was Tyven's choice. If I were to bed you it would end the same as if you were with Tyven," Madok replied, impatiently. "Now, your refusal to be with the Irishman has ensured he'll be beaten."

He walked toward Broccan who stiffened, but Rhianwyn stepped between them.

"I don't need your bloody protection, Lilliana!" Broccan blared.

"You may be an exceptional warrior," Madok said. "In truth, Tyven and Gronow rave about your skill with a sword, but you don't possess a weapon just now and you have an injured shoulder, so I'd take my chances."

Rhianwyn still stood between the two men. "Broccan does have an injured shoulder. Would beating him make him fit to bed me?"

"I'll spare his cock any impairment." Madok didn't crack a smile.

"You're a fiend!" she snapped.

"You'd better entice him, Princess, or he *will* be taken to the dungeon and perhaps put on the rack tomorrow. Maybe you'd like me to remain and watch the two of you mate?"

Rhianwyn sneered. "Maybe I'd like you to fall upon your sword. Wouldn't watching us mate arouse you, Madok? Although of all Tyven's brothers, you're the least likeable."

Madok shrugged. "I don't require your favor." He

looked deeply into her eyes.

"I suspect I could make you favor me," she said, seductively moving closer and sensually grazed Madok's forearm.

He jumped and stepped back.

"Best stay away or you'll be tempted. It's the second night of the dragon moon." She unlaced her gown and Madok's eyes turned immediately reptilian.

"How foolishly you toy with danger, sister-in-law! Seduce him!" Madok pointed to Broccan. "And I'll not be forced to take him to the dungeon."

He went out without another glance and Rhianwyn smiled.

"I don't think he's jestin'." Broccan looked serious now, too.

She shrugged. "He didn't take you to the dungeon. Which would you rather face, Sir Broccan? Two nights with me or time in the dungeon?"

Broccan's eyes narrowed as though he wasn't certain.

Rhianwyn sighed, sat on the window seat, and gazed at the silvery full moon. "Do you think they'll let you go free even if we do as they request?"

"I know other truths about Tyven, and he's let me live. Maybe none so clandestine as attemptin' to bed a married princess and leave her with child but…I'm hopin' he'll let me live."

"I have to see Tyven!" Rhianwyn jumped up. "If he won't promise you'll be released unharmed, then I'll not even consider this." She pointed to the bed.

Broccan shrugged. "You may earn a bloody beatin' yet. Have you seen the rack or other implements of torture in a dungeon?"

She shook her head, not wanting to think of those. She inhaled, summoning strength. She'd need to do this. She crooked her finger, beckoning Broccan to her. He swallowed. She saw his uncertainty, but his interest, too. He *was* a man, and she well knew of his healthy need to frequently couple.

"Come here, Sir Broccan. See it done. Must I seduce you?"

He made no attempt to draw nearer. She removed her boots and stockings, untied her gown, and slowly removed it. She stepped out of her petticoats and unlaced her shift. He fidgeted uncomfortably and turned away. She went to him and stared into his very blue eyes. She saw the desire even though he fought it.

She suspected Madok would eventually kill Broccan if they weren't together. She prayed the brothers Dafyddson would permit him to leave once the dragon moons were ended.

She ran her hand down his impressively well-formed arm. He flinched.

"Is your shoulder still painful?"

He shook his head. "Not noticeably."

"Don't you long to kiss me, Sir Broccan?"

"No," he said, but the muscle in his jaw twitched.

"Not even a little?" She attempted to flirt as Lilliana would, but she also had to be cautious. She couldn't do anything he might recognize and suspect she was actually his wife.

She ran both hands along his gloriously muscular chest,

then placed her face to his chest and inhaled his desire-provoking masculine scent. She pulled her hand through his thick hair. He still hadn't touched her.

Seduction was clearly not her strong suit. But she was certainly well aroused. She touched her lips to his neck, and he jerked his head away. Persisting, she whispered in his ear as her hands went to his breeches' ties.

"I want you, Sir Broccan. You do make my heart beat faster and my skin become heated. If we must do this...then perhaps you might at least attempt to enjoy it."

She put her arms around his neck, then rubbed her peaked nipples against his bare chest and felt his body react even if his mind wasn't agreeable. She finished untying his breeches and released his erect manhood. Still, there was no sign of him intending to touch her.

"You're being difficult, Sir Broccan."

She bent to pull down his breeches; her lips brushed his manhood. He sucked in his breath and when she stood, he made a tortured sound. He stepped out of his breeches and tossed them on the nearby chair. She stared at his magnificent naked body and her breath hitched. Christ, she wanted him.

"You are an impressive man, Sir Broccan. How could any healthy warm-blooded woman not want you?"

She met his eyes as she removed her shift slowly, enticingly. She stood before him naked, too, touching her body to his. She dared him with a glance, but he shook his head.

"So be it, go to the damn dungeon, you bloody stubborn man!" She blew out her breath and fluttered her fringe, then reached for her shift she'd let fall to the floor.

But he pulled her to him hungrily and gazed into her eyes. Fury remained in his deep blue pools. Still, he kissed her so hard, her mouth hurt. He lifted her into his arms and placed her on the bed ungently. He kissed her throat, then her breasts, but didn't touch her womanhood, before he entered her. She cried out as her maidenhead was pierced.

Lilliana had still been a virgin.

"Just see it done," she said when it seemed he'd stop.

Therefore he thrust within her apparently with little more pleasure than being ordered to do anything he didn't agree upon.

She closed her eyes, tears threatening as he moved above her. There was no joy and little pleasure. His eyes remained closed. When he groaned, his body trembling above her, an involuntary sob escaped. He opened his eyes. There was regret within them.

He moved from her, lay back staring at the ceiling, and covered himself with linens. She found her shift, pulled it over her head, turned to face the wall, weeping silently into her pillow.

"God's bones," he whispered. "Why didn't you tell me you were innocent?"

"Don't let guilt assail you, Sir Broccan."

She looked back to see him staring at the droplets of blood upon the bedsheet.

"Being virginal doesn't mean I was innocent. I'm far from innocent."

"I regret it wasn't more pleasant for you. If I'd known...I would've been gentler or..."

He reached for her arm, but she stiffened and pulled away. She suspected neither would sleep.

BROCCAN STOOD OUTSIDE the bedchamber speaking with Madok and his brothers. Tyven was oddly absent. Several other knights with swords drawn were nearby ready to prevent escape should he attempt it.

"It was done!" Broccan snarled.

"Still, you must stay together another night to ensure greater possibility of leaving her with child...and apparently—" Maddock looked accusingly at Broccan "—she wasn't satisfied."

"I doubt she would be when we've been ordered to be together under threat of my torture or death."

Angry pounding on the door stopped their discussion.

"Let me out of this chamber at once!" Lilliana demanded.

Madok opened the door.

"We did what you ordered done." She wouldn't meet any of their eyes. "Now permit him to return to Wessex."

"You'll remain together one more night," Madok replied, unfaltering.

She glared, fire in her dark eyes. "Truly, this makes me no better than a whore!"

Madok exhaled loudly. "Understand this. Your husband wants to save your life."

"I wish to speak to him!"

"He's indisposed," Madok replied.

"Send in his entire order of knights. Have them sard me morning till night and still I won't conceive," she said, assuredly.

Madok glanced at her, head tilted. "Have you been declared barren by a healer?"

She lifted her chin, regally. "No. It's women's intuition. I won't conceive when this is forced upon me."

"If that were so, why do a good many women carry a child after they've been raped?" Gronow asked.

"I didn't request your opinion," Lilliana snarled. "And *that* was no better than rape, except he hadn't any choice either." She spared Broccan a glare, too, and he couldn't help feeling brutish.

He still didn't know if the many rumors he'd heard about the princess and the knights she invited to her chambers were true. But clearly, she hadn't been with a man fully until last night and her first time wasn't a pleasurable experience. Was he actually sorry about that? Not wanting any woman he'd bedded to be left unappeased.

"Go back inside the bedchamber, Lilliana," Madok ordered, "or he will be taken to the dungeon."

"I want to see my husband. Surely he owes me that."

"Let her go to Tyven," Gronow suggested. "Take him, too."

Madok exhaled loudly but pointed to the guards. "Chain him and hold tightly to her."

RHIANWYN WAS ROUGHLY escorted down the steps by one guard.

"Why are you taking me to the dungeon? You said you'd permit me to see my husband."

Two others accompanied Broccan even though his hands and feet were chained.

"They probably intend to beat and torture me while you watch," Broccan suggested, struggling against his chains.

They walked by a dark chamber. Madok, leading the way, shone his flaming torch inside. "Let her see what's in store for the Irishman if she doesn't comply."

The guards shoved her inside. The smell was rank, and she espied shelves with bloodied, gruesome weapons. Some, like the morning star and mace, she was familiar with, for knights used them in competitions. Others were more horrific. There was blood on the floor, along with torn fingernails, severed hands and feet, and presumably cocks though they were shriveled, and some burned. She placed her hand to her mouth, gagging.

She spotted the large rectangular wooden frame with iron rollers that must be the rack. She understood how it worked. The unfortunate victims' ankles would be tied to one set of rollers, their wrists to another, then the rack would be stretched till their bodies were eventually pulled apart.

"You *are* barbarians. I thought tales of Welshmen and their brutal cruelty were exaggerated."

Madok glowered but Gronow didn't take offense.

"Ask your Irishman if he's seen implements of torture

before," Gronow said. "Women are sometimes sheltered from such barbarism. But I'd wager any castle dungeon in Wessex, Mercia, Ireland, Rome, Egypt—nearly anywhere has such items."

Rhianwyn looked at Broccan, disbelieving. He nodded solemnly.

"He's correct. Though I'd not want them used upon me."

"Why do you keep those?" She gestured to the grizzly items on the floor.

"Fear is often the best torture," Madok said. "We could sever just one hand...maybe his sword hand." Madok looked to see her reaction.

"Or a foot, since a lame knight is useless," Gronow added.

"If he doesn't bed you—and bed you well this night—we might take his cock!" Madok threatened.

"I doubt his pretty Saxon wife would favor that notion." Gronow raised his eyebrow.

No, she would not.

"You said I could see my husband."

Madok gestured to the guard, and he clasped her arm again and led her to another part of the dungeon. She felt her eyes widen seeing Tyven chained to the wall.

"Why are you here?" she asked. "Why is a prince chained in his own castle's dungeon?"

"Because you arouse him and he doesn't trust himself not to have you when you're in season," Madok explained.

"Is that true?" She pressed her face against the bars.

Tyven looked ashamed, but nodded.

"He cares for you, likely even loves you, so the pull is stronger," Gronow explained.

"Let me inside to speak with him," Rhianwyn insisted.

"You cannot!" Tyven shook his head.

"You're chained to a damn wall!" Rhianwyn placed her hands on her hips.

"Should you go in there with him he'd easily pull free should he transform," Madok said.

"He'd sard me here in the dungeon?" she asked, flippantly.

"You truly believe he'd care when he's filled with draig lust?" Gronow asked.

"His only thought would be mating," Madok affirmed. "Believe me, the location wouldn't be a consideration."

She gave Madok an even more unfavorable look. "So be it. Let my husband have me. But in human form in his bedchamber."

Gronow and Madok shook their heads impatiently.

"Take her to Vala," Madok ordered.

"Don't!" Tyven roared, pulling at his chains.

"Your princess should know part of the reason you protect her." Madok stared at his brother. "Do you want her to willingly mate with the Irish knight?"

Tyven growled, his eyes reptilian, smoke rising from his nostrils, but he nodded.

They were taken to a nearby dungeon cell.

"Come here," Madok ordered.

Vala, the mature woman Rhianwyn had seen in Wessex, apparently Tyven's lover, stepped forward. She looked at Rhianwyn with dislike, perhaps jealousy.

"Pull down your gown, woman?" Madok ordered.

Vala spared him an equally distasteful look but complied. She unlaced her gown, keeping her breasts covered, then turned and Rhianwyn gasped. Her back was covered in long scars. Like those left when someone was lashed, but also like claw marks after an animal attack.

"Would you like your lovely soft skin to look like that?" Gronow asked. "During the mating someone with draig blood can be enthusiastic if they suffer a partial change."

"And if they suffer a full change?" Rhianwyn asked.

"A human woman wouldn't survive." Madok didn't hide the truth.

Broccan wore an expression of disgust.

She and Broccan were marched up the stairs and taken to the corridor outside her chambers.

"Tyven's found a man who appeals to you," Madok said.

"So go get busy with your Irishman and enjoy yourself this time." Gronow smirked.

"Burn in hell, the lot of you!" She went in, slamming the door yet again.

THE DOOR VIBRATED with how hard she'd closed it. Broccan longed to fight the men presently surrounding him. Christ, he wanted his sword.

"She's a passionate sort," Gronow said as he gestured for Broccan's chains to be removed. "Yet, I'm not sure I envy you, Irishman."

"Will you permit him to leave come dawn?" Lilliana came back out, as riled as him.

No one replied.

"Will you permit him to leave unharmed if this is done?" she repeated.

"I suppose that depends on what occurs between now and then," Madok said.

"Give me your word!" She stared into Madok's face.

"Tyven will make that decision."

She looked like she wanted to scratch Madok's eyes out, but instead she screamed and went into the chamber. Broccan simply followed.

He could see her enragement as she paced. He felt bloody useless to do anything to calm her. Well he could. He was experienced in making a woman calmer. He could make her experience release, which was what the bloody Dafyddson brothers wanted.

He met her eyes. There was fury, but longing, too. He didn't want this, yet when she looked at him, not all of him was opposed. He had an immediate cockstand. She looked ready to jump out of her skin...or maybe just ready.

His eyes roved up and down, taking in her shapely body and shiny hair, her stunningly lovely face, dark sensual eyes, and full lips. Her essence seemed unusually beautiful. He was attracted to her. Judging by how she was gazing at him, it was mutual.

She suddenly hurled herself at him, just as abruptly as she had when she'd sent him over the cliff. He thudded against the wall, grimacing as his shoulder smarted again. He didn't have time to dwell on it, for she pulled his head down and kissed him torridly. He wrapped his good arm around her and pulled her closer.

She smiled then, probably sensing his arousal. She untied his breeches straightaway and tugged them down, fondling his cock, tip to ballocks. He moaned. Turning her, he pulled up her skirts, placed his arm under her thigh and took her against the wall. She cried out and moved with him as he exuberantly thrust into her till she quivered, her warmth tightening around him. He held back his culmination, ensured she climaxed time and again before giving way to his own release.

FINALLY LILLIANA HAD drifted off to sleep. She'd been ravenous, insatiable. There were some benefits to that beyond the obvious pleasure. At least when they were filled with lust and sarding like rabbits there wasn't time to think or feel guilty.

She moved closer. He was about to tell her he was exhausted, there was no damn way he could service her again. Yet what she did next distressed him more. She placed her head on his chest, her hand on his heart, her bent knee across his thigh. By God, that was precisely how Rhianwyn used to sleep beside him, though she hadn't done so in some time.

He closed his eyes. Content and half asleep now, too, he could almost imagine it was his wife with him. They had the same body type. Same rounded hips, same firm breasts, same soft skin. Christ, why was he comparing Rhianwyn to a princess he'd just had heated relations with? She sighed softly then kissed his chest.

"I love you, Broccan," she whispered though she didn't waken.

Bloody hell, that sounded like Rhianwyn.

He was probably overtired and riddled with guilt. He needed sleep but when he moved his shoulder pained him. He groaned and cussed, which wakened her. She abruptly moved.

She'd insisted on no affection between them but, apparently, he wasn't to get any sleep, for she teasingly touched his chest with her fingernail, making him hard...again. Then she placed kisses down his body, took him in her mouth, and he could think no more.

SHE'D LOST COUNT how many times they'd coupled. It was a wild, frenzied, mostly sleepless two days and one night of salacious, primal pleasure.

They'd been placed in an impossible situation, and she'd been mad to have him love her. Though it had nothing to do with love on his part.

Yet now as they lay together breathing heavily from the latest ardent encounter, he reached out and brushed her tousled hair from her face, then leaned closer and kissed her gently. She pulled away and he sat up.

"There was to be no affection...no tenderness," she reminded him.

His eyebrows rose and he reached for his breeches.

They'd both been unclothed since soon after he'd first sarded her against the wall.

"Prince Tyven will see you now," a voice called from outside the door.

Wasn't he supposed to avoid her? Perhaps not now that the dragon moons had passed.

Rhianwyn found her clothes amongst their scattered garments but only attired herself in shift and gown. She pulled her fingers through her hair, glancing at her reflection in her mirror. She jumped back seeing her true reflection. But it was no longer a full moon. She turned away hoping Broccan hadn't seen.

OUT OF HABIT, Broccan reached for his absent sword after he'd donned his garments. Lilliana opened the door. Tyven stood waiting. He, too, sniffed the air and his eyes widened.

"Yes, we did as requested," Lilliana said. "We coupled heatedly and repeatedly. Does that please you, husband?"

Broccan wouldn't have stated that in such a bold manner, but it was the truth. He was wrought with guilt, but the time spent with the princess had been primally pleasing.

For a man who'd insisted on the pairing and had his brothers threaten Broccan with torture and death if he didn't follow through, Tyven didn't appear pleased. He looked at Lilliana, cleared his throat, and cast a jealous glare at Broccan.

"Will you permit Sir Broccan to leave?" she asked.

"Since you do apparently favor him quite a lot, I've decided he'll be kept here until the next draig moon to…be with you again at that time."

"But that's not what you said," Rhianwyn argued.

"It isn't what was agreed upon," Broccan fumed. "Not that we actually agreed to any of it." Broccan approached Tyven, hoping to look tall and formidable even without a weapon. "I must return to my wife."

He felt damn guilty saying that.

"In truth, I regret I mightn't ever be able to permit you to leave. It can't be known that you two have been together." Tyven looked sheepish.

"You're not bloody serious?" Broccan threw his hands in the air, then winced when that jostled his shoulder. "Do you suppose I'm about to become a town crier and publicly announce my infidelity? I considered you a friend, Tyven. Besides, you trusted me with other secrets. Why is this different?"

Lilliana seemed even more distressed than him. The most peculiar look crossed her face. She walked into the bedchamber, headed straight for the window, threw open the shutters, and glanced downward.

"If you cannot promise Broccan's safe return to Wessex," she called, "and my fate's only to wait till the next whole moon till he or another man beds me in hope of siring a child…or you eventually give in to your lust and sire a half-dragon beast that'll end my life anyway, tell me why I shouldn't throw myself from this window."

Tyven started inside the bedchamber. "Lilliana, don't make such reckless threats."

She grasped the walking stick and stepped up onto the window's ledge. Broccan's heart raced when in her nervousness her fringe fluttered again. That was so like Rhianwyn. Come to it, she'd reminded him of her a good many times since he arrived in Welshland.

"Get down, Lilliana." Tyven warily drew closer.

"That's damn dangerous," Broccan warned.

She continued to gaze downward.

"Rhianwyn! Don't do it!" Broccan called, though he wasn't certain why he used that name.

She glanced back at him, eyes wide as shields, then teetered precariously. He raced toward her, tried to grab her, but missed. She screamed and began to fall. He heard a whoosh behind him. An immense green creature with scales, wings, and a long tail pushed past him, knocking him to the floor before flying out the window. Christ's cross, he'd just seen a full-fledged dragon.

Broccan hurriedly stood and hung his head out the window. Gronow and Madok joined him. The winged creature caught Lilliana before she landed. Tyven was nowhere to be found, thus must be the dragon, and he'd just saved her life. Was she truly Rhianwyn or had Broccan only startled her by calling her that?

The dragon flew back inside the window holding the princess, whose eyes were wider now, but she said not a word. Then the massive creature gently placed her on the bed before changing back into human form and reaching for bed linens to cover his nakedness.

Her mouth fell open. Broccan likely wore the same dumbstruck expression. Gronow, however, appeared distraught.

Madok shook his head. "Brother, that's the last purposeful transformation permitted during this trip round the sun. Do it again and you'll remain in draig form."

"I'm well aware," Tyven replied, "but I wasn't about to watch my wife die."

"You shouldn't have done that," she rebuked. "The walking stick is a wand. It would've saved me...if I hadn't dropped it when I fell."

She closed her eyes and waved her hand. The walking stick hovered outside the window, then came to her dripping with muddy moat water.

"Morwenna was correct. You do have magic." Tyven shook his head.

Gronow gazed at her in awe.

"It's the wand that has magic," she said dismissively.

The others were likely no more convinced than Broccan, for he could now sense her mysticism.

"Why did you call Lilliana by your wife's name?" Tyven asked.

Broccan shrugged. He honestly couldn't answer that.

"The more pertinent question is why did you respond to the name?" Broccan looked at her.

"I was merely startled," she began. "When you called Rhianwyn, I thought perhaps she'd followed you to Welshland. I looked to see if she was here. Now, Tyven, promise me you'll permit Broccan to return to his wife."

"And what of next month, during the draig moons?" Tyven asked.

"I'll lie with you," she replied.

All men stared now.

"You know why that can't happen," Tyven said even as he looked at Lilliana with unhidden attraction. "After the transformation you witnessed you must realize how dangerous that would be."

"You apparently risked much to save me; therefore I *will* spend time with you. Now, please see Sir Broccan escorted safely to the borders of your land."

Madok worriedly paced. "He shouldn't be freed after he's seen you shift."

"You intend to kill him then?" Lilliana asked. "And me, too, for I've seen it as well."

"Sir Broccan won't be killed." Tyven shook his head. "Gronow will accompany him to the Wessexian border. Broccan, I trust you'll never speak of what you've seen or any of what's happened during your time in Cymru."

Gronow grinned. "Do you suppose he'll blab that he's lain with a married princess and possibly impregnated her? How long would that take to get back to his wife? Or if he spouted off about seeing a dragon, everyone would think he was mad or spent his time in Cymru drinking himself senseless."

Broccan barely paid attention, for suddenly the thought of leaving her was distressing.

"I'll be safe here, Sir Broccan," she said as though knowing his thoughts. "Return to Wessex and give your wife my best wishes."

Broccan nodded but wouldn't meet her eyes.

"May I have a word with Lilliana alone, Tyven?" Broccan asked.

The prince nodded. Madok glanced curiously at them and Gronow raised his eyebrow, but the brothers left them.

RHIANWYN SHIVERED AS Broccan looked at her differently now. She shouldn't have summoned the wand.

She sat down trying to appear aloof. "If I were you, I'd leave straightaway before they change their mind about letting you go."

"I don't want to leave you here...with them."

"They're not going to hurt me. Tyven saved me."

"You can't truly intend to be with him...to *mate* with him?"

"I'm not afraid." She turned away from Broccan's intense eyes and he grasped her arm.

"Tell me why you looked at me when I called her name? The truth."

She shrugged. "I thought perhaps you'd struck your head during the fall from the cliffs...that I'd caused the revered Sir Broccan to go mad."

He looked unconvinced.

"You should leave, Broccan...unless you intend to take me to bed again? I wouldn't be opposed!" she said seductively.

He narrowed his eyes, probably disliking her flippancy. She loathed the thought of him leaving yet wanted him out of danger.

He looked from her face to her body and back again. Did he truly suspect she was Rhianwyn? He leaned forward and brushed his lips to hers, then grazed her cheek with his hand, making her tingle head to toe.

She stepped back. "You should go. What's occurred here in these chambers will never be spoken of again."

"Agreed."

"Nor will any of it be brought to mind," she said.

He sighed. "We both know that's unlikely."

"Best be on your way, Sir Broccan."

She reached up to move a tousled lock from his forehead then went to the door. It was unlocked. The corridor was empty.

"It seems you're free to go."

"I must retrieve my sword and get Dubh."

"Are you through talking?" Gronow startled them both like he appeared from thin air. His nostrils flared and he looked at her more intently.

"Thought you were maybe partaking in another hasty coupling?"

The exasperating man couldn't hold his tongue.

"See that Sir Broccan's horse and sword are returned."

Gronow looked at him. "After bedding a princess are you truly keen to return to your wife, Irishman? However, she's a lovely woman, too. I saw her at the feast while in Wessex. Rather unusual pale blue eyes. Quite mesmerizing. Pretty face and hair, lovely curvaceous womanly form. If I were you, I'd get back straightaway. There's probably any number of men wanting to…spend time with her should you tarry on returning. I wouldn't turn down some time in her bed."

"I dare you to say that after my sword's returned,"

Broccan muttered through gritted teeth.

Gronow only grinned.

Rhianwyn touched Gronow's arm. "Give me your word Sir Broccan will meet no ill will on Dafyddson land."

Gronow dipped his head. "It will be so, Princess."

Broccan nodded to her—formally. They purposely avoided looking into each other's eyes. She prayed he'd make it home safely even as she despaired being parted from him again.

CHAPTER ELEVEN

L IKE MANY TIMES when distressed, Rhianwyn soaked in a hot bath, trying to forget all that had occurred in this chamber. Through the window she'd watched Broccan ride off with Gronow and Madok. He'd glanced back once. She hastily stepped away, not wanting him to know how deeply she'd been affected by their time together or by his leaving.

"Hello, Princess." Teg flew in the open window.

Rhianwyn sunk deeper in the water.

"Hello, Teg."

"There's been much excitement since you've returned to the castle."

Rhianwyn wondered how much he knew.

"I heard Tyven used his last transformation. Should he transform again he'll remain in dragon form...unless of course the centuries-old curse should be ended. He must care a great deal for you to risk that to save your life."

Rhianwyn sighed. She'd dwelled upon that much to-day, too.

"How do you know of it?" Rhianwyn asked.

Teg shrugged. "Morwenna told me. She knows most of what occurs with magic."

"Turn away. I'll leave the bath and dress for dinner."

"Did you enjoy your time with your Irishman? It seems

you barely left these chambers."

"How do you know of that?"

He lowered his head, sheepishly. "I fell asleep and woke to you and that Irish knight moaning, breathing heavy, your breasts heaving."

Rhianwyn wrung out the washcloth and tossed it at the ellyll, who smiled with his wide-gapped front teeth.

"Turn around," she repeated, and he complied.

She was barely attired when someone knocked.

"Enter," she said.

Tyven stood there looking dashing in his green and white robe emblazoned with a red dragon symbol. His long hair was unplaited. His green eyes were intense. It was difficult to imagine he was the immense dragon who'd saved her.

"I request you join me in the hall to dine," he said but wouldn't meet her eyes.

"Since the draig moons are over, we could have food brought here." She pointed to the table and chairs.

He shook his head.

"Or go to your bedchambers."

She glanced around to see if Teg was hiding. She didn't want him overhearing their conversation, since that had sounded damn seductive.

"If you wish," Tyven agreed, but looked uneasy.

She went to him and took his arm. He was tense as they walked down the corridor. They met a manservant.

"Please have food for my wife and me delivered to my chambers."

He looked at Tyven curiously. "Yes, Your Grace." He

bowed.

Approaching two large double arched doors, Tyven cleared his throat.

"Let me go in first." He sounded like he was hiding something.

Rhianwyn nodded. After he'd gone inside, she heard a displeased female voice. Likely Vala. Tyven stepped back out, looking guilty.

"If you prefer not to dine with me," Rhianwyn said, "perhaps that would be best."

She turned and walked away. He followed silently.

She stopped and faced him. "Dine with *her*, Tyven? Surely you owe her that since she's been the one to see to your needs for God knows how long."

Just then Vala, who must be nearly two decades older than Tyven, came from his chambers. The look she cast Rhianwyn was laced with jealousy. Was she in love with Tyven?

"I asked you to leave by the back door," Tyven whispered.

Vala scowled.

"I'll go to the hall," Rhianwyn said.

Tyven threw both women a frustrated gaze but nodded.

She picked up her skirts and hastily left. Arriving at the great hall, she was stunned to find Tyven already there. He was as stealthy as Gronow. She supposed having dragon blood might cause that.

"Sit with me, Lilliana." He gestured to the chair beside him.

She complied, noting his serious face. When they were

both seated, he reached for her hand.

"I've come to care for you far more than I ever expected. I believe I'm falling in love with you."

That stunned her. She didn't know how to reply. She couldn't deny she found Tyven attractive. They had a good rapport. Obviously chivalrous, he'd protected her against her overbearing father and he'd saved her life today. She liked him, but to hear he was falling in love with her took her off guard. She couldn't tell him she loved him when she didn't.

She'd lied and deceived people for months now. She should be a worthy liar.

"I know you don't feel the same, Lilliana. I realize you're in love with Sir Broccan. I suppose a lot of women fall for him."

"Even so, he's married to one of my best friends," she replied.

He wore a far-off look. "I wanted you to know I've made a decision that will better your life...at least I do hope so."

He looked weary. His eyes lacked their usual sparkle.

"What is it?" she asked.

"I intend to release you from this marriage."

She felt her eyes widen and shook her head. "Father wouldn't accept that. He'd believe I disgraced him. I'd be unmarriageable and despair having to live with him the rest of his days. In truth, I would've rather drowned in the moat."

"Hear me out, Lilliana," Tyven insisted. "There'd be no disgrace if you're widowed and bequeathed coin, to live as you wish till you find a man you'd be agreeable to marrying."

She cocked her head not understanding. "I'm not a widow. You're very much alive."

"I'll not hold you to a marriage you'd never have chosen and will one day end in your death. Nor will I continue to make you suffer indecency by having you lie with other men, even if it's to save your life."

He curled his fists, exhaled, and looked up at the high castle ceiling.

"I won't permit another woman I care for to die because of the Dafyddson curse and that *will* happen should you remain. Then Father would expect me to take another wife who'd be sentenced to the same fate. He'd find ways to force it."

"What do you suggest, Tyven?" She touched his hand. "Surely you wouldn't take your own life?"

"I won't actually be dead…I'll simply live in a different form."

"You plan to transform permanently?" she guessed, again stunned.

He nodded nonchalantly. "Unlike the pitiful halflings, I'd remain able to think. I'll truly still be me, just in a different form. I assure you it isn't as terrible as that horrified look on your lovely face suggests. There's some thrill and advantage to being full dragon. The ability to fly is remarkable." He smiled then—a happy smile.

"You only make this sound compelling to console me. You can't give up your life here." She motioned to the grand hall.

"My life isn't as I'd want it. I'm under Father's thumb and must avoid women other than Vala, who I feel I use every time we're together. I look upon your beauty and vivaciousness and want you without question. You're youthful and alluring. Like my Seren."

He closed his eyes, looking sorrowful remembering.

"My life consists of days planning battle strategies or warring to appease my father and to avoid guilt because of Seren and lustful yearnings for you. I'm honestly ready to be done with this life."

"Your brothers certainly won't approve!"

Rhianwyn tried to think of ways to convince this man what he was suggesting was foolish.

"True," Tyven said. "But they will understand."

"They'd surely blame me if you've told them you care for me."

"Dearest Lilliana." He caressed her hand. "I nearly made full transformation straight after losing Seren, but I felt I must honor her memory by living. Yet, this isn't the life I'd wish for me or you."

"Why did you inform me of your intentions?" She was curious.

"Because it's imperative you know this decision was made of sound mind. I also want to assure you you'll be provided for and safely escorted back to your kingdom. Cadfael will ride with you."

"Cadfael knows of this?"

Tyven bobbed his head. "He's my truest friend. I've always trusted him with my life and my secrets. He'll stay in Wessex to serve you or marry you, if you want to wed him. He's attracted to you. Unless your Irishman chooses to leave his wife for you."

Pray God, no.

Would Lilliana yearn for a life with Sir Cadfael? She had an affinity for knights.

"Don't do this, Tyven—not for me."

"It's not only for you, Lilliana."

She reached out and touched his face. The handsome face of the man to whom she was now wed. She thought of the majestic creature he'd been this afternoon. The intense green eyes of both. An immense lump formed in her throat at the thought of him giving up his human life.

"If you're truly set on doing this, I won't attempt to dissuade you."

They were both startled when the other Dafyddson brothers hurried into the hall looking alarmed. Did they sense what Tyven planned?

Tyven glowered. "Why are you here? I told you I needed to speak with my wife alone."

"Was there trouble in taking Broccan to the border?" Rhianwyn asked.

"No. He's on his way to Wessex," Gronow replied.

Madok went to the arched window and opened the shutters. "Look," he said.

"What is it?" Tyven asked.

Gronow pointed. "Look at the damn sky."

Tyven stood and went to the window. His eyes widened. Rhianwyn waited to be informed why they wore such baffled expressions.

"There are still red rings around the moon," Cynfawr

said.

"Apparently once in a long while four nights of draig moon appear," Tomos added.

Tyven gazed at Rhianwyn and inhaled deeply.

"Don't you feel the powerful urge to couple, still?" Madok asked Tyven.

He nodded. "I thought it was only because I have affection for Lilliana."

"No, we all feel it," Gronow ogled her lecherously. "Madok and I have already mated with women repeatedly. Cynfawr has been to the draig caves, and Tomos, wearing his hood, went to the brothel. Yet we all maintain powerful lust."

"I will spend the night with my husband." She went to stand with him then led him to a corner so they could speak privately.

Tyven's eyes grew wide, then reptilian. He shook his head and turned away. She took his hand and spoke lowly.

"Tyven, I promise I won't conceive, and I don't believe you'd hurt me."

He exhaled deeply and kneaded his brow.

"Mating can be dangerous. The woman sometimes incurs wounds."

She nodded. "I've seen. I'm not afraid and apparently, I have magic. If you fear that, then I'll wear chain mail."

He smiled.

"If you intend to go through with this colossal transformation to save me, let me stay with you this night."

His eyes clouded. "I do yearn to be with you...and my desire grows the longer I know you."

She reached for his hand again. "Then we'll go to your chambers."

Avoiding the stares of the other men, she and Tyven left the hall.

RHIANWYN AWOKE IN Tyven's arms. The night had been one of tenderness and gentle coupling. He'd said that would better ensure no unwanted happenings. He'd looked at her with such gratitude and affection afterward, Rhianwyn almost wished she was free to love him. Or find a way to end the curse at the very least.

Tyven stirred beside her. When his eyes opened to see her there, he smiled at her in such a way that if her heart didn't belong to Broccan, she thought she could fall in love with him.

"If the curse was ended, would you go back to human form?"

"Good morning to you, too, lovely Lilliana."

She smiled, then blushed when he stroked her breast, but he nodded.

"It's said once the curse is undone, all affected would return to human form."

"Then I'll locate Morwenna and see if she's made progress in finding a means to end it."

He sat up looking startled. "Morwenna would never do so…not for our line."

"She doesn't wish anyone else to be affected by the curse. I sense she's fond of you. Her daughter loved you.

Surely, she knows how much you love her. I can feel that love still."

He lay back down and took her in his arms again, was tenderly caressing her when without warning the door was thrown open and King Eurion stepped inside their bedchamber. He loudly sniffed the air. His lips curled back in an unsettling smile. The man was clearly aware and pleased they'd spent the night together.

How fortunate he hadn't arrived the morning before and found her with Broccan. They'd both have been dead already.

Rhianwyn gathered the bed linens, covering her breasts. Tyven glared. She could see he loathed the man.

"Son, I'm gladdened knowing you and your bride have been together during the draig moons. With the fortuitous fourth night, my hope is my grandson will be born next summer. I'd thought I might need to accomplish the deed myself."

He looked at Rhianwyn with lascivious eyes that became reptilian. She shivered with repulsion.

"Leave our bedchambers, Father. Your rudeness apparently knows no bounds."

They were all equally stunned when Morwenna entered the chambers unannounced and wearing a grim expression. She cast a surprised look at Tyven and Rhianwyn but glowered at Eurion.

"Have you been injured?" Morwenna asked Rhianwyn. "Do you bear scratches or bites?"

Rhianwyn felt her cheeks flame. She wasn't eager to have this conversation even if Eurion hadn't been here.

Still, she turned her back to show them she'd not been wounded.

"It seems my son's the one to bear wounds. She's a feisty Saxon woman!" Eurion guffawed looking at Tyven's shoulder. There were tiny arcs on his skin from her thumbnail when meeting her release. Rhianwyn's face became warm again. It had been refreshing reacting naturally during physical relations—not always with that on her mind when she'd been with Broccan after the soul switches.

"But now, son," Eurion's voice thundered. "We must plan war. The Powys Kingdom's been causing a ruckus near our borders. We'll teach them a lesson they'll not soon forget." Eurion left the chambers as quickly as he'd entered.

Morwenna glanced at Tyven. "Better go. Wouldn't want to disappoint your father."

"My wife will meet you in the hall," Tyven said not yet leaving the bed.

Morwenna rolled her eyes. "I'm a healer and not a virginal maiden. I've seen my share of naked men," she murmured as she left.

Tyven donned his garments and met Rhianwyn's eyes. "I'll see you this night, Lilliana. We'll continue our previous discussion."

Rhianwyn nodded and he kissed her before he left.

MORWENNA WAS PACING when Rhianwyn came into the hall.

"You actually permitted him to bed you?" She sounded disgusted and worried. "Do you know how foolish that was?"

"Because of the pact," she whispered, "I've been assured I'll not carry a child; therefore I won't meet the same fate as your Seren."

"Even mating can be dangerous. Bite and claw marks can become purulent," Morwenna scolded.

"Why did you come?" Rhianwyn motioned for Morwenna to sit, for the sorceress's pacing made her unsettled.

"I had a vision of Eurion finding you in bed, not with Tyven but with the Irishman whom you apparently knocked over a cliff and then bedded. I'm almost sorry I missed seeing that. You knocking him over the cliff, not the bedding." Morwenna smirked. "But you both would've been killed if he had found you that way. Likely burned alive!"

Rhianwyn shivered. "Thankfully that didn't occur."

"While you were with the Irishman, I was searching the mountain caves. I haven't located any part of the book."

Rhianwyn wondered if the book that allegedly contained knowledge of how to end the curse was only a tall tale.

"Maybe it's only myth." Morwenna's low voice mirrored Rhianwyn's thoughts. "However, I wanted you to know you have another cousin. My brother's daughter. She might assist with ending the curse if I can locate her."

Morwenna and Mererid had a brother? But Rhianwyn hadn't even known her mother had a sister till only recently.

"Meic and his wife were killed years ago. Their daughter was raised by peasants in another Cymruian kingdom. She doesn't know of her lineage."

Rhianwyn stared as Morwenna spoke on.

"If you should remain in Cymru and are restored to your true form, perhaps together we might find her."

"I must return to Wessex on the anniversary of the pact."

"I doubt you'll be permitted." Morwenna shook her head. "If Eurion believes you carry his grandson he mightn't let you out of his sight much less this kingdom."

She'd be out of his sight permanently, Rhianwyn thought, if Tyven carried through with his plan or should Eurion catch wind of it.

Morwenna nudged her from her musings. "When you're my niece, body and soul, remember your mother's land and castle are yours. I'd like to get to know you better."

"I'll make no promises, Morwenna. I know not what the future will bring. In truth, I might never be in my true form if the other women aren't agreeable to returning to our original lives."

"You could use magic to influence their decision. I suspect you have potent powers you aren't aware of. That probably kept Tyven calm during the mating, for Seren bore no mating wounds either."

Rhianwyn shrugged. "After the pact has ended, I doubt I'll ever want any association with magic. I certainly wouldn't go against the crone's powers. She seems unconscionable."

Morwenna stood. "I do hope we'll see each other again."

"Surely, for the pact anniversary isn't for another moon," Rhianwyn said.

Morwenna shook her head. "No, you'll be leaving within days."

Rhianwyn didn't argue. Morwenna had powerful intuition.

"Therefore, this could be a forever farewell. But know this, the curse placed upon you by the servant is ended. I've had a vision. The curser has indeed died. Therefore you'll suffer no further from it. Do be careful of taking potions from now on. I believe you're a fine healer, like your mother. Now, I must take leave. Remaining in a Dafyddson dwelling ravages my soul...especially here where my only child took her last breath."

Rhianwyn embraced Morwenna firmly.

"Whether in joy or sorrow, hold on tight during an embrace, for it leaves both people better for it," Rhianwyn said with a smile. "I *am* glad to have met you, Aunt Morwenna." She let go of the other woman and kissed her cheek.

"I don't possess the same countenance as your mother, not by any measure. She was sunshine; I am darkness."

"I'm drawn to both," Rhianwyn replied.

"You have trace of each, my niece, but now, I'm leaving before I'm given to frivolous emotion."

Morwenna pushed her dark red hair behind her ear and Rhianwyn smiled. That habit had been passed down from an aunt she'd not even known.

CHAPTER TWELVE

W ITH JUST THE two of them in the enormous hall, Tyven wore a contented smile throughout the meal. Was he truly at peace with his decision? He chatted happily and looked at her with adoring eyes. It only made her feel guiltier that his life would be severely altered to save her. Lord knows she already felt enough guilt on many counts.

"I intend to follow through with my plan this night," he finally said.

"Tyven, no. Not so soon."

"It isn't that I wouldn't like to make love and hold you as you sleep for one more night. But now that I've made up my mind, I want to do this, Lilliana. Please respect my wishes."

She nodded, feeling tears welling. "Your father and brothers might hold me accountable. They'd want to know why you made another transformation."

"I've left a note explaining my reasons and requesting you be permitted to leave when the funeral's concluded."

"The funeral?" She was confused.

"A funeral must take place so others in the kingdom believe I've died. I often partake in dangerous battles. My death will come as no surprise. Then you'll be free to return to your father's kingdom, accompanied by Sir Cadfael.

You'll be safer and happier, I hope."

"Do you even know my father?" she attempted to jest.

Tyven's green eyes grew momentarily concerned.

"He's an unpleasant man who doesn't afford you the respect you deserve. I do hope you'll marry someone who pleases you."

Her tears fell at the sacrifice Tyven would make. He reached over and gently wiped her cheeks.

"Don't weep for me nor pity my fate, Lilliana. It's my choice. The first of few I've made of my own free will. The only other was when I chose to wed Seren."

He cleared his throat.

"There's gold and silver in the trunk in your bedchamber beneath your petticoats. My brothers wouldn't begrudge you those, but Father would."

"Madok, too. He dislikes me."

Tyven shook his head. "In truth, Madok's quite taken by you, as are all the Dafyddson brothers. But none so much as me."

He kissed her cheek and then her lips.

"May I request something of you, Lilliana? Two requests if you'd be agreeable?"

She waited to hear, wanting to agree without question, but felt wary.

"I'd like you to take Gwynna. She's become fond of you, and she'll not tolerate many."

"Of course. I'll love and care for her and her foal when it arrives."

Rhianwyn didn't yet know what life she'd live, but she'd ensure the beautiful mare and her offspring had a home after the pact ended.

"I suspect it'll be a fine foal, with such a grand sire and splendid mare," Tyven said. Then his brow furrowed. "The next request you might be less likely to consent to." His eyes were intense again.

"What is it?"

"I want you to be with me when the transformation occurs."

Her body tensed. Her immediate thought was to refuse.

He grasped her hands pleadingly. "I wish you to know…that I'll still be me." He pointed to his chest.

She nodded, the lump in her throat disallowing verbal response.

"Where?" she asked, finally.

"I've selected a location. We'll ride upon Gwynna. When it's done, you'll take her back to the stables."

Tears flowed in earnest, but she nodded.

THEY CANTERED FROM the courtyard outside Tyven's castle atop Gwynna. They rode across the rolling green hills to a gnarled tree, uniquely shaped like a dragon. Tyven lifted her off the horse and took her hand. They gazed at the sea in the distance. She inhaled the salty sea air and looked up at the waning moon. Tying the mare to the tree, he pulled Rhianwyn to him. He was warm and smelled musky. He smiled looking at her.

"It pleases me that I make your heart beat faster, too."

"You do, Tyven. I wish you…"

He placed his fingers to her lips, grazing them lovingly before kissing her. They coupled beneath the tree. Afterward, she touched his chest with a familiarity that startled her. If not for Broccan, she'd truly fall for this man...who'd soon not be a man. If not for the pact and her being in Lilliana's form, would he still be doing this? Would he have cared for Lilliana, too?

"You're plagued with worry over me," he said. "I wouldn't wish that upon you."

She cleared her throat. "Why do your father and brothers not sense what you intend to do?"

He shook his head. "The draig moons have ended. They've perhaps mated till they're content or drunk themselves into deep slumber."

"You chose this night because of that?"

He nodded. "And because I'm ready, although if things were different, I think I could spend a lifetime with you...but I see prolonging this causes you pain."

He gently moved from her and held out her garments, though made no attempt to attire himself.

"I'll not need such possessions," he explained.

Then he went to his beautiful horse, her white coat gleaming in the moonlight.

"You've been my loyal companion for better than a decade, my lovely Gwynna, but I must leave now. Lilliana will watch over you and you her. Although..." he paused and looked over at Rhianwyn "...I suspect she'll soon take on a different form as well."

Rhianwyn opened her mouth, but no words came out. She felt her stomach dip and twirl, felt the blood leave her face, felt the ground shift beneath her feet. He couldn't know. How could he know? How was this possible?

"Occasionally, I'm able to hear thoughts. When we were joined, that truth came to me. I'm aware of the soul exchange," he said. "I suspect the reason you love Sir Broccan is because you're actually his wife, Rhianwyn?"

She nodded. Her mouth was dry, her tongue thick, but she managed to reply. "I'm not to speak of it, but yes, that's true."

What must he think of her sharing intimacies with him?

He looked back at the mare. "Then you, Gwynna, will have a fine home at Brockwell Manor's stables and a good amount of land to run free."

Even if Rhianwyn didn't return to her life there, Broccan would surely take the beautiful mare and her foal. His steed *was* the sire. She nodded, again silenced by deep emotion.

Tyven passed the reins to Rhianwyn. The horse nuzzled her as though in comfort. Rhianwyn burst into tears. Tyven shook his head and went to her again.

"Weep not, sweet maiden." He brushed the tears from her cheeks. "I promise, this is my desire. And one day perhaps this curse will be ended, and I'll find a woman whose heart doesn't belong to another."

With that, he smiled, stepped beneath the tree, closed his eyes, and inhaled several times. With no apparent discomfort, the man turned to dragon form. A beautiful, majestic creature, with immense wings and large expressive eyes.

She held her chest, watching, and jumped in earnest when he spoke.

"You're a rare woman, Rhianwyn. Like my Seren. Accepting of magic and the unexplainable. Go now. When the funeral's over, make your way directly to Wessex."

"Thank you, Tyven," she whispered.

"Will you do one more thing for me?" he asked.

"If I'm able." She nodded.

"Be happy, Rhianwyn."

That said, he unfurled his massive wings and flew off. His silhouette against the moon was a sight to behold. She stood fascinated until Gwynna nudged her. She mounted the horse and returned to the castle.

KING EURION LOOKED enraged enough to strike her dead when he learned what his son had done. But Tyven's brothers either convinced him it was Tyven's wish or insisted no harm come to her. All four looked ready to battle him to protect her.

The funeral was attended by surely all in the kingdom. Vala looked at Rhianwyn with as much contempt as Eurion. She was probably in love with Tyven.

Rhianwyn was relieved when the following day, her monthly courses occurred. Eurion demanded to see evidence of the bleeding. With some indignance she showed him the stains upon the bed linens. Now, whatever occurred after the pact was concluded, Lilliana—or whoever inhabited her body then—wouldn't need to face Eurion.

She and Morwenna shared another hasty farewell, unable to speak alone with so many about. Each of Tyven's brothers embraced her, wishing her well. Then she set off wearing her black mourning garments, riding upon Gwynna, with Sir Cadfael, two other guards, and two small trunks. One with a few garments, the other with the gold and silver Tyven provided.

Rhianwyn wondered what Selena, Elspeth, and Liliana might've faced in the weeks she'd been in Cymru. At the top of the hill looking back at Tyven's castle, a large green dragon in the distance tipped his wings to her.

PART TWO

CHAPTER THIRTEEN

I T WAS LATE evening when Rhianwyn, Sir Cadfael, and the two guards, rode into Hengebury. The village seemed unnaturally quiet, therefore the horses' hooves clomped noisily on the cobbled streets. Several of the sheriff's men in their black tunics and breeches met them near the castle, blocking their way.

"What are you doing about when it's nearly dark?" one man called. "The bell announcing curfew has already rung."

That was odd. Thaddeus's kingdom had no curfew.

"Princess Lilliana has returned, now widowed after her husband's death," Sir Cadfael replied.

The men bowed their heads. "Our condolences, milady," one said.

"We regret to inform you your father's also ailing," another added.

"Was word not sent of the king's failing health, Princess?" Winston, the sheriff asked, riding up on his horse and also bowing.

"No. This is the first I've heard of it," Rhianwyn said.

Winston drew nearer and whispered, "The bishop and the king's head advisor, Hankin, are attempting to control everything now that your father's unable."

"The bishop?" Rhianwyn asked.

Winston nodded. "Bishop Clements. He's a vile, unscrupulous man, Princess. He's wreaked havoc in our kingdom since he arrived. The dungeon's full and overflowing. I fear the very people who *should* be imprisoned are making the decisions now."

"That's alarming," Rhianwyn whispered back.

"It is," Winston said. "Clements is ruthless. There've been more beheadings the past week than in all the time I served as a man-at-arms. People are being held or executed for unsubstantiated crimes. I know not how to stop this madness. If I oppose them, I'll be thrown in the dungeon alongside the others. Half my men and the castle guards have been paid off or promised positions in the king's court."

This wouldn't sit well with Winston who was a good sheriff and an honorable man.

"Where are Sir Severin and his knights?" Rhianwyn asked.

"Severin's hands are also tied. He couldn't be bought, but they've apparently threatened to harm his wife. Some knights have been dungeoned. Cassian and Broccan included. Your friends, Elspeth, Selena and Rhianwyn, too, each held for ludicrous reasons. The brothel harlots have all been hauled in. Clements has a particular dislike for women. But I shouldn't be speaking of all this during your time of mourning and when you must go to your father."

She touched Winston's arm. "No. I'm grateful you alerted me to this distressing situation."

He nodded and gestured for the guards to let them pass.

RHIANWYN RODE GWYNNA to the royal stables, then brushed and fed her. Cadfael told the two Cymruian guards to rest overnight and return home at daybreak. He carried Rhianwyn's small trunks and accompanied her to the castle afterward.

"I don't believe it's safe for you here, Princess," Sir Cadfael said in a low voice.

"Do you think I'd be safer in Cymru with King Eurion?"

Cadfael shook his head, long blond hair partially covering his furrowing brow.

"Besides if my father's ill and perhaps dying, I must see him."

Cadfael nodded but exhaled deeply. "How will I protect you as I promised Tyven?"

"I won't hold you to that, Sir Cadfael. If you wish to return to your homeland…"

"No, my princess," Cadfael interrupted. "My place is with you."

Was he following through with his promise or did he have feelings for her, as Tyven suggested?

Upon entering the castle, Rhianwyn felt an unsettling, almost palpable tension within. She'd have to try to speak with her friends and Broccan. Maybe locate Severin. She was startled to meet Oliver Barlow in the corridor. His eyes grew wide, and he grasped her arm. Sir Cadfael nearly dropped the trunks seeing that.

"I assure you, I'll not hurt the princess," Oliver whispered. "Come with me, Lilliana, and you, as well." He gestured to Cadfael.

"Lord Barlow, this is Sir Cadfael," she said. "Cadfael, Oliver Barlow."

The two men nodded hastily. Oliver took her arm again and whisked her inside her chambers, then closed the door and locked it. He began to pace.

"What is it, Oliver?" she asked.

"Everything's a right mess, Lilliana."

"Is my father truly near death?"

Oliver nodded. "Regrettably, that's true—especially now when I've heard you suffered the loss of your husband."

Rhianwyn took off her black mourning cloak and placed it upon the bed. The chamber smelled musty from being closed. She went to the arched window intending to open the shutters, but Oliver grasped her arm yet again and shook his head.

"Keep your damn hands off the princess," Cadfael warned Oliver.

"Aren't you a gallant one! Believe me, it's for her own good." Then Oliver looked at her. "It's best no one here at the castle knows you've returned, Lilliana. Bishop Clements and Hankin were nearly gleeful when they learned of your recent loss."

Rhianwyn stared at Oliver. "The bishop doesn't even know me and why would my bereavement please them?"

"Because you're now free to remarry." Oliver's expression was intense, his usual calm demeanor jittery. "You must know Hankin has coveted your father's throne for years. If he marries you, he'll gain full authority as king."

She surely looked appalled. "Me marry Hankin?" She cringed. "He's decades older, discourteous, and emits a foul odor. He can barely tolerate being near me. Believe me, I feel the same."

"Marrying you would give him power, for you're from a royal line, which the people expect."

"What ails my father?" Rhianwyn asked.

Oliver shrugged. "That imbecile Dorsett and his nephew are hopeless physicians. It's been a week since your father took ill. They think the king might have been poisoned. The bishop and Hankin seem eager to accept that.

"They've locked up Radella and Rhianwyn, suspecting the poison might've been from their supplies. They're suspicious, for remedies were found at Brockwell Manor, when Rhianwyn wasn't meant to be offering healing. Elspeth is being held since she had opportunity to administer the poison. As is the Welsh woman Heledd, and other servants who had access to the king's chambers when he took ill."

"Heledd's in the dungeon?" Cadfael bristled.

He undoubtedly felt protective of his countrywoman.

Oliver nodded.

"Why dungeon Broccan and Cassian?" Rhianwyn struggled to understand.

"Because they have scruples and questioned what was being done," Oliver explained. "Broccan was enraged when upon his return from Welshland he learned his wife was imprisoned. Cassian was already there for speaking out.

"Severin, Winston, and I are outwardly agreeable. We can be of no use if we're in the dungeon or, worse still, go to the block ourselves. That's where the other advisors who disagreed with the bishop ended up."

This was a damn mess. Rhianwyn sat upon the bed, overwhelmed. "Thank you for informing me, Oliver, but I must go to my father. Surely the bishop and Hankin will soon discover I've returned at any rate."

Oliver sighed and nodded. "And you—" he glanced at Cadfael "—won't be welcome if your loyalties lie with the princess, not the bishop or Hankin who's happily taken over the king's duties."

"They'll not send me away," Cadfael avowed, hand firm on his sword's hilt.

"You'll be of no assistance in the dungeon either, Cadfael," Rhianwyn warned. "I'll attempt to discover what I can of my father's condition. Surely they won't expect me to wed if he's near death."

"I wouldn't count on that!" Oliver scoffed.

"What can I do?" Cadfael asked him.

"Try not to get yourself killed or dungeoned. Believe me, that might be a feat."

AFTER OLIVER LEFT, Cadfael stood protectively inside Lilliana's chambers. If anyone knew, that impropriety alone could be grounds for imprisonment, but they needed to form a strategy.

"I want you to accompany me to the dungeon," Rhianwyn said.

"Why would you wish to go there?" Cadfael asked.

"I must speak with my friends and assess their condition."

"And learn of Sir Broccan as well." Cadfael's eyebrow rose and she looked away. "You needn't deny it. Tyven told me of your feelings for him...and of the magical pact."

"Shhh!" She placed her fingers to her lips. "I can only surmise that speaking of the pact didn't kill them because Morwenna has magic and Tyven was cursed with dragon blood. Yet here in Wessex where the pact was sworn, we mustn't discuss it, for that could be fatal. Although if I'm forced to marry Hankin, death would be less objectionable."

"The bishop sounds dangerous," Cadfael said. "You'll need to be cautious."

She exhaled. "We must visit the dungeon before I go to my father. Once Hankin knows I'm here, I won't be free to move about."

Rhianwyn looked through Lilliana's armoire. Hidden at the back was the peasant's garb she'd left before she'd gone to Cymru. Cadfael turned away as she changed garments.

"You still look like a princess," he said when she was attired.

She untied her hair, shook it so it was messy.

"Better?"

He shrugged. "It's not the garments and hair that give you away. You have a regal elegance."

Rhianwyn was beginning to see the fondness Cadfael held for her.

Now full dark, the castle was quiet. They walked the corridor leading to the dungeon. The guard at the top of the stone steps stopped them. When Cadfael grabbed her arm roughly, she didn't pretend the gasp.

"I'm taking this pathetic woman into the pit to see her husband. She's been granted the privilege for giving us names of those who've spoken out against the bishop and Hankin."

That was quick thinking on Cadfael's part and done with a believable Saxon accent, too. The guard motioned for them to pass. Rhianwyn shivered. The last time she'd been down these steps was to see Godric.

Moans and weeping were heard when they reached the bottom. They should've brought a lantern; the two candle sconces on the walls emitted little light.

She peered into each small-barred window. The cells were crowded; most people were sitting or lying down. Glancing in one, she jumped back. Broccan was looking out. His face was bruised, his eye nearly swollen shut. He would've fought whoever placed him in this dungeon.

Oh my love! My brave knight.

When their eyes met, he appeared startled.

"What are *you* doin' here?" he whispered.

"I hope to better your plight."

"Meanin' no offense, but unless you've a key and a means to end the bloody tyranny that's occurred here, it's unlikely even a princess can do much."

"Princess?" someone questioned.

She recognized Cassian's voice and espied him in the next cell.

"Why the hell are you here, Lilliana?" Unlike Broccan, Cassian smiled on seeing her.

"In the dungeon or in Wessex?" She smiled back, glancing at the guard at the top of the stairs.

"Lilliana?" someone else asked. She saw her three friends gathered at the barred window of another cell. Heledd was with them. Rhianwyn drew nearer, noting their anguished expressions.

When a thought suddenly came to her, she hurried off deeper into the dungeon.

"Where are you going?" Selena whispered frantically.

"What *are* you doing?" Cadfael asked, following her. "If that guard comes down, I'll be thrown in with the lot of them." He gestured to the cells. "I couldn't protect you then."

"I'm trying to find another chamber that connects to the dungeon."

It was even darker here; therefore she struck the walking stick on the ground, and it began to glow. A few gasps were heard from nearby cells. At the end of the corridor she found it—a partially hidden wall with a shuttered window. She pushed on it but to no avail. Cadfael threw his shoulder against it. The wood splintered and gave way.

"I hope that guard didn't hear that," he hissed.

Apparently he had, for the man came rushing down the steps. Maybe he'd fall and break his neck. They quickly made their way back to the guard.

"What by Christ's cross is happening down here?"

"Had to put the woman in line," Cadfael said, gruffly shoving her against the wall. "She was bemoaning her husband being imprisoned. I told her to be grateful she's permitted to see him. I'll let her talk with him for a bit."

The guard snarled a reply and stomped back up the stairs.

"You should consider becoming an actor, Sir Cadfael."

He grinned. "Now what?"

"You'll see." She went to where Broccan and Cassian were being held and touched the walking stick to the doors' padlocks. They burst open.

Cadfael cussed in Welsh. Broccan came out immediately. Cassian's eyes were wide as shields as he stepped out, too.

"Not everyone will be able to escape this day," Rhianwyn whispered. "But I swear with the assistance of these brave knights we'll do what we can to see all of you released."

Broccan stared but nodded gratefully. Cassian, on the other hand, pulled her into his arms and held her tight.

"I'm damn glad to see you, Lilliana." Then he kissed her.

"I doubt we have time for that." Broccan sounded jealous.

"I'm going to release you five, too." Rhianwyn gestured to her friends and Radella and Heledd. "We may need your help."

"I'll stay where I am," Radella shook her head. "I'm too weak to walk up those stairs just now."

Rhianwyn loathed leaving her behind, but the old healer likely wouldn't be persuaded.

"Surely we can't simply escape." Trembling, Heledd

looked like she mightn't leave either.

"We can't simply go up those stairs when he's there." Lilliana motioned to the guard.

Rhianwyn looked at Elspeth and Selena. "Remember the abandoned chamber we once found and the stairs leading to a door out of the castle that's known by few?"

Elspeth nodded.

"I've found it." Rhianwyn placed the glowing walking stick to the padlock on the door of their cell, too, and the women came out. Selena embraced her as tightly as Cassian had. That would appear odd since Selena was in Elspeth's form, and Elspeth was seldom given to affection. However, they all seemed relieved to see Rhianwyn.

A few other women tried to push out. Rhianwyn regretted having to tell them to stay and quickly reset the lock.

"I promise we'll be back for the rest of you," Rhianwyn said. "But we mustn't draw too much suspicion."

There were a few grumbles.

"The lot of you must be quiet or that bloody guard will hear," Cassian warned.

"You think six people won't be missed?" a surly old man asked.

"Do you honestly believe they've kept count of how many are in this damn dungeon?" Broccan replied.

The man shrugged. Cadfael clasped Rhianwyn's arm as they walked back down the dark corridor. Cassian climbed in the opening to the adjoining room. Broccan reached up to procure one of the sconce candles and passed it to Cassian.

One by one they climbed through the opening into what had once been the mage William Albray's chambers. The shelves remained cluttered with dust-covered mortars and pestles, bottles and jars.

Rhianwyn and Cadfael stood nearby. Cadfael kept watch for the guard.

"Is it now nighttime?" Broccan, the last one to climb into the other chamber, asked.

In the dungeon it would be impossible to determine time.

Rhianwyn nodded. "I expect the monastery bells will soon ring declaring midnight."

"Best we make it out of the castle under cover of darkness," Cassian urged.

"Where will we go that we won't be found?" Elspeth spoke for the first time.

"I'll take the women to Brockwell Manor," Broccan suggested.

Broccan hadn't even embraced Lilliana. Was he not on friendly terms with the woman posing as his wife, or was he intent on seeing them out of this dangerous situation first?

"Will you come with us, Lilliana?" Broccan asked.

She was well aware he avoided meeting her eyes. The last time they'd been together they *had* wildly coupled; therefore this was undeniably awkward. But she needed to pretend she was unaffected.

"I must go to my father," Rhianwyn replied. "And likely prepare for a wedding."

"What?" Lilliana and Broccan both asked.

Those in the dungeon probably weren't aware of

Tyven's passing. She glanced at Cadfael.

"Prince Tyven was recently killed leaving your princess widowed. Lord Barlow's informed us he believes she'll be made to wed the advisor Hankin."

The other women stared at Rhianwyn with expressions of horror and disbelief.

"That's disgusting!" Elspeth said. "The man's foul!"

Lilliana shook her head. "You can't marry him. He's reprehensible."

"I agree," Selena replied.

Heledd stuck out her tongue in repulsion.

"Like most women, I don't suppose I'll have a choice," Rhianwyn said.

"Maybe you can use that stick on Hankin." Selena motioned to it.

"It may well come to that," Rhianwyn said. "But now, make haste. If it's learned you've escaped, it's likely you'll be hunted down."

"I'll see them to the manor's cellar," Broccan assured them. "There are several concealed chambers. Once we have everyone settled, Cassian and I will find Severin and try to stop that asinine bishop and the lout Hankin, too."

"Hopefully before your wedding night." Cassian winked and Rhianwyn sneered.

By Broccan's tight jaw, and the way he glanced at her, she believed he was reluctant to leave her.

Cadfael took Rhianwyn's arm as they left the others.

"Be cautious," Broccan called softly from where he stood near the shattered opening. Rhianwyn turned back to him.

"And you," she replied praying he and the others would make it to the manor without being seen.

AFTER ATTIRING HERSELF in regal garments again, Rhianwyn went to request time with the king. The smug look on Hankin's face made Rhianwyn want to strike him. She hadn't brought the wand, for she couldn't risk it being taken. Hankin boastfully sat on Thaddeus's throne in his hall as though already named king.

What a pompous arse.

"I must see my father," she pled. "I've heard he's gravely ill."

She spotted the other man in the corner and her stomach knotted. He wore rich green robes and a miter, the pointed headdress donned by bishops. She'd heard the man was an uncle to the former sheriff, but his appearance was so like Godric, she fought a gag.

"This is Bishop Clements," Hankin said following her gaze.

She nodded, immediately disliking the man even beyond his appearance and the superiority he emitted.

"Princess." He spared her a nod. "My condolences on the loss of your husband."

Even his voice was like Godric's. She shuddered. Both men observed her black mourning gown and veil.

"Your unfortunate situation will soon be rectified." Hankin smiled.

"You're able to bring my husband back to me then,

Hankin?" she asked, discourteously.

Hankin growled. Bishop Clements narrowed his eyes, his expression disapproving.

"I'll make you a married woman again," Hankin announced.

"That's your version of a marriage proposal? While I'm still grieving my husband and have yet to be permitted to see my ailing father, whom I'm told may be near death, too."

Bishop Clements rose and walked toward them, with an alarming presence that made her shiver. He was a dangerous man. She shouldn't be flippant.

He stopped before her and stared as though she were a rodent to be exterminated. Then he stunned her when without warning, he struck her hard across the face. She gasped and her hand went to her cheek. It burned fiercely. Her eyes watered. The memory of being beaten by Godric came to her in a torrent of fear and anger.

Sir Cadfael started toward them, but Rhianwyn put her hand up to stop him when two guards unsheathed their swords.

"I don't want you hurt, Cadfael," she whispered.

"You obviously don't know your place, woman!" The bishop's voice was menacing. "It's clear you must be taught to hold your tongue and obey men."

"I don't even know you," she dared to say. "I want to see my father. He's still king and I'm his daughter."

"You may visit him." Clements nodded arrogantly. "When you return, I'll see you and the king's head advisor wed."

She was appalled. "I won't marry today. My place is at my father's bedside."

"You'll be permitted to return to him after the marriage is consummated," Clements said.

Hankin's usual grim countenance brightened.

She couldn't hide her revulsion. Hankin was twice her age and then some. He smelled of bad breath and stale sweat. She doubted he'd washed in an age.

Beginning to panic, she could barely catch her breath. "You won't allow me to observe the usual time of mourning?"

"If your father dies with no one named as next ruler, the entire kingdom will be in anarchy," Hankin said.

"It seems the kingdom isn't flourishing even now." Rhianwyn couldn't bite her tongue. She stepped back when the bishop raised his hand to her again. She met his stony gaze with loathing.

"It probably wouldn't do for a princess to bear bruises on her wedding day. The people mightn't approve!"

Clements's lip curled back like an angry wolf's. "If you're unwilling to behave accordingly and observe expected obedience, perhaps I'll cut out your tongue or maybe…you'll meet your end soon, Princess." His tone was caustic. "Thus far I've not resorted to sending heretics to the stake here in your kingdom. However, the smell of burning flesh often sets a worthy example. If their princess met such a fate, the peasants would certainly realize they mustn't step out of line."

"You threaten to kill a princess?" Cadfael roared. "I think you're not a holy man at all!" He looked like he might charge the vile bishop.

Clements turned his gaze. "You, Welshman, have thus far been excused for your shortcomings, being from an uncivilized country, but I'll have you sent to the block if you question my authority."

"May I request Sir Cadfael be permitted to return to his homeland?" Rhianwyn begged. "He's a valuable knight and only accompanied me at the request of the Dafyddsons. Surely you wouldn't wish to wage war with Welshland when you're not yet king, Hankin?"

She saw that distressed the elderly advisor. Most knew of the Welsh, their history of fierceness in bloody battles.

"Allow him to return," Hankin agreed with a nod.

"I'll not leave you, Princess." Cadfael shook his head.

"You can't protect me if your head and body are parted." She gave him a smile. "I thank you for your loyal service."

She curtsied to him. His eyes filled with uncertainty.

"I'm certain you'd be welcome to stay at the knights' keep till rested for your journey. God speed!"

Cadfael bowed. Hopefully he knew she meant he should find the others.

RHIANWYN WAS FINALLY led into the king's chambers. It was dark and gloomy. Windows were shuttered, drapes drawn. Upon entering she smelled the strong elixirs and potions. Dorsett and Hadley stood looking entirely useless as usual. They had the decency to move from the bedside and permit her to go to the king.

By the bedside candle, she barely recognized Thaddeus. He was much thinner with an unhealthy gray pallor. His breathing was shallow. She touched his face to find his skin clammy.

"Father," she said. "Can you hear me?"

The man slowly opened his eyes. They were glazed. Filled with pain, but a result of potions, too. She leaned closer. She could smell elixirs on his breath and skin. Too many to detect individually.

He moaned. "Lilliana?"

"Yes, Father. I'm here."

She sat on the chair beside his bed. His thin hand shook as he reached for hers.

"I'm sorry, daughter," he rasped. "I've failed you and not been a good father. I…"

He began coughing and his body shook.

"You mustn't tire the king," Dorsett warned.

"Tire him?" He was clearly dying. She longed to ask the incompetent physician what elixirs he'd administered. But a princess wouldn't know anything of healing.

"He shouldn't be talking," Hadley added.

The king was weak, but it was clear he wanted to make amends for the strained relationship with his only legitimate child.

She gently clasped the ailing man's hand. "I bear no ill will toward you, Father. It cannot be easy to be king."

"Nor to be a king's daughter," he whispered.

"That's long enough," Bishop Clements called as he opened the door.

She glowered. "You'd deny me this precious time with my father? You're as heartless as your nephew and his son. It would be fitting if you met an equally wretched end."

The man's cold eyes filled with fury. She doubted anyone dared insult or oppose him. He stepped nearer and the king lifted his head.

"Don't harm my daughter."

The bishop's lips twisted in another cruel smile. This man, even though a king, near death he couldn't protect her.

Dorsett and Hadley waited wide-eyed to see what would transpire.

"Perhaps Your Grace should be given a taste of wine brought from Rome," the bishop suggested. "It's finer than any found here in this cold, damp country and blessed by his holiness himself."

"Wine won't assist my father." Rhianwyn shook her head.

"If he'll be meeting our heavenly father soon, let it be with this sweet nectar on his lips."

Would the man blatantly poison the king with others to witness it or make her seem hysterical if she accused him of that?

"May I taste it as well?" Rhianwyn asked.

"A woman given wine blessed by our pope?" Clements snorted, dismissively. "Physician, give the king the wine."

The bishop poured it into a goblet and passed it to Dorsett. The drunkard physician's hands shook. He licked his lips as he carried it to the king. Clements left with a satisfied nod. Maybe Rhianwyn was being overly suspicious because she already distrusted the bishop.

"Wouldn't you like to taste it, Dorsett?" Rhianwyn taunted. "It's surely the finest wine you'll ever know."

The man inhaled the scent and closed his eyes, nearly salivating.

"May I smell it?" Rhianwyn asked.

Dorsett sighed but held it beneath her nose. If poisoned, it wasn't detectable by scent.

"Wine might not mix well with the potions and elixirs you've given my father," she said.

"It won't matter, Princess," Dorsett said. "It's unlikely he'll live more than a day."

"I concur," Hadley added. "So let him have the wine."

"As loyal physician to my father, surely you're owed the honor of drinking holy wine."

The man nodded and took several greedy gulps, then exhaled happily afterward. Rhianwyn waited. It could be slow-acting poison, or she could be entirely wrong. The king looked at her questioningly.

"Will I not be permitted to taste that wine?"

Dorsett seemed regretful he couldn't drink the entire goblet. How could she deny the king this? She couldn't prove it was anything but wine.

Dorsett placed the goblet to the monarch's lips. He managed a few sips but smiled.

"It is very fine wine," he whispered. "Now, I'm weary, daughter. I think we shan't see each other again. I pray not to waken if my life's only to be weak and bedridden. I do hope you know I love you, Lilliana. Although I might never have said it, and rarely showed it, I adore you and always wanted to shelter you. I regret I won't be able to protect you from whatever future you're fated for."

He coughed deeply, leaving blood on his lips. Was it from a poison or did he suffer an ailment of the lungs? She placed her ear to his chest, hoping she appeared a grief-stricken daughter not a healer. There was a rattle within his ribs.

King Thaddeus wasn't elderly and had lived a regal life with ample food and no back-breaking labor. Still, she could see he was resigned to death. She'd witnessed it often.

Lilliana, the *actual* Lilliana, should see her father again. She should be the one hearing his words of apology and love. But alas, Lilliana's soul was in Rhianwyn's body, now believed to be in the dungeon. This was yet another travesty of this wretched curse.

Thaddeus smiled then, his eyes brightening as though he saw an angel or the spirit of his late wife. He squeezed Rhianwyn's hand, let out a slow breath, then breathed no more.

Clearly it wasn't the wine, for Dorsett remained alive. Keeping her back to the men, Rhianwyn picked up some of the potions and elixirs on the bedside table and sniffed them. Potent herbs used in remedies but none detectable as poison unless it was the mixture with the wine. Dorsett noticed even though she'd tried to remain sly. She quickly set down the potion she'd been holding.

"Are you thinking to drink them to avoid marrying Hankin?" Dorsett suggested.

"You know I'm to wed him?" she asked.

Dorsett nodded. "I heard him and the bishop whispering of it earlier."

She glanced at a second doorway leading to the kitchen. She could possibly make it down the steps, out the kitchen door, and into the forest. Anything to avoid being married to Hankin. Thinking of the consummation nauseated her.

"Planning to make a run for it, Princess?" Hadley asked. "Can't say as I blame you."

Instead, she reached for a valerian root remedy used to induce sleep. Too much might kill her, but if knocked out, she couldn't be wed. That would buy time. She purposely caught her bell sleeve on several of the elixirs and they fell to the ground. She bent to retrieve them and clandestinely drank the sleep potion, then lay upon the bed next to the king, and pretended to cry mournfully. Hopefully she'd appear distraught about losing her husband and now her father.

CHAPTER FOURTEEN

B ROCCAN WAS TIGHTLY wound as he waited on the manor's back stairwell. He felt he might jump out of his skin. He'd sent Chester to find Severin and any other knights who might join them. The bishop and Hankin had to be stopped.

Hearing footsteps on the stairs, he watched Rhianwyn holding her skirts and making her way to him. She looked weary and forlorn as did all who'd been held in the dungeon.

"Will you be able to prevent Lilliana's wedding?" she asked.

He blew out his breath. "God knows. But we must do something."

She shivered and he took her in his arms. She jumped when the monastery bells pealed. Not the typical chimes declaring noon or midnight. They were louder, more urgent, and they didn't stop. There'd only be two reasons for that. They were either being invaded by an enemy army...or the king had died. Since he'd reportedly been ailing, that was more likely.

Rhianwyn gasped and began to weep. That was peculiar. She had no love for King Thaddeus. However, the kingdom would be in upheaval if Hankin was named king.

She probably feared for Lilliana, who'd apparently be forced to wed the offensive man.

"Rhianwyn?" he said. "Are you unwell?"

"I'm…" she sobbed "…heartsick for our kingdom and for Lilliana. How dreadful to have to wed that loathsome man."

A knock at the back door disrupted their conversation. Severin stepped in with Everard, Zachary, and several other knights, including the Welsh knight Cadfael. Rhianwyn gazed at Zachary lingeringly.

"Broccan, Christ's cross," Severin cussed. "The king has died. We're sure to be in chaos by day's end. I've brought a few men." He motioned to the knights. "More will gather, but we couldn't all leave together without drawing suspicion. The streets are teeming with unsettled people, which I suppose could work to our advantage."

Broccan nodded. "Come down to the lower chambers. We'll speak there. Haesel and the kitchen staff have prepared food aplenty."

"You can't stop to eat when Lilliana may even now be marrying Hankin and…sharing his bed!" Rhianwyn pled, looking like she might collapse.

Broccan lifted her in his arms and carried her down the steps.

"Rhianwyn, we must be nourished," Broccan explained. "Like you and your friends, Cassian and I have gone without ample food for days. Besides, we can't charge into the castle without formin' a viable plan."

She nodded as he set her to her feet in the large cellar chamber. Selena and Elspeth were whispering in the corner, looking as distressed as his wife.

"Is the king truly dead?" Selena asked.

"It is so." Severin nodded solemnly.

Elspeth came to Rhianwyn and took her hand as though in comfort. That was damn unusual. Elspeth wasn't usually given to emotion or empathy. Since she'd lost Ulf, she'd seemed quieter. But why would she feel Rhianwyn should be comforted?

Loud footfalls were heard on the stairs and several other knights emerged. Broccan was surprised, but pleased to see Winston, and several of his men-at-arms, too. Their help would be greatly appreciated. But who was presently keeping the peace amongst the villagers?

The pandemonium could benefit them but how many people might be hurt? They'd need to make a move soon. He hoped someone had a reasonable scheme, for he could think of few options that wouldn't see them on the block by day's end.

RHIANWYN AWOKE TO something odorous beneath her nose. She coughed and pushed it away, her head fuzzy. Dorsett held a vial, likely smelling salts. She was on her bed in her chambers with several maidservants around her.

"Thank the Lord, she's awake," one said.

"Yes, thank God." Dorsett breathed a sigh. "I was ordered to rouse you or go to the damn block."

He wasn't even concerned for her.

"You're to be dressed in bridal attire," an older woman

ordered in a brusque tone. "The bishop commanded it be done as soon as she was revived."

Rhianwyn saw an array of luxurious garments already set out including a bejeweled silk gown of royal blue.

"I'll inform them she's awake and that the wedding may proceed." Dorsett sounded almost cheerful.

Rhianwyn glanced at the walking stick inside the armoire. How could she use it to assist her? She couldn't simply sail out the window. Couldn't use it as a weapon. If anyone saw she'd be accused of sorcery, which might find her tied to a stake and set aflame.

Dorsett left with haste. The bedcovers were pulled back as the group of servants tugged at Rhianwyn's garments, pulled them off, and hurriedly saw her garbed. They worked together without speaking. Still somewhat groggy, they assisted her to a chair and two servants fashioned her hair.

The door was thrown open. Hankin and Clements stood there.

"Finally, she's nearly prepared," the bishop said.

No…she wasn't marginally prepared.

Hankin wore finer garments, too, but already large stains formed beneath his arms and the odor was noticeable even from across the chamber. Surely, she'd spew if he bedded her.

"Leave us now!" Hankin ordered the servants. They hastened off.

Clements whispered something to the guard at the door. Although the man grimaced, he nodded and left.

Rhianwyn caught a few words. Were the servants

who'd just attended her to be silenced?

"People must believe the two of you were wed with the king's blessing before he passed," the bishop proclaimed. "Therefore you must be married straightaway."

"I wholly oppose this," she said, wobbling as she stood.

The bishop waved his hand dismissively. "I care not of your opposition."

He motioned to the other guard at the door.

"Take her to the castle's chapel. The union must be sanctioned by God."

Rhianwyn scowled. "God must shudder at all you do."

"Take her now!" Clements ordered.

The guard grabbed her arm, roughly. She could fight, but she'd surely be injured.

"Please allow me to take my walking stick. Grief-stricken at the loss of my husband and now my father, I'm feeling unsteady. This belonged to my mother," she lied. "With no father or mother to witness me wed, it would console me to cling to it."

"So be it!" Clements barked. "However, should you attempt to harm me, Hankin, or any men in our employ, I *will* see you sorry."

Rhianwyn held tight to the stick while the guard held tight to her arm…so tight she could feel her skin bruising as she was hastened away.

THE CHAPEL WAS nearly in darkness; perhaps a dozen candles flickered near the altar. Shoved up the three steps, she nearly tripped. Hankin stood waiting, his thin lips smiling. He took hold of her arm, and his stench overpowered her. She placed her hand to her nose.

The bishop stood before them, opened a Bible, and began speaking in Latin. She understood some, for William Albray had been fluent in the language. She heard their names being said. Then the bishop looked at Hankin and he nodded.

"It is done. A holy union, in the eyes of the Lord."

Rhianwyn shook her head. "But I didn't vow to be his wife."

"Hankin proclaimed intent to wed you and it has been done. Now, we'll go to the royal chambers where the marriage is to be consummated."

"We?" Rhianwyn asked.

"I'll witness the consummation and declare it done."

This was getting better and better. Pray God something saved her from this. She grasped the walking stick.

THEIR HORSES TIED beyond the castle gardens, Broccan and the others moved stealthily. Knowing the back entrances to the castle would work in their favor. They'd need to be ruthless with the guards and whoever stood in their way.

RHIANWYN WAS RUSHED to the king's bedchambers. His

body had been moved and evidently Hankin had already taken up residence. He appeared well pleased at his good fortune. Soon to be declared king and married to a beautiful young woman.

The bishop tipped his head toward Hankin. "See it done."

The guard stood at the door. Obviously, he'd remain here for the coupling, too. She should've drunk poison.

Glancing at her, then back to the bishop, Hankin looked anxious. Had he perhaps never been with a woman? He certainly wasn't appealing in appearance, hygiene, or personality. She gazed at the walking stick, surprised they'd permitted her to keep it. If they knew her thoughts—how she was now wondering if she could knock them over the head and run—they'd take it.

But she'd never be able to render three men unconscious. Even with magic.

Hankin took a few steps forward and she stepped back. He looked at the bishop again.

"You're larger and stronger. Bend her over the bed, pull up her skirts, and see it done," Clements ordered. "If you fight, woman, the guard will hold you down."

The guard didn't appear eager, but fear of losing his head would likely impel him to obey.

Hankin cleared his throat. He'd gone pale. Maybe he wasn't keen to do this with others watching if he had little or no experience. His eyes roved her body, resting on her breasts.

He reached for her, attempted to kiss her neck. She turned away. His breath was foul. When he squeezed her breasts, she was repulsed by the protrusion against her stomach.

"Could we drink to celebrate?" She moved from Hankin and looked at the bishop. "Since it seems we'll have no wedding feast, might I not request a drink?"

"Take the woman now! Have her!" The bishop's sinister voice echoed off the walls.

Spurred on, Hankin yanked her hair, then brutishly threw her against the bed on her back. He was sweating more profusely now. Even his hands were wet. She shuddered. She would not be raped…not again. Yet even if she struck Hankin, there was Clements and the guard. If she used magic, she'd probably need to kill the bishop to avoid going to the stake. What a bloody mess!

Rhianwyn picked up the walking stick, willing it not to glow.

"Dare not strike him!" Clements snarled. "Lie still, close your eyes, and permit it to be done. It's your duty as a wife."

She threw him the most furious glare she could manage.

The bishop nodded to the guard who unsheathed his sword and walked toward her.

"If I'm dead, how would the marriage be consummated? Would you defile a corpse, Hankin?"

He looked like he might spew at that consideration.

The guard tried to take the walking stick from her, but like with the old crone, he couldn't pull it from her hands.

"See this done. I'll announce you're wed, declare you king, then you must address your subjects!" Clements gestured to the raucous sound of the crowd outside the window.

The guard placed his sword near her throat. She gasped. Hankin pushed her on her back on the bed. The sword remained dangerously close. She couldn't die now. They were so near the end of the pact.

Hankin unfastened his breeches. She closed her eyes tight, felt her skirts being lifted and fought a sob. Maybe it would be soon over.

She suddenly heard a familiar high-pitched voice. "Princess, I leave you for mere days and you get yourself in the worst situations."

Rhianwyn smiled up at the ellyll upon the chandelier, then watched him transform into a beautiful white-faced barn owl and swoop down. With the men distracted, she kneed Hankin in the groin, sending the groaning, bare-arsed man to the stone floor.

The guard slashed his sword at the bird but missed. The owl flew at the bishop, knocking off his miter and raking his claws across his face. Clements put his hand to his cheek, now bleeding from four long scratches.

Rhianwyn jumped up, righting her skirts. She knocked the sword from the guard's hand with the wand, just as Broccan burst through the door. Several knights including Severin, Cassian, and Cadfael barged in, followed by Winston and his men.

Broccan hit the guard over the head as the man reached for his sword.

"Have you been married?" Broccan asked.

"She is wed," the bishop answered, curtly.

"I never spoke any vows, nor did he." She pointed to Hankin now red-faced, picking himself up off the floor and hoisting up his breeches.

"Has he…bedded you?" Cassian looked appalled.

"No!" she assured them.

"Then it's not a holy marriage," Severin said.

"Nor legal," Winston added.

"I'm a bishop ordained by the pope himself and…"

"And guilty of murdering a king," Oliver said rushing into the chamber holding a vial, a frightened-looking woman beside him.

"This woman was found hiding in the woods," Oliver explained. "She admitted she and her sister, the alewife, were forced by Hankin to add this potion to the king's special ale before it ever got to the castle. She believed it might be poison, but their daughters are in the dungeon. They were told they'd be killed if they didn't comply."

"That's a lie!" Hankin trembled.

The bishop didn't reply.

"The two of you are guilty of the deaths of many!" Severin blared, glowering at Hankin and Clements. "None given fair trial, therefore neither shall you."

"You can't kill me!" Hankin's voice trembled. "I was the king's advisor for two decades."

"Yet you conspired to kill him," Broccan accused.

"It was his notion." Hankin's hand shook, pointing at Clements.

The man glared at Hankin.

"You won't kill *me*!" The bishop nostrils flared. "My presence would be missed in Rome, my death investigated."

"Who'd know what became of you?" Rhianwyn said. "You might've met misfortune by bandits wishing to steal your expensive garments." She approached him. "Who'd know if you were fed to hogs or left rotting in a dungeon till you're dust?"

She threatened nearly the same as the Dafyddsons had to Broccan. He actually smiled. Their eyes met with unmissable attraction. He cleared his throat and turned away.

"You wouldn't murder me in cold blood!" The bishop still sounded confident.

"You, Bishop Clements, ordered the deaths of innocent people and the murder of our king," Severin charged. "That's treasonous and *no one* is above the crime of treason."

A fiercely intimidating man, Severin drew nearer. For the first time the bishop looked uncertain. He glanced nervously at the door like he'd try to get past the knights with swords raised.

"Maybe the princess should end your life," Cassian suggested. "You killed her father and nearly had her raped."

Rhianwyn shook her head. As much as she wanted these men punished, she'd sworn an oath to her mother not to harm others.

"They deserve death, but not by my hand," she said.

"It'll be done in public view so the people will know their king is avenged," Severin replied.

"Straightaway while the crowd below watch." Winston nodded.

"Will my sister and I be put to death, too?" the woman

with Oliver asked, trembling.

"No, woman; you had little choice," Severin replied. "Go to the dungeon with these guards. See your daughter and niece released."

"And the healer Radella and all those held for crimes they didn't commit," Rhianwyn said.

Cassian nodded. "I'll go with them to see it done."

"Let us through!" Lilliana pushed by the knights and sheriff's men. Elspeth, Selena, and Heledd were close behind.

They glanced her way, then at Hankin, unspoken questions in their eyes. She shook her head. "The marriage isn't legal and wasn't consummated."

They all breathed a sigh, but none looked more relieved than Lilliana.

"I'd like my friends to accompany me to view my father's body," Rhianwyn said.

Lilliana glanced at her, clearly grateful.

"I'll go with you, too," Broccan said.

Although kind and chivalrous, Rhianwyn didn't want Broccan there when they saw the king's corpse. How would Lilliana's probable reaction be explained? Lady Brockwell was empathetic but wouldn't be distraught over the king's death. Although accustomed to hiding her feelings, Lilliana might be stoic even after losing her only kin.

"Do you wish to watch these two go to the block?" Severin asked the woman who appeared to be princess.

Rhianwyn shook her head. "I suspect I'll know it's done by the sound of the crowd."

Severin nodded. He and several knights escorted

Hankin and Clements out the door, ungently.

Teg sat on the window ledge. Broccan stared like he mightn't see him as an owl yet didn't comment.

"Your father lies in the hall, Princess," Oliver said.

Broccan gestured for the women to go out the door and he followed. Rhianwyn noticed tension between Selena and Elspeth. Lilliana was quiet, too. Her somberness surely due to grief.

The king was laid out not in the glorious regal garments of a monarch but still in nightclothes, unshaven, his hair unkempt as he'd been upon death. The bishop and Hankin had shown him no respect.

Some of what Thaddeus had done during his reign wasn't respectful. His penchant for very young women was perverse, yet his advisors and many others knew of it and readily supplied him with girls barely women.

"He must be adorned in garments fitting of a king," Rhianwyn said on seeing Lilliana's eyes dim at the sight of her father in such a state.

Elspeth, abused by the man for years, still looked like she'd offer to go for the garments. Now in Selena's body, she couldn't.

"I'll select his garments, milady," Heledd suggested. "Employed by royalty my entire life, I know what's expected."

Lilliana and Rhianwyn, their backs to the others, stepped forward. Rhianwyn reached for her friend's hand as though needing consolation, hoping it comforted the other woman. Then she held her close and whispered.

"I'm so very sorry, Lilliana."

The princess nodded, sniffling. "I know he wasn't the most honorable man or the best father, but…"

"But he was your father, and we cannot choose who we're born to."

Rhianwyn remembered saying that to Elspeth the day their mothers were laid to rest.

"Thank you for asking me to come along, Rhianwyn," Lilliana said while the two continued to embrace.

"His last thoughts were of you, Lilliana," she whispered but their conversation was cut short when Heledd returned with fine garments including Thaddeus's robe and small silver crown.

"I'll wash, shave, and garb him, milady," Heledd offered. "So everyone can view him as a king should be seen."

"Thank you, Heledd," Rhianwyn replied. "I appreciate your kind understanding."

Elspeth nodded to Rhianwyn and Lilliana, then threw a peculiar look at Zachary as she stepped out of the hall. Zachary glowered at her, his jaw tight. Lilliana gazed at Zachary, too, but appeared truly lovelorn.

Rhianwyn would need to inquire what occurred while she was away, but not this day.

How intently had Broccan been watching them?

"Come to the castle tomorrow," she whispered to Lilliana. "I'll request you accompany me again to discover what type of poison was given to your father."

Lilliana nodded, her eyes wet with tears, which would probably be interpreted as empathy for her friend.

Pray Broccan saw it that way.

"Thank you, Rhianwyn, for being here for me," Rhianwyn said when they approached Broccan. She still found speaking of herself in the third person peculiar even after all this time.

"May I assist with anythin', Lilliana?" Broccan asked, concerned.

Just hold me in your arms, she longed to say.

"No, take your wife home," Rhianwyn replied, instead. "After being in the dungeon, I'm certain she'll wish to bathe. Perhaps you should both go to the hot pool. It's good for body and soul."

Would Lilliana even know of the hot pool? Rhianwyn shouldn't have said that. Broccan lifted an eyebrow curiously, but then Cadfael approached.

"I'll see you to your chambers, my princess," Cadfael offered. "It's been a most difficult day for you."

She gratefully took his arm, feeling she might stumble in her weariness. The incident with Hankin had evoked horrific memories. She trembled even now.

Broccan looked like he didn't want to leave her, but Lilliana reached for him, needing comfort, too. He placed his arm around her shoulder, and they left the hall.

UNABLE TO SLEEP, Rhianwyn went to the chapel. Everything that had recently occurred deeply haunted her. The cheers of the crowd as the two men were executed disturbed her, too. She longed to be in Broccan's arms so desperately her heart ached. She was sorrowful for many reasons.

She couldn't help thinking of Tyven, too. His curse had ruined his life. The pact had probably destroyed her and her friends as well.

Even though she'd been here earlier with the two despicable men, she liked this chapel. She gazed at the candles she'd lit. For her mother, Ulf, Tyven, and the king. She wondered if she should light one for the mage William Albray. She sighed, longing to weep endlessly.

How sad that Lilliana couldn't be here. Would that comfort her? Oddly, Rhianwyn felt she knew her friends not much more than when this pact had begun and soon, finally, it would be done. But there was no certainty afterward. Lilliana's future was more unsure with Tyven and Thaddeus both gone.

The women would soon need to decide what life they'd choose. Just now Rhianwyn didn't feel strong enough to decide whether to stay here or return to her chambers.

Cadfael stood at the doorway, surely exhausted, too. He hadn't rested since arriving in Wessex. She'd told him she didn't wish to see anyone. There'd be many who'd surely come offering condolences.

Eyes closed, weeping softly, she was startled on hearing the voice.

Broccan.

"Lilliana, may I sit with you?"

She nodded, hastily wiping her tears, for she doubted Lilliana shed many tears in plain view. Broccan sat not far from her.

"How are you holdin' up?"

"I'm well enough." She hoped she sounded courageous.

"Why aren't you with your wife?"

"She was weary and wanted to sleep. I couldn't."

"A stay in the dungeon must've been wearisome."

She had to make conversation, not dwell on how she yearned to be in Broccan's arms.

"I'm sorry for your loss," Broccan said.

"Thank you," she replied, unable to prevent a deep sigh.

"And Tyven?" He lowered his voice. "Is he actually lost?"

"Tyven, *the man* is…gone, at least until the curse is ended. He transformed to protect me." Tears flowed again.

She wasn't good at hiding emotions.

"He clearly loved you then," Broccan replied.

Rhianwyn shrugged. "He was a valiant man."

Broccan reached for her hand, lacing his fingers through hers. His touch only brought more tears.

"I'm sorry for what happened…between us, too," he whispered.

She dared look into his eyes, which only made her weep in earnest. He took her in his arms and held her close. Whispering Gaelic words of comfort, he touched her hair, then kissed her head.

She needed to end this, for she had the greatest desire to kiss him, passionately. To take him to her bed to ease her sorrows. She believed he wanted that, too. She moved away and stood. Spending the night together now would further damage their marriage.

"I must return to my chambers. I'll probably meet with Father's advisors tomorrow to learn who'll be named king and who I'm expected to wed."

Broccan stood, too. "Don't be frettin' of that now. Sit in this quiet place and allow yourself time to mourn."

She swallowed hard but sat again.

"Do you want me to leave?" he asked.

By God, how could she reply? She wanted nothing more than to spend a night making love with him.

She said nothing, so he sat and placed his arm around her. She nestled into him. His strength and warmth soothed her enough to temporarily let go of her worries.

BROCCAN LOOKED DOWN at the woman sleeping against him. He couldn't understand his desperate need to console her this night. He'd left his wife sleeping knowing there was nothing for him to do but return to Lilliana. He deeply desired to protect her and ease her grief.

He'd barely dared to dwell on what they'd shared in Welshland—what had been forced upon them. But since then his heart, mind, and body had known no peace. *Again.* During winter and spring, the seasons he'd been drawn to Selena and Elspeth, he'd bedded them both only twice, believing he might be falling in love with them because of the soul-switch spell. But with Lilliana, his summer indiscretion, they'd spent days and a night together and shared many intimacies. He shook his head and took a breath. Remembering that would benefit no one.

He'd been stunned when he returned to find the kingdom in an uproar, his wife in the dungeon along with half of Hengebury. He'd followed soon after when he offered his opinion of Hankin and the bishop.

He'd watched both men go to the block earlier. Rhianwyn, usually opposed to violence, peculiarly asked to witness it, too. Maybe she needed to know justice was served. Hankin had wept, begged for his life, and pled for redemption. When the hood was placed over his head, he'd wet himself.

The bishop watched with no emotion. Broccan shivered thinking about it. The man gave off an essence of evil. He hoped he went straight to hell for his crimes and having no remorse. When asked if he wished for atonement, Clements only sneered and placed his head on the block.

Lilliana sighed in her sleep. The sound made him remember her sighs when he'd loved her. His loins tightened. By God, what was wrong with him? He wanted to make love with her.

He lifted her into his arms and stood. Cadfael and Cassian were talking outside the chapel door as Broccan approached. Cassian gave him a sideways glance. It probably seemed odd he'd be carrying the princess. He hoped they didn't notice his fondness for her.

"She's finally asleep," Broccan said. "I'll carry her to her chambers. Unless you'd like to?" He looked at Cadfael.

Cadfael shook his head. "I wouldn't wish to wake her."

The other two men walked with him. When they reached Lilliana's chambers, Heledd was waiting. She smiled sweetly at Cassian. Clearly, they'd become close. She hurried to turn down the bed for Lilliana. Broccan laid her down, gently pushing strands of hair from her face.

Bloody hell, why was he showing affection for another woman...a princess no less and in plain sight of others?

"I'll ensure she's cared for," Heledd said.

Cassian kissed Heledd's cheek, and the three knights stepped outside the door.

"You look like you need sleep." Cassian gestured to Cadfael. "Come to the keep. There are spare bunks."

"I shouldn't leave my princess." Cadfael shook his head.

Broccan could see the man had feelings for her and though Lilliana wasn't his to feel jealous or possessive of, he did all the same.

"You won't protect her when you're dead on your feet," Broccan said.

"True, I must rest," Cadfael said. "But who'll stand watch?"

"I'll stay outside Princess Lilliana's door," Winston offered, approaching, obviously having heard.

"That'll be appreciated," Broccan said.

"I'll send Zachary over, too," Cassian added. "He's been so bloody on edge he barely sleeps after what happened with Selena and Chester."

Broccan looked at Cassian for an explanation.

"I'll tell you on the way to the keep. Walk with us."

Broccan nodded to Winston, and they left.

"Well?" Broccan asked, longing to take his mind off Lilliana.

"Chester apparently went to the brothel asking for carnal *experience*, for he'd never lain with a woman and didn't want to disappoint Mirtha."

Cassian's distaste in discussing this was obvious. He'd once been smitten with Mirtha, but now he seemed taken by Heledd. Broccan could say nothing, for he was obviously equally fickle in how quickly his affections changed.

"Why is Zachary so riled?" Broccan asked.

"Because it was Selena who Chester requested." Cassian shrugged. "Or maybe she offered. I only know that Zachary's in love with Selena and when he found out…"

"He became infuriated with his twin brother?" Broccan guessed.

Cassian nodded. "Wouldn't you be if your brother sarded the woman you loved?"

Broccan nodded. Thankfully his brothers were in Ireland; he had enough to contend with. He was married and bloody smitten with a princess. This time it was apparently with no magical attraction.

He left Cassian and Cadfael at the keep and went to get Dubh.

CHAPTER FIFTEEN

G ARBED IN BLACK, Rhianwyn walked into the chamber off the great hall where the king and his advisors usually met and important decisions were made. There were only a few men here. The others had been executed for disagreeing with Hankin and Clements.

Oliver sat in the head advisor's chair. Severin and Winston were here. Broccan and Cassian, too. She didn't believe knights usually attended meetings with advisors. Not that she knew everything that occurred in the castle. The men stood respectfully. She lifted her black veil.

"Thank you for joining us, Princess," Oliver greeted her. "You have our sincere condolences."

She nodded and he pulled out a chair next to him. She tried not to look at Broccan. She'd gone to sleep in his arms and dreamed of him. Damned erotic dreams. She felt her cheeks flush.

"Have you asked me here to inform me you'll be the new king, Lord Barlow, and that I'm to be sent to God knows where to marry God knows who?"

Oliver grinned. "In truth, we'd like to make a very different proposal, Princess."

"Go on then." She was curious to hear.

"Would you like to be queen?" Oliver asked.

She wasn't expecting that. She held her hand over her mouth. It probably wouldn't look regal if her jaw dropped.

"There's never been a ruling queen in this kingdom," Rhianwyn said.

"Don't you think you could do better than Hankin?" Oliver asked, eyebrow raised.

She rolled her eyes. "A village idiot could do better than Hankin. But the people wouldn't accept a queen ruling over them. Most would believe women incapable or untrustworthy."

Oliver shook his head. "I believe they would if she had the support of the advisors, the sheriff, the grand cross, and his knights."

She tucked her hair behind her ear. "People do take heed of Severin and his knights and respect you as sheriff, Winston," Rhianwyn mused.

"You're an intelligent woman, Lilliana," Cassian offered with a grin. "A little manipulative and underhanded. You'd make a fine queen."

Was that a compliment?

"I believe a woman might be more liable to listen to the people," Broccan said, "and perhaps better empathize with their plights."

Rhianwyn considered that Lilliana might revel in being queen. Elspeth, too, if she ended up living Lilliana's life. Selena, probably wouldn't, yet she'd learned to be princess remarkably fast and had excelled.

Rhianwyn looked at Oliver. "May I request my own advisors?"

There was a rumble amongst the men, muffled comments. A few shook their heads.

"Would I be free to take a husband of my choice?"

"You could perhaps pick some of your own advisors," Severin suggested rubbing his chin.

"You'd certainly have a say in who you wed if it was someone who'd be seen as suitable for a queen's husband." Oliver looked serious.

"So long as you didn't choose the village idiot," Cassian snorted.

She smiled. A little humor was welcome, even in dire times or maybe especially then.

"Who would you name as advisors?" Broccan asked.

"I'd have to think on it, but probably Friar Drummond, for he's wise and caring. I'd name some female advisors, too. Perhaps Radella and Rhianwyn. Maybe even Marlow. As healers they'd know what would benefit the people. I'd sack Dorsett for good—unless he agrees to quit the drink. Maybe Elspeth could also advise us. She knows how the castle runs better than most."

"Those sound like reasonable suggestions," Oliver agreed.

"Would you request to remain head advisor?" Rhianwyn asked him.

Oliver nodded. "Unless you're opposed?"

She shook her head. "You're also respected by the people. I'd keep you on in that position."

"You're saying you'll agree to be queen then?" Sir Severin asked leaning closer.

"She's very young." One of the other advisors wore a stern expression.

Severin looked at her proudly. "No younger than her father when he took the throne. And she's of royal bloodline."

"May I have the day to think on it?" Rhianwyn asked.

The men looked at each other as though they couldn't believe she wouldn't accept straightaway.

"That's the sign of a good leader." Oliver gave her a winsome smile. "Someone who thinks and isn't prone to impulsiveness."

"You've given me much to consider." She tried not to sigh at the enormity of the decision.

RHIANWYN HOPED FOR time alone to discuss this with Lilliana, but there were always others around. When her friends were in the hall where the king now lay in elegant regalia, the people poured in to pay their respects.

The king's throne was placed near his body and Rhianwyn was directed to sit upon it. Oliver took a chair nearby. As her maidservant, Heledd was permitted to be close, too.

Several knights stood guard as the people came to her. They knelt at her feet and grasped her hand—weeping and offering words of condolence and numerous gifts—sheaths of wheat, lambs, vegetables, baked goods, and preserves. Most subjects were poor, therefore she tactfully assured them their gifts weren't necessary—their presence and kind words were all she required. Most seemed warmed by her response and not insulted, which she'd feared.

Lilliana appeared envious, gazing longingly at Rhianwyn from her position at Broccan's side.

I'd far rather be with him.

Selena and Elspeth came to her and shook her hand in the endlessly long line of loyal subjects. Again, she sensed tension between them; they'd barely look at one another. What had caused the rift?

From early morning till darkness fell, Rhianwyn greeted the people. She'd been brought food and ale twice, left once to use the privy, but her body ached from sitting stiffly, regally. Her throat was raw from speaking.

The great hall, though large, was hot with the staggering number of people here. Her heavy gown and robe were too warm; she itched where they tugged at her neck.

Lilliana left not long after Selena and Elspeth. Broccan remained and Rhianwyn glanced up to see him watching her. Their eyes met and he must've sensed her weariness. He went to Severin and the two men spoke.

Severin looked at Oliver and waved his hand. Oliver, Severin, and Winston clapped their hands, raising their voices above the drone. Once the crowd lulled, Oliver called out, "Our princess must now retire to her chambers."

That brought wails of disagreement. Some began pushing and shoving to get to her.

"We must respect the princess in her time of mourning," Winston shouted.

"Princess Lilliana will see you come morning," Severin's deep authoritative voice resounded even in this gargantuan hall.

The people finally began filing out. Rhianwyn longed

to fall into a heap upon the floor and weep. Cadfael, Broccan and Cassian came to her. Oliver, Severin, and Winston approached, too.

"We'll use the back stairs, Princess," Severin said.

Wearing a concerned expression, Heledd took Rhianwyn's hand. "You're weary, milady."

Rhianwyn only nodded. The life of a queen wouldn't be for the faint of heart. When a group of them stood outside her chambers, Oliver touched her arm.

"This has been a difficult day, Princess," he said. "But will you give us your answer now?"

"The people must be informed of their next ruler," Severin warned. "Upheaval will ensue without that assurance."

The knights and the sheriff agreed.

Oliver touched her arm. "Your father's subjects have another day to view his body and speak with you before his burial. It would be best if you were crowned before he's laid to rest."

Even bone-tired she knew they were correct.

"*If* you choose to become queen," Broccan added, pulling his hand through his hair as he often did when distressed. "Don't feel obligated to accept if you think it a burden and not an honor."

By God, Rhianwyn's heart despaired, he had come to care for Lilliana.

"If I don't accept, who'd be appointed monarch?" she asked.

Some shrugged; some shook their heads.

"It'd be a bloody mess, Princess," Severin admitted, his beard now partially bare from rubbing his chin.

"Maybe Oliver," Broccan suggested. "He's a wealthy lord and respected."

"Perhaps Severin or Winston," Oliver said.

Winston shook his head. "I'm too young and haven't held the sheriff's position long enough."

"I wouldn't want to be king for all the gold on earth." Severin gave a heavy sigh. "You're the best choice, Princess. Think on it this night. You'll have to tell us yea or nay come morning."

She nodded, suddenly feeling weak. She couldn't collapse as that would make them believe she was incompetent or fragile, but these damn garments would drain anyone. Broccan and Heledd both wore looks of concern.

Cadfael who'd remained quiet, stepped forward.

"You're exhausted, my princess."

"Go to bed, before you keel over," Broccan said brusquely when she'd caught him gazing at her again.

"Give us your answer at dawn's light," Oliver relented.

Heledd took her arm and led her inside Lilliana's chambers.

Despite Rhianwyn's exhaustion, sleep refused to come. She knew the decision she must make, but doing so alone, without consulting Lilliana, or their friends, or Broccan, weighed heavily on her and it was dawn before an uneasy peace allowed her to rest.

THE ANNOUNCEMENT PRINCESS Lilliana would be queen was made shortly after daybreak. It was met with cheers and applause by the people. Then Rhianwyn spent the entire day receiving them. Having a woman ruler, even if only for a short time, had to be beneficial. She hoped.

She was crowned queen the following morning. Rhianwyn walked up the steps to the throne, looked down upon the king's body as his crown was taken from him and placed on her head—his red robe draped over her shoulders. The great hall was filled to bursting and more people lined the corridors near the hall and out the castle doors. The crowd erupted with exalted joviality.

Rhianwyn didn't meet Lilliana's eyes. She'd be most displeased she missed the elation of this monumental honor. First task as queen was to walk behind the carriage that was pulling Lilliana's father's casket and to watch the king buried in the noble cemetery.

Although Lilliana might relish the honor, Rhianwyn hoped not to remain in Lilliana's form. She longed to return to a simple life...of course with Broccan, but that wasn't certain. If he learned the whole truth, would he want a life with her? The anniversary of the pact loomed near. She both longed for and dreaded what that might bring.

KNOWING SHE HAD to go to the sunstones later, Rhianwyn insisted Cassian take Heledd out to dine. Cadfael remained loyally standing outside her chambers. She expected a battle from him but would stand her ground.

"I must go alone," she said.

"This has to do with the magical pact?" he whispered.

She nodded, wondering why nothing untoward had occurred when she spoke of this to Cadfael here in Wessex. Perhaps because the pact would soon be ended it no longer mattered. But how could she be sure?

"Will you be safe?" His eyes filled with concern.

She reached up and touched his shoulder. "You're a fine knight and an honorable man, Cadfael, but even you couldn't protect me against the crone's magic."

His brow furrowed and his hand instinctively went to his sword.

"Believe me, if I thought the infernal old hag could be killed by an earthly weapon, I might attempt it myself."

"What am I to do tonight?" he asked.

"Go to a tavern and drink yourself worriless."

"I don't even like Saxon ale!" He scowled.

She smiled. "After the first two or three, you'll not notice the taste. You could find a woman," she suggested.

"The woman I want is beyond reach." He dared to touch her cheek. "Be cautious, Princess."

She nodded. With walking stick in hand she made her way to the sunstones.

BROCCAN SAT IN the manor's hall, presently on the receiving end of a glare from his wife.

"You'd truly deny me a night away with my friends?" she asked with hands on her hips. "I didn't believe you were a controlling man." She cast him another furious gaze.

Why was she so combative?

"You're twistin' my words, Rhianwyn. I didn't say I was opposed. I said it was peculiar that you'd be invited to spend the night with the princess…rather, the queen."

Maybe it was because he wouldn't mind such an offer himself. He shook his head at that desirous thought.

Still, Broccan believed there was more to this. Rhianwyn seemed evasive. Lilliana had been behaving peculiarly earlier. She'd barely look at him.

"Is it so difficult to believe Lilliana would wish to spend time with her old friends after losing her father and her husband? She needs our company. She wants to share some mead and conversation, perhaps to the wee hours."

Broccan shrugged. That was possible. But intuitively, he felt there was more to it.

"Am I permitted to go then?" she asked, chin lifted defiantly.

"Do you really believe you need my permission?" he said. "I'm not your keeper."

That likely sounded damn irritable.

"Yet you appear opposed. God's bones, you certainly spend enough time drinking with the knights and recently hanging about the castle as though Lilliana doesn't have dozens of others protecting her."

She seemed jealous again. If she knew the truth, she'd have good reason. He'd had wild relations with Lilliana in Welshland. Since then he couldn't stop thinking about her. He even believed he could be falling in love. Until recently he'd thought her pompous, vain, cool, and manipulative. Now, he couldn't fight the pull she had on him.

"Should I take you to the castle in the wagon?" he offered.

She shook her head. "I've asked Chester."

"And tomorrow? How will you return home?"

She wore a far-off look he couldn't ascertain and took some time to reply. "Lilliana will send me back by royal coach."

He nodded.

"I'll be leaving then." She held a jug of mead and a pouch with presumably a change of garments.

"Enjoy your time with your friends then."

He gave her a peck on the cheek. Lately he couldn't muster passion for his wife, being too bloody besotted with the queen. That saddened him, for when he and Rhianwyn wed, he couldn't have loved or lusted for her more unless there were two of him.

She stared at him, her eyes suddenly filling with tears.

"What is it, Rhianwyn?"

Did she know how he felt about Lilliana?

"You're a good man, Broccan Mulryan." She reached up and brushed a lock of hair from his forehead. "I'm sorry I haven't always been easy to live with."

Now he was confused and plagued with guilt. Good men didn't lust for other women. She also sounded like this was maybe goodbye. Had she plans to leave him?

"I knew you were strong-willed from the day we met," he replied. "Besides, I'm not always a ray of sunshine either."

She smiled at him, opened the door, and set off.

THE WIND WAS warm, yet Rhianwyn shivered making her way across the grassland. It was the autumn equinox, equal time of day and night. The stars were already bright, the full moon high. Another time she might have relished the nighttime sky.

Now, her stomach was in knots, her mind a muddled mess. Unlike when they'd gone to the stone circle the night they'd made the pact, she walked alone. Then she'd laughed and joked with Elspeth and Selena. Now there seemed little to laugh about and she felt a wide chasm between her and her friends.

She heard a screech above her, watched the owl soar and dive, then land near her and transform.

"Teg," she said. "Why do I see you in owl form sometimes now?"

"Because you've developed an abhorrence to magic."

That was true.

"I never even thanked you the other night when you saved me from being raped."

"You have been rather busy, Queen Lilliana." The impish little creature grinned. "You did kick the man in the stones, and you would've eventually called upon your own magic."

"I'm very grateful you appeared when you did."

"At your service, milady." He bowed amusingly.

"Why did you come to Wessex when Morwenna declared you free of our binding?" She continued to walk as Teg flew beside her.

"Truth be told, I missed you." He smiled the wide-gapped grin she'd become fond of.

"I've missed you, too."

"I sense your wariness tonight," he said.

She nodded. "I am wary. I don't know what my future will be after this night."

"We seldom know our futures, Rhianwyn, and those who do likely prefer they didn't."

She sighed. "You're being very philosophical, Teg."

"Well, lovely Rhianwyn, I'll go now and leave you to it." He motioned toward the towering stones.

"Will I see you again?" she asked, hopeful.

"I'll be around."

"Teg, will you sense me even if I'm in a different form?"

"I see your brilliant essence even on the days you mightn't feel it."

Tonight, she felt as brilliant as a snuffed-out candle.

Teg flitted near and she pressed her lips to his cheek. Even by the moonlight, she saw him blush.

"Kissed by a queen!" he gushed, flew upward, then changed to owl form again.

She was disenchanted with magic but appreciated her little friend.

Rhianwyn stepped into the circle, glancing at the towering stones. Was she the first one here? Although eager to be done with this pact, she was filled with dread. Maybe the others felt the same.

Selena arrived next. Even in Elspeth's strong body, she took hesitant steps. She came to Rhianwyn and held out her arms. They embraced.

"I've missed you so, Rhianwyn," Selena said.

"And I you," she replied. "We've had no time alone to speak since my return. Have you been well since your release from the dungeon?"

"Well enough," Selena sighed.

"You've had a falling-out with Elspeth?"

Selena looked like she'd weep but nodded. "Ever since Ulf was killed and Agnes was found dead by her own hand…"

"Wait, Agnes took her life?" Rhianwyn asked.

"Drank a poison." Selena nodded. "Since then Elspeth's been withdrawn. She stays at the brothel sarding men day and night. She caused the rift between Zachary and Chester."

"How? What did she do?"

Rhianwyn really had missed out on much while away.

"She took Chester to her bed. He evidently came asking instruction on how to please a woman, for he was a virgin and didn't want to disappoint Mirtha who he believes isn't and…"

"And I thought he might as well learn from the best!" Elspeth interrupted as she approached.

"Hello, Elspeth," Rhianwyn greeted her. Elspeth only nodded.

Selena scowled. "But, Elspeth, you knew Zachary was in love with me, well likely he fell in love with Lilliana, but in my body, and still you bloody sarded his twin brother! Now they're not talking, Mirtha's furious, and Chester and Zachary are both heartbroken."

Elspeth shrugged, indifferently. Rhianwyn didn't even offer her opinion.

"You're not the only one who's suffered loss, Elspeth," Selena accused.

"I didn't say I was," Elspeth spat. "I don't know why your kirtle's in a knot over Chester and Zachary anyway, Selena. And besides, you didn't even know that Maxim was your father when he was killed."

"Maxim's dead?" Rhianwyn's gasped, her heart already aching.

Selena was in tears now, too. "When the guards hired by Clements came to take Fleta and the other harlots to the dungeon, Maxim tried to stop them. He was killed. I only learned he was my father after his death."

"I'm sorry, Selena. Maxim was an honorable man. I'm deeply sorry about Ulf and Agnes, too, Elspeth."

"I don't want your pity!" Elspeth snarled.

"You'll get none from me any longer, Elspeth!" Selena sounded unempathetic. "You've hurt many people while you were in my form."

"She's certainly not alone in that." Lilliana's tone was accusatory as she drew near.

Rhianwyn placed her hand on the back of her neck. She'd longed for this bloody pact to be ended. She'd hoped they'd be more understanding of the others after what they'd each gone through. It seemed their friendships were unlikely to ever be restored.

The stones began to glow, and an eerie sensation overcame Rhianwyn just like the night of the pact. Precursors to the old crone appearing. Rhianwyn held tight to the walking stick. A peculiar thick mist enshrouded the stone circle and when it began to swirl and dance, the old woman stood before them.

"You're all in fine form this night," she croaked.

"Sarding superb!" Elspeth replied.

"You've learned very little in this year." The hag glanced from one woman to the next.

"I've learned I'd like to strangle the life out of you!" Elspeth took a step forward and the crone cackled, amusedly.

"And the rest of ye, have you nothin' to say?"

"Nothing you'd like to hear," Lilliana replied.

"I just want this pact to be over…and I never want to see you again!" Selena sounded courageous considering she was once so timid.

"You, healer, you're quiet." The old woman stared at Rhianwyn.

She shrugged. "I'd also like to end this and then be done with magic for all time."

The crone shook her head. "That's unlikely when you possess a powerful magic in your own right, else you wouldn't still have that wand."

She stared at the walking stick.

"Have the four of you decided what form you wish to take? Which life will you choose to permanently live after samplin' a season in each of the four?"

No one replied.

The crone shrugged. "First I'll change you back to your original forms while you make the decision."

Rhianwyn immediately became dizzy, then looked

down to see she was attired in the clothing Lilliana had worn. She recognized her own body shape. She touched her head, relieved to feel her own hair.

A squawk was heard overhead. An owl circled again, then flew down and transformed to an ellyll.

"You should not speak of this now," Teg warned looking at Rhianwyn, concerned.

"Of course we can." The crone sounded indignant. "I'm the one who stated that condition. Since the pact will be concluded this night, we'll speak of it with no ill consequences."

Teg shook his head vigorously and glanced toward the mist still surrounding the sunstones. Rhianwyn froze though her heart raced when she saw Broccan step from the fog. Her breath hitched on noticing the angry look he wore. It was clear he'd heard everything.

The old woman was the only one who didn't seem bothered he was here.

"So that's the truth of it, then?" Broccan asked. "You were part of a soul switch? You were each involved?" His voice was gruff, his tone accusatory. His entire countenance rigid.

When no one replied, he stared stonily at Rhianwyn.

"That's what occurred," the crone finally said.

Rhianwyn wouldn't meet his eyes. She felt queasy and still couldn't catch her breath. This was what she feared. What she'd dreaded most of all.

"I think I'm owed an explanation!" His voice became lower, but fiercer.

Rhianwyn opened her mouth but couldn't find the

words.

"Was it forced upon you?" He stepped closer, his eyes boring into Rhianwyn.

"It wasn't forced," the hag seemed pleased to tell him. "They each agreed of their own will."

"Is that true?" Clearly, he needed to hear it from her.

Rhianwyn nodded. "It wasn't forced," she whispered. "I'm so very sorry, Broccan. I..."

"When?" he interrupted. "When did you agree to the pact?"

"Perhaps we might discuss this alone, later, Broccan," Rhianwyn suggested as she approached him. He stepped back, holding his hands up like she had a contagion.

"Sure we can talk about it plainly with your *friends*." He said that word with distaste. "It's not as though I haven't shared intimate discussions and much more with all of them before."

Rhianwyn couldn't believe Elspeth wasn't making a sarcastic comment. Maybe she sensed the depth of his fury, too.

"Tell me when you made this pact? I'd at least feel somewhat less betrayed to know it was made perhaps when you were girls...young and foolish."

He glowered as he stood waiting, and she loathed having to tell him.

"It was..." the crone began but Broccan raised his hand silencing her.

"I want to hear it from my wife...if you're actually my wife just now, for how in the bloody hell would I know? It seems you've each been my wife at one point."

"It was a year ago this night," Rhianwyn said, fighting tears.

"Last autumn at the standing stones," he whispered, for she'd twice nearly told him, and he clearly remembered.

His eyes widened, blazing with temper. He took several deep breaths, then turned away and looked toward the sky. He shook his head again, then looked back at her.

"Therefore, on the day we were wed, when you promised to love me always and be true to me, you already knew you couldn't keep those vows?"

"I wish I could undo it, Broccan. I'm so very sorry."

"You're sorry! You think that makes it better then, do you?" He placed his hand on his sword's hilt and she knew in this instant, he would've liked to take her life.

"It's not as though she had much choice," Lilliana said. "She was ordered to marry you. Her father had disappeared. She was losing her home."

"The three of us wanted the pact," Selena explained. "But Rhianwyn didn't."

"Do not make excuses for her!" Broccan blared. "She's a strong woman who has a mind of her own!"

His fury was disturbing.

"Oh don't bloody well whinge about it!" Elspeth finally spoke. "It's not like you didn't enjoy yourself a good deal of the time, Sir Broccan."

He growled then and glared at Elspeth with a look that frightened Rhianwyn. The stones glowed brighter and began to rock. Three fell over; two crashed together breaking apart. That wasn't caused by the crone's magic. He was a son of the high king of Tara. Ulf had told her

Broccan had magic. Elspeth closed her mouth and Broccan turned back to Rhianwyn.

"You made a sardin' mockery out of our love. You destroyed the sanctity of our marriage by all this sordidness. You knew you couldn't be true. That I'd bed other women and you'd be with other men. You knew how I loved you, yet apparently that meant bloody nothin' to you!"

"That's not what...it wasn't. I...didn't," she stammered, unable to discredit his accusations.

"It was all simply a lie then? Did you...pretend to love me?" His voice broke.

"Through it all, I loved you...I love you, still, Broccan."

"You have a bloody mad way of showin' love, Maiden Albray."

That shook her to her core; he couldn't even refer to her by name or as his wife.

"Now," he said with another snarl. "I'm goin' before I say somethin' I can't take back, do somethin' I regret, or I tell *you*—" he stared hard at Rhianwyn "—and all of you what I think of you just now."

He turned to walk away then called back over his shoulder.

"And when I find out your identity," he growled at the old woman, "and what you had to gain from all this, and sure I bloody promise you I will, you'll be sardin' sorry, woman!" He glared at the crone.

She sneered back though Rhianwyn thought she might fear him, too.

When Rhianwyn heard his footfalls in the distance, she

crumpled to the ground, trails of tears wetting her cheeks.

"I'm very sorry, Rhianwyn." Selena sat beside her and took her hand.

"As am I," Rhianwyn sobbed.

"You have to make the decision now!" The old woman demanded, looking almost smug at the chaos she'd caused. "Sure the lot of you will be queuin' up to be Lady Brockwell!" She actually laughed.

If Rhianwyn could summon the strength she'd strike her.

"I only know I don't want to be queen," Selena finally said. "The other lives, I'll accept if that's what's agreed upon."

"I bloody well don't want to be Lady Brockwell," Elspeth said. "No matter what a fine lover he is. I can cope with the other lives."

"And you, Princess? Or queen now I suppose?" the old woman asked.

Lilliana took a breath. "I'd choose to be queen, the regal life I know, but hopefully with more freedoms than before."

"And, Lady Brockwell, what do you wish for?"

"I wish I'd never met you," Rhianwyn whispered, and the wand glowed red now.

"Be that as it may," the hag replied with a smirk, "you must choose."

"I honestly couldn't care less," Rhianwyn said, emotionlessly. "I'll be a queen, a servant, or a whore. It matters not."

"But not Lady Brockwell? It is your birthright after all,

though by the look your husband wore, I doubt he'll wish to remain married to you. He might even return to Ireland to be far away from you."

Was that her intention all along? Did the woman want Broccan to return to Tara? She did have an Irish accent.

"Tell us who you are," Rhianwyn insisted. "You owe us that at least."

"Owe you? I owe you nothin' at all. I gave you a magical opportunity you all chose to go along with. The fact you seemed to have learned nothin' and appreciated none of it, can't be blamed on me."

"You're a coward!" Elspeth accused.

The old woman snorted. "I don't need to tell you."

"But why *did* you do this?" Lilliana pressed.

"It brings me joy to offer such opportunities to those who bemoan their own fates."

"Joy!" Rhianwyn scoffed.

She couldn't feel less joyous.

"You must make the decision now!" the crone ordered.

Rhianwyn stood shakily. "I'll go along with whatever they choose." She started to walk away.

"You must state your choice!" The crone insisted, her tone firm.

"The three of you decide. I'll be made aware soon enough if my image changes before daylight."

The crone started after her, but Rhianwyn raised the wand and held it before her. It glowed hot, turned bright red, and shook in her hands.

Selena gasped. "Rhianwyn, your eyes glowed bright blue."

Lilliana and Elspeth nodded disbelievingly.

"If you come near me, old crone, I swear I'll drive this wand through your sarding heart and send you straight to hell!"

"Rhianwyn?" Selena ran after her.

"I need to be alone. I truly don't want to see any of you for a long while."

"Where will you go?" Selena asked, surely aware she'd avoid Brockwell Manor when Broccan was so infuriated.

Rhianwyn shrugged. "Don't worry of it, Selena."

Selena was weeping profusely. Rhianwyn needed to get away. Where *would* she go? Did she even care?

CHAPTER SIXTEEN

"GOD'S TEETH, WHAT the hell's wrong with you?" Cassian asked when Broccan entered the tavern. "Why do you wear that murderous expression?"

Broccan pounded on the counter. "Ale—the strongest you have and lots of it! I don't care about the cost," Broccan growled, and the barkeep hurried off to the cellar.

"What's happened?" Cassian asked. "You look like someone shit in your best ale or maybe walked on your grave!"

"Do you not think when I'm not replyin' to your annoyin' questions that I mightn't want to talk about it?"

"Yet you chose to come to the tavern when I suspect you've got finer ale at your manor," Cassian said.

He didn't want to be anywhere near Brockwell Manor should Rhianwyn return home. He was livid! Disappointed! Betrayed!

Maybe he'd come here because if he'd gone to the manor and saddled Dubh, he might've ridden straight out of this bloody village—maybe gone back to Ireland. He supposed he shouldn't make rash decisions in his fury, yet he couldn't see ever making amends with Rhianwyn...not knowing the whole truth.

Much was explained now. But that she'd chosen it, not

had it forced upon her was what galled him most. He felt gutted. As a youth, on a dare, he'd once gone into the pen with an unbroken stallion and been kicked in the ballocks. Even that hadn't taken the wind out of him like this.

"So you and Rhianwyn…?"

"Don't bloody ask of her!" Broccan roared. "Don't sardin' mention her name!"

Cassian looked already well on his way to being drunk. He eyed Broccan up and down but didn't comment.

"I thought you were spendin' the night with Heledd, or have you moved on to fancyin' another woman by now?"

Cassian's eyebrows rose. "Don't take your ill temper out on me. Heledd says she won't become involved with anyone till she knows if she'll be staying in Hengebury or returning to Welshland."

The barkeep brought two jugs of ale and set them before Broccan.

Broccan pulled out a coin pouch and tossed it at the man. "Just keep bringing ale."

A jug in each hand, Broccan went to a table in the back of the tavern. He'd finished one and started on the second when Cassian came to sit with him.

"Ready to talk now or at least not liable to run me through if I sit with you?"

Broccan shrugged so Cassian sat, tankard in hand.

"I'd wager by how enraged you are, your wife must've broken her vow of faithfulness?"

"That's a bloody understatement!" Broccan snarled under his breath as he pulled his hand through his hair and curled his fists till his knuckles were white and his arms shook.

"Is this somehow to do with your absurd suspicions a while back? When you thought that Elspeth and Rhi…"

"I warned you not to mention her name! Not ever!"

"That's a bit infantile, but if you won't tell me what's happened, why did you come here?"

"It's not as though I knew you'd be here!" Broccan slurred chugging another hearty swig.

"I don't know that ale has ever helped a man overcome whatever's ailing him when it comes to a woman."

"Is that the wisdom you offer, Cassian? Don't over-drink? You should maybe take your own advice."

"Have it your way, my friend. I'll leave you to your misery. But if you get into a drunken brawl with no one to assist you, you'll be sorry. Or if you take to easing your sorrow in a whore's bed, I doubt it'll increase your chances of making things better with Rhi…"

Broccan slammed his fist so hard the empty jug fell on the floor and smashed and the other one tipped over, spilling ale on the table and floor. "Say her name and I'll sardin' draw my sword!"

Cassian placed his hands before him, then walked away.

RHIANWYN WALKED UNTIL her feet ached and sobbed till her throat hurt. Dawn was breaking and still she remained in her own form. For better or worse, evidently the other women had chosen to stay in their own lives.

Her regrets were many and her options few. She

wouldn't go to the manor. She'd perhaps return to retrieve a few possessions when Broccan wasn't there, but she doubted she'd live there again.

She thought of all the pain the pact had caused. All the lives it had cost. All the time they'd never get back. How it had changed everything.

"You should sleep, Rhianwyn." Teg's voice startled her. She hadn't been aware he'd been following.

She nodded. "I'm so very weary—mind, body and soul."

"He might come round," Teg said, unconvincingly.

"Did he look or sound like he'd ever come round?"

Teg made a peculiar whirring sound with his lips. "No, he certainly did not, but he was stunned and enraged. Once he has time to think about it."

"He'll only feel more betrayed."

"Where will you go?" Teg asked.

She thought for a while. "To someone as unsociable as I now feel."

RHIANWYN LIFTED HER head and moaned, looking around the back of Radella's cave. When she'd arrived, the old woman had been as understanding as she ever was with her brusque manner. At least she didn't ask for details. Rhianwyn only told her that she and Broccan had a huge row—that their marriage was probably unsalvageable.

The old woman who'd been her mother's friend had looked at Rhianwyn with a modicum of sympathy, briefly touched her hand, and given her a blanket and pillow.

Rhianwyn had Teg procure some ale, mead, a few sleeping potions, and she'd been blissfully drunk or asleep for days. How many she couldn't determine.

She heard Radella's clucking tongue. "You'll not remain here indefinitely, drinking yourself senseless, and crying yourself to sleep each night."

Rhianwyn only reached for more ale, but the older woman kicked it away from her.

"You're a strong, intelligent, skilled woman. Whatever's happened with your husband must either be mended, or you'll have to move forward without him. That's the plain truth. I'll not stand by watching you wallow in self-pity."

Rhianwyn stood with some difficulty, holding her throbbing head. She folded the blanket, set the pillow neatly upon it, wiped up the spilled ale and picked up the jug.

"Thank you for letting me stay here these days," Rhianwyn said.

"It's been a damn fortnight, Rhianwyn. You've barely eaten and not bathed or even changed your garments. I'll…"

"Not stand by while I wallow in self-pity. I understand."

"Your mother would be dearly disappointed, lass."

"My mother's dead!" Rhianwyn said, coldly.

She shielded her eyes as she walked into sunshine that nearly blinded her. She did need to bathe. She'd go to the hot pool.

SHE'D BATHED, PUT on her outer garments, and left her shift behind when she met Matty on the path.

"Rhianwyn, dear lass, tell me what's happened between you and Broccan for I tell ye, he's in a bad way."

She looked at Matty, worry flooding her mind.

"He's ailing?" Rhianwyn asked.

"He's drunk mornin' till night and in a nasty temper. He's not been workin' on the ledgers, not gone to the knights' keep. Even snarled at me when I asked him what's happened. I just saw Radella. She said you've been wretched, too."

Wretched! Was that what she was?

"I'm sorry he's been unwell," Rhianwyn managed.

"I won't ask what's gone on 'tween you. But if you'd maybe come talk to him…perhaps you could mend it."

"Some things can't be mended, Matty. Some pain runs too deep to be forgiven."

"I'll pray that's not true. Come to the manor. I miss you so. Even Haesel misses you."

"I miss you, too, Matty. But I suspect the lord of the manor doesn't and wouldn't welcome me."

"Sure you must need to come for your possessions?"

"One day."

"Where are you goin' to stay, dear? Radella said you left in a state, displeased with her."

"I'm weary of disappointing others, Matty. But worry not for me. Broccan will need you."

"You do still love him then?"

"I'll always love him." Her voice broke.

"Where there's love, there's hope," Matty said.

She only shook her head and walked off.

RHIANWYN FOUND HERSELF back in the clearing where she'd once lived. She wished her old cottage hadn't burned. In the distance smoke curled from the chimney of the cottage that had been Maxim's. She despaired again for his death, too. There weren't enough tears for how downhearted she felt.

She found Keyon sitting near the fire surrounded by Maxim's three large dogs.

"Rhianwyn." He stood and the dogs came to her, tails wagging.

"Keyon. I didn't know you lived here now. I'm pleased you're looking after Maxim's dogs. I was deeply saddened to hear what befell him."

"As was I, Rhianwyn. He had a heart as big as the rest of him. We'd become good friends. I thought the least I could do was care for his dogs."

"You don't still feel the need to wander?"

"Probably come spring, but I'll take the dogs with me. They're good company."

They sat silently for a bit.

"If you don't mind me saying so, Rhianwyn, you're looking unwell. You're thin and pale. The shine's gone from your lovely eyes."

She hadn't looked at her reflection in some time.

"Is it true you and Broccan no longer live under the same roof?"

"It's true," she replied, her heart squeezing.

"You have friends, Rhianwyn. Lean on them. You've helped many in need. You can stay here with me if you like."

He gestured to the small cottage. "I'd play for you day and night if it'd cheer you."

She saw the lute leaning near the door and thought of Tomos. Maybe she should go to Cymru. She had an aunt—apparently a castle. The thought of leaving Broccan shattered her heart. Yet staying knowing he loathed her made her soul despair.

"Thanks for your kind offer, Keyon, but I'd be poor company. I'm blessed to have such a wonderful friend." She touched his hand.

"At least stay for some stew. I'm not so fine a cook as you, but I'm learning."

"I'd like that," she replied.

His wide grin brightened her mood some. They sat together, Keyon speaking mostly. The three dogs lay near her surely sensing her distress. She welcomed the stew. She couldn't recall when she'd last eaten though she thought she remembered Radella urging her to eat.

Afterward, Keyon played some cheery tunes.

"You could sleep inside. I'll stay here by the fire," Keyon suggested. "For I'd not want you to be tempted by my handsome face and brawny body."

She smiled for the first time since the night at the sunstones. Keyon had peculiar darting eyes, unruly red hair, and gangly arms and legs. But his kindness, humor, and cheerful nature made up for his appearance. She hoped he'd find someone who'd love him for the good man he was.

Warmed by fire, food, and friendship, she felt encouraged and decided to go to the manor. She'd have to face Broccan sometime. It might as well be now.

SHE APPROACHED, REMEMBERING the first night she'd gone to see Broccan. She'd been nervous then, too.

Candles burned in the hall windows. Broccan was surely still awake. Perhaps drinking. Was this wise? Her legs shook and her breath quickened.

Should she knock? This was her home, too. She opened the door. The corridor was empty. She heard voices. Maybe Broccan and Matty talking. Perhaps she should leave. She turned, nearly went back out when she heard a woman laugh. That was *not* Matty's laugh.

Heart thumping, she silently made her way down the corridor. The doors to the hall were open. Her mouth went dry as she approached and heard the recognizable sounds. No use backing out now. She peeked in the room and must've gasped though she wasn't aware she'd made a sound.

Both Broccan and Mirtha looked up. They were lying upon the table, both unclothed. It was clear what had just occurred. Mirtha's face colored and she reached for her gown though Rhianwyn had never seen her in a gown before.

She thought her knees would give out. Her cheeks flamed along with her jealous temper. Mirtha sat up and held the gown over her breasts. Broccan didn't cover himself or look away as Rhianwyn stared.

"Lady Brockwell!" His tone was mocking; his voice slurred. "I did wonder when you might make an appearance if only to retrieve your possessions or boot me out of the home that belonged to your dear father."

Rhianwyn stood stock-still, longing to be anywhere but here. Mirtha boldly remained sitting by Broccan.

"Should I give you time to speak?" Mirtha looked at him.

"You could ask the lady of the manor if she intends to stay long enough to speak."

"I do not!" Rhianwyn barked.

Broccan shrugged and finally stood unabashedly unclothed, reaching for his breeches.

"Where's Fairfax?" Rhianwyn asked. "Does he approve of his sister sarding a married man? I recall him once rebuking another of Broccan's women."

Mirtha pulled a face on hearing that. Broccan tugged on his breeches.

"Do you leave your brother, whom you seem so very protective of, unattended in the guesthouse, while you carry on with Sir Broccan or have you been moved into the manor as his private whore?"

"Why are you taking your wrath out on me? I'm not married."

"Sarding a married man makes you equally blamable."

Mirtha shrugged. Collecting her other garments, she glowered at Rhianwyn as she walked through the open doors.

Broccan tied his breeches. Remaining bare-chested, he took the jug of ale, sat down, and took a long drink.

"Why should me sardin' Mirtha even matter to you, Lady Brockwell? Maybe you're just riled she's not a woman you made a pact with. Someone you didn't give your blessing for me to sard! Maybe you'd still like to control which crannies my cock finds its way to!"

"You're purposely being crude and offensive. I thought you above using women, Broccan."

"Using?" he snorted. "She came to me."

Rhianwyn's heart was beating so fast she heard it pounding in her ears. She longed to scream or weep but wouldn't give him the satisfaction.

"You couldn't possibly resist?"

He stared unblinking. "Give me one good reason why I should've resisted? It's not like marriage vows mean anythin' at this point."

His eyes looked bloodshot, his hair tousled. Void of his tunic she looked away from the marks of passion Mirtha had left on his neck and chest.

"If not to respect her, then for your own self-respect."

He only glowered again.

"You're so damn typical, behaving like any man who's been wronged. Easing your woes with drinking and whoring. I thought you above that, Broccan. And you had her on...*our* table."

The memory of when they'd made love on that table

the first time they were intimate and several times afterward, tore at her heart.

"Our table? Our table?" He abruptly stood, voice dripping with rage. "That's damn ironic. Do you know how many women I've bloody well sarded on that table?" he bellowed. "Of course you do. You bloody well agreed to it, arranged the whole sardin' thing! I'll tell you what I think of *our* table and of *our* marriage, Lady Brockwell."

His body grew rigid, and he flipped the immense weighty chestnut table and hurled it across the hall. He was a powerful man, but that show of strength was not only fueled by rage, but also by magic.

"There! We've no table! No marriage—no life together! Not any longer!"

He picked up shattered pieces of wood and began tossing them in the huge hearth. The fire hissed and spat and the flames roared higher.

The walking stick in her hand hummed. Even in his fury he turned to look at it. She felt the power running through her. In her jealous anger she wanted to inflict pain upon him, too. Instead, she pivoted and started toward the doors when both loudly slammed shut, preventing her exit.

She turned back angrily. He strode toward her and backed her against the wall, grabbing hold of her shoulders. She wasn't certain what he intended. When he boldly tried to kiss her, she slapped him hard across the face.

"You dare come near me with her kiss still on your lips—her scent still upon you!"

She thought her temper pleased him. His eyes roved her body, resting on her breasts.

"How many men sarded you, Lady Brockwell, when you were the harlot, the servant, and the princess? Did Tyven have you, too, maybe in the form of a beast?"

"You're more of a beast this night than he ever was!"

When she looked into his eyes, she saw the reflection of her own, eerily glowing bright blue. She turned away and pointed the wand at the doors. They not only flew open but were pulled from their hinges and thrown against opposite walls smashing goblets and bottles, knocking down trophy animal heads, swords and shields mounted on the wall. The noise was nearly deafening.

Her own potent magic stunned her. She rushed down the corridor nearly bumping into Matty. She must've known what Rhianwyn had seen. Mirtha was even now lacing her bodice. Matty shook her head, wrung her hands, and looked like she'd weep.

Rhianwyn walked toward the door.

Mirtha foolishly drew near. "Do you honestly believe you have any right to be angry? You don't even live with him. Surely you don't expect a man that grand to be celibate?"

Glaring, Rhianwyn tried to sidestep her, but Mirtha blocked her path.

"You'd be wise to get out of my way," Rhianwyn warned, enragement still coursing through her.

Mirtha wore a smug smirk. "In Mercia, I fought daily just to keep alive. Do you think threats from a sarding lady frighten me?"

Rhianwyn raised the wand, fighting the urge to employ magic against the other woman, but instead she pulled back her fist and punched her in the nose, hearing the bone crack. The stunned look on her face as Mirtha placed her hands to her bleeding nose was marginally gratifying.

"I never professed to be a lady!" Rhianwyn blared, slamming the door.

CHAPTER SEVENTEEN

RHIANWYN GLANCED ACROSS the street at the busy tavern, tempted to go in, maybe even find a man. Considering she'd just chided Broccan about self-respect, she wouldn't start down that path. She headed for the monastery instead, where she'd be safe and not tempted.

Rhianwyn knocked on the heavy wooden door, then shook her bruised fist. Mirtha had a hard head. Friar Drummond appeared, wearing his brown cassock, tied with a rope. He held a candle.

"Rhianwyn." He appeared surprised seeing her at night, especially with no babe needing a place to be cared for. Shining the light upon her, he must've seen her woefulness.

"What ails you, child?"

"May I stay here for a time, Friar?"

He looked closer. "We offer safe haven for any who are sick or downtrodden with nowhere to go. But you have a home, Rhianwyn."

She shook her head. "I'm heartsick and not welcome at my home, nor do I want to be there."

His already kind face softened. "Then come in, child." He gestured to the door.

"Wait," she said. "Will you berate me if I weep or over-drink ale?"

He smiled warmly. "So long as you don't drink our ale supply dry or wail so loudly you disrupt our prayers, you'll not be chastened."

He motioned for her to enter, closed the door, and patted her arm.

THE CHAMBER GIVEN her was small with one tiny window. The bed had little straw; the blanket, thin and worn, had clearly been a feast for moths. But it was clean and the room quiet except when the monastery bells pealed. Rhianwyn was grateful to be here.

Pitcher, basin, soap, and cloth were left for her, and a robe like the ones the friars wore. A goblet of ale and tray of simple but tasty food was set outside her door morning and night.

She'd asked to be left alone and requested no visitors...though who'd come to see her even if they learned her location, was uncertain. She needed to sort through her thoughts and future options. Broccan had made it clear he believed their marriage was over and the image of him and Mirtha gave her no peace.

She slept a lot. She'd hear the monks' morning and evening prayers being chanted in Latin and wondered what she should pray for. She kept the wand with her, but cautiously, remembering how she'd longed to harm Mirtha with magic. No one should have such power. Clearly Broccan did, too. Maybe it was best they never reunite. Still, her heart despaired at that.

Rhianwyn was startled by a knock, for she'd seen no one since she arrived.

"Rhianwyn, child, may I come in?"

It was Friar Drummond.

"Of course," she called.

He smiled seeing her wearing the robe. "Do you need anything?"

She shook her head. "I've appreciated the food, drink, and quietude."

"I sensed you required solitude, but perhaps you need a friend, too. Do you wish to share what torments you? I recognize the look of someone whose heart and soul are suffering."

He was correct on that count.

"I've betrayed my husband," she sighed. "I don't believe he'll forgive me. I also found him with another woman and…I don't know what lies before me now."

"Perhaps if you were to speak with the man?" the friar suggested.

"He doesn't want to talk to me."

"The Irishwoman from Brockwell Manor stopped by recently asking for you, as did the wandering minstrel, the red-haired woman from the brothel, and the blonde castle servant. Even the queen sent a messenger asking to be told of your condition."

"How did anyone know I was here?" Rhianwyn put her hands before her.

Friar Drummond's eyebrows knitted. "Your husband apparently followed you the night you arrived. Perhaps he needed to know you were safe."

"Or wanted to murder me?" she said under her breath.

The friar stiffened. "Is that why you're truly here? You feel you must be protected from him?"

"No. Broccan doesn't approve of men using their brawn to harm a woman. If he'd been inclined, he would've done so the night I arrived, for he was as angry as I've ever seen him."

The friar seemed reassured. "Have you made any decisions in the fortnight you've been here, Rhianwyn?"

Had it been that long?

"I have an aunt in Cymru. Perhaps I'll go there."

"You're welcome to remain here till you're strong enough to travel or until you decide to speak to your husband. With time apart perhaps his temper has cooled, and he'd be more inclined to forgiveness."

"Perhaps." She held little hope but didn't want to sound completely forlorn.

"Have you forgiven him?"

She took a breath. "I understand why he strayed."

"That's a start," the kind man said. "If you're weary of these four stone walls, you might come to the gardens or the orchard. Too much solitude can cause despair. We have a fine herb garden. Perhaps you might brew some of the tea you once brought me when my stomach ailed me."

When he touched her hand in a fatherly gesture, she suddenly missed William Albray, the only man she'd ever think of as her father. She always wondered what had become of him. Even to learn he'd died would give her closure.

Father Drummond patiently awaited her reply.

"I'd like that," she said.

BROCCAN NUDGED DUBH'S sides, urging him to gallop. The cold wind on his face was welcome. No matter how he attempted to calm his rage, he couldn't manage it—or the despair. Severin had given him a moon away from the training field to *sort himself out*, as he'd gruffly put it.

In truth, Broccan didn't trust himself with sword or other weapons. He was too infuriated to control his emotions or his enragement.

Matty had stopped telling him he shouldn't be drinking so much, quit looking at him with accusation after the night he'd been with Mirtha. She didn't even ask about the destroyed table, or the state of the hall's doors that he'd propped against the wall—hinges bent, doors damaged.

He looked down at his battered knuckles. Punching tree trunks wasn't even the most foolish thing he'd done these past weeks. Not resisting Mirtha had been an immense mistake.

He knew he'd have to talk to Rhianwyn. But to what end? When he thought of her, his heart squeezed, and his stomach churned. He'd followed her at a distance after the chaos that ensued at the manor that night, wondering if she'd go to a man's bed in retribution for his infidelity. He was relieved when she'd gone to the monastery. He knew they couldn't live together just now.

He'd drunk himself senseless most nights and slept when the sun shone. He continued only with his daily ride.

Dubh shouldn't suffer because his life was a bloody debacle. Cassian tried to talk to Broccan a few times, but he'd shut him down straightaway. How could he explain the depth of the betrayal he felt?

Broccan rode into the stables after a long ride. Dubh snorted, spotting Chester mucking out the stables. The man looked as downcast as Broccan felt. He and his twin brother apparently remained estranged. Chester was obviously regretful about going to the brothel and likely bemoaned losing Mirtha.

Broccan cleared his throat and looked away on that count. But Mirtha *had* come to him, ready and willing, and in his fury, he didn't turn her away. He hadn't planned for Rhianwyn to find them together, yet maybe in some cruel way, he was pleased she'd seen. That she'd been angry and jealous. Maybe he wanted to hurt her, make her feel as betrayed as he did. But the stunned look on her face and the pain in her beautiful pale blue eyes had gutted him. Not to mention seeing her eyes glow. Few had that level of magic.

"I'll tend to your horse, Broccan." Chester sounded low. "Dubh's come to like me a little."

"Thanks, Chester," Broccan managed.

He dismounted and affectionately patted his cherished stallion's neck. He glanced over at Blath, Rhianwyn's horse, and the pregnant mare that once belonged to Prince Tyven. He'd ensured they were both ridden daily, too.

A memory flashed to when he and Rhianwyn used to ride the meadows. They'd laughed and talked, raced sometimes, gone to the river with the dogs, and often stopped to make love. He closed his eyes and curled his fists.

"Are you unwell?" Chester asked, concerned.

"Drank too much last night."

That wasn't a lie.

"I've heard Zachary's requested a position in a knights' order in Mercia." Chester's voice sounded strained.

Broccan shrugged. "I've not been to the keep for some time and haven't spoken to Zachary recently."

Chester hung his head, carrying on with his chores. Broccan could feel his discontentment, too. He'd offer the man a drink if he hadn't not long ago sarded the woman he loved. Mirtha had come to Broccan twice more, but he'd spurned her advances, and she hadn't returned.

Broccan began walking out of the stables.

"You should go talk to your wife," Chester called.

Broccan didn't reply. He liked the young man and wouldn't want to beat him for his unsolicited advice.

THE WEATHER REMAINED warm, but the trees had shed most of their colorful leaves. Now at the monastery for a moon and a fortnight, Rhianwyn had helped harvest the vegetables and apples. She'd learned some about the process of ale making. She and Friar Springham, the resident herbalist, had struck up a friendship. It felt good to kneel in the dirt, and to work with mortar and pestle again.

Against her better judgment, one November day, Rhianwyn agreed to see the women who came requesting visitation. Matty, Radella, and Mabel, Severin's wife.

They walked to the orchard and sat on a crudely built wooden bench under a dogwood tree.

Matty spoke first. "Your color's better."

The last time she'd seen Matty, Rhianwyn had been so angry she'd probably looked red as a beetroot.

"You've put on a little weight," Radella added. "You don't look like you'd blow away in a wind gust now."

"How are you, dear?" Mabel touched Rhianwyn's arm.

"It's peaceful here," Rhianwyn replied.

"But how are you?" Mabel pushed.

She only shrugged.

"Whatever's happened, you can weather it," Radella said.

"Your friends each overcame adversity," Matty added. "The wee harlot, Selena, suffered a sword's wound and recovered."

"Elspeth was beaten horribly and violated by her husband," Radella continued. "She healed."

"Even the princess suffered the death of her husband and father," Mabel said. "Severin told me she was nearly violated and wed to that horrid Hankin. Now she's ruling queen."

Rhianwyn remembered every damn detail of all that, for she'd bloody well endured it. She bit her tongue. "Yes, my friends are strong women. I should aspire to be as valiant."

That sounded damn bitter.

Matty's lips pursed. "Broccan's hurtin', too, lass."

Her heart ached knowing she'd caused this. His pain

and hers. No matter where she was or how far she journeyed, she couldn't avoid that guilt.

"The monks make a lovely apple cider." Rhianwyn changed the subject as she stood. "We should try a sample."

The three women looked at her with varying degrees of concern and sympathy but didn't offer further advice.

AFTER BIDDING THEM farewell, Rhianwyn spotted Oliver Barlow with Father Drummond. He noticed her, too, and waved.

"Rhianwyn, it's good to see you," Oliver said. "I heard you were staying here. Have you taken up residence permanently?" His smile was pleasant.

"Lord Barlow," she greeted him more formally. "No, I wouldn't wish to wear out my welcome."

"Walk with me?" he asked as he nodded to Friar Drummond.

"Lilliana says you're welcome to stay in the castle if you're growing weary of this meager existence."

Rhianwyn snorted. Oliver grasped her arm affectionately as they strolled.

"Have you learned anything regarding Corliss and the other women born at the brothel?" she asked. "Is that why you're here?"

Oliver nodded. "I was just thanking Friar Drummond. Because I believed Corliss might've partaken in the violence and murder there, the friar showed me hidden records in the cellar. Some were damaged from the damp. Fortunately the ones we required were legible."

"You've discovered Corliss's birth mother?"

Oliver nodded. "It's a bit peculiar, for some babies born at the brothel weren't born to harlots. Some pregnant women apparently went there knowing the harlots would assist and wouldn't judge."

The brothel women were understanding; Rhianwyn remembered that from her time spent there.

"Who is Corliss's mother then?"

Rhianwyn was curious.

Oliver's brow furrowed. "The cook at Brockwell Manor."

"Haesel?" Rhianwyn must've appeared stunned, for Oliver grinned.

Rhianwyn doubted Haesel had ever looked at a man, much less lain with one.

"The father was listed as Lord Easton," Oliver explained. "The elder Lord Easton. Apparently, friends with the late Giles Brockwell, over twenty years ago Lord Easton had his way with Haesel. Forced or by choice, I couldn't say."

Rhianwyn doubted it was by choice. Men of power and position simply took women who appealed to them, regardless of how the woman felt. Or maybe he *had* seduced her. Some men were charmingly persuasive with young women.

"The irony is, Corliss was noble born," Oliver said. "Well her father was—probably a lecherous arse, but a noble."

"It's fortunate the former sheriff told the younger Lord

Easton he'd learned she was common born. That prevented Corliss from marrying her half brother," Rhianwyn replied.

God's bones. Rhianwyn knew how that felt.

"It turns out Halsey Winthrop is Mabel's child," Oliver said.

"I'm pleased of that." Rhianwyn smiled. "They've already become close. Mabel thinks of Halsey's daughter as her grandchild."

"Severin must be tickled, too," Rhianwyn said. "What of the others born at the brothel?"

"The castle servant, Cora, was born to the harlot, Dora."

Had Dora named the girlchild before she gave her to the monks?

"The brothel's former enforcer, Bartlett, was apparently Dora's child, too."

Dora, who'd seemed maternal, probably couldn't see the babies disposed of while she carried them. Pity she couldn't have raised them. Maybe some of this recent violence would've been avoided.

"Have you discovered more regarding Corliss's involvement in the crimes at the brothel?"

Oliver frowned. "I spoke with the harlot, Stena. She finally admitted Corliss talked her into it. They both committed the violence. It was Corliss's notion to use a cross, thinking it might remove suspicion from them and hoping pious churchgoers would be blamed for hurting harlots whom they deemed sinful.

"It all sounds very calculating," Rhianwyn replied.

He nodded. "Cora and Bartlett were involved, too.

They killed Ackley Coutts, also at Corliss's suggestion. He apparently saw them together outside Godric's house. They thought he'd heard them speaking of the brothel murders. Sheriff Winston has dungeoned them all. They now await judgment."

"I'm sorry, Oliver." Rhianwyn squeezed his arm. "I know you care for your sister. Your parents must be devastated."

Oliver let out a long breath. "They certainly don't need this in their elder years. But those unfortunate women were injured and killed. Justice must be served. I suspect Corliss would prefer the noose to years in the dungeon. I doubt she'd cope."

"You're a good man," Rhianwyn said. "Fair and just. I'm glad you're head advisor."

A pensive expression crossed his face.

"I've heard of the trouble you and Broccan now face. He knows the truth then—about the soul transfers?"

She narrowed her eyes wondering just how much Oliver knew. The day Godric died he said he was aware of some of what was occurring.

She only nodded.

"I'm glad the magic that plagued you and your friends is finally over," Oliver said.

"But the aftermath is long-lasting and far-reaching."

"You think Broccan won't come to terms with it?" Oliver's eyebrows knitted.

She only looked away, her heart aching again.

"If I'm able to assist you, Rhianwyn, please let me know."

He took her in his arms and held her. She simply accepted his consolation. Then he abruptly released her.

"Oh, I nearly forgot." From a pocket inside his overcoat he produced the book she'd found in William Albray's chambers in the castle. He'd been keeping it for her.

"Oliver, do you know what became of my father?" Rhianwyn asked. "I'm aware he was a Druid, like you. Are you able to determine if he yet lives?"

He shook his head again. "I've been trying to learn of it since he went missing. I believe it involves magic, yet not William's. A mystical force that wanted him gone from this place. Maybe from you."

Rhianwyn didn't understand. Maybe when she felt stronger, one day she'd ask Oliver more about it.

He glanced at the book. "I believe some's written in another language, maybe Welsh."

"Thank you, Oliver."

"Well, I'm off to see the queen. She's requested a meeting."

"How goes the queen?" Rhianwyn asked.

"You could come see for yourself. Lilliana inquires for you often and says Selena and Elspeth do as well. I suspect they maintain a good amount of guilt at the present state of your marriage."

"They're no more to blame than me. As Elspeth often pointed out, I wasn't forced into the pact."

"Coerced by what Lilliana and Elspeth told me," Oliver said.

She shrugged. "All water under the drawbridge. I must quit living in the past, take responsibility, and stop laying blame."

"I wish you luck with that." He smiled again. "And if your damn Irishman is who you want, then I'll hope you'll be able to make amends. And if not." Oliver only winked.

Rhianwyn took the book to her chamber.

CHAPTER EIGHTEEN

RHIANWYN LET THE heavy doors swing shut behind her, on her way to attend the market with Friar Springham, the herbalist, where they hoped to procure ingredients for the monks' winter supply of remedies. It had been more than two moons since she'd left the monastery. The trees were bare now; the grass was brittle and brown.

She'd hoped to see Elspeth and Selena, but if they were there, she'd missed them. She'd heard through bits of gossip that trickled even to the monastery, that Elspeth worked in the castle by day, the brothel at night. Rhianwyn wouldn't judge. Elspeth had always used sexual relations to cope with hardships.

Earlier today Rhianwyn told Friar Drummond, the abbot, that she'd make arrangements to reside elsewhere. They'd been kind permitting her to stay, but she'd become too comfortable. That prevented her from making necessary decisions.

Keyon was playing a merry tune at the market, the three dogs at his feet. Rhianwyn smiled at that. She and Friar Springham parted ways. She planned to go to the hot pool to bathe. Weekly, she used the cramped, round wooden tub brought to her chamber. But a long hot bath would be welcome.

When Keyon finished playing, she visited with him. They shared a honey cake before she made her way to the hot pool.

BROCCAN FINALLY LOCATED a hammer to repair the hall's doors after Rhianwyn's display of magic. Chester had offered to fix them, but he'd declined. They stood as a reminder that Rhianwyn, too, had powerful magic and that their combined powers when infuriated weren't a good mix. Maybe pairing their lives hadn't been wise.

Matty eyed him when bringing his tray to break fast. The other servants stayed away. His foul moods and quick temper probably earned him a reputation as being as dislikeable as the former Lord Brockwell.

"It's about time you got round to mendin' those." Matty scowled. "Maybe you might think about mendin' your marriage as well!"

He pounded harder, straightening the wrought-iron hinges and cussing loudly when he hit his thumb.

"Your opinion is duly noted, Matty. But you know nothin' about what's occurred between…her and me."

Christ, he still couldn't bring himself to say Rhianwyn's name. Clearly, he wasn't ready to consider forgiveness.

"It's good you're not usin' a sword these days or you'd have more than a bruised thumb or heartache."

Broccan didn't reply hoping Matty would leave.

"Now I don't pretend to know what's happened between the two of ye but…"

"You'll not hear it from my lips!" Broccan cut her off.

"So you intend to continue mopin' about, cavortin' with maidens and whores alike, and drinkin' yerself into an early grave? That's not what I'd expect of the principled person I've known for three decades. Not how the son of a king of Tara…"

"Matty." He shook the hammer before him as he spoke. "I know you're concerned, but I'll thank you to keep your opinions to yourself."

Just then Ida, a maidservant, came to the door. She stepped back on seeing him. Jesus, had he become that much of an ogre?

"Sir Cassian's here to see you, milord?" She nervously dipped a curtsy.

"And I will be seen!" Cassian stepped in eyeing the hammer. "Strike me with that and I'll bloody well run you through." He unsheathed his sword. Ida gasped and scurried away.

"Hello, Matty." Cassian nodded.

"Sir Cassian." Matty smiled. "I'll leave you two to talk then."

"It'll be a short discussion." Broccan hammered the other hinges and cussed again when he couldn't make the doors hang straight.

"Severin wants to know when you'll resume your duties as joint knight commander. He intends to take some time off."

Broccan looked at Cassian. "Since when does our grand cross ever do that?"

"He and Mabel are planning to go to the seaside."

"That'll be enjoyable in November," Broccan said sarcastically.

"While Severin's away I'll name someone else knight's commander if you're too busy drinking and whoring. However, keep in mind, you've not been released from the order and could be dungeoned for shirking your duties. Perhaps you could take up with Corliss while you're there."

Broccan scowled and pounded the hinge till it snapped.

"Sardin' hell!" Broccan threw it across the hall where it struck a shield he hadn't yet rehung from the night Rhianwyn's temper erupted.

"When does Severin leave?" Broccan asked.

"At week's end." Cassian still held his sword in his hand.

"I'll be there." Broccan exhaled.

"You'll need to sober up."

"I haven't had a drink in…hours."

Cassian rolled his eyes and took a wide berth when walking past Broccan.

"By the way," Cassian said when partly down the corridor. "You've been requested to take audience with the queen."

Broccan groaned. "When?"

"I'm to accompany you straightway, with force if you're opposed."

"Of course I'm sardin' opposed. I don't want to see her or any of them."

"Them?" Cassian asked, head cocked. "Your wife and her three former friends who now seem mostly *unfriendly*?"

Broccan growled. "Yes."

Thinking of them, and all that had occurred during the year of the pact, renewed his fury straightaway.

"You'd truly try to haul me in to meet with the queen?"

"I'd rather not, but I will if I must. If you'd change your garments first that would be preferrable. I doubt you've time to bathe, though you sarding need to. You smell like a damn ale house or a stable."

"The queen can see me as I am or bloody well wait."

"I'll tell her you'll be there later, but she'd likely oppose your smell even more than me."

"I don't give a goddamn what she thinks. Maybe I'll roll in stable muck, and she'll get the message I don't want to be in *her grace*'s presence."

"Suit yourself, Sir Broccan." Cassian smirked, sheathing his sword. "I'll see you at the castle. Make it quick."

Cassian left and Broccan tossed the hammer against the wall, leaving a large mark.

RHIANWYN LINGERED IN the glorious hot water. She'd missed frequently bathing. With the soap made at the monastery, she lathered her hair, and put on clean garments she'd sent for from the manor. She brushed out her hair, then gathered her possessions. She lifted her head at the sound of approaching hoofbeats.

Broccan.

When he spotted her, he looked down from atop Dubh, glowered, and started back from where he'd come.

"I'm leaving," she called. "You'll not be made to suffer my company."

He sneered but startled her further by dismounting. "I suspect we will need to speak soon to make some decisions."

That didn't sound hopeful.

She nodded. "Whenever you're ready."

"I need to bathe; perhaps you could meet me later at the manor?"

"I'll not go there!" She couldn't dismiss the image of him and Mirtha.

"The guesthouse then?"

She put her hands on her hips and glared. "That would be ever so much better. Perhaps we could include your mistress in our conversation, too?"

"As I said, I doubt who I take to my bed should be of consequence to you. But if it consoles you…we were together only once."

She shrugged. "That makes it better then, does it?" She repeated what he'd said the night he discovered the truth.

He threw his hands in the air. "This is bloody pointless. It seems we can't have a civil conversation."

"Clearly," she snapped before walking away.

BEING FRESHLY BATHED and in clean attire didn't improve Broccan's mood. Seeing Rhianwyn weighed heavy on him as he was shown into the queen's court. When he saw Selena and Elspeth sitting with Lilliana, he stopped short.

"Hell no!" he snarled and turned.

"Guards!" Lilliana called. "Bring Sir Broccan back or take him to the dungeon if he'd prefer."

Two burly guards grabbed hold of his arms.

He swatted them away. "Sard off! I'll walk on my own."

He glowered at all three women and certainly didn't bow to the queen.

"Take a seat, Sir Broccan," she said.

"I'll stand!"

"It wasn't a request." She lifted her chin and pointed to the table where the women sat.

"Maybe you'd like to order me to your bed, too?"

Elspeth snorted and covered her mouth. Selena only looked away.

"You've not requested the fourth person in your infernal magical pact be here, too?" he asked.

"Rhianwyn doesn't know of this meeting," Selena said.

Elspeth crossed her arms, wearing a scowl. "She'd probably disapprove as much as you."

"Well get on with it," Broccan said, slumping in the chair.

"We wanted to tell you about the night we made the pact," Lilliana began.

He wouldn't meet their eyes.

"Rhianwyn didn't want to agree to it." Selena reached out to touch his hand. He pulled it away.

"We didn't really give her a choice!" Elspeth nodded. "We played on her protectiveness of Selena."

"We manipulated her," Lilliana admitted.

"*You* manipulate someone, sure I'd never believe that!"

Lilliana ignored his sarcasm. "When offered the chance to live a season in each woman's life, Elspeth, Selena, and I could only see the advantages we might find in the others' lives and the despair in our own futures."

"Still, Rhianwyn had a choice." Broccan wouldn't let them justify it.

"But you know how protective she is of me," Selena said. "She tried to explain the possible disadvantages to the pact. She didn't want to go along with it. If she'd not been angry with the king for disallowing her healing and ordering her to be wed. Then displeased at you for behaving so boorishly the night she was fitted for her wedding attire."

He saw the warning look Lilliana and Elspeth threw at Selena and her cheeks pinked.

"So you're sayin' in her anger she agreed to the pact to spite me?"

"No, that's not it at all." Sounding woeful Selena twisted her hair.

"We just want you to understand and forgive Rhianwyn," Elspeth said.

"Is that all?" he said.

"Surely you know how much she loves you?" Selena said.

"She has a damn peculiar way of showin' it. She toyed with my emotions. Made me think I was goin' mad for bein' attracted to other women when it was her all along. Agreed to havin' me sard three of her friends and lettin' a slew of other men have her."

"By recent gossip, you're trying to even that score." Elspeth sneered. "Sarding Mirtha and God knows how many harlots while Rhianwyn pines away in a bloody monastery. I'm certain the brothers must've had to double their supply of monk's pepper to calm their natural urges with beautiful Rhianwyn in their midst."

"As I've said before, Elspeth," Broccan snapped, "I don't how know how you've managed to live this long with that bleating tongue."

"I remember you rather liked my tongue." She licked her lips provocatively. He jumped up, enraged.

"Elspeth!" Lilliana rebuked. "We're trying to help Rhianwyn not make this worse."

"You'd think he was the only one who suffered during the pact," Elspeth growled. "It can't be changed now. God's bones some married men would be pleased to sard different women and deflower two virgins in that lot."

"I didn't agree to your sardin' pact! I had no damn say in it!" Broccan paced, feeling he might explode in fury. "I know I wasn't the only one gravely affected by the pact. Ulf and Agnes didn't exactly fare well!"

He knew that was cruel. Elspeth curled her hand into a fist but then simply looked at the floor.

"Zachary and Chester were affected by your heartless game, too."

"We do all regret the pact," Lilliana said. "Everyone suffered, Broccan."

"Rhianwyn did...terribly." Selena's eyes filled with tears. "She does love you very much."

By Christ he didn't want to hear any more—certainly didn't want to feel empathy for Rhianwyn or any of them.

"Do you forget Rhianwyn stepped before a sword meant for you when she was Selena?" Elspeth said. "She saved your sarding life."

"She was raped and beaten by Godric when she was Elspeth," Lilliana added.

Selena dabbed her eyes. "Rhianwyn suffered poisoning and a curse and was nearly raped again while living Lilliana's life. Who knows what occurred in Welshland when Prince Tyven was killed."

He despised knowing all Rhianwyn had suffered, but it didn't change his resentment. "I'm not sayin' she didn't suffer," Broccan admitted, in a low voice, "but do you honestly believe I can simply forgive and forget all that happened?"

Broccan sat again and put both hands on his head, wanting to pull his bloody hair out. No one spoke for a time, and he exhaled several times.

"Is that it? Am I free to go, Your Grace?"

The three women looked at each other and Lilliana nodded. "Please think about what we've said."

"We're very sorry for all you endured." Selena lowered her head.

Lilliana and even Elspeth nodded. "We are," they said together.

BROCCAN'S MIND WAS a muddled mess and his heart remained raw as he walked from the castle. Should he go the tavern? The manor? The brothel?

As he mounted Dubh, again he considered riding away and never looking back. However, he'd sworn an oath to the knighthood. Until he was released from that by his grand cross and the king—well now the queen, he'd be deemed an outlaw if he left. He could be hunted down and killed.

Besides, could he simply leave without talking to Rhianwyn? He closed his eyes, for they burned with tears. He was deep in thought when someone called to him.

"Sir Broccan, you looked far away."

It was Keyon with his three dogs. The merry minstrel had a satchel over one shoulder, his lute over the other.

Broccan cleared his throat. "Goin' somewhere?"

Keyon looked down the path. "I thought I could maybe stave off the need to wander until spring, but when it hits, I simply must go. At least I'll have these fine companions with me now." He pointed to Maxim's dogs—now Keyon's dogs.

"Safe journey then, Keyon."

"Will you be here when I return, Sir Broccan?"

He shrugged. "I can't say, Keyon."

"I saw Rhianwyn at market today. She's staying at the cottage now. I told her she'd be doing me a service keeping the place up till I return. I'm certain she's been at the monastery long enough. All that praying and those deafening bells would drive me mad." Keyon's eyes darted back and forth.

"That was good of you," Broccan said.

"It's not as though she'd get a warm reception at the manor." There was accusation in the always affable man's voice. "She was happy in her simple life in her dilapidated cottage and would've likely remained there if she hadn't been ordered from her home and forced to marry."

Bloody hell! He was meeting reproach from everyone. He sometimes felt like shouting aloud he'd been the one wronged. However, he supposed Rhianwyn's name had already been sullied. He'd heard whispers that most people believed she'd been with another man or men and that Broccan banished her from the manor.

"I asked her more than once if she wanted to marry me," Broccan defended. "Even on our wedding day I gave her a choice not to wed me!"

Keyon turned up his nose. "She'd only have been forced to marry another man. Besides, you can't tell me you weren't aware she was already deeply in love with you. I hope Queen Lilliana changes those rulings, so women aren't forced to marry or leave their homes simply because others deem them of an age to be wedded, bedded, and bred."

"You mightn't believe me, Keyon, but that'd be my wish, too."

Keyon nodded, gave him a lopsided grin, and called for the dogs to follow. He was whistling when Broccan rode away.

HE HAD NO conscious intention of going to the cottage. Broccan was deep in thought and didn't direct Dubh to head into the woods. Yet when he looked up the sun was setting, and here he was at Keyon's cottage, not far from where Rhianwyn had once lived.

She was inside; he heard pots or crockery being rattled about. She didn't sing or hum as she once had when happily attending to chores. She likely didn't feel any more like singing than he did.

He dismounted and tied Dubh to a tree. There was still some green grass for him. Should he knock—ask if she'd be willing to speak to him? Would he be able to conceal his acrimony long enough to have a conversation?

He was probably behaving like a heartbroken adolescent, not a grown man. He was startled when she opened the shutters and peeked out.

"I heard a horse," she said. "I sensed you were here."

"Would you be willin' to speak with me? We could start a fire," he suggested. The wind had become brisk.

"I've just made some soup and tea. If you wish to eat, I admit I don't relish sitting on the ground." She put her hand on her back. "The beds at the monastery are probably no more comfortable than the bunks at the knights' keep."

By God she was beautiful. Her hair was unbound, and she looked radiant by the light of the sunset. She wore a simple kirtle like the one she'd been wearing the day they met. Although she wouldn't meet his eyes, he saw hers were filled with pain. For that he was sorrowful. He swallowed the lump in his throat.

He knew he still loved her. Else his heart wouldn't ache when he was near her. He knew he still wanted her, else his loins wouldn't tighten at the sight of her or when he caught the scent of her hair. He also knew he still felt the need to shake her when he thought of all that happened.

"I'll come out." She reached for her shawl. "We'll forgo breaking bread together and I know you dislike my tea."

"The wind's cold. I'll come inside."

She opened the door and he ducked to enter the low doorway.

"Do you want soup?" She wrung her hands, nervously.

He nodded. "It smells good."

God's nails this was awkward.

She took two bowls from the shelf, ladled one nearly full, one with only a smattering. She buttered two thick pieces of bread and set them on a plate near him but took no bread herself.

"You're not eatin' much."

"I've not had any appetite."

She was thinner than he remembered. There was a sharpness to her cheeks and her collarbone that he'd not noticed before.

The soup was delicious. She'd always been a fine cook. He managed to eat everything even though he wasn't certain he could manage it. They ate in silence. She took mere mouthfuls then sipped the potent tea.

"Would you like more?"

He shook his head. "It was good. Thank you."

This was so bloody uncomfortable he wanted to rush outdoors. At one time he could talk to her like no other— pour his heart out. Now, if he told her what he felt within his shredded heart, she'd only wear a more maudlin look.

How he longed to see her smile. For her to laugh with him again. Yet, he couldn't deny his fury. The disappointment. The betrayal.

She cleared the crockery, put the lid on the iron pot, wiped the table and sat down again, eyes lowered.

It was her who finally spoke. "I'll not hold you to this bleak marriage, Broccan."

That stunned him, yet he shouldn't have been surprised. He didn't know how to reply. The thought of losing her forever struck terror within him. Yet the notion of trying to return to how it had been before seemed inconceivable. He wasn't ready.

She must've seen the accusation in his eyes, for she tucked her hair behind her ear and nibbled her bottom lip. He could see her trembling, fighting tears. He longed to take her in his arms and simultaneously wanted to throttle her.

"You believe I should accept all that happened and forgive you so easily?"

She didn't speak.

"After what happened with Doirean, it took a long time for me to trust again. Then I fell deeply in love with you, trusted you with my heart and...you betrayed me and ruined the specialness between us. I thought myself a lecherous shite when I was attracted to you no matter what form you were in...when I was drawn to your soul."

She only nodded, tears now falling down her lovely cheeks. By God, he didn't want to hurt her. He nearly reached out to take her in his arms.

"I've said I'm sorry," she whispered. "I've told you how regretful I am. If I could change it, I swear to God, I would. If I could've told you about the pact without risking you befalling harm I would have. At least then you would have known why and…"

He believed her and still he wanted to scold her.

"I know not what to do, Broccan." A sob escaped. "You *will* eventually have to forgive me or…"

"Or what, Rhianwyn?" He stood and stared down at her. "If I can't forgive you, then what?" His voice caught.

She finally met his eyes. "Then you'll have to let me go."

That bloody well gutted him. His chest tightened. Tears welled in his eyes, and he angrily swiped at them.

"By Christ. You think that could be easily done? When thoughts of you plague me day and night. You're like a sardin' parasite in my mind." He slapped his head. "A constant torment to my body. A curse to my soul!"

It was easier to be angry than reveal his sorrow. It was regarded as weakness for a man to weep.

"I'm sorry," she whispered again.

He stepped toward her and saw the uncertainty in her pale blue eyes as they widened. Did she think he'd harm her? She'd experienced enough violence at the hands of men during the last year.

He reached for her, lifting her to her feet, then pulled her to him. His lips claimed hers. She moaned, full lips parted whether to protest or in mutual attraction, he wasn't even sure. But when her arms tightly wrapped around his neck, he knew she needed this, too. Tugging at her kirtle and shift, he kissed her neck and shoulders, bared her breasts, and suckled them till she pulled his hair and cried out. He rid her of her garments while she tore as his, too.

Pulling off his tunic, she hastily unfastened his breeches, her hands shaking.

He was so damn aroused he nearly had her against the wall. Instead he lifted her into his arms, laid her on the bed indelicately. He couldn't wait to touch her. He placed his hand between her thighs, his fingers inside her. She arched her hips, groaned, and firmly squeezed his cock. Their gazes finally met.

There was passion in her eyes when he thrust into her as eager as the first time he'd ever bedded a woman, or perhaps as a man sentenced to death and knowing this would be the last time he'd ever know such torturous pleasure.

They moved together vigorously. She called out his name, but no words of love passed between them. Only moaning and panting, until he took her to her crest and then groaned as he succumbed to his own release.

There were no tender caresses afterward. He felt like a lout, but he moved from her straight after, procured his garments, and attired himself. The mark on his shoulder from her thumbnail angered him. She must have shared that intimate information with her friends, too.

She held the bedcovers over her breasts. He didn't look at her face—couldn't bear to see if she was weeping.

"That shouldn't have happened!" he said, pulling on his boots, securing his sword, and reaching for his overcoat. "For this changes nothing."

"I know," she whispered. "As I said, I won't hold you to this marriage. I'll go to the priest, tell him I'm an adulteress…that…"

He shook his head. "You'd be sent to the dungeon or hanged. Besides, I've betrayed my marriage vows recently and not even while I was bound to a pact."

He couldn't meet her eyes.

"Half the village once believed I was mad. On the grounds of my madness, you could tell the priest you want to be released from your vow."

"You wish our marriage ended then?"

Would he want to hear her reply?

"I'll always love you, Broccan, but I can't live eaten away by guilt—trying to make up for something I'll never be able to. As I said, if forgiveness isn't possible then you must let me go."

His heart thundered in his chest and his mind whirled. He wasn't sure his knees wouldn't buckle.

"You think the two of us could remain in this small village together...yet not together?"

"That depends on you, but I can't endure your wrath and disappointment indefinitely."

He tipped his head and went out without looking back, more tormented than when he'd arrived.

CHAPTER NINETEEN

RHIANWYN SPENT MUCH of the next fortnight poring over the book that once belonged to her father. She realized some of what she'd thought were potions or spells were in Welsh. She spoke some Welsh but read very little. There were references to dragons written in feminine penmanship. Her mother's she suspected. She hadn't noticed that before. She'd not been in possession of the book long before she'd transformed to Lilliana. Her mind had been on other worries.

"So what does it say?"

She jumped hearing the squeaky voice.

"By God, Teg! Are you trying to stop my heart?"

He only grinned.

"You stayed away so long I thought you'd returned to Cymru."

"I suspected you needed time alone. Besides, those monastery bells nearly deafened my tender ears. Since I'm no longer bonded to you, I come and go as I please. I spent some time with the queen listening to the conversation she and your friends had with your husband."

Rhianwyn arched her eyebrows.

"They tried to make him understand you truly didn't want to agree to the pact," Teg said.

"I'm certain he appreciated that!" she replied, sarcastically.

He shook his head. "Not noticeably. I think he would've liked to strangle Elspeth. But why don't you wish to see your friends?"

She shrugged. "Being with them reminds me of the pact. Seeing them brings it all back. I want to move forward."

"You seem very melancholy," Teg said.

"I *am* melancholy. I pray one day this gloom will lift. I suppose it won't until Broccan decides about our marriage."

"I believe something will cheer you soon."

"Tell me," she urged, leaning forward.

The ellyll shook his head. "I want it to be a surprise."

"Is this about Broccan?"

Teg shook his head. "No. He's sleeping at the knights' keep and is back training. He's looking skillful again and not like I could best him in a swordfight."

She was glad, for she'd worried for him.

"But if not a reconciliation with your Irishman, this news might be second best."

"By God you're annoying. I'm of half a mind to place a spell on all the fungi in Wessex and have it taste like horse shite!"

"It's not far off now." Teg fell on the table laughing. "You really are quite beautiful!"

"What?" Rhianwyn asked.

"I thought you were striking as a princess, but when in your true form, you shine. Lovely hair, unusual, bewitching blue eyes. You're far prettier than that blonde Mercian woman who'd maybe give her eye teeth to be Lady Brockwell and not because she wants to live in a manor."

"I thought you were trying to cheer me. Telling me how the most beautiful woman wants my husband when she's already shared intimacies with him, definitely won't."

"You used your magic that night."

She whirled to face him. "How do you know?"

"There are other creatures about that maybe even you haven't seen. They're abuzz with news of your magical abilities and your husband's, too. You make quite the pair."

"Sadly, we don't."

A knock on the cottage door made Teg smile broadly. Rhianwyn opened it to find Cadfael and Cassian.

Teg frowned. "I wasn't expecting them." He sounded disappointed.

"Rhianwyn." Cassian stared. "Why the hell do you have an owl on your table?"

Cadfael grinned. She suspected he saw Teg's true form.

"He had an injured wing, but it's healing."

That probably sounded unconvincing.

"We've come to escort you to the castle," Cassian said. "The queen's requested you attend a meeting with her advisors."

"Why would she want me there?"

"Wasn't it you who said the queen should have female advisors?" Teg asked.

Rhianwyn didn't reply. Cassian wouldn't hear Teg; therefore her response would seem peculiar.

"I'll get my cloak," Rhianwyn said.

SEVERAL PEOPLE WERE already present when they entered the castle's meeting area. Queen Lilliana of course. Oliver, and the other advisors, but Elspeth and Radella were here, too, as was Marlow, the old healer. Winston was in attendance and Sir Severin, apparently back from his time away. Next to him was Broccan who narrowed his eyes and shifted uncomfortably seeing Rhianwyn arrive accompanied by Cadfael and Cassian.

When everyone was seated, Lilliana stood. "Thank you for coming," she said, warmly. "I know not how long I'll be permitted to rule, but while I *am* queen I want to rule well. I know some of running a kingdom and have some fine advisors whom I trust.

"However, I want advice from all of you, too—suggestions of what would make this a better place for common born as well as nobles."

No one spoke and Lilliana lifted her chin.

"Now's your chance to help me make some necessary changes."

"Castle servants should be given more than one half-day off each week," Elspeth began. "Their days should be shorter as well. They'd be more productive and less resentful if they're rested."

"That sounds like good advice." Lilliana motioned for the advisor holding the quill to mark it down.

"Girls and women should be permitted to learn to read and write," Rhianwyn suggested. "As well as all low- or common-born people.

"I agree wholeheartedly," Lilliana replied and Radella nodded.

"The spinster market should be done away with," Radella said, "and the rule that a woman must be wed. If she can provide for herself, let her remain unwed. And the rule a man can beat his wife with no reproach must be abolished."

"A lot of men will oppose that," one advisor stood.

"Of course they will," Elspeth said. "But if they're permitted to beat their wives, perhaps wives should be permitted to kill them in defense."

The knights and Winston shook their heads.

"We're trying to lessen the violence in the kingdom for women and men," Winston replied.

Oliver nodded. "To that end we're most pleased the knights and your men-at-arms have become more affable, Winston."

"I agree," Winston said. "I do think it'd benefit everyone if our roles were more clearly defined."

"That's sensible." Severin shook Winston's hand. "You'll meet with my knight commanders and me. We'll draw up a proposal for you and your advisors to view, Queen Lilliana."

"Thank you, Sir Severin," Lilliana replied.

"Dorsett should be sacked," Radella said.

"Unless he's given the ultimatum to quit drinking," Rhianwyn added. "He's a decent physician when not filled with drink."

"Since that seems unlikely, would you take over as healer, Rhianwyn?" Lilliana asked. "Everyone knows you're the best."

"I learned from the best." Rhianwyn looked at Radella. "My mam and Radella."

"I'll not take the position so don't bother asking!" Radella snarled.

"And I can barely see my nose in front of my face," Marlow said.

"Rhianwyn?" Lilliana waited for her reply.

She looked at the queen, her one-time friend, but wouldn't glance at Broccan.

"While I appreciate your confidence in my abilities, I won't be responsible for others' well-being any longer. Besides, it's unlikely I'll be staying in Hengebury."

Broccan's head turned sharply at that. There were several muffled comments.

"However, I'll agree to stay to train any others who'd be interested in healing. We need more midwives also. I believe Selena might like midwifery. I'd gladly assist with that training, too."

There were other suggestions and much discussion. Lilliana would make a good ruler.

Rhianwyn felt Broccan's gaze on her. She despised how awkward it was between them. Made worse since they'd lain together. He looked like he didn't want to be here.

"You're quiet, Sir Broccan," Lilliana said. "Surely you have some notions how the kingdom can be bettered? As someone not born in this kingdom nor lived here long, what would improve life for others?"

Rhianwyn saw the scowl Broccan gave the queen. He likely wanted to say don't swear to pacts that affect the lives of others.

"All suggestions made today have merit," he said, "well other than killing men."

"You think men should be permitted to abuse women then?" Elspeth asked.

"I didn't say that!" Broccan sat up straighter. "As Severin and Winston said we want to curb violence."

"What of the women dungeoned for unlawful carnal knowledge?" Elspeth asked. "Do they deserve to be there or to meet the noose?"

"The priests will expect that," an advisor said. "It is breaking one of God's commandments."

"Then men and women should be held equally accountable." Elspeth stared at the man and Radella nodded.

"If you make such a ruling, Queen Lilliana, then you can expect to be overthrown straightaway," Oliver said.

Elspeth stood, fists curled like she might punch Oliver. All the women there glared at him.

He put up his hands. "I'm not saying I agree. I'm just telling you that you must begin with small changes—accept small victories. Then everyone will be more likely to go along with it."

Severin nodded. "He has a point."

"Men suffer injustice, too," Rhianwyn said. Everyone looked at her, waiting for her to elaborate. "Your knights for instance, Sir Severin."

"What in the bloody hell, Rhianwyn?" Severin looked affronted. "How am I unjust? Should I mollycoddle them? How will they become warriors if…"

"I didn't say you were unjust, but some of the age-old

followings should be changed."

"Go on," Broccan said with arms crossed.

"Boys not old enough to lift a sword, or to decide beyond what childhood games to play, begin training as a page, then a squire. Next, they're asked to swear a lifetime oath—to remain a knight, loyal to the king or queen—" she glanced at Lilliana "—for as long as they live. I believe that's unfair. Some don't want that once they've seen what a knight's life entails. Others grow weary or disenchanted."

"How is that different than making a vow to stay wed to the same person all your life?" Severin looked from Rhianwyn to Broccan.

"Being wed to someone doesn't often end in being maimed during training, in tournaments, often being parted from loved ones, or killed in battles in far-off kingdoms," Rhianwyn said.

"Much time and training are put into readying a knight for service," Severin countered. "They're needed to protect our kingdom against invaders and keep the peace."

"Then let them begin at an older age—definitely older when they swear an oath, and instead of a lifetime pledge, make it for a set amount of time they'd agree to serve—perhaps five years after they've been knighted. Then let them re-swear if they want to commit longer or to leave the knighthood if they don't.

"Some knights, like Severin or Cassian—" she pointed to them "—are gladly sworn for a lifetime. The knighthood's in their very bones. Yet, others have different reasoning. Everard only remains to honor his father's memory and to earn his brother's approval."

Cassian touched her arm. "You honestly think Everard doesn't want to be in the knighthood?"

She nodded. "I do, and some men never wanted to be knights in the first place."

Rhianwyn looked at Broccan. This time their eyes held. He'd know this suggestion would give him a way out of his sworn oath—therefore from remaining in Wessex.

"We'll speak on that longer after Severin, the advisors, and I have thought on it," Lilliana said.

A few other topics were discussed. Rhianwyn believed Lilliana had begun her reign impressively. She thanked them for being there and they poured out of the chamber.

"May I walk with you?" Cadfael held the door for Rhianwyn, and they descended the many castle steps.

"If you like." She nodded and he took her arm.

"You're thinking of returning to Cymru?" he asked.

"How did you know?" She looked up at him.

"I know you're Morwenna's niece and that you've found a section of the book that may have answers to ending the curse on the Dafyddsons."

She must have looked stunned. He smiled.

"Your little ellyll keeps me informed."

"I have decisions to make, Cadfael. Even if I should decide to leave Hengebury, I've just agreed to train others to be healers and midwives."

"When you're ready to make the journey, I'll accompany you, if that pleases you?" He bowed.

She eyed him curiously.

"I liked you as a princess, but I admit I like you better now. However, I suspect the feistiness you displayed back in Cymru was your own."

They heard footsteps. Rhianwyn turned to see Broccan. His expression was dour.

Cadfael drew nearer and whispered in her ear, "Your Irishman doesn't like me walking with you."

She shook her head. "I doubt that causes him consternation."

"I know when a man's consumed with jealousy."

"Did you wish to speak with Lady Rhianwyn?" Cadfael asked.

Broccan nodded. "If she'd spare me the time."

Cadfael kissed Rhianwyn's hand, bowed, then winked at her and walked away.

"You're keepin' company with the Welshman then?" Broccan blurted. "A knight? I thought you were opposed to being linked to a knight."

"I was walking with him, yes."

"You seemed rather *cozy*."

"He's aware of magic and knows of the pact. I welcome being able to speak to him of it."

"That would be refreshin'—to have someone to talk to of that sardin' chaos."

"It's clear you and I can't speak of it. Brooding doesn't become you, Broccan."

That wasn't true. He looked damn appealing with his unplaited hair and jaw unshaven…even with the scowl that was often on his handsome face of late. She longed to reach out and graze his stubbled jaw.

He growled at her comment.

"Besides," she said, "you could talk to Cassian about

the pact. He knew of your suspicions. You did, after all, toss a coin to decide which woman's bed you might go to. Mine or Elspeth's."

Broccan's face became ruddy. "How the hell did you hear about that?"

"Cassian runs off at the mouth when he's been drinking…or when he's sharing intimacies in bed."

Broccan stiffened and stopped walking.

"You've gone back to *his* bed then?"

Rhianwyn glowered. "If I'm not to inquire who frequents your bed, then I expect the same courtesy from you."

He puffed out his cheeks looking riled.

"Are you truly leaving this village?" he asked. "Or did you make that suggestion today only so I'd be released of the oath I swore and you expect that I'll leave?"

"I don't know what my future holds, Broccan. I am considering going to Cymru. I'll regret hurting you till I draw my last breath, but I can't remain like this."

He exhaled. "What's in Welshland?"

"I've discovered an aunt, my mother's sister. I've also found a book and learned I might assist with ending the curse."

"You'd simply leave…when nothin's resolved with our marriage?"

She shook her head. "I don't see anything being resolved when you can barely look at me. And if I can help others…"

"Bloody hell, Rhianwyn," he interrupted. "Our marriage doesn't stand a chance—not if you never put me first."

"That's unfair."

"Unfair? We're speaking of fairness then? Did you not put Selena before me when making the decision to agree to the pact?"

She looked at him and sighed. "Selena had no one. She was timid and fearful, innocent and being forced to become a harlot. You're a warrior, strong, self-assured, with a means to support yourself. People adore you; women flock to your bed."

"You sound like you'd make the same choice again."

She shook her head earnestly. "I will *always* avoid magic. And I'll never be placed in a position where I must choose between those I love."

"By all accounts you avoid most everyone."

She nodded. "It's easier that way."

They neared the edge of the clearing leading to the forest. "You shouldn't walk alone through those dark woods."

"I won't ask for your accompaniment. I think it best we don't end up in the cottage alone together…again."

"On that we agree," he said, but still he looked at her with a hunger she recognized, for she felt it herself.

"I'll make it there before the sun sets. Good night, Broccan."

He exhaled. "I cannot permit you to walk alone."

She tucked her hair behind her ear. She'd be resolute not to invite him inside.

BY GOD, THEY had as little willpower to keep away from each other as feral animals, Broccan thought. If only the rest of their relationship had such certainty as their physical need for one another. One look of longing outside her door, one kiss inside and here they were, again, in bed unclothed, breathless, panting, coupling desperately.

Here he was again, furious at not being able to keep his cock in his breeches when he was unable to commit or forgive.

She got up first this time and dressed straightaway. She started outside, leaving him in the bed still catching his breath. He'd only just attired himself and pulled his hand through his hair when he heard a man's voice. Oliver? Did he visit her here and bloody well share her bed, too? That riled him to no end.

Broccan stepped outside to see Rhianwyn, weeping. But the man who comforted her wasn't Oliver. He was older, with long unkempt white hair.

"Dear daughter, don't weep so. I'm back. Finally I'm back."

"But where have you been all this time?" she sobbed. "I've worried much for you, Father!"

William Albray, the eccentric mage Broccan had heard much about. He looked at Broccan and cast him an unappreciative glance. By their tousled hair, and her partially laced kirtle, he probably could well see what had just occurred.

He didn't know Broccan or that they were wed...that sexual relations wouldn't be considered sinful. However, not actually living as man and wife, Broccan couldn't help feeling like he'd sinned when he couldn't promise her a life together.

"Father, tell me where you've been?" she repeated.

"It's all confoundedly confusing." William appeared vexed. He touched his hair, then his chin. He seemed absent-minded.

"I remember walking into the village when I spotted him." William pointed to Broccan. "I'd heard the new Lord Brockwell had arrived, but I'd never met him. I sensed straightaway that he was affected by magic.

"I had a drink in the tavern, then upon the road back to our cottage, I was overtaken by peculiar dizziness. When I awoke, I was in a place I didn't recognize. Kept in a warm, dark chamber, I wasn't mistreated. I was fed regularly. Yet no matter how I called for explanation and demanded to be returned to you, daughter, no one obliged me. I believe someone with powerful magic kept me there."

Rhianwyn took his hand to comfort the perplexed man.

"Today, when I awoke, I was simply on the very road where I'd been when I was taken. I met Oliver and he took me here to you, for he said our cottage is no more."

The man did sound mad. But Broccan knew much was possible with magic. Rhianwyn appeared relieved he was home. Maybe she wouldn't leave now William was back.

She looked about to introduce them, but perhaps wondered how. She wouldn't likely refer to him as her husband. Just then Cassian rode through the trees on his horse. By God was he here to see Rhianwyn, too, or perhaps he'd heard William was returned?

Cassian hastily dismounted. "Good. I've found you,

Broccan. A messenger just came to the keep. He's left this. It's from Ireland. The messenger said it was urgent you receive it straightaway."

Cassian passed him the paper with a wax seal Broccan recognized. It was from Tara and in his father's hand. Broccan broke the seal, removed the letter, and read it by the torchlight Oliver carried.

"Christ," Broccan said under his breath. This was bloody bad timing.

"Untoward tidings?" Cassian asked.

Broccan nodded. "My father's ill. Probably dying. He's requested my presence."

"Bloody hell!" Cassian said.

"I'm sorry," Rhianwyn whispered as she held tight to William's hand like he might disappear again.

"Severin's already said if the news was unfavorable, he'll grant you temporary compassionate leave from the knighthood. You'll have to go."

Dammit. He *would* have to go. He and his father didn't see eye to eye, but he couldn't deny him his deathbed request. He gazed at Rhianwyn. This was sarding inopportune timing.

"When will you go?" Cassian asked the unspoken question in Rhianwyn's eyes.

"Probably tomorrow. Maybe the day following. I'll arrange things at the manor…although everything is in your name Rhianwyn. You can still manage it…if you wish."

William looked even more befuddled.

"Matty and Chester will do fine," she replied, "maybe with Oliver's advice and assistance."

Broccan nodded. Did she truly have no interest in her birthright, or would she go to Welshland even though her father was here?

"The profits will still be yours," Broccan said.

"How long do you think you'll be gone?" Cassian asked as he stared at Rhianwyn, too.

Was he worried about her or wanting to swoop in while Broccan was gone? No, Cassian was his friend. He shouldn't be so damn suspicious. Did anyone really believe their marriage was salvageable?

"Maybe Matty would like to go back to Ireland with you?" Rhianwyn suggested.

"I doubt it." Broccan shook his head. "She's plagued with achin' bones and she's content here helpin' care for Fairfax and Maisie."

Rhianwyn nodded. "Best you get the ledgers in order and pack up your possessions then," she replied.

She stepped inside the cottage with William, but not before he'd seen tears glistening in her eyes.

BY EARLY MORNING Dubh was saddled. Fionn and Oisin, his dogs, were eager to set off. Broccan was not. The manor's affairs were settled. He'd spoken with Chester who'd agreed to assist with running the estate. Adam would help, too. Matty basically managed the manor and the servants. Oliver would tend to the ledgers. He told them all Rhianwyn had full authority to make changes and distribute the coin and profits as she saw fit.

He'd hoped she might come by the manor to see him off, although that wouldn't be easy for either of them.

"You'll be cautious now, Broccan, won't ye?" Matty affectionately patted his cheek. "Don't let your father or his advisors hold you to that life, for I know you've no fondness for it."

He embraced the old woman who'd raised him and heard her bite back a sob.

"Don't stay away too long or you might dearly regret it, lad. The two of ye…you should be together."

"Take care of yourself, too, Matty. You're not as young as you used to be." He managed a smile he didn't feel.

"Oh be off with ye. I'm liable to live to be a hundred."

He mounted Dubh and set off. He had to stop at the knights' keep before he left. By God, it was market day—the village already bustling with people and the vendor stalls were set up. Just like the day he'd met Rhianwyn.

After he spoke to Severin and Cassian, the entire order came out to see Broccan off. His breath caught on spotting Rhianwyn in her worn cloak, basket in hand, looking much as she had the day he'd first seen her. Lovely, mesmerizing, intriguing, but maudlin now.

Christ's cross, he didn't want to leave her. Their eyes met and she attempted a weak smile, but he saw her sorrow. Should he ask her to accompany him? What if she turned him down? And William had just returned. Besides, *his* father wasn't a pleasant man even when he wasn't ailing. Broccan didn't even know how long he'd be gone.

She looked away and kept walking. Cassian and Cadfael both stared, urging him to go to her. By God he hated farewells. He thought of when he'd left to go to Mercia, how they'd bemoaned being apart. He recalled making love most of the night before—the lingering kisses and embraces when parting. Now, they weren't together even when they were both here.

She walked nearer. He knew she could hear him. He loudly explained his intended route. The roads he'd take and where he'd cross the sea to Ireland. She didn't seem to be paying attention, but sure she'd hear.

He realized she'd crossed the road not to bid him farewell, but to say goodbye to his dogs and horse. With tears in her eyes, she bent to pet them. Then she stroked Dubh. Broccan had to look away; the lump in his throat was bloody painful.

RHIANWYN FELT HER heart might break. How grand and handsome Broccan looked upon his horse. She petted Fionn and Oisin, then Dubh. She whispered to each of them.

"Please take care of him. I love you all so very much."

Why couldn't she say that to her man? Because he wasn't her man any longer and she wouldn't want him to feel guilty when he couldn't say it to her. Or when he must leave perhaps never to return.

"Safe journey, Broccan," she said, her voice breaking.

"Be well, Rhianwyn," he replied.

He nodded and started toward the edge of the village. When he got to the gates, he turned and raised his hand.

She thought he might put it to his heart, as knights did when they intended to return to their true love. But instead, he only waved again. Therefore she did the same. Then she turned and hurried away. She couldn't prevent sobbing and couldn't watch him ride off this time.

WHY OF ALL days would she choose today to return to the manor, she wondered? Maybe because when she'd gone to the cottage, she and her father didn't have much to say to one other. She knew he loved her, and she loved him, but he spoke only of magic, and she wanted nothing to do with that.

He'd patted her on the head like she was a child, then said he'd be off to have a pint with Severin, then go see old Marlow and perhaps fish with him.

William had been happy to spend time with her when she was a child but had never known what to do with her once she approached womanhood, especially after her mother died.

She chastised herself with a growl for when she arrived at the manor, she couldn't bring herself to go in. Matty must've seen her through the window and came out. She carried Broccan's overcoat, the one he'd been wearing the day they met. The one Rhianwyn had wrapped around her the morning after they made love. She'd worn it home as an excuse to see him again.

"He left it behind…I think for you," Matty said.

Her hands shook as she took it from the old woman.

She held it to her chest, inhaling Broccan's scent. Champion, Anslem's old dog, slowly approached.

"He senses your sorrow," Matty said.

Rhianwyn nodded and knelt beside the dog, put her arms around his neck and wept.

Swift-moving horses' hooves startled her. She looked up half hoping Broccan had come back for her, but it was Cassian, Cadfael, and Zachary. She thought he'd intended to go to another knights' order.

"Why are you here?" she asked.

"To get you," Cassian said.

"Me? Why? Is someone hurt?"

"No. We'll take you to Broccan."

She shook her head. "He would've asked me if he wanted me with him."

"Lord knows he's a stubborn man." Matty nodded.

"Stubborn as a damn mule," Cassian agreed. "But he didn't go over his route for good measure or for our benefit. He spoke so damn loudly he must've thought you were deaf. He wants you to follow."

She shook her head. "I won't. Not without him requesting me."

"Bloody hell, woman," Cassian said. "You're the most stubborn woman I've ever met. The two of you are quite the sarding pair."

"It's clear you love one another," Zachary said. "Don't throw that away if you have a chance to be together."

She could see Zachary was still hurting over all that happened with Selena.

Cadfael nodded and an owl swooped overhead.

"Why is an owl flying in daylight?" Zachary asked.

Cadfael smiled.

"Well come on," Cassian ordered.

She inhaled several times. Should she go?

Cassian decided for her. He threw her, rather unceremoniously, upon his horse.

"I have two horses of my own I could take if I intended to go," she argued.

"We don't have time. Broccan's horse is swift, but we'll try to catch up." Cassian mounted behind her. With a quick nod to Matty they galloped off.

UNPREPARED FOR THE journey, Rhianwyn wrapped Broccan's overcoat around her. The wind was icy. She felt suddenly unwell, too. It reminded her of her journey to Cymru when she'd been poisoned. Her head even felt dizzy, and her stomach protested.

"I need to stop," she mumbled, covering her mouth. "I'm going to spew."

Cassian jumped off and lifted her down. She made it to the bushes just in time. That happened several times along the way. Each of the men wore concerned looks.

"We're never going to catch him if we have to stop so often," Cassian groused. "If we're not stopping for you to spew, we're stopping for you to piss."

"God's bones, she's ill. Don't be such a cad," Zachary said, empathetically.

"Maybe I'll ride with Cadfael," Rhianwyn grumbled

still feeling nauseated.

Cassian rolled his eyes but placed her on his horse.

"We must find Lady Rhianwyn something to eat," Cadfael warned. "She needs to be renourished. She's pale as a ghost."

"By God, she is!" Zachary gasped.

Cassian nodded and put his arm around her as they set off. After stopping at a tavern she felt considerably better with her stomach full.

"You still don't look well, Rhianwyn." Zachary glanced at the other men. "We need to let her rest in a proper bed."

"If we stopped overnight, we'd not reach Broccan in time," Cassian warned.

"Do you feel up to riding through the night?" Cadfael's brow furrowed.

She nodded. She wouldn't admit she didn't.

It wasn't long till everything she'd eaten came up again.

"What the hell's wrong with you, Rhianwyn?" Cassian asked.

"You didn't drink anything that could've been poisoned?" Cadfael sounded concerned.

"I'm not poisoned."

But something was wrong.

They rode through the night. At least with no food in her stomach there was nothing to spew, but still she stopped several times to heave.

"Should we find a healer?" Cassian asked come morning.

"I am a damn healer," she muttered.

When they finally neared the harbor and dismounted,

Rhianwyn glanced out at the rough sea. This time she didn't make it to cover before spewing bile.

The men stared like she might have a plague.

"Even if you've missed Broccan's ship, you'll simply take the next one." Zachary sounded chagrined.

She looked out at a ship in the distance. She held her hands to her chest, trying to stop the pain in her heart. Even her breasts ached.

God's nails. Tender breasts, unsettled stomach, frequent urination. How long had it been since she'd bled? Too long. Come to it, she hadn't had her courses since she and Broccan had relations after they'd shared soup. How could she have been so distracted not to consider that with the pact over, she was fertile again?

"Let's go see when the next ship sails," Zachary suggested.

Cassian took her arm and started to walk off.

"I can't go," she said.

"Of course you can," Cassian insisted. "You have to."

Broccan's words suddenly haunted her mind.

"If you can't put me first, then our marriage has no chance."

She was with child; therefore, she truly couldn't put him first. Nor could she tie him down, not when he still hadn't been able to forgive her.

"Listen to her, Cassian," Cadfael urged. "Lady Rhianwyn's saying she can't go."

Cadfael looked at her like he knew what she was thinking.

"I just want to go home," she said. "I need to go home."

TEG AND CADFAEL both looked at her with sympathetic eyes, even though she hadn't spoken of her condition to anyone.

She passed the book to Cadfael.

"Please take this to Morwenna. With it she might help end the curse. I can't travel just now. But, Teg, I'd like you to accompany him."

"Why me?" Teg asked.

"Because I don't want Cadfael to journey alone."

Cadfael embraced her. "We will do as you request, but I promise to return when it is done."

She kissed them each on the cheek and they set off.

PART THREE

CHAPTER TWENTY

Wessex

RHIANWYN PLACED AUTUMN wildflowers on her mother's grave and whispered a farewell. She still liked to come talk to Mam even after all this time.

Years. A lifetime. Sometimes it felt like several lifetimes. And so many loved ones, gone.

Life had settled in the time since the pact had been broken, but she couldn't claim peace. Not entirely. Not yet. Would she ever?

There was a chill in the air. Today when she'd made her bed, she'd been plagued with dread at the thought of spending another winter without Broccan.

But she wouldn't permit herself to feel lonely. She was far from alone, she thought with a smile.

Leaving the graveyard, she glanced over to see Elspeth, Selena, and Lilliana standing under the huge oak where they all used to meet. She hadn't been in that cemetery for years, not since King Thaddeus was buried.

They must've noticed her, too, for they looked up from their conversation. Selena waved. Rhianwyn waved back. They wanted her there with them but had given up asking.

She sighed and clasped her satchel with her soap and drying cloth. She'd bathe in the hot pool while she had this rare time alone, then go start supper.

BROCCAN RODE OVER the hill and spotted the village below, tensing. What welcome would he find here, after all this time? Dubh, who didn't share his apprehension, whinnied, and took off at a gallop.

Broccan winced as pain shot from his back down his leg.

"Whoa, boy! I'm not recovered enough to hurtle at that speed."

His loyal steed obediently slowed.

Broccan glanced at the village gates, the castle, and the knights' keep. All unchanged. Stone took centuries to crumble, unlike people.

It had been a long time since he'd been here…too long. Maybe he should've stayed away. But the brush with death all those months ago triggered a powerful need to return. To her…to his Rhianwyn, even if she was no longer his.

There was no sense putting it off. He'd go straight to the manor. She might refuse to see him. Maybe, if she maintained her feisty temper, she might throw something at him. He wouldn't blame her. She'd be justified. He hoped she'd been happy these years…that she'd made a life without him and moved on. Even if he never could.

As he neared Brockwell estate, he heard children laughing.

Rhianwyn's children?

Probably. Even though she feared dying in childbed,

she adored babies. It would stand to reason she'd have several. But by God, not this many. Half a dozen children of various ages played on the grass and even more in the garden. He'd been gone seven years. How many could be hers?

He rode closer trying to determine if any looked like her. They seemed too enthralled with their games to notice him. Broccan dismounted with some difficulty. Damn those injuries were taking an age to heal. He tied Dubh to the grand hawthorn tree near the manor.

This fence hadn't been here when he'd been lord of Brockwell Manor. He unlatched the gate and simply walked through the open doors.

Glancing down the corridor, his heart warmed on seeing Matty. She was frailer, more bent. Her head lowered, she was muttering under her breath. She must've heard his boots on the stone floor. She'd always recognized his footsteps. Her head shot up and she held her hand to her throat like she'd seen a ghost.

"Broccan," she whispered. There was a hint of relief in her wearied eyes, followed by an unmissable scowl.

Of all the people in Hengebury, he'd thought Matty would be most pleased he'd returned or least likely to be *displeased* on seeing him. Apparently, he'd been wrong.

"Matty. You're lookin' well."

He wanted to embrace the dear woman who'd raised him, but by her expression he doubted she'd favor that. Her lips tightly pursed, she still hadn't smiled.

"You might've sent word you were comin'...or at the very least been considerate enough to let us know you were still alive!"

He met her eyes. "That was thoughtless and…this was an impulsive journey."

His voice was drowned out by a ringing bell. Then several children rushed by him toward the great hall.

Matty clapped her hands to get their attention. She'd done that when he was a child. "Don't you young gaffers be racin', or you'll knock the wee ones over. Haesel has your meal ready, but she'll make you wait if you're behavin' like unmannerly hooligans!"

Her words were harsh but her tone and smile kind. The children beamed happily and slowed down. Two young women patiently herded the enlivened children into the hall. One pretty lass smiled shyly like she knew him, but he didn't recognize her.

Matty must've seen the unspoken question in his eyes.

"The manor's an orphanage and a place for motherless children to safely spend their days and get a warm meal while their fathers are workin'. The guesthouse has been extended. It's now home to abused women and their children or women in the family way who've no husband, even harlots. Widows, and the elderly are also given food and shelter till a home's found. No one's turned away."

This was surely Rhianwyn's doing. She'd always advocated for the less fortunate. Broccan nodded, still glancing about hoping to see her.

"If you're lookin' for your wife…well the woman you abandoned all those years ago, you'll not find her here," Matty said.

Was she going to make him ask?

"You'd have to search for her in the graveyard."

Broccan felt his heart was being ripped from his chest; he couldn't catch his breath, saw dark spots before his eyes. He reached for the doorframe grasping hold to brace himself.

Matty shook her head. "I apologize. I'm bloody annoyed with you, Broccan Mulryan...but that was cruel." Her eyes softened only slightly. "Sure Rhianwyn will be visitin' her mother's grave as she does weekly."

Broccan exhaled, closed his eyes, and put his hand to his chest trying to make his heart beat steadily again. Relief flooded his senses, but it was true, Rhianwyn could very well have died. He'd be none the wiser with how long he'd stayed away.

"At any rate, I must be off to help with the children," Matty said. "I'm glad you're not dead. I'm not certain everyone will feel that way!"

Christ, she really was annoyed with him.

"If you're in need of food, you're welcome to join us. As I said, we turn no one away...as per Rhianwyn's rules. But I warn ye the manor's not as quiet as when you lived here. Under her management Brockwell estate has flourished. She uses most coin earned to keep this place afloat so she can help others. Giles Brockwell mightn't approve, but I'm damn proud of her."

"I'm grateful for the offer." His voice sounded shaky from his fright. "But I'd like to go speak with Rhianwyn."

Matty nodded but he saw her disapproval.

"Don't disrupt her life if you're only here to stem your curiosity before you'll be takin' off again."

With that she left him standing there. How the hell would everyone else greet him if Matty, whom he'd hoped would welcome him with open arms, did not?

BROCCAN CAUGHT SIGHT of Rhianwyn on the path to the hot pool, and even from a distance, her beauty awed him. Even after all this time, his heart sped, and his loins tightened. It had always been that way with her.

He turned back. Even with his injuries, he could have caught her before she reached the pool, but he refused to disturb her privacy, no matter how much he was tempted to look upon her loveliness.

Coward! Face her.

He was stalling.

Squinting in the late afternoon sun, he saw her three friends talking under the oak tree where they all used to meet. Did Rhianwyn no longer join them? Had she still not made amends with them after that wretched pact?

He didn't want to speak with them before he'd talked with Rhianwyn, but Elspeth saw him and beckoned. He started toward them, trying not to limp.

"Sir Broccan!" Lilliana addressed him coolly.

Elspeth lifted an eyebrow. "Look what the wind's finally blown in."

Selena offered a hesitant smile. "Are you here to stay?"

"Or just passing through?" Lilliana added.

"Ladies." He shrugged, not feeling overly friendly himself. He noticed that they were all ripe with child. "It appears congratulations are in order. Have you other children?"

Selena smiled, sweetly now. "This is my fourth."

"I carry my third child," Lilliana said.

"My first." Elspeth patted her stomach. "But my husband and I previously adopted two others."

They weren't readily offering information about Rhianwyn.

"You're all married then?" he asked.

"We are." Selena nodded.

They didn't tell him who they'd wed. Not eager to continue conversing, he didn't ask.

The silence became awkward. Even after all this time, he maintained some guilt, some embarrassment, and admittedly, some fury over what occurred during the magical pact.

"I should be gettin' on. I'll drop by the knights' keep. See if I've any old acquaintances still there."

"You don't fear being dungeoned for breaking your knight's oath and not returning long ago?" Lilliana tilted her chin with the same superiority.

Elspeth crossed her arms over her very round belly. "It's not *that* vow he should be concerned about breaking."

"In truth, I don't fear much anymore, Elspeth." He sighed not wanting to squabble or throw accusations. "I wish you well with your babes."

"Safe journey," Selena replied.

He nodded and walked away, shivering, not from the cool wind, but due to the chilly reception. He heard someone come after him and turned to find Selena wearing a serious expression.

"Have you seen Rhianwyn?"

He shook his head.

"She's no longer at the manor," Selena said.

He hadn't asked Matty if Rhianwyn still resided there.

He looked at Selena. "Will you tell me where she lives?"

She nodded. "They live where her original cottage once was."

They?

"Thank you, Selena."

"Please don't hurt her, Broccan." Selena sounded worried.

"I assure you, I only want what's best for Rhianwyn."

"Which is why you stayed away all this time?" Elspeth said, though he hadn't heard her approach.

"By the discourteous looks you wear, I'd think you'd have preferred I stayed away."

Broccan already regretted letting so much time pass; he didn't need their contempt.

"She hasn't wholly forgiven us for the pact," Lilliana added when she joined them. "She probably never will."

"You've not renewed your friendships?" He was sorrowful about that.

"She's not unfriendly," Elspeth said.

"But Rhianwyn won't truly let us back in her heart...not after all that happened." Selena sighed. "I do hope you two can resolve something so she can move on."

BROCCAN WALKED THROUGH the woods to Rhianwyn's cottage, recalling the first time he'd done so. He'd been nervous then, too, after their initial meeting when he hadn't made a good impression. But that was nothing like he felt now. How would she react? If everyone else was annoyed, she'd likely be livid. His legs grew heavier with every step. He should've gone back for Dubh.

He took a deep breath as he rounded the last turn, and came upon a well-built stone cottage, far bigger and sturdier than where she'd lived before they were wed. There was a well-maintained garden with vegetables, herbs, and fragrant flowers. There were other buildings...a barn, stables, and likely a henhouse.

But why would she choose to live in this simple home when she could've remained at the manor? He'd left it in her name. Did she give that up for the orphaned children?

Or was she now with someone who wouldn't live where she'd once resided with him?

Then he spied her, his wife, his heart, and he knew he'd give up everything only to know that she was happy now, with or without him.

IT HAD BEEN delightful soaking in the hot pool. Rhianwyn finished drying her hair by the cottage, then placed the kettle on the hook over the fire. Old habits die hard; she still preferred cooking outdoors. She'd sit and enjoy her tea. She lifted her face to the breeze, reveling in the last autumn days. The leaves were an array of stunning colors, and the scent was invigorating.

She'd despised autumn for a long while—the season they'd made the damnable pact and when she and Broccan experienced so much emotional tumult before he left. But bitterness and pain benefitted no one, and she'd finally let it go.

She brushed her hair while the tea steeped. It was still waist length. She'd thought of cutting it, but Broccan liked her lengthy hair. He *had* liked it. How long would she continue wondering of his opinion on every damn aspect of her life? Maybe she should change her hair…cut it midway down her back.

The vegetables were washed and peeled, ready to be boiled. The chicken roasted over the fire. It sizzled as fat dripped into the flames. The breeze carried away the smoke, but the smell made her mouth water. She'd churned butter early this morning and Haesel had sent fresh bread.

She glanced toward the cottage, the bountiful garden, the fenced area with the coop and clucking chickens, the pen of hogs, the small barn with her two cows, and the stables with her beloved horses. She was content with her life. *Mostly*.

She poured her tea, added honey—had taken only a sip, when she heard footsteps approaching. The children must be back. She smiled knowing they'd be filled with excitement and recounts of their day. But these steps were slow…hesitant.

"I see you're still drinkin' that pungent tea."

Broccan.

She whirled around and dropped the cup. Tea splashed her skirts. Her mouth fell open as he limped toward her.

"I didn't mean to startle you." He stepped closer, but then stopped, unsure. "That tea's obviously been beneficial. You haven't changed. You're maybe even more beaut...you're...a...sight for weary eyes, Rhianwyn," he stammered.

Her heart beat so fast and so loudly, he could surely hear.

Don't weep. Say something.

"Broccan. It's...good to see you," she managed.

Fighting the desire to fling herself into his arms, she went to him, embraced him slowly, as a woman of seven and twenty years should. He wrapped his gloriously powerful arms around her and pulled her to him. She pressed her face against his firm, broad chest, inhaling his musky scent she'd missed so much. The scent she'd alternately tried to forget and make herself remember. She didn't want to leave his arms. Still, she had to learn why he was here and what his intentions were.

Did he have a woman? Did he share his bed with many women? He didn't seem eager to end their embrace either. Even by the quick glance and in being dumbstruck on seeing him, she could tell he was even handsomer and just as grand.

BY GOD, SHE felt perfect in his arms. Just as he'd remembered. What he'd dreamed of every day and night since they'd parted. And she'd come to him…was clinging to him like no time had passed and she didn't want to end their closeness either. Her hair smelled exactly the same. It took him straight back to how it had once been between them…the love, the passion, the joy in being together newly in love. That scent, and her breasts against his chest, might be his undoing.

The lump in his throat was so large, he thought he'd choke. He needed to step away before he acted upon his desire to kiss her or blurted out how much he still loved her. Then she just might slug him. If she had a man, he certainly would, if he came home to find them like this.

She cleared her throat and he realized he was holding her too firmly. He released his grip, regrettably, for he never wanted to let her go.

RHIANWYN WILLED HERSELF to move. She'd be wholly humiliated if she seemed desperate to be in his arms when he mightn't feel the same. But he *had* held her tightly. Maybe he only felt guilty for not returning sooner or he pitied how pathetic she seemed.

Traitorous emotional tears escaped down her cheeks. When she moved away, he swallowed hard. Tears glistened in his eyes, too.

He cleared his throat, but his words were raspy. "That's the warmest greetin' I've received today."

Wiping her tears she took a long breath, searching for something benign to say.

"Would you like some tea?" she asked, nervously.

"It seems you'll be needin' another." He bent, picked up the cup she'd dropped, then brushed off the soil. He moaned when passing it to her.

"You're hurt?"

"Ever the healer?" He smiled.

She shook her head. "I haven't been a healer for a long while."

He eyed her closer. Since she'd always adored healing and once told him it was what gave her life purpose, he was likely wondering why she'd given that up.

"Your leg's injured?"

He shrugged. "Wrenched my knee when thrown from my horse durin' a battle."

"Dubh?" she asked, looking around.

Broccan nodded. "He's well and made the journey with me."

"And the dogs?" she asked.

He shook his head. She saw the sorrow in his eyes.

"Both gone. Fionn was old even when we were here in Wessex. But Oisin died a few months ago...protectin' me."

She fought tears again on remembering his loyal dogs. She'd met them the night she and Broccan first made love. She recalled waking the following morning with one dog on either side of them.

"I'm sorry, Broccan. I loved them, too."

He glanced at her oddly. Did he think she'd just professed her undying love for him?

She tucked her hair behind her ear. "Where is Dubh?"

"I left him tied at Brockwell Manor."

"You've seen Matty and the children then?"

He nodded. "You don't live there now?"

"Sit. Rest your leg, Broccan." She pointed to a felled log near the fire. "I've another tea you might favor."

He nodded, grimacing as he sat down. She felt his eyes upon her as she procured dried herbs from the cottage. He waited for her reply.

"I help at the orphanage some and offer reading lessons to the children. I keep up the estate's books, but no, I couldn't live there. Too many memories." She sighed. "I wanted a quieter life here in the forest like when...I was younger."

Placing herbs in a cup, she poured boiled water over them, then made another tea for herself. The teas steeped while she and Broccan silently assessed each other, trying not to look too obvious.

He had no receding hairline. His hair remained thick, too, but it was longer, with a few streaks of gray—a bit more at the temples. The lines on his forehead and by his eyes were slightly deeper. Yet it made him only more attractive and undeniably sensual. Her heart quickened. She looked away. Those thoughts hadn't entered her mind for an age.

She strained the herbs, added honey, and passed him a cup. Taking her own, she held it tightly and sat next to him—not too close. They sighed in unison. There was much to tell him and to ask.

"This is pleasant." He nodded to the tea he sipped.

"It's mint. Even Elspeth and Selena like that one."

"I saw them and Lilliana at the cemetery."

"And they didn't run you out of the village?" She smiled trying to make the conversation lighter.

"They weren't overly friendly. Even Matty was cool."

"They're all protective of me."

"You're not displeased with me for stayin' away so long, then?"

How would she reply? There'd been several times through the years when she was far more than displeased. On occasion, she'd gone to the middle of the forest and screamed in lonely frustration and anxious pondering. Other times she was regretful or sad—worried he'd been killed as many suggested. Lilliana had been adamant she should have him declared dead so she could remarry.

He's here now.

Wasn't that all that mattered? How long would he stay? She needed to have a very serious discussion with him—but not until she knew his future intentions.

She saw him glance at the woodpile.

"Looks like you're set for winter. You'll not be needin' me to chop wood like the first time I came to your cottage."

She nodded, fondly remembering. He shuffled his long legs, fidgeted uncomfortably. She didn't believe it was because of his injury.

"I could get you a chair. I should've offered. We used to like to sit on this old log."

"No. I'm content sittin' here." He smiled. That smile still made her heart flutter, but his eyes held distinct weariness. He'd probably faced many difficulties while he'd been away.

"You look fatigued, Broccan."

"It was a long ride," he replied dismissively.

She resisted the urge to take his hand or caress his chiseled jaw, which was presently covered in the closest she'd ever seen to a beard. It, too, bore traces of silver. He gazed at her. When their eyes briefly met there was still the compelling attraction between, even if she'd believed that part of her was long buried.

"Rhianwyn?" He lowered his eyes. "Are you happy?"

How would she respond?

SHE STOOD, PROBABLY only busying herself to avoid his question. She added more wood to the fire and looked off toward the trees. He shouldn't have asked. Yet he had to know. She wore the oddest expression. One he couldn't discern.

She finally nodded. "I'm happy enough."

He stood, too. His knees unsteady again. He'd waited too long. He should've known a woman as lovely and special as her would fill her life with joy. But she was a woman meant for love. Had he ruined that for her? She'd once had twenty-seven marriage bids by the king's invitation. Broccan had been honored when Thaddeus granted him the privilege of her hand. That seemed long ago...so much water under the drawbridge.

"I'm glad. I always wanted to ensure your happiness. I..."

What more could he say?

She closed her eyes, emitting a sob that made his chest tighten.

"I have many blessings," she sniffled.

Shite—he'd made her cry. How could he let her know he *was* happy for her when his heart was breaking? He wanted to hold her again. Comfort her and himself.

She kept looking toward the forest like she was expecting someone. A lover? Would he be displeased to find her conversing with the man she'd once loved? The man who still loved her and could never forget her or what they'd shared.

"And you, Broccan? Are you happy?"

He shrugged. "I'm happy to see you well. I had to know you were taken care of."

Now she seemed more distressed...uneasy. Guilty maybe that she'd moved on? Yet Selena said she hadn't.

Silence again.

"Maybe I should be goin' then?"

Her eyes grew wide and her face paled. She looked stricken. Because he was leaving or because he'd shown up in the first place?

Broccan heard voices approaching from the trees. He looked up to see William, Rhianwyn's father, holding hands with a lovely little girl, with long, wavy, dark-brown hair and eyes that were nearly identical to Rhianwyn's. He'd never seen anyone else with eyes like that. There was no mistaking she was her daughter—a wee thing, perhaps four years—five at most. Rhianwyn had at least waited some time before finding another man. She hadn't gotten over him quickly. Did that make him feel better or more guilty?

"Mam," the child called, running toward Rhianwyn. She lifted her in her arms and the loving smile they shared warmed Broccan's heart.

"Hello, my lovely girl." Rhianwyn kissed her cheek. "How was your afternoon with Papa?"

William stared at Broccan with the look of a protective father who didn't want a rogue breaking his daughter's heart...again. A gentle man, he didn't speak, but nodded to him probably out of consideration for the child.

"I caught two fish, Mam. Papa says I'll be as good a fisherwoman as you."

"I'm sure you are already, my girl."

Then the child's eyes welled with tears. Broccan noted the sudden apprehension on her mother's face.

"Sweetheart, what is it?"

"Promise you won't be displeased, Mam?"

"I can't promise that, my precious daughter, but, still, you must tell me."

The child's lip quivered.

Rhianwyn glanced at William. "Father? What's happened?"

William looked chagrined. He rubbed his balding head. "She had a wee incident. I knew you'd worry; therefore, I took her to Everard to be patched up before you saw her."

"Patched up?" Rhianwyn voice rose slightly higher as she threw her father a questioning glance, set the child to her feet and gently pulled up her sleeve to reveal a bandage wrapped around her thumb and wrist.

"Some hooks had to be cut from her skin," William

said apprehensively.

"Uncle Everard poured remedy on it after. It burned like fire. Then he sewed it closed, but I was very brave, Mam."

"I'm certain you were, lovely girl, but I don't expect you to always be brave."

Uncle Everard? Had Rhianwyn borne Cassian's child? Cassian had loved her before Broccan even met her. But the child didn't have Cassian's fair hair; it was even darker than Rhianwyn's beautiful light brown locks. Chester or Zachary? They were also Everard's brothers. But Everard was a knight. Why would he be mending wounds?

"Are you angry, Mam?"

"Oh, my darling." Rhianwyn knelt beside the child and held her close. "I'd never be angry you're hurt. I'm just relieved it wasn't worse."

"Don't be riled with Papa. He was helping Marlow since he can't see anything. Two hooks were caught together, and I tried to pull them apart even though Papa said to wait." She looked down, sheepishly. "Tell me I can still go fishing with him."

William waited for her reply, too.

"I wouldn't disallow you from spending time with Papa. You adore one another and both love fishing."

The child and the old man released matching sighs. The girl just then seemed to notice Broccan. She eyed him closely.

"Mam, who's that?"

Rhianwyn looked at Broccan, eyes serious again. William scowled once more.

"This is Lord Brockwell." She cleared her throat. "We were friends some time ago."

"I haven't been called that in a long while," Broccan said. "It's lovely to meet you, young lady, and what's your name?"

"I'm Mererid."

"After your grandmother?" Broccan wasn't sure whether to extend his hand.

The child gave him a sweet, rosy-lipped smile like her mother's.

"Did you know Mam's mam?" Her voice was cheerfully high-pitched.

"No, but I've heard about her. Your mother must love you very much to bestow the honor of the name of the woman she cherished?"

Rhianwyn gave Broccan a grateful nod.

William looked from Rhianwyn to Broccan, uncertain. "Well, I'd best get back."

"You won't stay for supper, Father?"

"I promised Marlow I'd cook today's catch. I'll clean the ones you caught, dear Merrie, then bring them on the morrow."

"Thank you, Papa." The smiling child went to her grandfather, offering a farewell embrace.

"Thanks for taking her to Everard, Father."

He nodded, then threw a cautionary glance at Broccan. William had just left when Broccan heard someone else hurriedly approaching.

"Mam, Mam!" someone called.

A boy, older and taller than the girl, burst through the

trees wearing a worried expression. Broccan noted his blond hair, more like Cassian.

She hadn't waited so long after all.

"Is Merrie hurt, Mam?" The boy rushed to the girl. "Merrie, I had a vision of you and there was blood!"

She smiled and shook her head. "Don't worry, Gwil. There wasn't much blood. Uncle Everard fixed it."

The boy reached for the girl's sleeve as Rhianwyn had.

His eyes grew larger. He pulled his sister to him. They clearly shared a powerful bond. Rhianwyn went to the lad, tousled his hair affectionately and embraced him, but then became suddenly serious.

"Gwilym, why are you alone?"

"Because he can run like a bloody deer," a familiar voice called, and Cassian came through the trees sounding winded. "He was standing there with me. Then he was just gone." Cassian bent over placing his hands on his knees as he caught his breath.

Broccan's heart thundered in his chest as his worst fears were confirmed. She'd settled down with Cassian. Borne his children. Made a life with him.

He felt sick.

But if she was happy...wasn't that all he wanted?

Rhianwyn crouched beside the children, now clasping both their hands. "Gwil, you must never leave without telling someone nor go through the forest alone. Those are my strictest rules."

"But, Mam, I was so worried."

"I understand you're protective of your sister, but I don't want anything to happen to either of you."

She gathered them both closer. Broccan saw the relief on her lovely face. She closed her eyes, mumbling under her breath. Probably a prayer. Evidently, she maintained the deep fear of losing those she loved. She'd nearly not married him because of that.

Cassian must've just noticed him, for his eyes became wide. He broke out in a broad smile as he walked toward Broccan. That wasn't the reception he'd expected. Unless Cassian no longer saw him as a rival.

He pulled him in for a gruff embrace. The two people he thought might be most displeased with him for staying away so long had warmly welcomed him.

Cassian clapped his back. "It's been a long time, friend."

"It has at that!" Broccan returned the affectionate gesture.

"You must come to the keep. Many knights will remember you although several have recently joined our order."

"Is Severin still there?" Broccan asked.

Cassian shook his head. "The old boy moved to the seaside with Mabel. Halsey and Adam went with them. They've half a dozen children now. Severin and Mabel are doting grandparents."

"I didn't think he'd ever give up the knighthood," Broccan said. "Who's grand cross then?"

Cassian puffed out his chest. "You're looking at him!"

CHAPTER TWENTY-ONE

R HIANWYN WATCHED THE two men, glad they were affable. She was grateful Cassian didn't mention Broccan by name. Her children had heard numerous stories about the nearly legendary Sir Broccan. They were closely watching the two men. Lord Brockwell had been the safest name to use.

"Who's that, Mam?" Gwil whispered. A polite child, he'd never do anything that might make him appear rude.

"A friend," Rhianwyn said, quickly. Too quickly. Mererid caught that. They were both clever and intuitive for their young age...or for her comfort level.

The men stepped back from one another, and Cassian cast her a sideways glance. She shook her head in silent warning.

"He's Lord Brockwell," Mererid said.

"I was once," Broccan corrected.

Gwil looked confused and Cassian thankfully came to the rescue.

"He's a knight, too. The others will want to see him, so we'll set off."

By Broccan's curious expression he was puzzled at Cassian's insistence they leave straightaway.

"I haven't had time to speak with Rhianwyn and not

even been introduced to her son."

"This is Gwilym," Rhianwyn said. "We mostly call him Gwil."

"Won't you ask him to stay for supper, Mam?" Mererid gestured to Broccan. "You say we should invite visitors to eat with us...because it's good to always be courteous. And if he's your friend..."

"And he's a knight," Gwil gushed, appearing greatly impressed. That struck fear in Rhianwyn's heart. She didn't want him to follow the path of knighthood.

"We'll both come back later for supper," Cassian replied though Rhianwyn hadn't actually invited anyone.

"My horse is at the manor," Broccan said.

"The children and I could fetch him and stable him here." Rhianwyn gestured toward the building behind the cottage. "Unless you'll maybe be leaving this day."

Her eyes met Broccan's, and he shook his head. "I'm far too weary to set off anywhere today."

"You must stay a while." Cassian clapped Broccan on the back again, which brought another baffled look from Broccan. "We'll have much to catch up on."

"We'll go get your horse." Gwilym's dark blue eyes lit up, for he adored horses.

"Sure your mam would be able to lead him, for she's a way with horses, but he's temperamental with those he doesn't know," Broccan warned.

"Gwil and Merrie are both very good with horses, too," Rhianwyn replied. "I wouldn't be surprised if Dubh permits them to handle him, too."

"Aren't you a bit small to be near horses?" Broccan

glanced at Mererid.

Rhianwyn cringed. That would not bode well. Mererid bemoaned her small stature. She scrunched her face and put her hands on her hips. She'd inherited that habit from her mother. Amused, Rhianwyn fought a grin. She doubted she'd feel that way when her daughter was older. She and her strong-willed Merrie often locked horns even now.

"I'm the same age as, Gwil, Lord Brockwell!" she sniped, eyes flashing, lips pouting. "We're twins you know."

Broccan shook his head. "I'm sorry I've offended you, Mererid. Forgive me. I honestly *didn't* know you were twins. I annoyed your mother the first day I met her, too."

Rhianwyn smiled remembering that day.

"I *am* bigger and taller, Merrie," Gwil said, kindly. "Everybody thinks I'm older."

"You're only *gigantic* because you stole *my* food when we were inside Mam." Mererid's expressive eyes widened dramatically.

Cassian snorted. Rhianwyn threw a reprimanding glance at Cassian and her daughter.

"Mererid. That's unkind and untrue. Your brother wouldn't steal a scrap of food to save his life."

"You said so, Mam." Again, Mererid placed her hands on her hips.

"No, Mererid," Rhianwyn corrected. "I said sometimes with twins, one receives more nourishment than the other and grows faster...which is why you were small when you were born and Gwilym was bigger."

"I was so tiny I almost didn't live." Mererid threw a

serious look at Broccan.

"That must've been frightenin' for your mam and your father?" Broccan looked at Cassian, then Rhianwyn.

"It was." Rhianwyn couldn't calm the tremor in her voice remembering the paralyzing fear the first fortnight of her daughter's life when she didn't believe she'd survive.

"You'll have lots of time to talk later." Cassian nudged Broccan's arm. "We should go to the keep."

Rhianwyn went to Cassian, embracing him to whisper in his ear, "Broccan doesn't know. Promise you'll not tell him. The children aren't aware who he is, therefore, you mustn't say anything that would make them suspect."

Cassian held her closer. "There'll all bound to put it together soon. You'll have to tell them."

"I need to know if Broccan intends to stay…otherwise, I won't mention it."

"He has a right to know, Rhianwyn…and so do they."

"Cassian. I must do this my way."

"If you keep holding me, he's going to think we're together." Cassian laughed.

"That might be best just until I know if…"

"Should I kiss you then?" he jested. "For old time's sake."

"I doubt your wife would favor that any more than I would," she said through gritted teeth. She pinched him and he laughed again.

"Mam, are you telling him not to drink too much ale and come back drunk?" Mererid spoke with her usual sassiness.

Rhianwyn laughed, which broke the tension. But Broccan looked more serious. He likely wouldn't want to think Cassian was prone to drinking if he was her man and their father.

"I'd rather no one drink too much, or you won't appreciate my food."

"It smells damn delicious," Broccan said. "You always were a fine cook."

"That hasn't changed." Cassian patted her arm affectionately.

He was playing this up well...even though he'd been the one through the years who'd often insisted on finding Broccan and hauling his arse back here, as he'd put it. He'd attempted it once.

"Why don't we forgo the knights' keep today?" Broccan said. "I'll stop by tomorrow."

"Maybe we could go with you, Lord Brockwell, to get your horse while Mam makes supper?" Mererid asked.

Rhianwyn glanced at her disbelievingly. She wasn't a child who usually warmed to people she didn't know. Perhaps she was intrinsically drawn to Broccan.

Because she was his daughter...or because she was female?

"I'll go with them." Cassian nodded.

"Someone should stay to help you, Mam," Gwil suggested though he looked eager to go along.

"Supper's nearly ready, my very thoughtful boy." She touched his jawline, so like his father's. "I'll finish my tea while the vegetables boil."

"May we take Morrigan with us?" Mererid asked.

Gwil whistled before Rhianwyn replied. The very peculiar-looking dog raced through the woods toward the children. She stopped short of knocking them down.

"What, by God, is that?" Broccan chuckled.

"She's our dog!" Mererid looked insulted again.

"She's part Irish wolfhound," Gwil chimed in.

Rhianwyn smiled. "I believe Fionn or Oisin left something of themselves behind when they departed Wessex."

She saw the look Cassian gave her but ignored it.

"The Ravencroft's corgi had puppies two months later," Rhianwyn explained.

Broccan tilted his head looking bemused. "How in blazes would a wolfhound and a corgi even...?"

Rhianwyn fought a smile. "I suppose where there's a will there's a way," she replied hoping she wouldn't have to explain to the twins what he referred to.

With a grin, Broccan observed the odd long-haired gray and fawn-colored dog. She had one pointed ear and one floppy ear, short legs, an overabundance of whiskers, a perpetually wagging tail, and a huge scar down her side. He shook his head and reached for the eager animal, who promptly rolled onto her back.

"She's a shameless hussy," Mererid said.

"Wherever did you hear that?" Rhianwyn asked incredulously.

"Aunt Elspeth," the child replied.

"I should've known," Rhianwyn mumbled.

"Morrigan?" Broccan lifted an eyebrow.

"Had to keep with the Celtic legends." Rhianwyn returned the affectionate smile.

"I'll get our coats," Gwil called.

Rhianwyn froze. Broccan would guess the truth. She

should've told him when they were alone, but it wasn't something she could simply blurt out.

"You don't think we need coats, Mam?" Mererid eyed her closer. They were both damn intuitive. "The sun will soon set. We might catch a chill."

"Of course, go ahead, Gwil." Rhianwyn nodded.

She held her breath as their son came from the cottage wearing one and holding the other small leather coat she'd made from Broccan's long brown overcoat. The one he'd worn the day they'd met. The one he'd left behind. The coat she'd slept with when she carried their babies to keep his scent with her and wept into and clung to for so long wishing it was him holding her.

Gwil passed the smaller coat to his sister and they both put them on. Rhianwyn knew she'd weep soon. She had to be strong.

"Those are fine-lookin' garments," Broccan said. He looked at her, his expression dark and unreadable.

"Mam made them for us from our father's coat," Mererid replied.

There it was. The truth.

Broccan blinked, wordless, looking like he might pass out.

"Father's a brave knight off on a dangerous quest and been gone a long while." Gwil looked proud, beaming as he touched the coat lovingly.

"He's fighting fierce enemies and doesn't even know about us." Mererid sounded sorrowful.

"Mam believes he'll find his way back when he's done all the important deeds he must do," Gwil, always positive, replied.

The twins shared a hopeful look.

Rhianwyn wanted to turn away from Broccan's gaze, but she wouldn't. She hoped he saw the apology in her eyes, for she certainly saw the flash of understanding in his. That, and accusation. Every line in his handsome face told her that he'd been gut-punched. She prayed the children wouldn't be aware.

"You two come with me." Cassian must've noticed. "We'll start on ahead. I think your mother might like to tend to Lord Brockwell's injury. It appears he's limping."

The children went to her and grasped her waist tightly. She kissed the tops of their heads.

"Mind your sore arm, precious girl. And only one honey cake till after supper, my sweet boy. Stay together."

"I won't let them out of my sight," Cassian called back.

They were barely concealed by the trees when Broccan exhaled deeply. He ran his hand through his hair but didn't say a word.

She touched his arm hesitantly. "I'm sorry, Broccan. I didn't want you to find out that way."

"God's bones, Rhianwyn, you bore my children?"

She nodded.

"Did you know you were with child when I left?"

"We have much to talk about. Sit down, please."

"I don't want to sit, Rhianwyn." There was an edge to his voice. "I just want the truth."

"You *need* to sit." She opened the cottage door and went inside.

He followed and she pointed to one of the chairs at the

finely crafted wood table. She lowered herself to one. Looking like his injured leg wouldn't hold him, he sat, too.

His gaze didn't leave her face as she tried to think of a way to explain.

"I realized I was with child the day your ship sailed."

He maintained a forlorn expression. "I had hoped you'd follow me," he said, softly.

She shrugged. "You couldn't tell me you'd forgiven me, Broccan. You were set on leaving…"

"Compelled to go to my father when he was ill." His voice rose. "He requested my presence."

"I understand that. But you didn't ask me to come along."

"I s'pose I thought I'd insinuated it."

Rhianwyn blinked back the tears.

"In truth, I *did* follow you. Cassian, Cadfael, and Zachary insisted. Cassian actually threw me on the horse and accused me of being the stubbornest woman alive."

"He's not wrong," Broccan replied with a hint of a smile.

"On the journey…I began to suspect. With all that happened, I hadn't paid attention to my moon days. When I realized I hadn't bled for a time, I was already easily sickened. Smells made me spew. At the harbor the sight of the moving water caused disturbing nausea. I knew I couldn't possibly board a ship. It broke my heart watching your ship sail off."

Elbows on the table, her face in her hands, she recalled the mingled joy and sorrow of knowing she carried his child.

"But you…and Cassian?"

She sighed and touched her hand to her chest. "There was no message from you or even *of you* in all those years." She hoped her own voice wasn't too accusatory. "Some suggested I have you declared dead so I might remarry. Lilliana said as queen, she'd proclaim it so. But I never considered it. Not once."

Their eyes met and held.

"You probably should've." He blew out his breath, raggedly. "Cassian's a good man."

She shook her head. "Cassian has helped much with the children, but he married Heledd and is to be a father himself. My father and Matty have assisted, too. She's told Gwilym and Mererid stories about you. As have many of the knights and even Selena, Elspeth, and Lilliana at times."

"Sure I'm glad you weren't alone, then." His usually strong voice sounded strained.

She nodded. She wanted to admit she'd been heartsick for him every day and loathed that he'd missed out on so much with their children.

"You chose Welsh names," he said.

"Named for my mother and her father. But they're Gwilym Broccan William and Mererid Tara Radella Matilda."

He nodded his approval with a sad smile.

"You haven't even asked me where I've been all this time…or why I stayed away?"

She sighed again. "I suspect you haven't forgiven me…or that something more important kept you away."

"There's nothin' more important to me than you." He grasped her hand. "There never has been. I wished you'd sent word when you were with child or after they were born."

She shook her head. "When we were bickering so terribly, you said until I could put you first, our marriage didn't stand a chance. When I learned I carried your child, I knew I couldn't always put you first.

"Besides, after all that happened with the pact, there was so much animosity between us, Broccan. You'd barely meet my eyes. I reasoned if you came back...to me, I wanted it to be because you desired to do so. Not out of obligation. In my defense, I didn't even know where you were." She held out her hands in dismay.

"You said you were leaving for Tara, but when Cassian and Zachary went there, they couldn't find you. I even thought you might've created that story of your ailing father to have an excuse to leave."

"Christ's cross, I wouldn't have done anythin' that low!" He stood up and began to pace though he limped even more noticeably now. "Cassian and Zachary went to Tara?" He looked stunned.

"Against my wishes," she assured him. "I didn't know until they'd returned."

"Sure I was likely imprisoned then. Father *was* unwell when I arrived, but his illness was much exaggerated, to get me back to Ireland. When I refused to agree to take his throne, he had me dungeoned, thinking I'd soon see reason."

She grasped his hand. "I'm truly sorry, Broccan. That

must've been distressing. Did you escape?"

He puffed out his cheeks, then blew out his breath. "Father eventually died, and my brothers released me. They're more inclined to the throne of Tara anyway. After all that happened *here*…I've no fondness for magic."

She nodded. "I won't use magic or permit Father to do so near me or the children either…even though both are magically gifted."

"I've missed so much with them…and you, Rhianwyn."

"You stayed away a long while."

"I was imprisoned for some time. When released, I remained to help defend Tara from invaders. I was still undecided what I'd do next when Leofwine came asking for assistance with a distressing matter of interest to me. I worked with him searchin' for and dealin' with nefarious creatures. By then, I thought I'd waited too long—that you would've found someone else. I didn't want to disrupt your happiness."

"Why do you return now?"

"About nine moons ago I was nearly killed. Believing I'd die, I could think of nothin' but seein' your lovely face again. I took considerable time to heal—still haven't entirely—but I needed to see you, to know you're well."

The heaviness of the conversation was nearly palpable. Still, there were more difficult topics to discuss.

"Broccan, I don't want to tell the children the truth unless I know you intend to stay."

"Of course I'll stay." He pulled his hand away, looking insulted.

"How can you know you'll be content here? You said yourself you've never stayed anywhere long enough to settle down. I can't let my babies' hearts be broken should you wish to leave."

"They're mine, too, Rhianwyn...and hardly babies."

"I'd never deny you a relationship, Broccan, but there can be no hard feelings between you and me. I haven't told them anything about the trouble we faced. They believe they were created of a beautiful, mutual love between two people who longed to always be together...if you'd not been called off on a quest to save many lives."

"We *did* share a powerful love. It *was* beautiful and at one time nothin' could've kept us apart."

She nodded and stood. "Yet our children were conceived of anger and desperation...no love passed between us that day."

He lowered his eyes, looking ashamed.

"I regret that more than you know, but not them...or you, Rhianwyn. Telling them they were conceived of love wouldn't be untrue. No one shared a love as powerful as ours. I want them to know me as their father...to be a part of their life and yours in whatever capacity you'll allow."

She needed to be firm.

"Surely this comes as an immense surprise. Take time to dwell upon it, Broccan. This can't be a hasty decision."

He looked into her eyes and her heart fluttered. She sat down, weak at the knees.

"The three of us are content. We speak of you with love—always keep you in our prayers. But I've misled them. I fear when they learn much has been a falsehood, it could crush them."

"Then we'll tell them I *was* away on a quest but now I'm back to stay."

He knelt before her, wincing. Clearly, he was injured worse than he let on. "Let me remain here to get to know them."

She didn't reply but saw him closely observing her home.

"When you first left, I stayed in Keyon's cottage. I couldn't bear to be at the manor...without you. When the weeks turned to months, I realized you might never return. I was filled with sorrow and regret. But when I felt the child move within me, I feared our baby would sense my sadness and be born with a maudlin disposition. I had to make a happy life for the child.

"So, I had this cottage erected. Cadfael was a stonemason before he became a knight. Cassian and Everard helped, Chester, Fairfax, Winston, and Zachary all assisted, too. Even Keyon. Of course I didn't know I carried two babies then. Besides this kitchen and sitting area, there are only two bedchambers. I did insist on having hearths in each room and there's another small chamber where we bathe.

"We have the garden, cows for milk, butter, and cheese. Chickens for eggs and meat. Hogs, too. Horses for work and pleasure. We lead a simple, peaceful life, Broccan. The way I want it."

He stood unsteadily. "I promise I won't complicate your lives. If you'd rather I didn't live here. I'll stay elsewhere...at least for a while."

She closed her eyes, deep in thought.

"Have you a man in your life?" His jaw tightened.

"Do you mean in my bed?"

"I don't have the right to ask that."

"I promised the children there'd be no man unless I heard you were killed. But I've often thought it would benefit the children to have a father."

She saw his wounded expression.

"A father who's here always. But the knights have all been kind. Many have taken on the role of their father."

"But not your man?" He stepped closer and looked down into her eyes. She recognized the desirous expression.

"You should go. They'll be waiting. I doubt Dubh will let them lead him without you."

He pulled her to him, gently though she felt the tenseness of his brawny body.

"I wouldn't want to disappoint them when they're expectin' me, but we've much to discuss, Rhianwyn. Whatever becomes of you and me, we must make things right for our children. I want them to know I'm their father. Please tell me you won't oppose that."

"If you commit to staying…at least most of the time, then of course I'll tell them. But they're bright and intuitive. They'll soon discover the truth. They must be told before they learn it elsewhere. They do know *Sir Broccan* is their father."

"I gathered that when you gave your son my name…even if it is only a middle name." He attempted a grin, but she saw it was half-hearted.

"Come with me." She took his hand. "We'll take my horses. It looks like walking is painful."

CHAPTER TWENTY-TWO

T HROUGHOUT THE MEAL, Broccan couldn't keep his eyes off the children.

His children.

They were delightful and amusing, intelligent, and beautiful. Like their mother. So like their mother. If anything she'd grown more beautiful. She smiled so easily at the children. So proudly. He could see the fondness Cassian had for the children and her. Yet, apparently, he'd married Heledd, the Welsh woman who'd once been Princess Lilliana's lady-in-waiting.

The meal was delicious. Broccan hadn't tasted food like that since he couldn't remember when. They'd kept the conversation light. Talked about the horses and the comical-looking dog.

They spoke some of Matty and the children at Brockwell Manor Orphanage. Broccan didn't ask about the people he'd known during his time in Hengebury. Rhianwyn barely mentioned the other three women other than to say that they, even Lilliana, helped some at the orphanage and that Selena was a fine midwife. He didn't know who they'd married.

After the meal they'd fed the chickens and hogs, fed and milked the cows. The children were eager to show him everything. They helped get hay for Blath, the mare he'd brought from Ireland for Rhianwyn, and Gwynna, the tall white mare that once belonged to Prince Tyven. The stallion born of that mare, sired by Dubh, was an exceptionally fine animal.

Dubh and Gwynna seemed pleased to be reunited. Broccan almost envied the animals. There was only primal attraction—no emotions or complicated pasts to get in the way.

The children had clearly been taught early to help out, for they carried on with their duties with ease and no argument. They weren't shy around him. After the chores were done, they returned to the cottage for Haesel's sweet cakes.

Broccan already felt the warmth and hominess of the place and the love the children had been raised with. The hearth fire crackled comfortingly on his back as Gwilym and Mererid sat on a chair on either side of him. It seemed so easy. So right.

He shared some stories of his journeys, but he longed to be able to tell them more. He couldn't reveal his name...even though they bore his surname Mulryan—her name, too. He must be Lord Brockwell for now, even though he was far distanced from being a lord.

They knew he'd once been a knight. Thankfully they didn't ask his title. He could see Cassian found it difficult not calling him by name. As he consumed more ale, that'd likely worsen.

"You should be getting home, Cassian," Rhianwyn finally suggested, probably noticing his drunkenness.

Broccan had partaken in more than his share, too. He felt more relaxed than he had in an age. It did his heart good to be here with her again and to spend time with all of them.

"You, my darlings, must soon go to bed," Rhianwyn said.

Mererid made a face but neither child protested. Gwilym seemed especially good-natured. They pushed in their chairs and cleared their plates.

"We'll do dishes, Mam," Gwil said. "We usually do."

"We started supper later than usual. I'll tend to the dishes. Tomorrow night, you'll help."

"Where are you staying tonight?" Cassian asked with an unmissable chiding glance and waggling eyebrows.

Rhianwyn threw Cassian a reproachful look.

"I hadn't thought that far ahead. I s'pose I'll find an inn or maybe stay in a room above one of the taverns."

"There're spare bunks at the keep. We have an extra room at our cottage if you'd prefer." Cassian looked from Broccan to Rhianwyn. "Although you'd maybe like to stay longer. You and Rhianwyn have much to catch up on…being such good *friends* and all."

Rhianwyn tucked her lovely hair behind her ear, a sure sign she was angry or uneasy. Cassian didn't know her well, if he didn't catch that.

"Lord Brockwell could have my bed," Mererid offered, smiling. "I'll sleep with you, Mam."

Gwil agreed with a broad smile. "Merrie and I share a room, but we have our own beds. You and I could maybe talk more about knights." His eyes shone with excitement.

Broccan shook his head. "That sounds grand, Gwil, but

I couldn't put Merrie out of her bed."

Mererid shrugged. "I like sleeping with Mam. She doesn't mind when Gwil and me sleep with her even when there's no thunder or we don't have frightening dreams. She says she loves having us close and that one day we won't want to cuddle her any longer." She looked up at her mother adoringly with the same long-lashed eyes. "But I'll always want to sleep beside you, Mam."

By God, Broccan was thinking the same thing. He hadn't been with a woman in a long while. Rhianwyn had always enticed him more than any other. He'd thought his love and attraction to her might've faded, but being here made him want to be in her bed...even if it was *only* to hold her...even if his manhood was standing uncomfortably firmer than it had in some time. He was damn thankful for the table.

"If you overnight here, it would give you time to *talk*." Cassian smirked.

"Uncle Cassian, you're annoying Mam," Merrie warned.

Cassian grinned. "I should probably go before she throws something at me."

"I'd like to see that." Gwil laughed, blue eyes twinkling.

Now that Broccan knew the truth, he could see the boy looked like him. The shape of his eyes and the color. The blond hair still puzzled him although Rhianwyn once told him as a child her hair had been lighter.

"I'll start the dishes while your mam tucks you in?" Broccan suggested.

"*You* do dishes?" Gwil looked surprised.

"I ate the delicious food your mam served. The least I can do is help with washin' crockery."

"How come you talk like Grandmam Matty?" Mererid asked.

Rhianwyn met Broccan's eyes.

"I'm from Ireland, like Matty." Surely that didn't give too much away.

"Our father is, too," Gwil added. "If you're a knight, Lord Brockwell did you...?"

"I was a knight," Broccan interrupted the lad.

"Still are as far as I know." Cassian touched his own knight's pin. "You swore an oath and haven't been released from that."

Broccan looked at his friend. Would he hold him to that oath?

"Did you know our father, too, like Uncle Cassian?" Gwilym asked.

Again Broccan glanced at Rhianwyn. Now'd be the perfect opportunity to tell them. She lowered her head. Apparently, she didn't agree.

Cassian stood and reached over to tug on a lock of Mererid's hair.

"Stop that!" she said even as she giggled.

Then Cassian tickled Gwil and he laughed, too. He shook his finger at Cassian before both children embraced him.

Broccan was glad his old friend and one-time foe had been a part of their lives. Even though it should've been him.

Why didn't I come back earlier?

"I'll see everyone day after tomorrow at the wedding." Cassian's voice stirred Broccan from his regrets. "And you—" he pointed at Broccan "—better come to the knights' keep tomorrow. I've been looking to find a capable knight commander since my last two left the knighthood. Everard to become physician, Zachary to buy a damn pub."

"You might truly stay in Hengebury, Lord Brockwell?" the children said together. Both looked at Broccan, sounding hopeful.

"I'm thinkin' I'd like that, but I've not much interest in bein' a knight. Especially with this." He pointed to his knee, trying to ignore his other injuries.

"I'm sure it will heal if Rhianwyn tends to it. She's still the best healer and you were easily the best knight at training others. Severin always said so."

The children looked more curious about that and Rhianwyn appeared worried they'd soon put it together.

"Maybe we'll talk about that tomorrow," Broccan replied.

Cassian nodded and waved goodbye, closing the door behind him.

"Run along children; wash your face and hands and get into your nightclothes," Rhianwyn requested.

"I'll take the bucket and heat the water for dishes," Broccan said. "I'm happy to see you have an indoor hearth. When I met your mother, she didn't."

"We'll go with you," Gwil pleaded with hopeful eyes. Broccan could see that melted his mother's heart.

"I'll get the door." Mererid raced ahead and opened it with a delightfully sweet smile.

Rhianwyn pretended annoyance, but grinned. "As soon as you help Lord Brockwell with getting water, you *will* go to bed. I don't want churlish little children for Fairfax and Maisie's wedding."

Broccan shook his head in disbelief. "Fairfax and Maisie are bein' wed? Why, they're just children themselves."

"Not any longer," Rhianwyn said. "He's nine and ten and she's a year younger. I wasn't much older than her when we met." She sighed, then blushed, which made his heart race. Not to mention his constant cock stirrings. She was a beauty. Her hair shone in the firelight. She caught him looking at her and cleared her throat.

"Well…are the three of you going for water before the food on these dishes must be scraped off with a sword?"

Broccan laughed and the children giggled now, looking at his sheathed sword. Picking up the bucket, he whistled happily and followed Merrie and Gwil out the door.

RHIANWYN CLEARED THE dishes, dropping scraps in Morrigan's bowl outside the door. She heard laughter coming from near the stream and smiled. She'd waited years to hear that. The dog wolfed down the food and looked up.

"All right then, you wee beggar." She pulled more chicken off the bones. "But that's it. The rest is for soup tomorrow." She ruffled the dog's furry head and went back in, leaving the door open a crack. She piled dishes on the table by the basin, trying not to think of how fast her heart beat when Broccan was near.

The door burst open, the three of them still laughing. Gwil was on Broccan's back, arms around his neck. Broccan had one arm tucked under Gwil's leg, the bucket in his hand. Merrie was snuggled in the crook of his other arm. They looked so happy and so small against his large, muscular body.

She should've tried to find him.

She'd denied them all these years together. She couldn't still her tears and rushed off to her bedchamber, closed the door and bolted it.

BROCCAN SAW THE concern on the children's faces.

"What's wrong with Mam?" Mererid asked, lip quivering.

Gwil took his sister's hand but looked equally distressed.

"Sometimes people cry when they feel strong emotions," Broccan tried to explain. "Your mam was worried about both of you today, then relieved. It seems she helps out at the manor and does a lot here, too. She's probably weary. Adults feel weepy sometimes, too."

"Mam doesn't cry much," Mererid said. "She did when Radella died and when she had to give Champion the remedy that would made him sleep forever so he wouldn't be in pain."

"She weeps sometimes at night...when she thinks we don't hear," Gwil added.

"Because she's worried our father might never come back...or that he's dead," Merrie said.

Broccan's guilt surfaced again. How many times had she wept for him?

Gwil nodded. "She cried when Uncle Chester and Uncle Zachary had that big row and yelled at each other. When Uncle Zachary said some things could never be forgiven."

That was like an arrow piercing Broccan's heart. He'd never been able to tell Rhianwyn he'd forgiven her for agreeing to that pact. Now he knew a lot more about the old crone...more he must soon relate to Rhianwyn.

"Mam?" While he'd been musing, the children had pressed their ears against her door. "Mam, we'll hug you," Merrie offered.

"Your hugs always make us feel better," Gwil said.

They were tender-hearted children.

He heard the bolt being pulled back and the door opened. Rhianwyn's eyes were still damp, but she smiled.

"Are you weary from working too hard?" Merrie asked.

"Might we help you more?" Gwil reached for her hand.

"No, my babies, you help me very much...and you bring me endless joy. I am weary, but I'm also very happy. Now give me that hug and I'll tuck you in and sing for you...or maybe Lord Brockwell could. He has a grand voice."

"As good as Uncle Keyon?"

"Better," Rhianwyn said. "But don't tell Keyon."

They all laughed at that.

"Do you play the lute as well?" Mererid asked.

"I do." Broccan nodded.

"Could we let him play Father's lute, Mam?" Gwil looked hopeful.

Rhianwyn glanced at him, hesitating.

"I'm sure your da wouldn't mind," Broccan answered for her.

The children went off to collect the instrument. Rhianwyn leaned against the wall.

"I'm falling deeper into deception," she whispered. "I promised I'd never again deceive anyone I loved. Not after the pact and now…"

She began to cry again. He took her in his arms, caressed her fragrant hair and whispered Gaelic words of comfort…and love. She held him tighter and wept into his chest.

"You can't be holding me when they return," she whispered.

"Do friends not comfort one another?" he asked though what he felt for her had always been more than friendship.

She nodded, patted his chest, then dried her eyes. He stared down at her wanting desperately to kiss her but released her just before the children returned.

"Uncle Keyon's been teaching us how to play, too. When he returns, he's going to show us more." Gwil grinned.

"Maybe you could show us, also," Mererid suggested.

"Not tonight. Just one song and then you must sleep." Rhianwyn looked sterner.

She led them to the chamber and Broccan followed. He

saw two small beds each against a wall—the neatly sewn curtains and quilts. He envisioned her sewing them for their children. The odd-looking dog ambled in. Broccan took the lute and sat on the end of one bed. The children jumped on either side of him. Rhianwyn sat on the other bed where the dog joined her.

Like a family.

He strummed the lute, longing to sing the song he'd once written for her, but instead he sang something he'd learned as a child and now translated from Gaelic. The children grinned gleefully. Rhianwyn smiled at him with unmissable gratitude and perhaps love. He prayed that was true and not wishful thinking. When he finished, they asked for another song, but he wouldn't rile their mother. She'd said only one.

"Another time, if your mam permits, I'll be singin' more."

"I like how you talk. The way you say singin' and laughin' and such," Merrie mimicked.

"I do, too," Rhianwyn admitted, almost dreamily, but then stood. "It's well past bedtime."

Broccan leaned the lute against the wall. The children bounded into their beds. Rhianwyn pulled the covers over their shoulders, then kissed their cheeks while Broccan stoked the fire.

"Mam, may Lord Brockwell tuck us in, too?" Gwil asked.

"If you like. If he'd like?"

Broccan was flooded with such overpowering love and protectiveness, it nearly drove him to his knees. The dog leaped on Gwil's bed, so Broccan went to Merrie first. He fondly tapped her tiny shoulder, then placed a quick kiss on her tresses. She smiled at that. Then he went to Gwil, patted the boy's back, tousled his hair, then kissed his head, too.

"Good night, children." His voice thick with emotion, he cleared his throat.

How many nights had he missed this when he didn't even know they existed? He could've returned soon after he'd been released. He still would've missed their infancy and younger stages, but he would've had years with them. He'd had justifiable reasons for staying away, but this family would now be his only purpose.

When he looked up, Rhianwyn was no longer there.

"You were to sleep here, Lord Brockwell, and me with Mam?" Merrie said.

"I'll discuss it with your mother and move you to her bed, if she's agreeable to me spendin' the night."

"She will be," Merrie said. "You make her smile."

"You made her cry, too." Gwil frowned. "But you do light her fire."

By God. He hoped that was true. Could the child actually sense it?

"Gwil means you make the glow around her brighten...like Gwil and I do."

"No, Merrie, he makes her burn differently."

Broccan cleared his throat again. "I'd best let you sleep, or your mam won't permit me to visit again."

"Mam will likely make you bathe if you're going to sleep here." Gwil made a face.

"I am dusty from my journey." Broccan nodded.

"You do smell of horse." Mererid giggled and Broccan laughed, too.

He happily lingered as they said their good nights at least twice more before he left their door open a crack by their instruction, so the dog didn't scratch and wake them.

He glanced at the table. Dishes, already washed, were drying on a cloth. The door to Rhianwyn's bedchamber was open. He hesitantly peeked in, but she wasn't there. He looked in the other room. There was a large wooden bathtub, an iron basin likely for washing garments, a large cupboard, and a commode. Everything was tidy and clean.

Rhianwyn came up behind him and he jumped. By the light of the candle she carried, she'd been weeping again. How he longed to hold her.

"I'm heating the kettle for your bath."

"Your...er...*our* daughter told me I smelled like horse." He chuckled.

"She hasn't the politeness of her brother. I'm grateful she isn't afraid to state her opinion. As a female, she'll surely need that determination, but being the mother of a strong-willed child isn't always easy."

She opened the cupboard and pulled out a vial from a worthy collection, then glanced at him.

"Do you want herbs in your bath? I thought with your injury a hot bath with an herbal remedy would help."

"Why don't you offer healin' to others?"

She sighed. "I made an oath to Mam never to cause harm. I broke it several times. Therefore I heal my babies when needed, but..."

"You're a skilled and experienced healer," Broccan argued. "Many could benefit from that."

"Many do!" There was an edge to her voice now. "I taught midwifery to Selena and healing to Everard. He was always interested. After suffering one too many injuries as a knight, he requested to learn. Radella and Marlow assisted with his training.

"Besides, I vowed never to put myself in the position where I had to choose between saving someone's life and being a mother. *Always* they come first. I wasn't about to drag them out of their beds in the middle of the night to go with me or take them to Matty. I hadn't the luxury of someone staying here while I went to deliver a baby or save a life."

He detected a trace of bitterness in her tone.

"You're sayin' if I'd been here, you'd still be a healer?"

"I'm saying if you'd never come to Wessex in the first place, I'd still be a healer. If I hadn't fallen in love with you, I would've fought the rule to be married. I might've lived my life like Radella." She shook her head and tucked her hair behind her ear. "But I'd not trade my children for anything."

"Our children," he reminded her.

"Do you want the herbs in the water?" she asked again.

He nodded. "I'll go to the stables to get clean garments from my saddlebag."

"I'll get them if you wish," she offered, wiping her hands on her apron.

"I need some air anyway." He exhaled.

He was admittedly on edge, too. She'd always evoked

an array of feelings.

RHIANWYN'S MYRIAD OF emotions were unsettling. She was liable to scream or weep in earnest. She was happy, sorrowful, relieved. Grateful and resentful. Cautiously overjoyed and damn well desirous. For that she was the most annoyed. It affected her usually logical clear-headedness.

She'd filled the tub with three buckets of cold water and one large kettle of hot when he came back in with another kettle of boiling water and his saddlebag.

"If you leave your dusty garments on the chair, I'll wash them in the morning. I suspect Cassian will come fetch you. He's missed you. He said he must be cursed as far as best friends. He lost Anslem, Ulf…and you. I swear he searched for you for his sake as much as mine…and theirs." She gestured toward the room where the children slept.

"You needn't wash my garments," Broccan said.

She shrugged. "I'll be laundering ours. It won't put me out."

She started for the door but looked back. "I'm sorry if I seem short-tempered. It's been an emotional day."

"It has…and you didn't. If I were you, I might've tossed somethin' at me."

She smirked. "Enjoy your bath," she said closing the door.

He glanced at the bathtub wishing it was like the old days when they'd share a bath and heated lovemaking.

Those thoughts only added to his growing desire for her.

SHE WAS WRAPPED in a blanket sitting by the fire when he came outside. She glanced up offering a weak smile.

"Revelin' in some quiet time or avoidin' me?"

"A little of both," she replied. "Was the bath to your liking?"

"I feel much revived." He nodded.

"There's more tea in that small kettle. A cup just there and the jar of honey." She pointed. "Help yourself. I suppose you should familiarize yourself with the place if you'll be living here."

He snorted at that, and she grinned. He'd said those words to her when she'd come to the manor to try to talk him out of marrying her.

"How do you know I'll be livin' here?" He took a cup and filled it.

She took a long breath. "They already adore you and they don't even know the truth. You're clearly enamored with them."

"I'm completely enthralled and fascinated by them...like I've always been with their mother."

He sat not far from her, winced but tried not to moan.

"You should let me look at your wound."

"Maybe later," he said.

If he removed his breeches in her presence, he hoped it wasn't only for her to observe his injury.

She sighed again. "It isn't always easy being a parent."

"I didn't suppose it would be."

He moved a little closer, again smelling her fragrant hair. Feeling her warmth beside him, he willed his loins to settle. He almost put his arm around her but thought better of it.

"You've done well, Rhianwyn. They seem delightful, well-mannered children."

Her lovely full lips smiled broader, her eyes sparkling with love.

"They are delightful. Merrie isn't always well-mannered with her quick tongue. They're both beautiful; they're unusually intelligent and fast learners. They already read exceptionally well. Merrie's too stubborn and assertive at times—so feisty I long to shake her."

Broccan grinned. Their mother often made him feel that way.

"She can wrap her brother around her little finger and does. Gwil's perhaps too tender and placid. Submissive and kind-hearted, he gives in rather than causing a stir. Sometimes I swear, Mererid could be Elspeth's daughter and Gwil Selena's son."

"You do have contact with your friends then?" he asked.

She shrugged. "A little. I see them at the markets and the orphanage. Gwil and Merrie like playing with their children but we adults don't spend much time together. I suppose I can't let go of the past as I'd like."

He took her hand then.

"I was sorry to hear Radella passed. I know she meant a lot to you."

She looked into his eyes. He could see that loss still pained her.

"She became unwell. Likely from living in that damn cave. But she lived as she wanted, and she loved the children, like Matty does. Even Haesel dotes on them."

"Tell me, who did your friends marry?"

"Selena's wed to Everard. They adore one another and have a happy family. Her great-aunt, Fleta, takes their children when Selena attends to her midwifery and Everard to healing."

"Their children go to the brothel?" Broccan asked, thinking it unlikely.

"No. Fleta's given up the brothel. Sabina runs it now. Fleta lives in the cottage where Maxim once stayed. She says it makes her feel close to him."

"And Lilliana and Elspeth?" Broccan asked.

"Lilliana pined for Zachary for some time. She fell deeply in love with him—when she was Selena."

She closed her eyes and sighed, like the pact still haunted her.

"Lilliana married Winston. They seem a good match. She's still queen, and he remains sheriff. He's well liked and she's respected."

"The advisors or the people haven't demanded a king?"

Rhianwyn shook her head. "Thus far it's gone well. The kingdom is thriving. Lilliana listens to the people and her advisors. Oliver remains her head advisor and he's Elspeth's husband."

Broccan shook his head. "I wouldn't have believed they'd be compatible. Not that I'm an expert on that.

However, I did think her preference for women might make marriage difficult."

"I've heard that preference hasn't changed and Isolde, Elspeth's former lover, now widowed, *does* live with them. She's one of their servants. But I ask no questions and try to pay no heed to gossip. I suppose not everyone's notion of happiness is the same. I mostly mind my own. The children and I are content that way."

"What of Zachary and Chester?"

Her eyes clouded then and she squeezed his hand.

"They're still estranged. As Cassian said earlier, Zachary also gave up the knighthood. He borrowed coin from Brockwell estate to buy *The Fighting Cocks* tavern where I first met the brothers. He renamed it *The Knight's Escape*. He's recently married a young woman from that village. He's made it a respectable tavern. He's been successful, repaid the coin, and insists a percentage of his profits goes to the orphanage."

"I'm glad he's doin' well." Broccan sipped his ale comfortably, nudging a little closer. "And Chester?"

"He, too, borrowed coin. He owns a large boarding stable and horse-breeding business. He's also done remarkably well. The knights get their horses from him now."

"Is he…with Mirtha?" Broccan cringed mentioning her after all that occurred before he left. "Did they reunite?"

Rhianwyn turned away. "No. She never forgave him for being with Selena at the brothel, who was actually Elspeth of course. Nor did Zachary. It breaks my heart that twins, once so close, don't even speak. I think of Gwil and Merrie…how that might happen one day." She sniffed.

He touched her cheek. "But Zachary and Chester have no parents to ensure that doesn't ever occur."

She smiled at him through her tears. "Chester's now paired with Sir Wymund."

She glanced at him as if weighing his reaction.

He shrugged. "Some people are attracted to both genders. I hope Chester and Wymund are happy."

"I believe so. Chester wisely says he's drawn to what's inside a person," Rhianwyn said. "Still, he and Wymund must be discreet, for many people are intolerant of their union."

"I don't doubt that," Broccan replied.

"Chester and Fairfax remain close friends. Chester takes the less spirited animals to the orphanage for the children to ride."

With them sitting together talking, it seemed like no time had passed.

"What of Keyon?" Broccan asked. "He's never settled down?"

"Never. He visits often, but his wanderlust runs deep. Keyon was with Mirtha for a time. She went with him on some journeys. However, it didn't last. She found another man. And another. She's been ridden more than Chester's horses."

Sensing her acrimony, Broccan didn't reply.

Rhianwyn exhaled. "That was uncalled for and unkind. I shouldn't harbor such longstanding disfavor for Mirtha. She's had a difficult life. In truth, I sometimes thought of her in understanding why you might stay away so long."

He looked into her eyes by the firelight. "Rhianwyn,

please know I never felt anything for her, beyond temporary lust. I was angry and hurt, in a wretched dark place then and she was…"

"I must explain," she interrupted. "I still feel absurdly jealous of Mirtha. I reasoned, if after seven years, I can't let go of that resentment knowing the two of you spent one damn night together, how long might it take you to forgive me for the pain and havoc caused by the year of the pact."

"That was long ago." He placed his arm around her. She cuddled closer and lay her head against his chest, which made his heart soar.

"Mirtha stays at the estate sometimes, for she's prone to overdrinking. Fairfax still lives and works there, like Maisie. They're both very good with children. Matty's offered Mirtha employment, too, but she always declines. Maybe because she knows she'll run into me or won't accept coin provided by me. She's probably never forgiven me either…for breaking her nose."

"Are she and Fairfax still close?" Broccan asked.

"Sadly, no. Something happened between Mirtha and Maisie, and Fairfax sided with Maisie."

"Blood isn't always thicker when matters of the heart are concerned," Broccan said.

She looked up at him. Their eyes met and held. By God, he wanted to kiss her. She must've felt it, too—that powerful attraction. But she moved away, stood, took a poker, and stoked the fire.

"Fairfax still speaks fondly of you and will want you at their wedding. Merrie and Gwil are excited about attending. Therefore, we only have tomorrow to tell them. They can't hear it from anyone else. God's bones, I don't want them hurt, Broccan."

He moaned as he stood.

"Nor do I. I want a simple life, too, Rhianwyn. Adequate food, a warm place to lay my head. A good woman beside me. If she happens to be the woman I've loved for years, longed for endlessly, and the mother of my children…and if she loved me, too, then it would seem almost too good to be true. I'd be content here the rest of my days."

"But Broccan, you could be a king in Ireland."

"I rejected that life long ago."

"We've no servants." She was clearly trying to dissuade him.

"I've had no servants all these years. I've slept on the ground, hunting creatures most wouldn't believe existed and fighting battles that've left me weary, body and soul. An uncomplicated life would be much to my likin', Rhianwyn."

He took her in his arms again and she didn't resist. He stared down at her, hoping she'd tell him they *could* have that life together. But he saw doubt in her entrancing pale blue eyes.

"I'm nothing like I was when we met, Broccan. I was fiery and spirited then."

"I remember." He smiled.

"Christ, I wish I had more of that boldness now."

"I'm not the same man either, Rhianwyn." He gestured to his leg that even now barely held him and she didn't even know of his other injuries. "But it was this face I saw every night before I slept." He cupped her cheeks in his hands. "And these eyes I longed to look into when I wakened every morning. That love and longin' hasn't ebbed in all these years."

"I've mostly buried my longings, Broccan. I've been only a mother all this time."

"I'd never ask you not to be a mother, first. But I'll see your passionate desires return to how they were when we couldn't keep out hands from one another."

"I see your tenacity doesn't fail you."

He wouldn't tell her she'd shaken his certainty more than once. She shivered. How he longed to warm her. She lifted her face to him, and he placed a tender kiss upon her lips. She moved nearer, put her arms around his neck, and the kiss turned instantly torrid, their tongues met eagerly. By God, he ached to make love to her. Was it too soon? Would she think he pushed her?

She finally ended the kiss. "Bedding me probably wouldn't aid your injury," she whispered, already breathless.

He was about to tell her he didn't give a damn about his injuries when they were startled by approaching footsteps. He turned to see a tall young man.

"Hello, Rhianwyn, Sir Broccan," the lad said. "I heard you'd returned but I wanted to see for myself."

"Fairfax?" Broccan asked. He had the same straight blond hair, but the face and body of a man.

He nodded and came to Broccan who embraced the lad.

"You're here to stay, then, sir?"

"I am." Broccan gazed at Rhianwyn.

"I'm glad. You must attend our wedding. Maisie said she saw you at the manor. She's still a bit shy, but she's so damn perfect, Broccan. Lovely as a vision. I can't wait to be with her *always*."

He cast a somewhat accusatory glance at Broccan, too.

"I'll gladly attend your weddin' and look forward to meetin' Maisie, again. I must've seen her. Like you, she's obviously changed much."

"I'll let the two of you get on with catching up then." Fairfax winked. "Merrie and Gwil must be excited having their father home?"

"They don't know the truth yet, Fairfax." Rhianwyn's voice was strained.

"Best tell them soon, then. But I'll be off. Good to see you, sir."

"And you, lad." Broccan watched him set off.

"I feel like an old man, seeing him grown and in love."

"He and Maisie have been in love since the day they met," Rhianwyn said.

"Like you and me." Broccan smiled.

She nodded, hesitantly. "We should turn in. You must be weary."

"I'll sleep in your stables if you'd prefer."

"Not with that injury. Are you certain it's only your knee?"

"My back and hip are maybe less than ideal, too." He downplayed his extensive injuries.

"That happened from a fall off your horse?" She sounded doubtful.

He grimaced. "After I'd been run through with a sword and shot with…a few arrows."

She shook her head, her face now wrought with concern.

"I was always terrified I'd lose you because of the dangerous life of a knight. Gwil sees that as something he wishes to emulate. Please don't glorify battles and violence."

"I wouldn't!" He stiffened. "You permit him to spend time with Cassian who believes the knighthood is the only life. And it wasn't me who told them their father was a brave knight off fightin' enemies."

"I know," she sighed. "I had to think of something important enough to keep you away. I couldn't very well tell him their mother had entered into a dark magical pact that made her betray the only man she ever loved. And how did you put it? Destroyed the sanctity of our marriage by the sordidness of all that occurred."

He clasped her hand. "I was hurt and angry, Rhianwyn. I said and did a lot of things I'm not proud of. If only I could take them back."

"God, how I wish I could, too." She was weeping again. "Unfortunately, we cannot…even with magic." Her voice trailed off in a sob, like the regret came from her soul. "Now, I must go to bed. The children wake early."

"I need sleep, too." He reached for the bucket and doused the glowing logs. They sizzled and smoked. He poured more water until no more burned.

She walked to the cottage, and he followed. The dog waited inside the door, and she let him out.

"Stay close, Morrigan. No getting into trouble with wolves again."

She stood waiting for the dog.

"That's what caused the massive scar?" Broccan asked.

She nodded. "It took nearly one hundred stitches and endless prayers to save that dog. Merrie and Gwil would be heartbroken to lose her."

"Pain is the price of love," he said softly.

"I don't want them to learn that hard lesson at their tender age. Losing Champion was difficult enough and he was old, blind, and lame."

"But you have a fence." Broccan pointed to the stone structure surrounding the clearing.

"She digs beneath the stones," Rhianwyn explained.

Morrigan returned. The scraggly dog ran straight back to the children's room. Rhianwyn stepped in and Broccan followed. She pulled the bolt across the door.

"You have a lovely home, Rhianwyn."

"It is lovely." She looked around and he saw contentment on her face.

"I'll carry Mererid to your bed...if you like?"

She nodded, then blew out the candles on the table and in the sitting area. She pulled the screen across the hearth and closed the window coverings.

Not wanting to appear too familiar, he waited till she opened the door to the children's room. The twins were snuggled together in Gwil's bed with the dog already snoring at their feet.

"They do that often." Rhianwyn looked at them with adoring maternal love.

She covered them with the blankets, kissed them again, then motioned to the bed where Merrie had been earlier.

"I'll sleep here. You take my bed. You'll be able to straighten out your long legs."

"You can't give up your bed."

He wanted to suggest they share her bed even to sleep, but he wouldn't push especially when the children didn't know he was her husband.

They stepped into the corridor.

"If you still sleep unclothed, it's best Merrie doesn't get a lesson on male anatomy just yet." She smiled, then blushed.

"Not for maybe twenty years," he jested.

She seemed jittery when showing him inside her chambers. The bed wasn't like the one they'd shared at the manor. It bore no lavish canopy or tall posts. But it boasted a fine wooden headboard and was wider and longer than most. Had she had it crafted hoping he'd return?

She'd taken one weighty armoire from the manor. A large chest bordered the end of the bed. The hearth fire was flickering.

"There's wood in the andiron." She pointed. "More blankets in the chest, for no, I won't warm you this night."

She met his eyes and he grinned.

"You know my thoughts, Rhianwyn?"

"You are a man," she replied sassily.

He nodded. "This man's been some time without a woman…but as much as I long to bed you, even if you were willin', I'm not certain I'd be able."

Her eyes grew wider. "Your injuries are considerably…more extensive?"

She glanced at the front of his breeches then looked away, cheeks rosy.

She must be interested if that bore relevance.

He shook his head. "No damage there. You've well reassured me of that this day." He smirked. "But I'm not as young as I was, and I am weary."

"You're as damn appealing as ever." She smiled and grazed his cheek, which set him afire. "Good night, Broccan," she whispered.

The tenderness of her touch and her whispering his name made him remember how she'd done so when they'd shared intimacies. He'd missed that tender touch, the passion they'd shared. But even more, he'd missed that miraculous, soul-deep connection, the sense of homecoming he'd always felt in her arms. How could he make her trust him again? How could he convince her that he was here to stay?

"Good night, *Suile Gorma*."

She turned sharply and gasped. He hadn't used that endearment since he'd learned of the pact.

Blue eyes in Irish Gaelic.

She looked at him with anguish in those lovely eyes, and fled.

CHAPTER TWENTY-THREE

"WHY CAN'T WE wake him, Mam?" Merrie asked for the dozenth time, groaning and flopping upon the chair.

"Be careful of your wound, Merrie. I've just rebandaged it."

"He *has* been sleeping a long while." Gwil flashed a winsome smile so like his father's. It would undoubtedly charm women one day.

"He's injured and needs the rest," Rhianwyn said.

He used to rise early when they'd been together. They both liked to watch the sunrise. She didn't even know Broccan Mulryan now.

"How come you're making such a lot of food?" Merrie asked.

"Men eat more than women." Gwil was always logical.

"When was Lord Brockwell Lord Brockwell?" Merrie asked.

"A long time ago," Rhianwyn replied, mixing flour, salt, milk, and eggs.

"He has a grand horse," Gwil said.

"Dubh is a grand horse and sire of *Tywysog*."

The Welsh word for prince.

The children looked at each other with startled expressions. She hoped she'd never mentioned the name of his horse before when speaking of their father.

"Was Lord Brockwell's dog really Morrigan's father?"

Rhianwyn nodded. "Either Fionn or Oisin, for I've never seen other Irish wolfhounds near Hengebury."

"We've already set the table and done all our chores." Mererid kept looking toward the bedchamber. "He's been sleeping for an age. Why did you give him your bed?"

"Because you and Gwil were asleep, and I wanted to stay near you."

"Lord Brockwell's much larger than Mam," Gwil said. "He'd need a large bed. He's got big arms and must be very strong. He's even taller than Uncle Cassian. I've not seen anyone taller than Uncle Cassian."

"Ulf was taller," Merrie said. "You said so, Mam."

"Yes, he was."

"Is our father taller than Lord Brockwell?" Gwil asked.

She gulped a sip of tea. Fortunately Broccan stepped from the bedchamber, saving her from replying.

Rhianwyn tried not to be affected by his presence even as her heart sped. He glanced out the window to the sun's position, then at her and the children.

"You let me sleep half the mornin'!"

"Mam wouldn't let us wake you," Gwil admitted. "She said you needed rest because of your injury."

"I thought maybe you'd died," Merrie chimed in.

Gwil's eyes widened at that.

"Mererid Tara Radella Matilda Mulryan, I don't abide rudeness," Rhianwyn scolded.

"I thought I might've died and gone to heaven, too,"

Broccan said. "To sleep in such a comfortable sweet-scented bed. Then to wake to delicious smelling food and the laughter of children."

"Are you a charmer, Lord Brockwell?" Merrie narrowed one eye. "Mam says people who compliment others are often just charmers."

"Your mother's usually a good judge of character," Broccan said. "Good mornin', Rhianwyn."

He came up behind her as she took the biscuits from the rack above the fire and set them to cool. His closeness made her tremble. When she turned, he touched her nose. She jumped at the heat that innocent gesture sent through her.

"You had flour on your nose, Mam." Gwil smirked.

"You might have told me, you wee imps." She laughed.

They both giggled.

"Sit down, Lord Brockwell. The ham, eggs, and biscuits are ready. Merrie, please get the milk from the cool box and, Gwil, it's your turn to feed Morrigan later."

"I'll help with feedin' the other animals after we eat." Broccan waited for Rhianwyn to be seated before he put food on his plate.

Merrie and Gwil looked at each other, giggling again.

"Have I said somethin' amusin' then?" Broccan asked.

"We fed them all just as the sun was rising," Gwil said.

"Even your horse," Merrie added.

"Lord Brockwell's our guest and needn't assist with chores," Rhianwyn said.

Broccan met her eyes. There was disappointment in those amazing blue pools. Clearly, he didn't want to be referred to as a guest or Lord Brockwell.

"You've not eaten then?" Broccan asked.

"The children wanted to wait for you," Rhianwyn replied as the food was passed around. "After we break fast, we must have a conversation." Rhianwyn addressed the children trying to keep her voice steady.

The twins fidgeted nervously and looked at her, concerned.

"It isn't something to be distressed about."

They stared at each other again then said something unintelligible. Broccan glanced at Rhianwyn.

"Since they could talk, they've had their own language—even I can't understand. They only speak it now when they don't want me to know what they're saying, which is a bit rude." She eyed them closer.

Broccan said a sentence in Irish Gaelic and Rhianwyn smiled at their curious expressions.

"Do you know what he said, Mam?" Merrie asked.

Rhianwyn shook her head. "Only some. Maybe I could speak Welsh, your...Lord Brockwell, Irish, and you two in your twin language. We'd all understand very little."

"It would be an odd conversation." Broccan grinned.

"Our Lord Brockwell?" Merrie asked.

That child didn't miss a thing. Broccan met her eyes and nodded. Rhianwyn's heart squeezed.

"*Ti* or *mi*?" Broccan used Welsh words for you or me.

Rhianwyn reached across the table and grasped Broccan's hand. For strength? Solidarity? She knew not.

"It should come from me," she said.

Broccan nodded.

She took a long breath before beginning. "I told you your father was a knight off on a quest and that when it was completed, he'd one day find his way back."

The children bobbed their heads, eyes wide.

"Has our father been killed?" Gwil asked, worriedly.

Merrie rolled her eyes. "That would be distressing, Gwil."

"No, Gwil," Rhianwyn and Broccan said together, then she gestured to Broccan. Her eyes met his and she nodded.

"I have found my way back to you." Broccan sounded as jumpy as she was.

The children's eyes got bigger and bigger. They looked from Rhianwyn to Broccan and back several times, then at each other but spoke not a word.

"This is your father—Sir Broccan." She pointed to him.

Merrie beamed, which Rhianwyn wasn't sure she expected. But her brother remained solemn.

"Why didn't you tell us yesterday?" Gwil asked, his face pinched like he was trying not to weep.

Rhianwyn swallowed hard. "I wasn't sure how long your father would be able to stay. I didn't want to disappoint you if he had to leave straightaway."

"Do you?" Gwil asked, his eyes now filling with tears.

"No…I won't leave again," Broccan said.

"But a knight must go on many quests." Gwil stared at Broccan, unblinking.

"You didn't even know about us? How can you be sure you'll want to stay?"

"Because I love your mother very much and I'm honored to know she gave me two children as bonny and bright as you and Merrie."

Merrie smiled again, climbed upon Broccan's lap, and put her arms around his neck. He held her close, patted her back, and looked at Rhianwyn with obvious joy. But Gwil remained sitting...tears slowly falling. Rhianwyn crouched beside him and took him in her arms.

"Gwil, I know you're worried things might change, and they will, of course, but for the better. Your father's a good man. He'll care for us. I believe that with all my heart."

"I swear that's true, lad," Broccan affirmed.

"I have to feed Morrigan." Gwil squirmed from her arms and rushed to the door, then came back for his uneaten food before closing the door behind him with rather a slam.

Even Merrie looked surprised.

"Should I go after him?" Broccan asked.

Merrie shook her head. "Gwil's not like me. I'm quick to become excited, angry, or frightened. He's quiet and brave. It takes more to upset him, but longer for him to calm."

Rhianwyn nodded. "We'll give him some time. Then you should go to him, Broccan."

"I'm very happy you're my father." Merrie kissed his cheek. Rhianwyn could see that moved Broccan. He swallowed hard.

"In Ireland children sometimes call their fathers da."

"I like that." Merrie smiled. "Now, I'll go tidy up so you and Mam can talk or...kiss." She scrunched her nose.

"But you haven't eaten, Merrie," Rhianwyn said.

"I'm far too excited to eat Mam…and Da." She threw them a sweet smile before closing the door to her room.

Broccan inhaled.

"Christ's cross, how do you bear it, Rhianwyn?"

"Bear it?" She cocked her head.

"How their feelin's become yours? How our hearts are intrinsically connected?"

She smiled and came to sit upon his lap and put her arms around his neck as their daughter had just done. "It's an innate overpowering feeling. I've had years to accept and sometimes, still, it overwhelms me," she admitted stroking his hair affectionately.

"Should I go talk to him?"

Rhianwyn took Broccan's hand again.

"Soon. He'll be embarrassed he wept in your presence. He doesn't even like me to see him cry. He tries to behave as a wee man even though I've hopefully never imposed that burden upon him."

"I suppose that was my fault. Sure he's thought he had to be the man of the house from the time he could think."

"You're here now." She caressed his jaw.

He grasped her hand and kissed it, then blew out his breath again. She moved and he stood, uncertain.

"He's our son not yet seven years old, Broccan, not a foe you're facing in a competition or in battle."

"Bloody hell that might be easier. At least I'd know what I'm doin'."

"Think of when you were a child and attempt to empathize. It sometimes helps me."

"You're a wise woman, Rhianwyn Mulryan."

"I feel a bumbling fool much of the time."

"You make parenthood look effortless, *Suile Gorma*," he said.

She kissed him fiercely then. "Gwil will be in the stall with Tywysog. That's where he seeks comfort."

Broccan nodded and trudged out the door.

THE LAD WAS brushing the tall black stallion with the white star on his head.

"You've a way with horses, like your mother," Broccan said.

"Mam says that I got that from my...from you." He scowled.

That wasn't a good sign.

"Mam has lots of men who want her, you know."

Broccan cleared his throat. "I suspect that's true. Your mother's a special woman. She's beautiful, kind, and intelligent."

"Then why did you stay away so long?"

The lad wasn't going to make this easy.

Broccan exhaled. "At first, I couldn't return. I was imprisoned. Afterward I helped a friend hunt some...sinister people. Then I thought I'd stayed away so long that your mam would've found someone else. I didn't want to disrupt her happy life."

"If you'd known about Merrie and me, you would've come home sooner?"

The boy pulled his hand through his hair. Obviously, a

habit inherited from him even though he'd never known him till yesterday.

"I would've come back as soon as possible." Broccan stepped closer but that brought a deeper scowl from the boy.

"You think we're more important than Mam?"

Bloody hell, he couldn't say anything right.

"Your mother's the most important person in my life. I love her beyond measure. I should've returned sooner. I would've if I'd known about you and Merrie, for I suspect she's needed help raising two children alone."

"Sir Cadfael loved her, but Mam asked him to return to Welshland. Uncle Cassian would've married her because he thought you'd died, but Mam said he should wed Heledd. She told them both her heart would always belong to you. She won't even dine with Sir Finley and he has loads of women wanting him. He's so besotted, he looks like he'll fall over when he sees Mam."

How did the child know all this?

Broccan inhaled deeply. "I'm proud to know she was loyal and waited for me."

"If you hurt Mam, I swear I'll…" His small fist curled. He sniffled, then wiped his nose with his sleeve.

"As a knight, I swear I won't. If she'll have me, I'll do everythin' I can to make sure your mam's only ever happy. And you and Merrie, too."

The lad sighed, then smiled. Broccan was damn relieved when he permitted Broccan to embrace him. Then they both tended the horses, giving them time to talk.

BROCCAN WENT TO the keep with Cassian, shared some ale and conversation with the other knights, watched them train for a while, but couldn't wait to get back to Rhianwyn and the children.

Once he was there, they shared another meal together and did the evening chores as a family again. It all seemed perfect. They'd tucked the children in for the night and sat together watching the hearth fire and listening to the steady rain outside.

"Are you tired, Broccan?" She glanced at him, shyly.

He stood and went to her. "No, but I am after goin' to bed." He grinned.

"You go on ahead. I'll join you soon."

He wasn't certain that sounded like her intentions were what he'd hoped for.

RHIANWYN NERVOUSLY SET about doing menial bedtime tasks. She'd gone out with the dog, locked the door, blew out the candles, placed the screen across the fire. She was procrastinating. She knew she wanted him. The thought of sharing intimacies sent shivers throughout her body. Why then, wasn't she in there now tearing off his garments?

Holding a candle, she looked in on the children, fast asleep, contented smiles on their faces. She entered her bedchamber to find Broccan sitting on a chair fully attired. Candles still aflame. She'd hoped he'd be in bed with the room barely lit. Their eyes met and held. The way he was staring at her with hungry eyes already made her weak at the knees. He was a gloriously handsome man. Time had only made him more appealing.

He stood appearing uncertain, too. She took a breath and went to him. He wrapped her in his strong arms, his manly scent caused delightful tingles head to toes and especially between her thighs. He lowered his mouth to hers. His warm lips on hers heightened her desires considerably and when his kisses trailed to her neck, she gasped. His worthy arousal pressed against her belly.

"Wait, Broccan," she said, breathlessly.

"Wait?" He sounded tortured. "I don't know that I can with you here lookin' so sensual and smellin' so lovely and feminine. Christ's cross, I need you, Rhianwyn."

"But I must tell you something."

He ran his hand through his hair and stepped back. "That sounds ominous."

"Not really, but…well…I've not been with a man since I was with you."

He eyed her as though doubting her words.

"It's true."

"You're a damn desirable woman, Rhianwyn. It makes me somewhat sorrowful that you haven't known carnal pleasure in these years."

"You'd rather I'd shared my bed with several men then?"

His jaw tightened. "Well no, I'm glad you didn't take a slew of men to your bed." He exhaled and looked away.

"You look like you have something to say that you

think I won't want to hear," she said.

He nodded. "I won't insult your intelligence as a woman or a healer by sayin' I've not been with other women those years away."

"I thank you for that…I think."

"But there haven't been many, and it was never anything but stillin' a base need…and there's been no one for some time."

"You needn't explain," she said.

He was a man with healthy needs and women were always ready and willing to go to his bed.

"You've not been tempted to be with young Sir Finley? Although he seems barely more than a whelp."

He sounded jealous.

"You met him?"

He nodded. "Today at the keep. He's tall and brawny but sure he's barely able to shave."

"I believe he's four and twenty so hardly a whelp and I don't much care for beards." She glanced at Broccan's stubble, and he placed his hand to his chin. "I haven't been tempted. But Broccan, you need to know not only have *I* changed, so has my body. I've carried two babes within me—nourished them at my breasts. I won't look the same." She lowered her eyes.

"Woman," he said, his voice husky with arousal. "You are ravishingly beautiful. You've always enticed me like no other. I did recognize your soul after all, no matter the body."

Her heart soared and joyful tears flowed. He could have said nothing more reassuring. She nodded and smiled happily.

"Besides," he added, "when you see the scars I bear, you'll know I've not the body I once claimed."

"Nonsense," she whispered, her hands roving over his taut, muscular chest and arms.

She helped him pull the tunic over his head and stared at the lengthy, raised scar caused by a sword. It ran from his belly around to his back. The others, on his right shoulder and near his left nipple, must be from the arrows.

"Oh, Broccan, my love!"

"I told you," he said.

"How strong you are to have lived through that, my gloriously handsome warrior," she whispered, and he hastily removed her garments. She untied his breeches, and he tugged them off. There was another raised scar on his thigh. How had he survived such brutal wounds?

"It must've been an accomplished healer who attended these merciless wounds?"

"An old woman who made Radella seem congenial." He smiled. "But I was determined not to die without coming back to you."

He stood gazing at her.

"You're stunningly beautiful, Rhianwyn. Your breasts still firm." He touched them and she quivered. "Your nipples wonderfully pert." His mouth went to one and her knees went weak. "Your lovely hips perfectly round." He touched her backside and she gasped.

"Broccan, I need you!"

He placed his hand between her thighs, probing intimately, and she cried out, trying to be quiet. "I have missed you...and your touch." Her arousal was heightening.

She tensed on hearing whining.

"Is that the dog?" he asked, incredulously.

"Yes."

"But you just let her out."

"I did." Rhianwyn kissed him again, soon lost in their passion.

"I wanted to take this slow, enjoy every caress, for I've dreamed of this since we were parted," Broccan rasped.

"Next time we'll be slow," she panted, fondling his manhood till he moaned. "But just now I need you...inside me."

They went to the bed, held each other, and were soon joined. Rhianwyn gasped at the long-missed sensation. They stared into each other's eyes, her hips rising to meet his thrusts as they blissfully moved together, when they heard the door open.

Broccan froze and his eyes widened. "Bloody hell," he said under his breath. "I suppose we should've pulled the bed linens over us."

"Or locked the door," she whispered, then looked at the child standing there wide-eyed.

"Merrie, you should've knocked," Rhianwyn chastised, gently.

Their daughter stood unblinking. "We've never had to knock before."

I should've set some new rules with Broccan home.

"Mam, are you and Da...making a baby? Wouldn't he have to be behind you?"

Broccan coughed and pulled the bedcovers over them

before moving off her. Rhianwyn stood, trying to still her heaving breasts and reached for her shift. "Merrie, what is it?"

"Morrigan did a huge liquid shite on Gwil's bed." Merrie held her arms out indicating a large amount. "She must've been eating deer shite again, for it's full of berries."

Rhianwyn sighed. "Oh, that wee nuisance. I'll let her outside then clean up the mess."

"But that's not all, Mam. When Gwil and I tried to clean it up, Gwil spewed. Now Morrigan's eatin' Gwil's sick and it's…makin' me want to spew." The child gagged.

Because Merrie said it with an Irish lilt, Rhianwyn had to fight a laugh as she reached for the basin and held it for Merrie, who did indeed spew.

"Oh, sweet girl, you'll feel better now. I'll go to Gwil and get this all sorted."

"*We'll* get it sorted," Broccan said and Rhianwyn threw him a grateful smile.

She looked back at him as she started out the door. "Still want this uncomplicated life," she whispered, and he chuckled.

"I'll put on my breeches and be there straightaway."

THEY CLEANED THE messes, changed the bedding, and bathed Merrie who'd gotten vomit in her hair. With the children's and dog's stomachs hopefully settled with remedies, she asked Broccan to take the exhausted children to the larger bed in their bedchamber. She placed the soiled linens to soak in the washtub.

She peeked in to see them all already asleep. The sight of her man's large arms around them, their small bodies pressed to his chest, the mutt at the end of the bed, brought tears of happiness. She didn't have the heart to wake them to take the children to their own beds. Instead, she found a spot on the very full bed and curled up with them.

CHAPTER TWENTY-FOUR

THE NEXT DAY Broccan took the twins to the manor to see Matty so Rhianwyn could get ready for the wedding at her leisure. Once there, they met a group of children. Excited, Merrie and Gwil asked to stay, and Broccan had just left them playing in the fenced yard when Fairfax called to him.

"I'd like to ask a favor, sir."

Broccan joined the young man near the hawthorn. "If I can oblige, I will."

"I know well enough, I owe you my life. If I'd remained in that Mercian city, I'd be dead or maybe only wish I was. You taking me and Mirtha, all those years ago, likely saved us both. Maisie was surely spared an equally disturbing fate if she'd remained at the castle. Though I do wish Mirtha were as happy as me and Maisie." The young man wore the same strained expression he often did as a child. "Anyway, I'd like you to stand with me when I'm wed."

"I've been away a long while. Sure there's another to whom you'd give that honor?"

"I want you." Fairfax seemed firm.

"Then it'll be my privilege. You've grown to a fine young man, Fairfax."

"Rhianwyn says I still swear like an uncivilized Mercian." He snorted.

"Some things never change." Broccan laughed. "Might I ask you a favor in return?"

"Anything!" Fairfax pushed his hair from his eyes.

"After your weddin' is through, for I'd not want to take away the attention from you and Maisie on your special day, I was wonderin' if you'd mind much if Rhianwyn and I were rewed? I want to surprise her and renew my pledge to her."

"Mind?" Fairfax shouted. "I'd be delighted. Maisie, too. She adores Rhianwyn. As do I. She's been so good to both of us. We've seen her lonely these years. Knowing you'll be together as a family would be a grand wedding gift."

"I'll talk to the priest then."

"Has Rhianwyn agreed?"

"She's agreed for us to be together but doesn't know I intend to repeat our vows today."

"Sardin' hell, Broccan. She'll need to find a gown."

"She'll be wearin' a gown. She'll not be naked."

"Now that'd be a sight!" Fairfax jabbed Broccan with his elbow.

"You wee shite. I hope your days of lookin' in windows at women are well over."

Fairfax's face turned ruddy. "It was only just the once and that was nearly a decade ago. I've my own lady, the loveliest by far."

"I'm happy for you, lad!" Broccan clapped him on the back.

"Well enough of that sarding sappy shite. I'm off to get ready."

"Christ's cross, Broccan Mulryan, of course Rhianwyn must be told," Matty said after he'd discussed his intentions with her. "I'm dearly happy for the two of you. But she'll want to find a gown to her likin', not one she'd wear to someone else's weddin' no matter that she adores those two young people as much as I. *We've* both been here to see them grow up."

"Matty, you've thrown in quite enough snide remarks for me to know you're displeased I stayed away so long."

She placed her hands together. "You're back now. Thank the Lord your wife's the forgivin' sort and willin' to have you."

"I'm relieved of that, too." He exhaled. "And the gown she's wearin' has much meanin' to both of us."

Matty wore a serious expression. "Broccan?"

"Yes, Matty." He was suddenly worried what she might say.

"Have you told Rhianwyn you've forgiven her? For whatever occurred that split you apart?"

He inhaled deeply, released his breath, and shook his head.

"Is it only because you've not said it?" Her weary eyes and careworn face spurred him to reply.

"I came back, didn't I?"

"You won't ever be happy with that hangin' over your heads."

He didn't even like thinking about what had caused the need for forgiveness.

"If you haven't forgiven her, then be on your way. Let her go to Welshland to Cadfael, for the man loved her fiercely...or let her make a life with young Finley. He'd move heaven and earth for her. Sure she'll sense your unwillingness to forgive, and it'll tear at her heart as it has for years."

"I intend to do it," Broccan said.

"*Only* if you can say it truthfully."

Matty was correct. The thought of disappointing Rhianwyn and those two precious children gutted him. Besides, he had to ask forgiveness of her, too. Now he had to set a plan in motion and talk to four women.

"RHIANWYN," HE CALLED entering the cottage.

"In here," she replied from her bedchamber. "You were gone a while."

He found her standing in a flimsy shift and wearing a damn seductive smile.

"God's nails, you're not attired."

She looked a bit wounded at his reaction.

"When you said you were taking the children to Matty, I presumed we'd finally share a bed since we were interrupted last night."

She stepped toward him. The sight of her nearly took his breath away and the scent of her hair made his cock-stand damn unignorable.

"We're both freshly bathed and alone. Shouldn't we take advantage?" She winked, kissed his throat, and reached for the fastenings of his breeches.

"By God, you're a sensual woman," he said, but then looked away.

"Broccan, is something wrong?"

"I must request somethin' of you."

She shrugged. "I've agreed to don the light blue gown that I wore when we were wed."

He saw it hanging on the armoire freshly pressed.

"I have another request."

"Not one I'm likely to favor since you'll not meet my eyes."

"I want you to come to the sunstones with me."

She stared, looking deep in thought, then shook her head. "I've not been there since that night when you were so displeased after you learned the truth. When I felt your fury to the core of my being, to my very soul. It hurts even still when I…"

She stopped speaking and bit back a sob.

By God, he loathed distressing her. He took her in his arms and held her as she wept.

"I don't want you sorrowful, Rhianwyn, but I need to go there to tell you somethin' and…"

"Tell me something?" Her voice rose. "Just tell me here…anywhere but there. I've never even permitted our children to go to that location despite their many requests. I won't risk meeting up with that bloody old crone."

"I've asked Selena, Elspeth, and Lilliana to be there, too."

She left his arms. "All the more reason not to go. It would bring it all back."

"It saddens me you're no longer friends when you were close since girlhood."

"We're friends of a sort. You once told me that I must put you first for our marriage to have any hope. That's partly why I couldn't follow you to Ireland when I knew I was with child. As to my friends, I never wanted to be put in the situation where I'd have to choose. My children...and you, will always come first."

"As mothers themselves sure they'd know you'd never choose anyone over your children?"

"They all damn well expected me to choose that infernal pact. But worse still, I went along with it."

She tucked her hair behind her ears. It was just as well Matty had the children—that Merrie and Gwil didn't see their mother maudlin. Gwil would think he'd hurt her when he promised he wouldn't.

Rhianwyn narrowed her eyes. "You meet them there if you like. But I won't go."

"You must all be there, my *Suile Gorma*."

Her eyes flashed stormily. "You think calling me that will change my mind?"

"I hoped it might," he admitted. "I wouldn't ask if it wasn't important."

"Did the others say they'd be there?"

He nodded. "They were reluctant, but each agreed."

"I suppose you still have the ability to charm them, too."

"I don't usually attempt to charm women nearly about to give birth," he muttered under his breath.

"I'll go on one condition."

He stood waiting, wondering what the condition might be.

"Make love to me first."

He hesitated.

"You don't want to?"

"What? No, I mean yes…of course, there's nothin' I'd like more. After last night I'm still nearly mad with desire. Bloody hell, woman, I think of lovin' you constantly. But we'll have tonight together, for Matty said the children can overnight with her."

He could see her hackles rising. "But I haven't spent one night parted from them."

"Then it's clearly time, Rhianwyn."

"You can't just make that decision." She put her hands on her hips.

"I am their father." His own ire was piqued.

She turned and began rebuking him as she attired herself. "After years away without a word, making we worry endlessly, looking to the west every damn morning wondering if that would be the day you'd return…or the day I'd hear you'd been killed."

He watched her pull on her petticoats, stockings, and boots. She reached for her gown and angrily pulled it over her head and tied her laces.

"You simply march back into my life in all your masculine glory, charming me and the children—making decisions. And now…you'd rather go to the damn sunstones than bed me."

She glanced in the looking glass at her hair, then walked out of the bedchamber and started for the door.

"Never mind. Go talk to the others; I'll head to the manor."

Angry and impassioned himself, he stood blocking her way.

"Are you through with your wee rant then?" he asked.

"For now." She let out a breath.

"Bloody hell, Rhianwyn, your temper and feistiness haven't changed in these years."

"Actually, I've been much calmer without your unsettling presence in my life."

"Dispassionate you mean?" he snapped.

She shrugged, took her cloak, and went out the door.

"Rhianwyn." He grabbed her arm, gently pulled her back inside, then closed the door and held her against it. "Listen to me, woman."

She glared.

"Christ, Rhianwyn, I wanted to surprise you by repeatin' our weddin' vows this day, but there's somethin' I need to tell you and it must be done inside the circle of standin' stones."

She wet her lips. "You might've asked and not simply presumed I'd go along with restating our vows."

"I actually thought you'd find it romantic." He exhaled and released her from his grip.

"You must understand, Broccan. I'm accustomed to making decisions. For the orphanage, the home for abused women, and certainly for the children and myself. I'll have to accept that you'll make some decisions, or we'd make them together. But we don't even know if we'll be compatible as a couple, much less as parents."

He held his hands out before him, at a loss how to convince her. "We were very happy together until the pact."

"We were consumed in lust and sarding each other senseless most of the time back then," she said. "We don't know that we can maintain a lasting relationship."

"Our love endured hardship, disparity, and years of being parted. Do you honestly believe we can't be happy together? I know we can make it work. We're both damn determined. I love you even more than I did then."

"I feel the same about you." She nodded, grazing his jaw. "You did well in the rough introduction to parenthood last night…an initiation by fire."

They smiled as their eyes met. He had cleaned up spew, and washed Merrie's hair well covered in it.

"I was thinkin' we'd be more relaxed if we were alone and had the whole night together. That damn wee dog can sleep in the stables."

They laughed together then. "She'll sleep at the manor with the children. Matty has a soft spot for dogs and children. But now, let's go to the sunstones if we must."

"Let them wait a bit," he said, before kissing her ardently.

She ended the kiss, both of them already breathless. "We'd be late for the wedding. We'll continue this later."

"If I can wait that long." He grinned and took her hand.

They walked together, but as they crossed the open plain toward the stone formation, Broccan saw how pale she'd become.

"We'll not stay long," he promised.

STEPPING INTO THE stone circle, Rhianwyn closed her eyes, fighting tears.

"I have so many regrets that began here," she whispered.

"You convinced her to come?" Elspeth said on seeing them. "I thought if Rhianwyn knew we'd be here, she'd refuse."

"Ladies," Broccan nodded, greeting them. "Thank you for meetin' us."

Rhianwyn noticed the other women's uncertainty, too. Even Lilliana and Elspeth looked nervous.

"Hello, Rhianwyn," Selena called as she approached.

"Hello, Selena, Elspeth, Lilliana," Rhianwyn said.

"Have any of you been back here since the pact ended?" Broccan asked.

Elspeth nodded. "Only once."

"I've had the royal carriage take me by a couple of times," Lilliana said.

Selena shook her head. "I never wanted to return. Much sadness happened for you, Rhianwyn, because of the pact."

"Not only for me," Rhianwyn replied. "For Broccan, and all of you. So much pain and loss."

"The one time I came here I was hoping to summon the old crone," Elspeth admitted.

Rhianwyn blanched. "Why would you desire to see her again? Don't you loathe her?"

"I wanted to know why she did it," Elspeth explained.

"Surely you're all curious?"

Twisting her hair, which Rhianwyn hadn't seen her do in years, Selena shook her head. "I just wanted to forget."

"Back then, I could only dwell on how aversely it affected me," Broccan said. "I know some of what you've all suffered." He motioned to the four women. "Of course I can't know it all." He looked at Elspeth. "But I believe you lost Ulf and Agnes at least in part because of the pact and didn't get to say farewell to either."

Elspeth's usually stoic face and countenance faded. Her eyes became sorrowful, and her shoulders slumped.

"Ulf's last words were of his love for you, Elspeth," Rhianwyn said. "I should've told you before."

Elspeth shook her head. "You tried. I didn't want to hear. It hurt too much."

Broccan looked at Selena next. "I've learned Maxim was your father and not only did you never get to know him, you didn't even know of your connection till after he was killed."

"That's true and I'm much regretful." Selena wept openly.

"And you, Lilliana, missed bein' with your father when he died."

"He said he loved you and felt he'd failed you." Rhianwyn touched Lilliana's hand and she sighed.

"She even missed her own damn coronation." Elspeth snorted and jabbed the queen with her elbow.

"And my first time being with a man while in my own body," Lilliana admitted.

At that Rhianwyn and Broccan looked at each other

somewhat sheepishly.

Lilliana sobered. "The first man I was with was Godric."

They all shuddered remembering that horrid man.

"Rhianwyn had to break her healer's oath never to hurt others," Selena continued.

"And my oath to you, Broccan."

Lilliana stared at him. "Surely you must've suspected things weren't as they should be when I took my season as Rhianwyn? Even after I lied and told you the magical occurrences causing the soul switches were over?"

"I think I didn't want to know." Broccan shook his head. "I just preferred to believe things were back as they once were for Rhianwyn and me."

"We shouldn't have envied our friends' lives," Selena said, looking tearful again.

"We should've seen the blessings in our own," Elspeth whispered.

"All of us would've done a lot of things differently if we'd known the outcome," Lilliana said.

"We learned a terribly hard lesson from the pact," Rhianwyn admitted. "But I will loathe it and the crone till the end of my days."

They each nodded sorrowfully.

"But why are we here, Broccan?" Elspeth asked impatiently, holding the small of her back. "I can't stand forever in this condition."

"We all have a wedding to attend," Selena, reminded them, looking equally uncomfortable with her very round belly on her tiny frame.

Broccan looked at Rhianwyn. "I want you to summon the old crone."

"I will not!" she refused adamantly.

Why would he dare ask that of her?

"I assure you it'll ease your minds and give you closure...and me, too." Broccan gazed pleadingly into her eyes.

"Rhianwyn doesn't even have her stick or wand or whatever the hell that was." Elspeth shrugged.

"She doesn't need the wand; she never did," Broccan replied. "Rhianwyn has powerful magic."

Lilliana's dark eyes were serious. "Even if that's so, none of us summoned the crone that autumn night."

Broccan took a breath. "She wasn't summoned, but purposely came to you. I finally discovered the truth during my travels. When I was nearly killed some moons ago, I had two main regrets. That I wouldn't get back to Rhianwyn to tell her I loved her and that I'd forgiven her." He took her hand and her eyes filled with tears.

"And that I know who the crone is and why she did what she did."

"That's more than two regrets." Elspeth rolled her eyes.

"If we stated all regrets, we'd be here till well after our babies are born." Lilliana sighed, rubbing her own swollen stomach.

Broccan touched Rhianwyn's shoulder. "Please summon her."

"You could do it," Rhianwyn said. "I've seen your magic, too."

"Believe me, she won't want to see me," Broccan replied.

They each looked at Broccan, questioningly, but Rhianwyn finally agreed.

Holding her hands before her, she spoke. "Come to us now, magical crone. Grant this last request and our association with you will finally be done."

Rhianwyn tensed, despising the thought of seeing the old woman.

The stones began to glow and rumble, bringing it all back and Rhianwyn longed to run away. When a glowing circle appeared, they shielded their eyes. They were startled to see a man accompanied by a woman in chains. Her face was covered by a hood.

"This is Leofwine," Broccan introduced. "He's a soul seer and bounty hunter of unnatural beings."

"Hello, Broccan. It's good to see you again." Leofwine nodded. "I've missed your company all these many months since you were injured. I'm glad to see you've recovered and pursued your heart's desire."

Broccan nodded and took Rhianwyn's arm. "This is my wife, Rhianwyn."

They shook hands and Leofwine gaped at Rhianwyn. "You have powerful magic, woman!"

She shrugged. "I've turned away from magic."

"These are the other women once involved in the pact," Broccan said to Leofwine, pointing. "Elspeth, Selena, and Queen Lilliana."

Elspeth nodded to the woman. "Who is she and why is she in chains?"

"She's a malevolent shapeshifter and accomplished

spellcaster," Leofwine replied. "Broccan and I tracked her for a long while. She evaded us for years by taking different identities. When we finally caught her, she and her companions nearly killed Broccan. He was run through with a sword and shot several times. I wanted to kill her rather than imprison her. But Broccan refused, for he wanted her to one day face all of you."

"Doirean?" Rhianwyn whispered when she caught sight of the woman's reddish-blonde hair beneath the hood.

Still, she didn't understand. Broccan could have told her she'd been captured. Why would he insist on them meeting her here? And what did it have to do with the crone?

"Now," Leofwine demanded, "change into the form these women would recognize."

Doirean lowered her hood, glared at both Broccan and Rhianwyn, made a disagreeable face—and shifted into the bent old crone.

The women looked at each other in disbelief after seeing the transformation.

"God's bones," Rhianwyn gasped.

It was finally beginning to make sense.

"You did all this…created the magical pact that caused such pain only because you wanted Broccan?" Rhianwyn asked.

"Of course I wanted him. He's all I've wanted since first I saw him, but I didn't act alone." It sounded odd for the crone to now speak in Doirean's Scottish accent.

Rhianwyn looked at Broccan awaiting further explanation.

Broccan nodded and took Rhianwyn's hand. "Apparently my father had spies sending messages to Ireland. They each reported I was happy and in love with you, Rhianwyn—that we were planning to marry, and I wasn't apt to leave. Desperate for me to one day take his throne, my father employed Doirean to do whatever she could to break us up. It's believed she had something to do with William disappearing, too."

"But Broccan, Father disappeared before you and I ever met," Rhianwyn said.

Doirean smiled unpleasantly. "The mage might've interfered with my magic, for he would've tried to protect you, healer. Although I admit I didn't know you had magic until I couldn't take the wand from you." She motioned to Rhianwyn.

"Therefore, you didn't offer us the opportunity to live other lives, so we'd learn a lesson?" Selena asked. "You did it for coin?"

"True, I got a fair bit of coin," she said. "But it was mostly because I wanted him and if he didn't want me, I'd ensure he was happy with no one."

"Now, I am happy," Broccan said, "and you'll live in an eternal prison along with others equally despicable."

"So we aren't even all to blame," Elspeth suggested. "She would've done anything to break Rhianwyn and Broccan apart?"

"That doesn't make us any less blamable for agreeing to the pact," Selena rebuked.

"Why did you tell us not to speak of it?" Rhianwyn asked the crone, not understanding that part.

"Couldn't let him learn of it." Doirean looked at Broccan. "He might have guessed the truth."

"Why would you risk Broccan's life if your intent was to force him to return to Ireland?"

Doirean snorted. "He wasn't ever actually in danger."

"But lightning hit the tree!" Rhianwyn argued. "It caught on fire and nearly fell on him."

The crone shook her head. "The tree nearly fell on *you*."

That was true.

"The wolf attack?" Rhianwyn said.

"Did any wolves hurt him?" the woman asked.

Rhianwyn thought back. One had bitten Fairfax and another had nearly gotten to her, in Elspeth's form, but they hadn't gone for Broccan. He'd killed them, but they hadn't attacked him.

She could have told him the truth, at the very beginning. He'd never been in danger. None of this pain was necessary. Fury roared inside her, but she couldn't let it out yet. She needed to understand everything.

"Why didn't you let me die when I suffered the sword wound while I was in Selena's body?"

"Once begun, I thought it best the soul switches were completed. And it entertained me endlessly to see you tormented—your friendships and your marriage slowly destroyed." Doirean cackled.

"You're demented!" Rhianwyn glowered at the crone. She could end her now, use magic to turn her to dust. She took a deep breath, resisting with all her might.

"Where will you go once you take her back to prison?"

Broccan asked Leofwine.

"To Welshland. The sorceress Morwenna's requested my help with the dragon curse."

Rhianwyn would be glad if that could be accomplished. Maybe Tyven would return to human form.

"You could at least apologize." Selena addressed the crone.

"Apologize? Not bloody likely. I'm not sorry for any of it. You four were easy to persuade. Well...three of you were."

"I hope your stay in prison is positively wretched!" Rhianwyn spat.

Doirean's evil dark magic billowed out from the crone's withered flesh. "When I came to visit you at Brockwell Manor, I did try to break you and your husband apart and considered killing you before the soul switches began. I would have if he hadn't agreed to taking me along with him to Mercia. Now, I wish I had killed you."

Rhianwyn shook her head at the malice, even as her true revenge dawned on her. "Death would be mercy for you." She looked at Leofwine. "Instead, may I request that she stays in her current form?"

The crone's face fell. Before Leofwine or Broccan could reply, before she could argue herself out of it, Rhianwyn closed her eyes, breathed out slowly. Golden streams of magical light streamed from her fingertips, and it was done. She knew Doirean would remain in the aged body.

The rage left. The pain lifted. She'd used her magic again, a healing spell, not just for her friends and for Broccan, but for herself, too.

With a shriek, Doirean looked down at her flat, wrinkled breasts, her bowed legs. She ran a hand down her thin, gray hair. "NO! You can't!"

Rhianwyn reached out and gathered her friends together. The four women looked at each other, their eyes shining with tears of gratitude and forgiveness.

"We just did," Rhianwyn whispered.

Then she turned to her husband and kissed him. They were finally free.

"Farewell then, Broccan." Leofwine waved. "I do hope our paths will cross again. We worked well together all those years."

"Perhaps they will, my friend. My wife has a castle in Welshland. She'd probably like to show our children her mother's homeland."

"Your children?" Leofwine looked stunned.

Doirean's jaw dropped. Then she pulled at her chains and howled. How this would torment her, Rhianwyn thought. Broccan, living happily with his family, while she raged, imprisoned in barren misery.

Broccan nodded, smiled, and pulled Rhianwyn closer. "Twins. A bonny lass and a fine handsome lad."

"Congratulations, my friend. Now, best we get you back to your dungeon." Leofwine tugged Doirean's arm.

"Is there a rack in that dungeon?" Rhianwyn asked.

"There's most definitely a rack." Leofwine winked as he and Doirean disappeared.

"I'll be leaving, too, lovely Rhianwyn," Teg said fluttering near her face. "I'm finally going home. Oh the Welsh fungi. I can taste it already."

She pecked his cheek, and he blushed before transforming into an owl and flying off in a magical glow.

"We've a weddin' to get to," Broccan said, as he and the four women left the circle.

Rhianwyn glanced back. For the first time since that fateful autumn night, she could look at the sunstones without regret. Broccan's arm remained around her waist as they walked. He smiled, bent down and kissed her ardently. He must have felt the same.

CHAPTER TWENTY-FIVE

B ROCCAN AND RHIANWYN attended Fairfax and Maisie's wedding in the manor where the two had met as children. Later, they repeated their own wedding vows, again in the lovely garden. Rhianwyn knew this time it would be "'til death do us part."

Afterward they ate, drank mead and ale, celebrating heartily with those dear to them. Keyon, whose once red hair was nearly white now, played his lute. She caught him and Mirtha, whom Maisie had insisted attend the wedding, exchanging looks that suggested they might be meeting up later.

William and Matty looked deep in conversation. Was there an attraction between them? Chester and Zachary were speaking amicably, too. Rhianwyn smiled. She knew her magic could be employed for creating happy outcomes.

Dancing, Broccan held Rhianwyn close when Cassian and Heledd approached. Cassian passed Broccan a formal-looking envelope with a wax seal. Broccan broke the seal and read it.

"You and the queen have released me from my sworn oath of knighthood?"

Cassian nodded. "But I'd still welcome you anytime you'd like to help train the new recruits or spar with us, Sir

Broccan."

"Thank you, my friend!" Broccan patted Cassian's shoulder.

"Now, I'm going to dance with my wife." Cassian touched Heledd's barely noticeable pregnant belly, and they both beamed. The kingdom would continue to grow and flourish with all these expected babes.

Broccan took Rhianwyn in his arms again. "Matty says she's happy the children will be sleepin' here, and they seem eager to remain with their friends."

"We all need friends." Rhianwyn looked at Selena, Elspeth, and Lilliana, each talking happily with their husbands and families. Finally she felt no resentment. They were on the way to forming endearing relationships again.

"And I need you." Broccan kissed her again, much more passionately.

"Do you think you could save that till you're alone?" Elspeth called. "There are children here."

Lilliana smirked. "You'd better not go into labor tonight, Selena, for the woman you want to deliver your baby will obviously be otherwise engaged."

"Yes," Rhianwyn said, "please wait a couple of days."

"I'll do my best." Selena grinned. "I could have my husband see to the birth."

Cassian laughed at Everard's worried expression. "You're a healer now, brother."

Everard pursed his lips. "And glad of it, but I'm uneager to see my wife in pain."

"Let's go then, my love." Rhianwyn felt giddy from the mead and aroused from Broccan's firm body against her.

"Wait," Elspeth called, motioning for Rhianwyn to come sit with her. Rhianwyn did. Oliver stepped away and Selena and Lilliana were beckoned, too.

"What is it?" Rhianwyn asked. "I want to be with my husband. It has been years."

"God's bones, there's probably cobwebs beneath your skirts." Elspeth chortled. The other women laughed, too. "We four are forever bonded." Elspeth held out her hand, tears now glistening in her eyes.

"We're forever bonded," Selena and Lilliana echoed, placing their hands on Elspeth's.

Rhianwyn took a deep breath, then smiled and put her hand atop the pile. "We *are* forever bonded, my friends."

BROCCAN EMBRACED HER when she joined him again. "I have another surprise for you, *Suile Gorma*. I've had the cottage where we used to go to make love readied for tonight. And there'll be no dog whinin'."

They looked at Morrigan lying contentedly by Merrie and Gwil.

"If we don't soon leave," Rhianwyn whispered, "I'll insist you bed me before we actually get to a bed like when we were first in love."

Together, they embraced their already sleepy children and left them with Matty. Broccan carried a lantern as they walked hand in hand to the cottage.

"You've yet to explain how our wee daughter knows how babies are created and why she believes I must be positioned behind you to see it done."

Rhianwyn laughed at his perplexed expression. "We often spend time at Chester's breeding stable. Of course they asked numerous questions. I thought the truth was best."

"We'll keep our bedchamber locked when we're more than sleepin'."

He grinned and squeezed her hand.

An owl shrieked overhead. Had Teg magically returned to Cymru, she wondered? Would Morwenna and her niece, Rhianwyn's cousin, end the Dafyddson curse?

She jumped, espying two spirits on the path.

Anslem and Ulf.

"I haven't seen you in an age," she said.

"Because you turned from magic, Rhi," Anslem explained.

"Like Teg, they've been spendin' much time with me," Broccan said.

"Now we know you're happy, Rhi, we'll be leaving." Anslem smiled.

"And my beauty, too," Ulf said looking back at Elspeth.

Both spirits waved and faded from view.

Once inside the cottage, Broccan and Rhianwyn kissed and caressed, wildly eager to make love. She pulled his tunic open and looked into his eyes when she spotted the item inside his garment. A lock of her hair tied with a now frayed scrap of fabric from the wedding gown she'd worn then and now. She'd given it to him before he'd set off for Mercia.

"You kept it all this time?"

"Always," he said. "It made me feel close to you."

She retrieved a note from her gown's pocket. Broccan had placed it under her pillow before he'd left on that journey. It was creased and made mostly indistinguishable by her many lonely tears.

"In this note, you said you'd always find your way back to me and I prayed on that every night that we were parted."

She showed him and he pulled her close.

"No one shares a love truer than ours, my *Suile Gorma*. By God, I want you," he said huskily.

He kissed her then, an all-encompassing kiss. Frantic to be joined after so long parted, the coupling was heated. Afterward, they made slow tender love, then held each other, hearts beating together, bodies entwined.

"Rhianwyn, would you like to journey to Welshland?"

She lifted her head to gaze at him. "But you said you'd be content remaining here all your days."

"I'll always be gloriously content with you and our children."

"And if we should have other children?"

He brushed a hair from her cheek. "Let's make more babies, my lovely Rhianwyn. I'd adore seein' your belly swell with my child. Sure watchin' you place our babes to your breasts would be a heartwarmin' sight, too."

He caressed her breast. She tingled again even though she'd just been gratified.

"I'd adore sharing all of that with you, too, Broccan. Merrie and Gwil would be elated to have siblings. But do you honestly think we could take our children to Cymru?"

"I saw your interest when Leofwine spoke of endin' the curse. Sure you'd like to assist. You'd get to know your aunt better and meet your cousin. Merrie and Gwil should see their grandmam's homeland."

She kissed him, now caught up in his excitement.

"Maybe one day we'll take them to Ireland, too, to where I was raised," Broccan said. "It is a magical place. We'll have many adventures and can always return to Hengebury."

"I'll go anywhere with you, my love." By the firelight she looked into his entrancing blue eyes. "As long as we're never parted again, not even for a day...and certainly not a night." She playfully arched her eyebrow.

He smiled sensually. Their lips met again and nothing else mattered. Not the season...the past...or even the future...only them, their unending passion and enduring love.

THE END

ACKNOWLEDGMENTS

There are always a lot of people to acknowledge when completing a book and a series. I'm truly grateful to the wonderful Jane Porter and the terrific Tule team, Meghan Farrell, Cyndi Parent, Nikki Babri, and Mia Gleason. You're all so great and have been amazingly helpful. I'm thrilled to remain a part of the Tule family.

Thank you to my fantastic editors, too. Thanks to Roxanne Snopek for the many hours you've put in throughout this installment and the entire Maidens series. Thank you for sharing the humor in this last book, *Fate's Final Season's* abbreviation which brought us some laughs. Your input and experience are much appreciated and have really bettered my stories.

Thanks to Helena Newton and Marlene Roberts, as well. I feel really fortunate to have such dedicated and talented editors with me on this writing journey. I applaud your diligence in making sure details are correct and errors are eliminated. That's no small task and so vital to an author.

I'd like to acknowledge Christian Bentulan from Covers by Christian for his fabulous cover designs. I absolutely love the covers in this series. I'm awed by his talent. A special thank you to Lee Hyat for her assistance in being the go-between regarding the covers.

Thanks to Tyler Steffensen for continuing to update my website. Technology isn't my strong point so I'm grateful he's willing to do this.

To my husband, Mark and my family, Katrina, Jerilyn, Shane, Darien, Daniella, Grayson, and Novak, you mean the world to me and your encouragement is what helps me get through even the most discouraging days.

To my extended family Kerry, Tannis, Grant, Matthew and Paige, and Elaine, even though we don't see each other as often as I'd like, I always know you're in my corner.

To my dear friends, who probably sometimes feel I'm a bit negligent in keeping in touch or meeting in person, I'm grateful to you for understanding and just knowing writing is my thing.

I also want to tell my readers how much I appreciate your loyalty in following me the past nine years through my different series. I'm so pleased when you reach out to let me know you're loving the books and characters. I'm also really thankful to those who leave ratings and reviews. Your patronage means a lot.

I can't wait for you to meet Fiona and Lorcan from my newest/next series, Witch and Demon Hunter. For those of you who have read The Irish Witch and The Witches of Time series, you might remember them for this is a spinoff/sequel series.

The first book, *Dark Irish Demon*, will release February 29/2024. Yes, leap year. Don't you think that has to be a magical sign?

If you enjoyed *Fate's Final Season,*
you'll love the next book in...

THE MAIDENS OF THE MYSTICAL STONES SERIES

Book 1: *Autumn's Magical Pact*

Book 2: *Winter's Haunting Pledge*

Book 3: *Spring's Mystical Promise*

Book 4: *Summer's Celestial Plea*

Book 5: *Fate's Final Season*

Available now at your favorite online retailer!

MORE BOOKS BY LEIGH ANN EDWARDS

THE WITCHES OF TIME SERIES

Book 1: *The Witch's Awakening*

Book 2: *The Witch's Compromise*

Book 3: *The Witch's Journey*

Book 4: *The Witch's Reckoning*

THE IRISH WITCH SERIES

Book 1: *The Farrier's Daughter*

Book 2: *The Witch's Daughter*

Book 3: *The Chieftain's Daughter*

Book 4: *A Chieftain's Wife*

Book 5: *A Witch's Life*

Book 6: *A Witch's Quest*

Book 7: *A Witch's Destiny*

THE VIKINGS OF HIGHGARD SERIES

Book 1: *The Norse Protector*

Book 2: *The Norse Sorcerer*

Book 3: *The Norse Explorer*

Book 4: *The Norse Conqueror*

Available now at your favorite online retailer!

ABOUT THE AUTHOR

Leigh Ann Edwards' fascination with history, romance, magic, time-travel and Ireland sparked her interest in creating the Irish Witch Series and her expanding collection of published novels. Growing up in a Manitoban village on the Canadian prairies left lots of time to create stories and let her imagination soar.

An author for thirty years, Leigh Ann is presently writing her fifth series with Tule Publishing. Besides writing, she loves spending time with her four grandchildren, reading, traveling, doing intuitive readings and reiki. Leigh Ann and her husband, their two cats, one large dog and Boston Terrier puppy, live in a small town near Edmonton Alberta, Canada.

Thank you for reading

FATE'S FINAL SEASON

If you enjoyed this book, you can find more from all our great authors at TulePublishing.com, or from your favorite online retailer.

TULE
PUBLISHING

Printed in the USA
CPSIA information can be obtained
at www.ICGtesting.com
LVHW050314310823
756768LV00004B/23